CRISIS OF COMMAND

DISJUNCTION

JON FRATER

aethonbooks.com

DISJUNCTION
©2023 Jon Frater

This book is protected under the copyright laws of the United States of America. No part of this publication may be reproduced, stored in a retrieval system, or transmitted, in any form or by any means, without the prior permission in writing of the publisher, nor be otherwise circulated in any form of binding or cover other than that in which it is published and without a similar condition including this condition being imposed on the subsequent purchaser. Any reproduction or unauthorized use of the material or artwork contained herein is prohibited without the express written permission of the authors.

Aethon Books supports the right to free expression and the value of copyright. The purpose of copyright is to encourage writers and artists to produce the creative works that enrich our culture.

The scanning, uploading, and distribution of this book without permission is a theft of the author's intellectual property. If you would like to use material from the book (other than for review purposes), please contact editor@aethonbooks.com. Thank you for your support of the author's rights.

Aethon Books
www.aethonbooks.com

Print and eBook formatting by Steve Beaulieu. Art provided by Phillip Dannels.

Published by Aethon Books LLC.

Aethon Books is not responsible for websites (or their content) that are not owned by the publisher.

This book is a work of fiction. Names, characters, places, and incidents are the product of the author's imagination or are used fictitiously. Any resemblance to actual events, locales, or persons, living or dead is coincidental.

All rights reserved.

ALSO IN SERIES

Disjunction
Dissonance
Dominion

PROLOGUE

"BROOKS! Straighten up that element. There are only a few thousand humans left in the galaxy—we can't afford to lose twenty more."

First Lt. Simon Brooks scanned his display and tightened his grip on the VRF-1/E Raven's controls. The Strike Raven was the newest of the Unified Earth Fleet's multiple-geometry fighters. He glanced at his positioning and saw that Dance and Ghost were edging away from him. Worse, Janus and Morrow were taking their cues from them and moving out of their own spots in the element to maintain spacing. Brooks toggled his com. "This is Section 3 Leader. You guys are all over the place. Lock your autopilots onto my beacon and keep the original distancing. Acknowledge."

He heard muffled replies and watched as his planes returned to normal. Then he glanced at the mission timer. Twelve minutes of life left.

In the year 2076, the Unified Earth Fleet's sole, space-worthy battleship, *Ascension*, fought the Sleer War and lost. Two years later, humanity had moved into the Sleer peace, or what passed for it. The Allied Sleer Fleet was its official name, decided in tandem by alien and human bureaucrats and military officers. The peace came at a price: the Sleer controlled their orbital ring around Earth, and the humans and Sleer together ran the matching one around Great Nest—the former Sleer capital world. The local Sleer leadership thought of it as a genuine partnership, but Brooks and Lt. Cmdr Rosenski saw it as each side holding the other's home world hostage. In the past two years, the surviving humans had made Battle Ring Great Nest more of a home, but its alien nature and the human crew's minority status were never far from anyone's mind.

The solution was for humans to re-take Battle Ring Earth. Missions like this one were how that happened.

Cmdr. Fairchild's rebuke stung. Worsening environmental conditions on Earth were slowly killing the six billion humans stuck on the surface, barred from moving into the safety of the Sleer's orbital ring. Only a few thousand humans lived on Battle Ring Great Nest. Forget communications; personal messages arrived once every few weeks, and what news they heard was censored by the Office of Military Protocols.

The greater truth was that Brooks was out of practice. Too much time talking to engineers, diplomats, and bureaucrats, and too little time flying planes or even simulators. He'd spent too much time and effort getting here to risk losing everything. He closed his eyes, trying to control his breathing and heart rate as the plane vibrated beneath him. He'd gotten rusty. His hands shook and his nerves were shot. And here he was, thinking his Sleer implants were supposed to fix those problems.

Rosenski's voice in his ear: "Uncle, you want to go over the plan one more time?" She was doing her job as squadron XO, trying to keep the lines straight and everyone focused. If Brooks's reaction was any indication, waiting for the countdown was just going to complicate things.

Fairchild's baritone rang out over the comm: "Why not? You

all know our objective—the command-and-control tower just above the ring spoke that's anchored on South Pico Island. Brooks and Rosenski especially know where everything is, so they'll be heading the run. Two-minute warning and *Gauntlet* launches her payload of Scatterpack cruise missiles. Those babies will break open and fill the sky with enough targets to freak out Tall Lord Fleet Master Nazerian or anyone else minding the sensors. That call goes out and Brooks guards the Prowlers as they jam whatever ring systems can be jammed and alert the rest of us to new contacts and enemy positions."

Brooks swept his eyes across his panel. His Raven could throw out a blanket screen of noise easily enough, but the VRF-1/P Prowlers were a new level of threat. A whole lot of pain could come from the Prowlers. They'd taken the jamming pods used on Lurker airborne early warning aircraft, miniaturized them, then installed them in a rotating frame in the Prowler's much smaller sensor vane. Blanket noise out to nearly fifty klicks, ten times the range of any stock Raven, meant a Prowler could target individual ships and break their combat computer's locks on friendly targets. Assuming that Brooks and his stock Ravens could keep them out of harm's way.

Fairchild continued: "Next phase: the missiles should draw fire from the point defense turrets, including fighters and surface rollers. Arkady will take her section and attack surface guns while covering *Gauntlet*'s approach. Once the troop carrier lands, she'll drop her load of battlers and move away to provide fire support. Rosenski and Brooks will lead their sections into the ring—followed by the battlers—and fight their way to the control center. Questions?"

None. They'd asked them all in the briefing room twelve hours ago.

"Hey, Genius. Nazerian does know that this is a war *game*, right?" Judy "Dances With Gears" Reagan's soprano jolted

Brooks, reminding him that he should have turned the general channel off. He needed his crew to hear his orders, but he didn't need to listen to their chatter.

"I don't know if he understands the distinction in our culture. Sleer games are rough."

"That's for sure. That kid's game they play with bowling balls...combination of dodgeball and lord knows what. We saw that in action. Nearly broke a couple of Underhill's ribs when she caught one. And those were little Sleer kids. The adults weigh a hundred times as much as the little lizards."

Marc Janus, who flew the lead Prowler, sniffed. "Dinosaurs, guys. A Sleer will bite your head off as soon as look at it."

Brooks toggled his comm, unsure why Janus's choice of word irked him. "They're living beings. Have a little respect."

"They have control of the orbital ring surrounding Earth, where we are freezing our collective asses off due to the environmental damage their construction project did to our ecosphere. Fuck them, and fuck all—"

"That's enough. Section leaders, ten-minute mark. If we can't find a way into that structure and gain control of it here, there's no hope of doing so back home. Concentrate, you little monkeys."

"Copy that, Uncle."

Not screwing around was the order of the day. Brooks led Section 3, a three-plane element armed with VRF-1/E Strike Ravens, fresh off the assembly line and filled with advanced avionics and weapons. Better armor, better engines, and the folks at the research division had somehow goosed the combat AIs, improving response times as well. So armed, Brooks, Dance, and Ghost ran interference for their support section, a trio of EWAR VRF-1/P Prowlers flown by Janus, Diallou, and Purcell.

The test of their competence was eight minutes away,

counting from Uncle's mark. Eight minutes until they hit the target's defense zone. Eight minutes to live unless they could pull this off. Uncle was running Section 1 and Rosenski had 2, above and behind Brooks. Arkady had Section 4, the big guns: twelve VRF-3/D Super-Ravens equipped with the new Armor packs. *Gauntlet*, their command ship, followed at a discrete distance, ready to disgorge her four dozen battlers for ground assault.

The plan was simple enough: Arkady would fly cover for the other three sections and the mother ship, picking out big threats and blinding whatever choice bits decided to primary her section. The trick was to gain access to the command tower, eliminate all opposition, and take control. Simple. At least on paper.

Happily, the unit had a functional orbital ring to practice on. Great Nest had been the capital world in the heyday of the Two Thousand Worlds (which Brooks and the other humans just called the Sleer empire). Humanity understood empires, but colonizing space wasn't a human success story.

Worse, Battle Ring Zekerys, while new, was a patched and repaired and partially restored facility. The ring around Earth was brand new and filled with unfathomable tech that they'd barely begun to investigate. Nobody had seen the inside of Earth's Sleer colony in years.

In the meantime, there was the hum of the Raven. The engines thrummed beneath Brooks as he adjusted the display, making sure he could verify the target area. They approached from the zenith, looking down as they swung toward the planet's north pole. At this range, the ring wasn't visible to the naked eye, even with the implants, but the Raven saw further and more accurately.

He toggled the laser-induction comm net that linked his section. "Section 3 this is Leader. I have the target on screen.

All hands verify and link your targeting computers to *Gauntlet*."

A flurry of acknowledgements, then Dance Reagan's voice filled his ears. "We miss this, there won't be a sling big enough to hold all our asses."

She had no idea. "We miss this and we set the whole mission to re-take Earth back another six months. Nobody screws up. We have a plan. Stick to it."

Brooks wished he felt as confident as he sounded. He knew the group plan. They all did. What he didn't know was the Sleer's (Red Team's) defensive disposition or strength. That they would use the ring as a staging area was only logical, but the Sleer had ways of attacking that tended to involve using large numbers of ships and troops. Overkill was their thing. Blue team had a fraction of that, but a lot more mobility and the best weapons the humans had been able to design and produce thus far in their association with the Allied Sleer Fleet. Both sides got to test the other in real time.

Part of the issue was that *Gauntlet*'s tracking and targeting systems hadn't been fully tested yet. That was part of why they were battling Nazerian's troops; *Gauntlet* still needed a proper shakedown cruise, but this was good enough for now.

"I really hate this part," someone said. The voice was distorted through the speakers, but it sounded like one of the replacements they'd taken on recently. Morrow, maybe. Skellington and Frost had transferred out months ago, leaving him with two spots to fill. Morrow was one of them; Purcell was the other. "A fighter plane should not make a habit of getting close enough to kiss the enemy."

"Gah!"

"Problem, Dance?"

"No, it's the thought of kissing a Sleer. Turns my guts."

Janus snorted. "What would they say if they knew we were talking about them this way?"

"They'd say 'Ah-heeeuuuaaaarhhhhl-zzzsssssss!'"

"Cut the chatter," Brooks chided, stifling a laugh. "Maintain your spacing and confirm status, people. Five minutes to target."

They could shit-talk the Sleer all they wanted, but it didn't change anything; Sleer tech was keeping them alive. The implants they'd taken early in the conflict while hiding aboard the Earth Ring were Sleer tech. The Ravens they all flew were developed from Sleer tech, reverse engineered from an AI algorithm that itself might have been stolen from the Cycomm Unity. The orbital ring around Earth that could comfortably house billions of Sleer and humans—if the Sleer Command was willing. Which they weren't.

Bottom line: the Sleer weren't the worst thing out in the universe, merely the one race that had come to reclaim its property and handed the Unified Earth Fleet its ass in the process. There were other races to work with or not. They'd known about the fleet of Skreesh titans heading in this general direction form over a year. That spelled doom for everyone.

"Fucking dinosaurs," he growled.

"Lieutenant Brooks, may I have a word with you on the command channel?"

Crap. He'd fucked up. "Yes, Uncle."

"Simon, you need to focus. Whatever is distracting you, cut it out of your head and manage what needs to be managed," Fairchild said. "Or do I need to hand your section to someone else?"

"No, sir. I got this."

"Very well." He switched back to general comms. "Three minutes to target. Section leaders report in."

"Rosenski, here."

"Arkady here."

"Joanne, have I told you lately how glad I am you're back with the team?"

"It wasn't hard, Uncle. They took the Silver Spars away from me and sent me here on the last re-assignment transport. Glad to be back with my Hornets."

"Former Hornets," Rosenski snarked. "By all naming rights, you're all Nightmares now. You're welcome."

"Whatever. General Hendricks still hates you, Uncle. You think they demoted me out of spite?"

"I think they've moving elements they see as uncooperative here to get us out of the way. Now that I'm gone, there are no UEF pilots from the original Icarus air group on Earth. That might mean something or not."

Rosenski clicked her tongue. "Brooks, are you in charge?"

"Yes, Ma'am. But I can't help think that the roles are reversed from that first day on South Pico Island. Now we're hitting them. It's a good feeling."

"That it is. Remember, I'm not bailing you out this time. Two minutes."

That's fair. He'd spent two years expanding his role and skill set. Time to stand up. Given his implants, aboard a Sleer vessel he could train the network to only give him what he needed when he needed it. But Sleer implant tech didn't work with Ravens. The next best thing to do was limit his inputs. He needed the command channel, so that stayed open. He needed his section to hear him, but he didn't need to hear them, so he switched that to talk on demand—his demand, not theirs. Balancers and directional thrusters worked on demand as well. Flight controls and targeting, along with weapons selection, he kept open, but shut the rest of it off his board, putting it out of his mind and allowing the autopilot to handle it.

And the world instantly became a quieter, sharper place.

"One minute. We have a launch detection."

New images popped onto the display as the Scatterpacks left their tubes; ninety-six rockets with all the range in the world and a flight speed nearly ten times that of a fully loaded Raven. Brooks took a last look at his own section. Dance, Janus, and Ghost flew the Prowlers in a triplet element far to his rear, with Morrow and Purcell backing him up in Raven-Es. "Prowlers, deploy your vanes. Thirty seconds."

They didn't verbally acknowledge him. They didn't have to. He saw their status on his board, green LEDs showing activity, blue LEDs showing their electronics coming on line, too low to do any good.

The battle ring was close enough that they didn't even need the cameras to see it. A thin ribbon of steel and complex organics, circling the planet, daring him to act. And here came the cruise missiles, a dense line of targets coming up very quickly from behind. Ten seconds. Five. The missiles shot past them, racing down into the battle ring's defense range.

Three. Two. One.

Enter the Zone of Death. Every defensive weapon could kill them at will. It made things interesting.

The Scatterpacks swooped and swerved, positioning themselves for maximum effectiveness, spacing themselves so that a minimum distance between each unit was observed. Then, BOOM, the display exploded with all the targets in the world as nose cones broke open and dispersed their warheads. Suddenly, instead of ninety-six blips, there were nearly a thousand of them, ten per rocket, all screaming down onto the ring's perimeter and blasting noise and heat. A veritable wall of interference.

Brooks toggled his comm. "That's it. Janus, Morrow, and Purcell, bring your EWAR vanes to full power, blanket all sections with noise. Scan for likely targets to jam when Red

Team appears. Dance and Ghost stay sharp. Anything comes within ten klicks, dies."

The space around him filled with more noise. This time blanketing a one hundred klick diameter sphere with energy opaque to Sleer sensors.

Uncle's voice in his helmet: "*Gauntlet* coming up behind us. Brooks, have your element cover her as she moves in to drop the battlers. Saint, move in and silence the defenses."

"Brooks. Copy that."

"Saint. Copy. On our way."

Brooks watched as Arkady's flight of Super-Ravens broke from the pack and descended, blasting afterburners. The ring's big surface guns were already pinging them as the ring's sensors began to recover from the attack, burning through the interference more quickly than any of them had a right to expect. Red and green energy blasts crossed their paths. Badly and slowly, but they were getting more accurate with each salvo.

By now, the ring loomed beneath them; a wide, flat surface studded with domes, hatches, and towers. His computer picked out the sites where energy spikes suggested sensors or weapons, but the one he paid attention to was in the middle of the mess. The main control tower, nearly half a kilometer high and armored within an inch of its life, loomed in his line of sight.

So close!

"New targets. Sleer Zithid fighters are deploying from tubes on the opposite side of the ring. Rosenski, take your section and follow me. Brooks, cover *Gauntlet*."

Brooks growled. This was where everything went to shit. *Gauntlet* was fifty klicks out and decelerating hard, looking for a place to land. Three of its prospective landing zones were shooting at them. The Zithids made things worse. They were small, one-man craft, each carrying short-range missiles and a triple-barreled auto-cannon that could shred a Raven in seconds. Faster than a stock Raven, too. But they had no armor worth mentioning; one lucky hit from a missile or a burst from a gun pod would cripple one. The Sleer had thousands of them on alert for just this kind of attack.

Simon Brooks wasn't a gambler, but he saw his opening and took it. He armed his payload—six heavy missiles with tactical warheads, meant to take out assault shuttles at long range—and designated his targets: the three big gun turrets at the base of the tower. The weapons officer on *Gauntlet* would see the flash, notice the dead zone, and direct the pilot to ground there to drop the battlers. "*Gauntlet*, this is Section 3 Leader. I'm making a drop zone for you, tower base. Stand by!" He thumbed the release, and adrenaline surged as he felt the bump and the jolt as the missiles dropped from their pylons and streaked toward the ring surface.

One. Two. Three flashes, then his display flickered and fluttered as his plane's electronics burped from the miniscule EMP. But the shooting stopped. "*Gauntlet*, tower base is open. Go! Go! Go!"

His headphones relayed a mishmash of dropped syllables and broken words. The speaker didn't even sound grateful, the bum. He checked his section. The newly arrived Sleer fighters were swooping around the far side of the ring, adjusting their course and speed to come at them in a giant Immelmann turn. He gauged relative speed and direction, made a decision. "Prowlers, jam as many of those fighters as you can. Dance, Ghost, go to Walker mode and follow me."

They heard him. A flipped switch, a pulled lever, and suddenly all three fighters had arms and legs and a third of their previous speed. They blasted hard to decelerate to *Gauntlet*'s approach speed and picked targets. Dance and Ghost used their planes like mobile SAM bases, dropping a dozen short-range missiles each. The fighters broke formation to evade the ordnance while Brooks used his plane's gun pod to pick off stragglers. Boom. Boom. Boom. Just like in the simulator arena.

The attack was faltering. The chatter between Fairchild and Rosenski dried up. They were cleaning the skies of Sleer fighters. Then he recognized Flower's voice on the alert channel. "Contact, contact. Slow-moving blob at twelve klicks, bearing one-nine-nine. Make it to be defense drones."

A hatch opened on the surface, a short tower dropped its walls and exposed a sheaf of stored missiles. Before he knew what happened, the payload burst up in trails of fire as they arced past his Raven and hit the Prowlers. One, two, three. The EWAR pilots never had a chance.

Brooks checked his position and saw that *Gauntlet* was under fire. A yawning chasm opened in his gut. Those were his people. He'd been ordered to defend them. No matter how this fight ended, he'd already came up a failure. He absolutely could not let the same thing happen to the assault shuttle.

The assault ship was only ten klicks from its drop zone, barely moving now, a big, fat target. Arkady's section was in Battler mode, dealing with Sleer rollers on the ring's surface. Hell, he could see the nearest wave of defense drones, at least twenty klicks distant, nowhere near a threat to any of his section members. And the tower's entry hatch was unguarded. A better target, which he should be able to open with his Sleer implants.

Fucking A.

"Dance, Ghost, cover *Gauntlet*. I have an idea." He switched his plane to Battler mode and pointed his leg thrusters toward the sky, diving toward the deck.

Fairchild pinged him almost immediately. "Brooks, you're out of position!"

"I have an opening."

"Get back in formation!"

"Uncle, I can see the entry hatch. I can—!"

The world flared white as a Sleer defensive projector swung to bear and a shield-zone appeared in front of him. A flash of light, a buzzing sound, and a jolt threw him against his harness as his ship spiraled down and impacted into the base of the tower.

His cockpit electronics shrieked and the world became a black hole. Nothing worked. No lights, no instruments, no noise. Except his status board. He watched the green LEDs flicker out to turn red. One by one, his section failed. The rest of the attack group were gone within minutes.

His canopy opened, the hard white light of the arena making him blink. Other canopies were opening in long rows. The training arena. All the pilots from all the sections. From across the room, Rosenski and Arkady glaring at him with murder in their eyes.

Uncle's voice in his headset. "You had one job, Simon. One. Job. Now you're dead, your section is destroyed, and the mission failed. In my office. One hour."

Fairchild's office was a cubicle in the building the air wing used for bureaucratic necessity. It might have been a jail cell for all the space it commanded. A desk, a chair for the ranking staff officer, and two more chairs on the other side. A laptop PC tied into the station's network. Uncle never used it.

Brooks knew he was in trouble, but he didn't comprehend just how angry Uncle was until he smiled from across the desk and steepled his fingers. "Got anything to say for yourself, Genius?"

Brooks dropped into old habits, hoping if he could talk his way out of this. "I don't think this mission was a fair test of my ability. You know I could have gone into the ring's computers with my implants and blinded their network. We all could have—at least those of us with the Sleer gear."

"No. We've been away for two years. For all we know, our implants don't even work anymore. That's why the plan dispensed with them."

That was ridiculous. Of course they worked. He could kick down a fire door if he wanted. "But I—"

"No." The smile vanished, leaving a cold stare. Fairchild ticked off his points on his fingers. "In the first place, you broke with the existing attack plan. In the second place, you disobeyed orders to do so. And in the third place, you didn't even manage to secure the objective. If this was a real mission, Katsev would be writing letters to all our families. And wondering where he was going to get twenty-four new Ravens." Uncle leaned back, stared at a seam in the wall, and seemed to re-evaluate several things. "Simon, until we can re-certify you for combat missions, I'm re-assigning you."

Oh-oh. "May I ask where?"

"Back to the techies."

Brooks held his breath to keep his heart from bursting through his chest. It was racing, reacting like he'd been insulted, hoping the affront wasn't intended... but wondering if it was. "You're putting me back in comms? That's where I started from!"

"It's also where you did the best. You helped get *Ascension*'s air base back up and running during the rescue and rebuild. You put together your own squad and ran them like a proper noncom. You got noticed by the right officers, and always kept yourself in their sights. You hooked the Hornets up with new fighters, graduated to flying a Raven, then built up the squadron as Arkady's XO. You're a solid officer, but when I put you in a combat aircraft, you lose the plot."

It was true. A slew of memories crossed his mind's eye as he recalled his screw-ups. Volunteering to have an alien AI insert Sleer implants into his body was probably the worst. The OMP had never forgiven him for that, or for supplying that same tech to his squadron mates. Although delaying an escape to from a troop transport to stuff a Sleer corpse into his ship's cargo bay for science came close.

"How screwed am I?" he asked.

Fairchild opened the laptop, tapped a few keys, and looked up. "It's not about 'screwed.' You show great potential. You're in the wrong role to realize it, that's all. This is my recommendation to Katsev." He read aloud from the screen, "'Lieutenant Brooks, while an excellent officer in most regards, lacks the instinct to excel on a modern battlefield against highly aggressive opponents like the Sleer. It's my considered opinion that he be assigned to a position where his exceptional skills in science and related applications can be most effectively utilized.'"

And there it was. Simon Brooks was out of rope. Katsev had once offered him the chance to transfer to his own squadron, the Specters, a formidable bunch of Raven pilots. "I don't suppose I can appeal to the CAG."

"I met with CAG. Commander Katsev and I agree. Simon, you're my boy and I promised your old man I'd look out for you. I appreciate that Rosenski and Arkady and I could take you this far. But you're not a killer and you never will be. I'm sorry. There it is."

Well. That was that. "Where are you sending me?"

"That's a bit of a question. Captain Rojetnick doesn't want to see you languish in a field science unit. The few we have are already packed with PhDs. Your best work is consistently observed in conjunction with Sleer equipment, so that's where you're going."

"Back to Earth, huh?"

"You wish. The Sleer high command is happy enough to ship humans out here to Great Nest, but God forbid any of us go back there. It's getting on time to push the Sleer into releasing a few of the prospective so-called 'New Worlds' to us for colonization. You'll help convince them it's in their best interest to do so. While you do that, I'll scout around and see what else you can be good at. Maybe put you on *Gauntlet* full time. You could be the Comms department head. You'd give Chief Amir a run for her money, I'll bet."

Brooks fidgeted as he imagined what Amir might say or do when she heard the news. Somehow, he didn't think his Thursday-night-coffee friend would be that understanding. Amir had high expectations for him. He didn't want to disappoint her. Hell, he didn't want to disappoint anyone in his weird little military family. "Why does that sound like a demotion?"

"I don't know. It shouldn't. You understand the Sleer better than anyone except Rosenski—hell, the two of you worked together to hijack a Sleer dreadnaught—so you'll go as a team, like you were back on Earth. Get us some 'New Worlds' to colonize. And then give the brass a rundown on *Gauntlet*. Why we need her and why we need bigger, human-designed ships like her. Get us some breathing room."

"But I'm out of Raven combat."

"Simon, there are hundreds of ways to soldier. Combat is only one of them. You have nothing to prove to me or anyone. Time to move on."

CHAPTER 1

"SO THIS IS our new world. What a dump."

Great Servant of Science Ship Master Metzek didn't try to hide his disgust at what his ship's instruments told him. Alpha Lyrae had some interesting features, to be sure. A bright young star, considerably brighter and younger than the one the primate race infesting the new home world claimed as their own. This one was at least a full magnitude hotter and was gulping down its supply of hydrogen. It would last another half billion years. Maybe not. Even if the primates died out before they witnessed it, this sun would expand into a giant and collapse to a dwarf sooner than their own. The primates had a saying: the bright candle burns twice as hot. Something like that. He was no fan of the primate race—humans—on the newly adopted home world —Earth, they called it—but he appreciated their mental process. Their music, for example. Metzek couldn't get enough of it. He'd ordered some of his favorites piped into the bridge on a rotating basis. One was playing right now. An old selection. Under My Thumb, about human mating practices. Humans made music about the things important to them. War, mating, and strong emotional states. Perseverance and despair were especially popular. Metzek didn't claim to understand any of it, but he liked what he liked. He didn't like Alpha Lyrae.

His XO, Zolik, tapped a claw against a console. "We've been here an hour. That's your description? A dump?"

"It means a disappointment," Metzek said. "Humans don't have recycler technology—at least not to the extent we do. A dump is a place where they haul their garbage for disposal."

"Disposal how?"

"It depends on the culture and their economy. Some burn it, some bury it, and some try to recycle it."

"Sounds exhausting and disgusting."

"It does," Metzek hissed. The passive sensors had pulled a selection of electromagnetic and spectrographic data. Now they needed to search further. "Deploy active sensors, full sweeps in all directions. Helm, plot a grand tour of the solar system spiraling outwards from the primary star to the outer planets. Drone masters, you may deploy your vehicles at will. We are a science vessel. Let's do some science."

"Indeed. Now we wait for the machines to do science for us," Zolik hissed. Their relationship wasn't exactly new. Zolik had come aboard his ship a year and a half ago, and Metzek had no issue with him. But he had a streak of emotion in him. He got frustrated when there was too little to do. You would think a science vessel—especially a new one like this *Zalamb-Duzen-*class ship—would be perfect for him. Yes, the machines did much of the work, but the crew needed to put their questions forward. Why was this blue-white star burning so fiercely so early in its life? Where were its planets? Why was the accretion disk so wide, and why were there so many different dispersion patterns running through it? What did the outer planets look like if there were any? All these had occurred to Metzek in the past few minutes.

"If you're bored, you can take one of the shuttles out to the edge of this system and take some readings. Great Servant of Science Telim will tell you what special equipment to install."

"I'm not bored. Just—"

"What?"

"You shouldn't be here," Zolik hissed, his shoulders and legs assuming the posture of discontent. "I know why I'm here, but you should be mastering a proper warship. Not running pointless errands for Edzedon."

There it was. Zolik was trying to be helpful. He was looking out for his commanding officer. Metzek chose to believe that, and so it was as good an explanation as any. "I won't discuss this with you. The fact that Fleet Master Nazerian chose Edzedon as his science officer has nothing to do with us."

"You're as good a science master as he is. Why is he serving the Tall Lord and you are—"

"I am learning about a new solar system that we may be called upon to colonize one day. You'll forgive me for taking a bit of pride in my assignment, even if we are looking over a dump. Especially if it's a dump. These primates throw away everything, or they did once. There might be something in the pile worth rescuing." He raised his voice to the rest of the bridge crew. "Continue with the operation. Acknowledgements from all departments."

This was the third stop on their deployment to the New Worlds. That's what the high command called the star systems within short range of Battle Ring Genukh. Everything within forty light years: over four hundred stars, at least sixty of which had planets. The New Worlds. No hint of how new. No real information about any of them except they might contain planets in habitable zones around their parent stars. They were looking for liquid water and oxygen. And while they looked, they made star maps, their cartographer teams paying close attention to each new system's features. It took weeks to map a single star system, but it might be worth it eventually. It wasn't for a mere ship master to know, but the migration from the Two Thousand Worlds to New Home—*Earth* to the primates who lived there—was as complete as it could be. They had organized a brief delaying action to give the civilians time to escape Great Nest. Almost three hundred thousand ships, each loaded with thirty or forty thousand refugees, gathered at Great Nest from all over Sleer space, then jumped to the New World they'd discovered thanks to Fleet Lord Nazerian's efforts. What a find! Air. Water. Sunlight. And a perfectly good, nearly complete battle ring under construction, too. It was almost too perfect for words.

Skreesh titans were still on the move and might well come this far down the Orion arm on this incursion. A battle ring would help them defend the new system, but could they organize a defense in time? That was the terrible question. Perhaps his star mapping would help formulate an answer. He hoped it would.

The map-making effort took weeks to manage. They utilized their strongest sensors, dropped hundreds of drones, and took countless photographs. They spiraled a course from ten million miles away from the primary star and traveled out in a pattern designed to cover as much territory as possible, crossing the plane of the ecliptic numerous times. Building a three-dimensional map of the system. The drones carried their own sensors and beamed their findings back to the mother ship. As time passed, the crew muttered and argued about aspects of their job and Metzek piped wilder, more aggressive music onto the bridge.

The crew constructed an astrophysical model while Metzek and Zolik worked in tandem for days on the accompanying report, adjusting the format and contents just so. They wanted to be sure the high command would note this world, but not be impressed. Zolik especially wanted no other science vessel to be dispatched. There was nothing here. Of what use was a too-bright star with a too-short lifespan surrounded by an accretion disk and no planets worth mining?

The next time Metzek came to the bridge, he addressed his comm officer: "Are we ready to transmit?"

"Yes, my lord."

Metzek was no lord, but he appreciated the effort of his officers to make him feel useful. He had a reputation. One great enough to command the first *Zalamb-Duzen* scout ship, which incorporated exceptionally powerful sensors and the new Meta-Pulse Relay Comm. Small enough to fit on a scout ship, but limited to textual data only. It would be enough to send Grossusk his report, though. "Then do so. Wish Ezedon a good day—and don't let him know how much we hate his guts. And let's prepare a spatial transition to the next destination. We have more systems to investigate. One of them has to be more interesting than this one."

The bridge crew agreed, chatting among themselves:

"I hope this next one has something to look at besides dust and one primary."

"Agreed. This was boring."

An hour later, the system blinked for attention. "New Home signals 'transmission received, and next assignment is confirmed.'"

Metzek shifted his weight forward, his claws clicking in an intricate dance. "Not a moment too soon. Navigation and helm, program destination and align us for..."

"Ship master! We have a magnetic anomaly."

Metzek and Zolik shared a look. Why were new problems

always cropping up during transitions? More importantly, why didn't sensor operators more fully describe the weirdness on their displays?

"Where is it?" Metzek asked.

"On the outermost edge of the system. It's barely registering, but the reading persists, and I can't account for it."

"We could call it random noise and nobody would know," Zolik hissed.

"I'd know. And one day, when Edzedon asks me why we left prematurely, I'll have to answer with something more substantial than 'I was impatient to leave.' Helm, plot a course and move us closer. We're a research ship. Let's do some research."

Reactive furnaces hummed and throbbed as they fed energy to the main drive. It still took the better part of four days, and the crew took the time to match as many of the current readings as possible with those the drones had already taken. Eventually, they had a solid contact to work with.

The bridge crew gathered around the display:

"Besides the fact that it matches nothing in our knowledge base..."

"It looks like a Movi planetoid. See the layered deck construction?"

"Bigger than any Movi ship I've seen. It's certainly bigger than any of ours."

"Threat level?" Zolik asked.

"None. It's dead. No power at all," Great Servant of Engineering Miressk answered.

Zolik pulled out part of the signature and glared. "It's not Movi. It's one of ours. Well, one of our ancestors' anyway. Here...you can see the hull structure. The way the latticework brings the armor into a honeycomb design. That's Sleer second migration technology."

"Which makes it at least twenty-thousand years old."

Metzek considered the implications. They were substantial. Twenty-thousand years meant it preceded the second migration—the time when the Two Thousand Worlds lived up to its name. It coincided with the Movi's third expansion period. The histories didn't have a great deal to say about that age, other than the Movi and Sleer were ebbing and flowing into each other's territorial claims. Neither had solidified into anything as permanent as a federal government. More like loose associations of local spheres of influence. The chance to examine—much less recover—such an example of Sleer history couldn't be ignored. The rest of the map-making expedition would wait. "This is a relic. We should we tell New Home about it."

Zolik hissed loudly. "No. They have all the data they need to catalog this system as unfit for habitation. This find is historic, but it won't change that description."

"You have an idea?"

Zolik stood in affirmation. "If we can restore it, we can always amend our previous communication. Our schedule will keep."

It wasn't a bad idea. But the chances that anything they used today would be applicable to a ship this old... "The empire had reactive furnaces back then."

"Oh, no. They had core taps."

"That long ago?"

Core taps were legendary in Sleer science communities. An array of probes opened a portal deep into hyperspace and linked the ship to a dimension of vastly more energetic quantum states. They were also notoriously fickle. A core tap mishap nearly always resulted in the destruction of its vessel. But it could power a ship the size of a small moon easily enough. Reactive furnaces were less powerful, but orders of magnitude more stable.

"If we transfer one of our own furnaces, we can probably bring its power core online within a few days."

"And win a scientific victory for New Home."

Metzek played with the notion of showing Edzedon something even he had never imagined. "We're not just a research vessel, we're a laboratory too. Let's perform an experiment."

CHAPTER 2

LT. CMDR SARA ROSENSKI got the news shortly after Brooks got his. She raged for a full ten minutes and then accepted what was. She'd seen his suicide run in the arena, same as the others. Simon Brooks was going to be the reason she resigned one day. After teaching him everything she knew about combat flying, he still hadn't learned that dead pilots couldn't kill enemies. She'd changed from her flight suit to a standard uniform and went to the Accidental Owl to drink. Today the CAG joined her. She was on her third scotch on the rocks while he nursed a Tom Collins.

His face was less frightening than it was a year ago. Commander Thomas "Butcher" Katsev, the Air Group Commander for the humans on Battle Ring Great Nest, was never conventionally handsome, but a miscalculated attack over Saturn had equipped him with a face that only a mother could recognize—possibly not even then. Scars and pocks turned his face into a lunar landscape. How he'd managed to keep both his eyes was something she'd never understand. As it was, he wore a black eye-patch over his left eye most times, but he took it off to fight. She appreciated the rakish charm it gave him. The

Butcher should have been a pirate. "I miss the days when a cryptic message written on a fortune cookie slip of paper in a mailbox was all we needed to pass orders from Layne," she groaned.

He shushed her. The room had ears. "Too easy to lose. And not everyone followed their orders. Probably didn't even always understand them. The new ways are better. Less chance of an interception and all the encryption you could ever ask for."

"I dunno. I can ask for quite a bit." She straightened her back, brushed the auburn bangs from her eyes, and waved to a black box behind the bar. The motion sensor picked her gesture up and a red eye opened to fix on her. "Two more, my tab," she said. The robot responded immediately, multi-jointed arms delivering her two drinks without spilling a drop. One more flash as the bar debited her account for the purchases.

She shoved one glass before him. "Did they ever get that data I sent from Mars?"

"That was two years ago. And you know better than to ask."

"I went through a fair bit of hell to transmit that."

"Yeah. You had to ask Brooks for a favor and everything. Boo hoo."

She got the hint. No more talking extracurricular activities in public. As if to punctuate the point, a rousing orchestral rendition of 'Katyusha' emerged from speakers in the ceiling. A crowd of drinkers raised glasses and cheered. A few tried to sing, badly. She turned to see the revelers were wearing Russian uniforms—very much like UEF livery but with red piping on the collars and cuffs. She downed one drink, then grabbed his and swilled that as well. The robot replaced them and she repeated her process.

"Not a fan of Russian folk songs?" Katsev asked.

"Just this one in particular."

"With a name like Rosenski? You should be all over it."

"Rosenski is Polish. My mother was the Russian. She's this short, round lady who can kill a man with a single lash of her tongue. Dad was built like a football player and couldn't sing a note. Guess who I took after?"

She ignored Katsev's side-eye. Six feet tall with auburn hair, Sara Rosenski would have stood out even covered in mud and dressed in rags. Her Sleer implants had taken her impressive natural physique and turned her into a Greek goddess.

"What's that got to do with an old song?" he asked.

"This is 'Katyusha.' It's about a woman who's out in the wild, singing to the world in the hope that her boyfriend who's at war can hear her and intuit that she's thinking of him. Well, the U-War came and everyone in my family joined up except for my mother and me. She'd play this damn song every day. All it did was fill me with dread that I'd never see any of them again. And now it's my turn. I'm sitting here five-hundred light years from home, with a drink and food to eat and a place to sleep and a job to deal with and tons of responsibilities. New York, Boston, and Philadelphia all took direct hits when the Sleer decided to teach us a lesson. But I think maybe he wasn't at home. Maybe he got out. Maybe—"

"Hey," he said, touching her hand, "you're past all that. Eyes front, not behind you."

"Too much work to do," she quoted.

"You know it."

"I can't stop. I keep thinking about what if this, what if that. I keep wondering if he—"

"You keep wondering. And the lists keep coming up from New Darwin. Boston took a direct hit, and there were no travel orders in his name at the time. If he's not here, he's nowhere."

"Yeah. What's that leave me with?"

"With me. With the Nightmares. With a career that has only picked up steam as we get our bearings on this space station. And with a certain first lieutenant who hasn't graduated from your care yet."

She snorted. "Simon Brooks. Fairchild's wunderkind and friend to alien AIs everywhere."

"Just get his ass trained. We need friends in high places, and he's on his way up there."

"I never want to hear this song again." She straightened and stretched and paid both their tabs. She felt the boozy fog falling away from her head, her implants already sensing she'd had too much and cleaning her bloodstream. "Have you seen the latest? The weather reports?"

"I see it all. I have Fairchild showing me everything he gets in the spirit of cooperation and mission goals. We don't have a lot of time left to make a move, and… well. It's being discussed at the highest levels."

"On Earth, not up here."

"Oh no. Up here. There's a lack of communication, but that doesn't mean the Brigade's mission is over. Get Brooks trained. We'll need him. Soon."

He hopped off his stool, stretched like a giant cat, and stalked off. She waited while her implants flushed the remaining alcohol from her blood, pushed the empty glasses back to the robot, and left to meet Brooks.

They'd come seven hundred light years in the past two years, and still had no idea how to get the Sleer to listen to them.

Bad enough that Simon Brooks was the only one the Sleer were willing to talk to. Commanders Katsev and Fairchild had both been specific about this meeting. Despite their presence on Great Nest, humanity was still very much locked into a single star system, while the allied races controlled thousands. Technically, humanity was a bi-system species, with a few thousand Unified Earth Fleet personnel inhabiting the orbital ring around Great Nest, the Sleer capital. The remainder were stuck on Earth, literally beneath the bulk of the Sleer. The aliens got the orbital ring, with safety and security, while the humans were forced to eke out what living they could amid accelerating natural disasters and environmental horrors. That had to change. Soon.

A raft of distractions buffeted Brooks's mind. Projects he owned, promises he'd made. The Allied Sleer Fleet was not supposed to work like this, with Sleer keeping their advantages to themselves and the humans begging for crumbs.

This meeting was typical. After long negotiations, the Sleer command figured the humans had earned a system of their own to colonize. A small gesture. A reward for having saved Great Nest from destruction at the hands of four Skreesh titans two years ago. The Sleer diplomat sat across from Brooks, a holographic display of the local neighborhood projected between them.

Project Polar Star. That was this plan's official name. Brooks still wasn't sure what name the Sleer used for his home world, but he knew where Polar Star came from: Earth was the star directly overhead when you looked up to the sky from the Battle Ring Great Nest.

He blinked, sitting straight in his chair, staring at the Sleer. The saurid diplomat seated across the table from him didn't move a muscle except to slide his nictating membranes once. Twice. Thrice.

Stick to the neighborhood. Nothing further than fifty light years from Earth.

"Cygnus?" he asked.

"No."

Brooks tried again. "Eridani?"

The Sleer blinked, his compound eyes flicking, examining data feeds. "No."

"Tau Ceti?"

"No."

Brooks kept his eyes on the display, trying to think like a chess master predicting an opponent's next move and countering. Every star system within fifty light years of Earth was lit in electric blue. With each refusal, a blue marker became red. They were running out of blue. "How can they all be taken?"

The Sleer placed both hands on the table and arched his crown feathers. "Space is crowded. Many races want resources. You are new to this. No one's fault. But you are very late."

Brooks bobbed his head. The alien had a point. It was an accident that a Sleer ship had crashed on Earth thirteen years ago. Without it, he'd still be there. Probably working with Dad to save what parts of the northern preserve hadn't already gone up in smoke. "Fine. Let's forget about constellations for the moment. Let's name stars. Alpha Centauri?"

"No."

"Sirius?"

"No."

"Betelgeuse?"

"No."

"61 Cygni?"

"No."

"36 Ophiuchi?"

"No."

"No? 36 Ophiuchi has the least compatible planet ever discovered. It can't be claimed already."

This time the Sleer flicked its tongue. "Claimed by Rachnae this morning. No."

"Fine." There were very few blue systems left on the board. "Delta Pavonis?"

"No."

"Why the hell not?" Brooks asked. "It's almost entirely covered by water. There's one land mass that's barely the size of Iceland—"

"Language, nest-mate."

Brooks inhaled, held it for ten seconds, and exhaled. "Why not?"

"Already claimed."

"By whom?"

"By the Decapods."

Brooks deflated. The Dec were an aquatic species. He couldn't complain without sounding churlish. "Oh."

The Sleer seemed to grin through tooth-filled jaws. "Yes, 'Oh.' No."

Brooks looked back at the map. "Chi Draconis?"

"No."

"82 Eridani?"

"No."

Brooks shook his head. "*Dim es meshugga,*" he blurted. "Look, I'm going to name the last two markers on that map," he said, "and if you say 'no' to both, I'll..."

"What?"

"I'll recommend that Unified Earth Fleet sever its ties with the Sleer."

This time, the Sleer burst into motion, both eyes 'blinked' like mad, while the tongue flicked. All at once the tip of the Sleer's nose was within an inch of touching his own. He seemed to shift position so quickly that Brooks could barely see it, much less react. Even his implants hadn't given him any warning. What kind of hardware did Sleer diplomats carry, anyway?

"Sever ties?" it asked. "You won't. Skreesh are coming. We leave, Skreesh will still come. Then others will follow. Decapods, Movi, Rachnae—"

Simon held up his hands. "We can handle them."

"With what ships?" the Sleer asked. "*Ascension* is inactive. *Paladin* is incomplete. No new ships from Earth arrive without orders from high command. You are alone. You would lose the fight. But you might try. How much of the battle ring would survive? A ring of particles, perhaps?"

Brooks looked back at the map as the alien sat back down. What the hell, he might as well give in to the inevitable. "Beta Hydri?"

"No."

Last one. "That leaves Vega."

"What is Vega?"

"Alpha Lyrae," Brooks murmured, sagging in his chair—his oversized Sleer chair, too big for a human—letting his feet dangle.

"Yes."

Brooks threw up his hands, then froze. "Wait, did you say yes?"

"I did. That system is worthless. Impossible to mine. Strategically useless. Take it."

Brooks locked his implants into the data network, swiped his hand, and the system of Vega turned from red to a frosty green. Earth's responsibility and opportunity. The only green mark in a sea of reds. "Thank you."

"*A dank*," he said. "You welcome."

Outside, the Sleer went one way and Brooks went the other. Rosenski met him outside the embassy meeting room. She looked tired. But then, being the head of *Gauntlet*'s battle group would do that to anyone. "Well?"

"Vega," he announced.

"Okay. What else?"

Brooks shook his head. "Nothing."

She shifted until her back was against the wall and her eyes closed. "Nothing? Like, 'hey Dad, what do you want on your hot dog?' nothing?"

"More like, 'hey Dad, what do you want on your hot dog? What do I want on my hot dog? I want you to call me. At the very least I want you to talk to me like a human being instead of ten seconds of small talk and then handing to phone to your brother. That's what I want on my hot dog.'"

She folded her arms and led him down the walkway. The shifts were changing and the hallway was full of people. All kinds of them. Humans, Movi, and Sleer mixed freely. The Rachnae had specialized atmospheric needs and the Decapods couldn't live out of water for very long. Both kept to themselves. "Ouch."

"Yep."

Brooks walked slowly, but not aimlessly. The commissary was only a few blocks away.

"Seriously, what'd we get?"

"Seriously, they gave us Vega. Twenty-five light years from Earth, more like five hundred from here. But it's close to home and strategically worthless to the Sleer, so we have something to experiment with. I want a muffin."

Rosenski grimaced. "Doc said your weight was up, remember? A muffin is the last thing you need."

"Bah. I just spent an hour of my life being shot down over every worthwhile and worthless planet within fifty light years of us by the only friends we have in the universe. I deserve a lousy muffin."

"They say it's for our own good."

"I'm sure. Just in case they fight another war with the Skreesh or Lord knows who else. They'll need allies. Guess who that will be?" he asked.

"Probably not the Movi."

"Not a chance. The Sleer love us for all the worst reasons.

They're the door to the universe, and we're their doormat."

"But you're not bitter."

"Not one bit."

She pounded his shoulders, making him flinch. "Good. Because we have less than two hours until we meet and greet about two thousand dignitaries, well-wishers, and assorted military and diplomatic types."

Brooks put his hands over his face. "Oh my God, that's right. First anniversary of the allied fleet treaty. God help us."

"I think he's done enough already. Let's get your muffin then get dressed. Party starts at 20:00 and division heads can't be late to their own shindig."

"Heh. You said shindig. Why are your eyes red?"

She answered him with a shove. "Come on, Genius. Let's get you home."

Brooks flexed his spine as Sara shoved him forward. This part of Battle Ring Great Nest was known as the Diplomacy Dome, and if you wanted a close look at the way this corner of the galaxy worked, this was the place to be. Since creating the new alliance between the Sleer and humanity two years ago, they'd set up this portion of the Ring as a unified area where all races of the galaxy could come together. It helped that Tall Lord Nazerian, the Sleer officer in charge of this station, had been watching a lot of Babylon 5 since arriving. Brooks and Marc Janus had pushed him toward other science fiction shows that involved a theme of many races gathering to overcome their problems in the face of continuing crises. Farscape was a favorite among the Sleer. Star Trek, not so much, but the humans enjoyed that one. In the end, there needed to be a place where the allied races could hash out problems and learn about each other. Diplomacy Dome was a section where that could happen. It made things simpler by getting everyone used to seeing each other. It was a slow beginning: Sleer, Movi, and humans were now learning how to greet each other on the street, and the few Vix that arrived seemed friendly enough. The first Rachnae were due to arrive in the next few weeks and the Decapods were already here, recently arrived in a ten-mile-long star ship in orbit over Great Nest. Waiting for something. At this precise moment in time, there was a single Cycomm in residence, and she was inseparable from her adopted humans.

Past that, they arrived at the airlocks that closed off the following section. Brooks leaned forward and used his Sleer implants to trigger a response from the security system. "ID confirmed. Rosenski, Sara. Brooks, Simon. Welcome to Primate Alley. Enter at will."

While the Diplomacy Dome was a hub of inter-species conversation, Primate Alley was a section for the humans alone, built according to specific instructions over the past year. Sleer could, of course, come through the section if needed, but considering that the section lay next to the diplomat's area, they tended to go around it.

The doors split open and they entered… Earth. Earth as it might have been had there been a distinct improvement of the human condition before the Sleer's arrival. A yellow sun shone down onto a human city, white and silver habitation towers clustered into a web of neighborhoods, each connected by tram lines and rooftop car ports. A grid of parks and canals wound its way through the space between the clusters. At the edge of town lay a wide hexagonal space filled with wild greenery, and multiple glass domes rose past it. In the center of the domed structures lay a sports stadium, and beyond that a marina that bordered on a rippling sea which surrounded the island, water as blue as the sky above it.

Brooks inhaled deeply. "Look at this place. We could fit two million people in this city, easy. The fact the Sleer only let fifty thousand of us up here is a crime."

"One good thing about being the only people living in it... everyone gets their own luxury apartment."

"You know what I mean."

"I do. Now that we're flying on all our thrusters, we have a chance to speed the immigration and assimilation game in our favor."

"Fifty thousand this year, fifty the next, then fifty the next. At that rate, we'll all be enjoying settings like this in a hundred and twenty thousand years. It's not even the fancy new Ring over Earth. This is the one we helped patch together after the Skreesh assault."

"Well, now that they're letting us have our own system to colonize, maybe that will give the Sleer high command a sense of security," she said.

"Or they hope that by getting our own colony world, we'll leave here, head to the new world, and forget about living above our own planet. Not a very friendly gesture."

"We'll come up with something. They can't stonewall us forever."

"They don't have to. Waiting us out won't take forever. How many people are freezing to death downstairs right now? Any idea? Millions? Billions?"

The air temp around them dropped a few degrees as Rosenski stiffened. Talking about Earth was a dick move. The rapid growth of the Earth Ring had destabilized the planetary environment, and things were getting worse. It was getting colder every day as new glaciers marched south. And the sector governors near the equator were balking at receiving refugees from the global north, despite OMP orders for them to do so. It was an ugly and depressing situation. "They're surviving," she allowed.

"Barely. I spoke to my dad a few weeks ago by way of the North American sector network. It's cold down there and getting colder. The crap in the atmosphere isn't filtering down quickly enough to make air transport viable, and ashfall is killing crops on some of the most arable land."

"Think about Vega. Hell, Dance and Binil live next door to you. Maybe that will take your mind off it."

"I'll do my best."

They parted ways in the lobby of their building, a forty-floor complex that could house a thousand people, and there were scores of buildings like it in this part of town. He did think about Vega, going so far as to pull data through his implants as he showered and dressed. It wasn't as if the Sleer diplomat had told him the humans couldn't go anywhere. They'd simply said no to everything except the one they didn't want. Was that because they knew Vega was worthless real estate? No planets had ever been observed there, but with the recycler and construction technology the Sleer brought to the table, a planet wouldn't be needed. The star was bright and young, and there were resources in that system orbiting it. All anyone had to do was drop a moderately sized space habitat in a useful orbit and populate it. The rest would take care of itself. So why hadn't the Sleer done that already? More importantly, did they expect the humans to inhabit that system any differently? If so, how? And why? Surely the UEF had shown that it could manage Sleer equipment as well as they could, if not always as intuitively.

Something smelled wrong. The Sleer had looked at Vega and found it wanting. But not off limits to the pathetic primates they meant to leave behind one day. They'd found a use for every other system they'd examined. A small voice in his head whispered a possibility he hadn't dared think about yet. What if the Sleer had rushed through because they hadn't expected to find anything...and didn't?

What if something useful *was* there... and they'd missed it?

CHAPTER 3

THE *BEAST* WAS GONE. Long live the independent freighter *Bastard*.

It wasn't the best vessel that money could buy. Money, as Sleer defined it, couldn't buy much of anything. None of the space faring races used currency the way humans did; they considered it barbaric. Modern economics were complex enough to fill a library, and the Sleer and Movi and others used massively parallel computer models to figure out exchange rates and values. Earth had centralized its money supply with the end of the Unification War, and now the Unified Earth Fleet credit was the standard unit of measurement. Not everyone was on board with that. Plenty of local currencies existed and remained in use on the planet, but all had exchange rates that changed with the price of work that went into any products. According to Frances Underhill, one of the OMP's AI, ZERO's, functions was figuring out how much everything was worth. Valri couldn't imagine having a job like that. It sounded like a ton of work and no fun. Maybe it was the perfect project for a mechanical intelligence who had a close relationship with alien technology.

Whatever it was, it was above her pay grade. If she ever got a pay grade. If she ever got paid. If she ever acquired clients, cargo, and markets. So far, all of that was a big fat nothing.

But now that *Bastard* was a reality, that would change.

She'd begun life as a *Nekezaken*-class freighter. The word, as far as Valri Gibb could tell with some assistance from the battle ring library, meant 'Family Cruiser.' Less of a cargo vessel than the word *freighter* suggested in English, but it was the equivalent of a station wagon in the Sleer navy. There was nothing military about her. She was designed and produced by the millions all over Sleer space for the express purpose of getting Sleer together for star-faring exploration and settlement. One hundred meters long and capable of spatial transitions of fifty light years or less, she was small and limited. Absolutely no threat to a Sleer warship or anything else. A few small-scale weapons, for defense against badly equipped pirates or privateers. But with five thousand metric tons of cargo capacity and a relatively spacious living area, she was exactly what Valri wanted.

That fact that her new ride's prow looked like a lobster—with wide "claws" on either side curving a bit toward each other—was icing on the proverbial cake. They didn't move, nor did they open or close. Just hollow workspaces—flight deck on the right, captain's quarters and lounge on the left. The tail thrusters even flared a bit like a lobster's. No missile launchers to be sure, but a few light lasers scattered on her hull promised to keep predators at a distance.

And she was all Valri's. All the Sleer had to do was approve her application to the Sleer Merchant Academy, and she could spend the next six months getting certified to run her baby as well as get licensed to broker trade deals. She'd looked carefully into every aspect of it. There were requirements, rules, regulations, and a host of other bureaucratic niceties to deal with. But getting her broker's license to work with On-Star Traveler had taken over a year while working full time at her desk job, and coding new apps for making money. She'd built PROFIT, the trading AI that had put her firm on the global map. She could do this. In the meantime, there was time and a small allowance from the UEF to get the ship ready. It needed repairs, but didn't everyone?

The rest of her crew wasn't as cooperative.

There was Richard "Grandpa" Frost, and "Skull" Skellington, and a repurposed self-directed service drone named "Assistant." Most days, Valri referred to it as "Ass" because it amused her and as a way of dealing with the stress of trying to open her own shipping business. It wasn't as easy as it looked from behind a desk. But she didn't have to think about those problems now.

She reclined in the pilot's chair in the right claw, transparent steel windows looking out on the workings of the hangar bay. The flights controls were far simpler than anything she'd seen on board any UEF craft, but then they were meant to be. Pilot couch on the left, co-pilot on the right, and two more couches behind them for a gunner and an engineer if needed. The couch closed around her, mimicking the way crash couches on Sleer warships locked their armored occupants into place. She'd never really trust Sleer designs, but they were easier to manage than the harnesses human crews had to rely on.

She could fly this if she had to. She surely wanted to. It had no way to work with her implants, but then it wasn't meant to. Implants were not generally available to non-military Sleer, and this was a decidedly non-military design. Being Sleer designed, the seats were bigger than she was. Maybe she'd need a pillow under her to see over the console.

A double beep from the speaker. That, at least, she understood. She hit the button. "Captain here. What is it?"

"Cap, this is Frost. If you could come to the deck, we'd like a word, please."

"On my way."

She pulled herself up and descended through the ship. It was a simple structure. Three main decks plus the two claws. The upper deck house the crew quarters and lounge and a kitchen and pantry, with mechanical closets for access to often used systems, and a ship's locker at the end. The main deck below it was the working area. Storage areas for cargo, hauled aboard through wide hatches in containers and locked to the deck using both grav plates and tie-downs. In the rear, the main engines, a small reactive furnace, and fuel supply to keep them running. Below that lay the ground deck, where the emergency supplies were kept. A Burro, an open topped anti-grav vehicle for local jaunts, three fly-cycles for the same thing but for a single passenger, and the freezer. The sort of thing that could double to store medical samples. It got that cold.

She didn't ask the obvious questions: why a family of Sleer colonist would need a freezer big enough to store a cow in at such temperatures? Or where the wiring for the upper hull defenses were kept? It was the only ship for sale and the price wasn't too obnoxious. Yes, buyer beware and all that, but...

She emerged from the main hatch and sauntered easily down the loading ramp. Frost and Skellington were in conversation with Kozzak, the Sleer who wanted to unload the ship. Tall, even for a Sleer, Kozzak towered over the humans by at least two full feet, with a mottled coloring around his head and long neck. He was dressed in a Sleer military coverall but wore no armor. His guild patches ran down his suit's entire left sleeve. The dude had been around.

And he apparently knew how to carry himself in the presence of strange primates. Frost stood to the side, arms folded over his chest, seething, while Ass made indistinct mechanical noises. The drone's English was choppy. They'd have to fix that eventually, but his machine pidgin served for the moment.

Ass met her at the foot of the ramp. "Captain! Assistance required. Immediate!"

She waved the machine off. "Skull" Skellington was the star attraction for this meeting. Skull had been teaching himself to speak Sleer over the past year, and by now he was quite good. Even with the physical gestures. He was quite animated even now, with his face puffed to three shades of red and his arms flailing while he rose from one stance to another, alternately hissing and shouting.

Valri strode to his side and placed a cool hand on his shoulder. He backed off immediately. She got the idea he was exhausted, and not just his patience. "What seems to be the issue?"

Kozzak blinked rapidly. "No issue. Merely explaining guild rules and regulations to your crew, Ship Master Valri Gibb."

"I see that. Mr. Skellington, can you recap for my benefit?"

"Lesser Servant of Guild Matters Kozzak rejected our application for an operating license," Skull wheezed. His tone set her on edge. Skull had never been anything but friendly and painfully dignified around her. For that matter she didn't think she'd ever seen Skull growl at anyone.

"Rejected? Denying my new ship a chance to fly? I haven't even paid you for it yet."

Kozzak raised his arms a bit and clicked his foreclaws: a conciliatory gesture for a Sleer. "Not my preference, Valri Gibb. In the time that primates—sorry…Umans—arrived on Great Nest, guild rules change. Again, not my doing. For guild merchants to operate, Lords Grossusk and Moruk create new rules for primate safety. Which includes new requirements for flight certification. Sorry for the delay."

"Delay? So, you're not denying my ship a license, it's merely delayed? That right?"

"I inform your crew of new requirements," Kozzak said, indicating the tablet in Frost's hand.

"And so he did. A list of demands." A flicker of a reaction crossed Frost's face. Valri knew enough about the man to know that in his imagination, he'd grabbed the alien, pulled off its hide, and made it into a jacket.

She took the gadget and scrolled through its contents. "We need to create a whole new bureaucracy just to deal with this," she murmured. There were reams of requirements. Safety inspections for new ships and existing vessels transferred to human agencies. Docking fees, flight fees, cargo transport fees, and licensing fees. Certification classes and examinations to be given by the Sleer Merchant Academy. Prohibitions against civilian humans serving aboard Sleer warships. The list seemed endless.

She looked up. "This is one hell of a straitjacket, my dude."

Kozzak blinked rapidly. "What means straight jacket? Is garment?"

"Is cage."

"You wear cage?"

She thrust the tablet into his face. "You're putting us in a cage. Leaving us behind while *your* people colonize every world within easy reach of *our* home world."

"Not at all. We elevate you to Sleer standards. For your own good, and Sleer's good, too. Apologies. I will remit all your applications to Sleer Merchant Academy today. If you pass requirements, you can be flying this ship in...two years, maximum. Contact me when you are ready." Kozzak gave a Sleer bow and bounded off. It was a disturbing thing to watch a Sleer bound. Nothing that weighed as much as a baby elephant had any right to sprint like that.

"Two years of night school," Frost growled. "Well, that's all kinds of fun. We might as well re-enlist with the UEF. We'd be back in uniform in a few weeks and we'd still be here."

"I'm sure Ray Fairchild would love to have you two back on his crew. I don't suppose there's a spare cargo ship built by human hands lying around?"

"Not that I know of."

Skellington took the slate from her, scrolled through the text with a fingertip. "Much of this doesn't even apply to us. See? The agency that needs to come up with these rules doesn't even exist yet. Those insignificant mealy-mouthed cretins."

"You're not speaking Sleer anymore, Skull."

"Hurt myself, ma'am."

"I thought so. Although we seem to have a fuck of a wait if you intend to call me that."

"What, ma'am? I'm being polite."

"You're making me sound older than you. Stop it please."

"All right, Valri. I'm open to new courses of action."

"You're the former intelligence wizard, you tell me."

"I'll need time to go over this. In the meantime, I don't think it's a bad call to take our scaly friend's advice. This part here says that admission preference is given to humans with UEF ranks. We all three have ranks."

"Some rank I have. Temporary Acting Captain," she recalled. She often wondered why these two had followed her into the private sector. Frost was a real CPO and Skull was an officer. Yes, she'd been their CO for a few days during the Skreesh attack on Great Nest, but...

"It qualifies. If you served, you have a better than even chance of acceptance. Shall we find a corner and fill out the paperwork?"

Valri sighed and nodded. They both stared at Frost, who grimaced. "I'm thinking," he said. "All right. I'm going to assume that you don't need to speak Sleer like a native for this to work. Plus, even if you do, my implants should get me through the literature, right?"

Skull slapped him on the back. "If you need practice, I can help."

"I'm sure you can, Skull. Fine. I was going to have to bump up my skills before long anyway. Let's go back to school."

CHAPTER 4

IN HER TIME as a quant for On-Star Traveler, Valri Gibb had attended her share of fancy business parties. Balls, galas, dedications—all designed from the ground up to woo funding for one project or another from those with wealth to spare.

Tonight's event was something in a wholly different class. If it was tonight: while so-called Primate Alley synched to Earth time over South Pico Island, the Diplomacy Dome ran in a world of perpetual twilight. Low lighting, enough for everyone inside to navigate, but bright lights were eschewed as a matter of inter-racial policy. Simon Brooks had explained it to her. Every species evolved to operate best in different wavelength of light. The Sleer apparently could see in the entire spectrum, or close to it, from X-rays to microwaves. Those damned compound eyes of theirs. The Sleer had names for colors and combinations that humans couldn't even imagine. The Movi home world, on the other hand, orbited the outermost edge of a dim K-dwarf star's habitable zone. It never got brighter there than dusk on Earth. So their eyes resembled some nocturnal species like cats or wolves: a wide iris and slitted pupils with a reflective retina.

But when great gatherings like this were held, the rules

changed. The sky was now the bright purple of Home Nest, the Sleer homeworld. A purple sky with yellow-orange clouds hovered above everyone. Right in the middle of the acceptable eyesight limits. It was one thing all the races could agree upon. That, and the fact that humans were in the universe now and represented a potential force to be reckoned with. The details as to how were still being discussed.

There were plenty of opportunities for discussion. The grand affair—officially the arrival of Tall Lord of Interstellar Trade Dashak from the ring around Earth—wouldn't start for a while. The Sleer sense of timing was different from the humans. In the Unified Earth Fleet, guests arrived at seven, schmoozed until eight, sat down for dinner until nine and departed after coffee and dessert at ten. The Sleer designated a full day for the event, and then it went on until things were done.

Valri arrived in her finest attire. In this case, her Allied Sleer Fleet uniform, really just a UEF dress uniform with the shiny bits removed. All except for her rank insignia, Temporary Active Captain, and her combat action ribbon. She'd earned both and had no problem reminding the world of it.

She strolled from one end of the garden to the other, over and over, trying to notice everything she could. Her implants helped her identify the military guests, but the civilians were another story. No implants, no transponder IDs, and the facial recognition gear the OMP used to monitor everyone's comings and goings was limited to human faces. She had to rely on her own senses and memory to tell one non-human from another. After a while, all the dinosaurs looked the same to her.

Then she saw Kitthen. The one Sleer she'd recognize anywhere, and not because he looked like a kitten. He was very short for a Sleer—only a few inches taller than she was—and his crown feathers were unique: orange, yellow, and purple. A saurian road flare in full bloom. She made a beeline for him and did her best to adjust her body posture to a formal greeting. "Lesser Servant of Trade Kitthen! It is a distinct honor to meet you here."

"Captain Gibb. I wish you well. Are you healthy?"

She popped her implants into translation mode and allowed her brain to start speaking Sleer as well as the alien tech translated. "I am. Is your nest well?"

"It is."

"That's good to hear. I wonder if I may ask a question."

"Of course."

"Has trade representative Kozzak been able to render a decision on my application to join the Sleer Merchant Academy? I filed my paperwork this morning."

"That's not my responsibility. I hope the process isn't making you unwell. I know uncertainty can be stressful for mammals."

He had no idea. Running a transport to the stars had been her dream for years. She bought a junk yard on South Pico Island just to harvest a crappy shuttle to make it happen. That ambition had introduced her to Ray Fairchild and his crew. "I am still waiting for an answer is all."

"There is time yet. Many humans ask to join the academy and other institutions, but we are limited in our time and attention. Adopt a stance of patience. Excuse me." Kitthen bowed and retreated into a crowd of other Sleer. Her blood pressure rose a notch as she realized she'd been snubbed. By *Kitthen*. She *had* to learn control. Lately, her heart had a way of jumping into her throat. She sometimes felt her blood pressure rising so quickly her eyes might explode. "Makes you wonder if they ever make up their minds about anything," she murmured, and took a sip of her drink. A very human Chablis, in a glass delivered from the officer's mess. Human glass, human wine, human digestive system. It would be hard not to think in those terms. The Sleer certainly did.

She sensed Ray Fairchild before she saw him. He approached from her right flank, stayed in her blind spot, and finally appeared at her side. A comforting wall of man. His scent alone was enough to take her anxiety down a notch. Standing next to the Deputy CAG was the safest place in the budding Allied Sleer Fleet.

"You're late," she scolded as she slipped her arm through his.

"Not at all. You were early."

"Someone had to make sure the bar was open."

"I'm glad you're taking your new job seriously."

She snorted and nearly spilled her drink. "A job is nine to five, five days a week, with lunch hours, pay, and benefits. Maybe a company car. A travel expense account."

"I think they can arrange that."

She glared at him, wondering if he was messing with her mind. That wasn't Ray's style. "I doubt they'd try. I'm no closer to my dream job as starship owner than I was this morning. They either lost my application to get a trader's license or they're ignoring it. Hell, Kitthen just told me not to get my hopes up."

"Ah, I see, you're behind the times."

"What's that mean?"

"Next time you pass the comm board, look for your name. You have been awarded the position of Undersecretary of Commerce for Interstellar Trade. That's a fully qualified department head spot in EarthGov." He raised his glass and clinked it against hers. "Congratulations, Madame Undersecretary."

She blinked and dropped his arm, then held her glass in both hands and drained it. Heady fumes drove into her sinuses and her heart rate doubled again. The two conversations could have taken place on different planets in different eras. How did anything work anymore? "I don't know what to say."

"Say, thank you."

"No. I mean...literally. I didn't apply for any government position. I asked for a spot in the Sleer Merchant Academy. I want to run transport ships between here and Earth. *That's* the dream, not another desk job." She twirled slowly, studying the room, seeking answers and finding none. She took in air, letting it come deep into her lungs, working to calm her pulse. "What happened?"

"Let's find out. Where's my comm guy?" Fairchild scanned the room, located his target, and led her away.

This section of the dome was given to a wide green expanse —a park. Low buildings surrounded a wide-open space paved with glittering flat tiles, and trees and shrubs formed a bit of a maze. Lots of private corners for discrete conversations. In the center, plenty of tables and benches designed for Sleer bodies. Uncomfortable for humans, but usable. Mammals would always be the children at the table.

They worked the room arm in arm, Fairchild pointedly greeting everyone they passed, Valri distracted and distant. When she came back to herself, they stood between a knot of Movi and another of Sleer. But in front of them stood Simon Brooks, Sara Rosenski, and Frances Underhill, all dressed in their UEF finery and nursing drinks and plates of finger food.

Underhill raised a glass. "Uncle Fairchild and Auntie Fairchild *de facto*. How nice to see you again."

She felt Ray stiffen as he looked them over. Underhill's signature blue-black hair had been done up in a bun for the event, her infamous silver headband nowhere to be seen. It blended perfectly with the black with blue piping of the OMP uniform. "What are you three conspiring about?"

Underhill gestured with her glass. "Not a conspiracy. Young Simon is telling me about his re-assignment, and I suggested he look at the Office of Military Protocols as a career. We love techies. They're worth their weight in gold."

"Then I thanked her for the opportunity and said maybe in twenty or thirty years," Brooks confirmed.

Rosenski popped an *hors d'oeuvre* in her mouth and spoke around it. "I just stood here and refused to say anything. While silently lamenting the fact that my career seems to be inextricably linked to this yahoo's."

"Hey, you demanded I join the Nightmares. Besides, I'm a nerd, not a yahoo."

"Bah! You can be both."

"What's this crap about me getting a government job that I never applied for?" Valri demanded.

Underhill raised her hand. "I did that. Sorry, not sorry."

"Nice of you to ask if I wanted it first, Frances."

"I don't make these decisions on my own, Val. The Sleer got your application to the Academy and sent it to me to verify you were you. I confirmed it, then sent it back. Then ZERO flagged you." She leaned in and whispered hotly. "ZERO was specific. You don't say no to the iron giant. Not if you know what's good for you."

For the millionth time in their relationship, Valri wondered who she was talking to: the Overcop or the woman. Frances made a habit out of intertwining herself with the job, and there were times when Valri wondered if it wouldn't be better just to part ways and stay away. "Is that a threat?"

"Not at all. Just saying. The OMP knows who we are now. Who you are. They want the new human-Sleer institutions to take on a certain shape. They found your application, did a background check, and figured you could do more for the home world than you could running cargo for the Sleer empire."

Now she at least had a sense of the mechanism behind the bureaucracy. "The iron giant give you a reason at least?"

"He did, but it would take hours to explain."

She cocked her head and gave her a look. "We have time. Cocktail hour can last all night. Spill it, boo."

"I'd like to hear the reason, too," Rosenski agreed.

Brooks gave a thumbs up. "Me too."

Even Fairchild nodded. "Seriously, I'd like to hear it as well. It's been keeping me up at night. Dish. That's an order."

Underhill sighed and looked up at a hissing sound. The Sleer were dressed in colorful robes, snarling at each other and drinking from metal goblets big enough to hold a human skull. "Not here." She led them to a clear spot some distance away, surrounded by a tall hedge on three sides.

"You all know the latest ASF transport fleet docked yesterday, right?" When they agreed, she continued, "You might not know everything it brought. A ton of new blood to staff the various academies and fleet posts that are being created. Human architects to study the battle ring's layout and to design new ships for us. News from Earth, too. On-Star Traveler, your old firm, Val? It just filed for bankruptcy."

"Jeez. For real?" Valri wasn't sure whether she should cheer or cry. The trading desk she'd run at that place had absorbed so much of her life for years. It wasn't what she was, it was who she was. At least until she'd left with a giant bank account and no rights to her own intellectual property, her trading algorithms. "I hate to say it, but I'm not sure what that means in this day and age."

"Neither did anyone on Earth. The OMP knows all about your deal with them. Your IP still lives on their servers, but if those get auctioned off to some Earth-based firm, your work goes with it. General Hendricks—"

"*General?*"

Underhill raised a hand. "Later. He decided trade with other planets could be a boon or a nightmare, depending on who ran it. If nothing else, he knows you won't use the data to put yourself above every human on the planet. So ZERO ordered the assets of the firm frozen and placed under OMP security. If you're in charge of the department that gets access…"

"Oh, no." A server drone ambled past with a full tray of drinks. Val exchanged her empty for two full ones and drank with both hands.

"Pretty much. As far as interstellar trade goes, you have a thick wall around you. Work for Hendricks, the wall stays up. Work for anyone else…law enforcement can detain you at their leisure. Gratz, Madame Undersecretary."

"Oh, dear God."

Brooks chewed his last bit of finger food and palmed his plate, flexing his arm like a discus player warming up. "So now that our Captain—"

"Temporary Active Captain."

"—excuse me, is in charge of trade with Earth, let's talk about Vega," Brooks said. "ZERO know about that, too?"

"Not that he's told me." Underhill traded her empty glass for a fresh one from a passing server bot and said, "But sure, let's have a talk. I'm told it was the only world the Sleer were willing to let us use for our own. Why do you think that is, Lieutenant Genius?"

"I have an idea," he said. "The rep I spoke to this morning said that Vega was impossible to mine and strategically useless. I thought about that, then I did a bit of research in the big databases. The Sleer are expanding out from Earth."

"The first scout wave, right?"

"Yes, ma'am. Zalamb-class scout ships. They're using our home system as a base and folding out to every star within a hundred light years of Earth. They know our names for them, the physical characteristics of each system, and they're making plans to bring them into the New Worlds."

"That's presumptuous as hell, don't you think?" Fairchild asked.

Rosenski folded her arms and scowled. "Makes sense. If I had an empire that was pulled out from under me, I'd want to start over in a region of space I could use my strengths on," she said.

Fairchild harrumphed. "Then again, it makes more sense to back track to your home world from a foreign location. That way, you link up with home and learn everything about the space between here and there. Still. That's a giant project. No way they'll be finished with that any time soon."

"They've got a two-year head start on us," Rosenski said. "They have an unlimited number of ships and crew. They'll have that database finished before you realize."

Valri didn't consider herself a military mind, but she recognized the truth in Rosenski's statement. When the Sleer put their full effort into something, it happened. Nothing stopped them. "What's different about Vega?" she wondered.

"That's a solid question," Ray decided. "I'm thinking we need to send our own people there ASAP to take a good long look."

Now they had Underhill's full attention. Always a problem. She'd demonstrated her trustworthiness over and over, but that uniform never stopped reminding them that she might work with them but reported to Hendricks. "What do you think they'll find?"

Brooks grinned. "Whatever the Sleer survey ship missed when they filed that report."

"Good luck with that. They don't miss much. That diplomat might have been telling you the truth."

"I still think we should—"

An uproar across the park. A gaggle of Movi women dressed in splendid robes and surrounded by holographic displays. Valri didn't spend much time with the delegation, and having heard about them from Judy Reagan's after-action report, she wasn't sure she wanted to. In any case she knew what bad news looked like. She polled her implants, shifted into their native language, and heard a crosstalk that she could barely parse. Body language helped her figure it out: the Movi were much closer to humanity that way than either would ever be to the Sleer. These folks were arguing frantically with unseen conversants, angry shouting and faces contorted by every emotion from rage to despair to petulance.

She left her own group to look more closely into the situation. Now she heard all the conversations at once, snippets and snatches at a time.

One Movi stood apart from the rest, a finger raised to her ear, speaking intently to the air in front of her. "If you cannot get me confirmation, then we have nothing to discuss. This is an opportunity to change everything! And it won't be long until the warlords and admirals decide the throne should be filled with one of their own. I don't care about the family. The family is gone. The idiot nephew is running things now. I am *not* shouting—" The woman brought up her head, slitted violet eyes filled with ambition and embarrassment. She stalked off and kept talking. The other Movi noticed Valri's presence and moved away. She imagined that similar conversations were taking place all over Battle Ring Zekerys right now.

"What was that about?" Fairchild asked when she rejoined the group.

"My Moviri isn't that great. And maybe the translator algos are out of whack, but it sounds like the Movi sovereign and his family have been deposed."

CHAPTER 5

THE MORE VALRI learned about her new job, the more she realized she wanted nothing to do with it.

In the time since the agreement between Captain Rojetnick and First Chairman Bon had gone into effect—as into effect as the Sleer occupation force and the *de facto* captive Earth government allowed—the humans had carved out a small slice of the Earthbound battle ring: EarthGov it was known on Great Nest. Essentially a 400 kilometer stretch of orbital ring positioned above South America, it housed what limited human representation the Sleer High Command was willing to allow aboard. The humans could make any rules they wanted to apply to other humans, but that was where their influence ended. Lords Grossusk and Moruk were not about to be dictated to by mere mammals.

The human leaders did their best to bring a semblance of their own governing practices to the stars. The Sleer were happy to accept new human populations into Great Nest's orbital ring, but no more than fifty thousand at a time, and only individual soldiers; no military units or their equipment. A ridiculous rule.

Even if humanity could somehow export every military unit on Earth, it wouldn't come close to approaching one percent of the total Sleer war machine present on Battle Ring Great Nest.

While the Earth cooled and the newly re-formed northern glaciers began their trek south, Antarctica had already increased its ice mass by ten percent. Winter had arrived, and it wasn't going away.

On paper, the Allied Sleer Fleet was an interspecies coalition for common defense against the encroaching Skreesh. In practice, the Sleer ran everything and threw the humans enough crumbs to shut them up. There was talk of allowing human climate refugees to occupy living space in the giant spokes that linked the planet surface to the orbital ring, but that was still mere talk. No agreements ever seemed to get signed.

EarthGov's Interstellar Trade Administration was even more complicated. The agency contained three sub-units: Industry and Analysis, Galactic Markets, and Enforcement and Compliance. Below Valri's position was a Deputy Undersecretary, an Assistant Undersecretary, and an entire plethora of deputies and assistants and offices. She had no idea what they all did, or even what they were supposed to do. She doubted she was that different from past bureaucrats. Politicians tapped their business partners or donors for help running the show all the time. Less of that since the OMP took the reins of human civilization, but it still happened. And now it was happening to her because she'd somehow made a name for herself as an on-again, off-again member of Hornet Squadron. In her own mind, she wasn't even a real soldier.

All she wanted was to fly her own space vessel. To make deals. Buy and sell without going through ten thousand pages of red tape for every transaction. It was finally possible. The battle ring held starships for the taking, ships of every size and description and mission. She could conceivably take any of them for her own use, but the Sleer High Command had rules against that, too. Starships were dangerous weapons, and humans were such *children*. Space travel was deemed too dangerous for them to be allowed access to anything bigger than a sports car.

Then there was Alien Megastructure-1, aka *Ascension*. Crashed on Earth thirteen years earlier, humans had spent a decade and countless billions to repair and recover her, turning her into an operational warship. Even though the AMS-1 was considered a Sleer flagship, it seemed that the rebuilt gun destroyer was always subject to supply shortages that didn't affect the rest of the Sleer fleet. Despite the fact her 6000-person crew had brought her this far, Sleer vessels were first in line for any supplies and repairs they needed.

Valri felt she could be useful running a space vessel. She'd done it before. But none of it was likely to happen as long as she was stuck here.

If this was her life…her job…her reward for a non-zero level of pseudo-military duty in service to whatever the Allied Sleer Fleet might become…she might as well bring all of herself to it. Her skill set wasn't insignificant. She was at best a middling spaceship captain, a figurehead with a crew that knew what to do without her being there.

She was also a skilled coder and quant. And the universe was utterly made by machines for other machines.

She felt a hole in her soul. A void shaped like her converted restored assault shuttle, the Beast. The Sleer had robbed her of a dream she'd built out of grease and grit and no small amount of help from Fairchild's Hornets. She didn't exactly want revenge, but she wanted to captain a ship. A real ship.

But first she wanted to know how bad others had it. She couldn't escape the image of the Movi woman who'd hissed into her comm at the party the other night. Something deep in Valri recognized a woman at the end of her rope, and thought the only difference between them was the length of rope they'd started with. Surely the Movi were experiencing a level of turmoil as bad or worse than her own.

Maybe there was an opportunity there. A chance for a newbie bureaucrat to find a way to link up two governments with converging aims: make trouble for the Sleer. She knew the Sleer and Movi had been at odds for centuries. They'd fought wars and trampled on each other's territories. And the Allied Race Treaty of decades past had included the Movi. Maybe they could be convinced to throw in with the humans this time around. Surly Bon wouldn't have a problem with that. And if he did, well, she was merely exploring opportunities for the UEF to secure its own new colony.

Vega. Everything came back to Vega one way or another.

Bur first she needed contacts she could talk to. She spent her morning tracking down the Movi trade delegates who'd attended the party, and made lists of names, titles, and job responsibilities. It was dizzying. Eventually she picked out her target, got ZERO to tell her where they were, and set off.

The Movi portion of the Diplomacy Dome was an upright cone, reminding her of the way big luxury hotels were built on Earth back in the day. Offices lay inside the building while wide terraces ringed the structure. They presented gardens, entertainments, and restaurants; places to relax and recover from a workday along walking paths. Plant life exploded around her. The entire setup was both spa and park. Looking up showed her tiers of balconies, and above it all, a holographic sky filled with a deep purple, punctuated by violet globes that flitted through the air. A dark fairyland was the best way she thought to describe it.

Valri found her target in a courtyard's cafe, reclining in a comfortable chair, a narrow table on her right and a floating display on her left. She sipped golden liquid from a fluted glass and lazily swiped through her display with a finger.

Valri bent slightly over the railing. "Miraled Makjit?"

The woman glared as her features froze in mid-sip. Then her eyebrows rose and her eyes widened. It was good to know that a surprised Movi looked similar to a human. "You!"

Valri smiled, wondering if baring teeth as a greeting would be taken as an attack or something less frightening. "Me. May I sit?"

Makjit put down her glass and scanned the park behind Valri before giving a single nod and pointed to where where the opening to the dining area lay. Probably wondering where the cameras and microphones were. Or the enforcers, henches, or soldiers. But Makjit was a gracious individual. "May I order you something? I'm quite impressed with the sparkling beverage your people made available in the cafe. 'Champagne,' it's called, I think. Would you like some?"

"It's a little early for me." Makjit's brow furrowed just a bit, and Valri amended her answer, "But why not? It's the end of the day somewhere, on some world."

"You travel as widely as we do, you learn to keep your own internal clock active and forget about the local time zones."

Valri settled into her chair. "I spent three years in an office. I didn't even have windows to look out of. Just walls and a console. I had to remind myself to get out of the chair every now and then to stretch."

"Sounds lovely."

"It was a bit hellish, but it led to the opportunity to be here." A server bot rolled over and deposited a glass in front of Valri.

She rolled the sweet vintage around on her tongue, allowing the bubbles to tickle her nose before swallowing. She wasn't sure what this stuff was, but it wasn't champagne. For all she knew, the bottle was less than a week old, but it hit the spot. "I have a question for you. Several, actually."

"You want to know about that conversation you overheard."

Crap. "Am I that obvious?"

"It's what I would have wanted to ask if our roles were reversed. Your Moviri is excellent," Makjit said, "but it's not a language we use to negotiate with strangers."

"Is this better?" Valri asked in Sleer.

Makjit smiled. Perfect, glowing teeth. "Much. You have a talent for this."

"And what is *this*?"

"Starting a conversation with a former stranger. You arrive, interrupting me while I'm working, and you're so pleasant about it that I'm not put off or angry. That's not always easy. Do me a small favor?"

"Surely."

"Smile for me."

Valri let her confusion show as Makjit pressed a fingertip to her forehead. Then she remembered that was how the Movi talked to someone else over a phone line. Makjit did have a few glittering buds over her eyebrow, but she'd assumed they were ornamental. Did they have implants of their own? She wanted to find out.

"There you are," her new friend murmured, her eyes dilating and looking at something unseen. Valri's implants detected nothing but the two of them and the access code to the general carrier signal that broadcast across the entire battle ring. But clearly, Makjit was doing research. On her. She wasn't sure if she should be flattered or wary. Maybe there was room for both. "I love your name, Valri Gibb. It's so compact."

"My job title is the opposite."

"Hmm. I see it: Undersecretary of Commerce for Interstellar Trade. Are you here to discuss opening a trade partnership with me?"

"Not exactly." She blinked, wondering how to proceed. A million questions flooded her mind, ranging over every topic she'd ever considered when the subject of aliens came up in past conversations. But one occupied more attention than any other. "Why *do* the Sleer run everything in this corner of the galaxy?" she wondered. She wasn't aware she'd spoken aloud until her new friend giggled.

"That's a long story. How's your knowledge of interstellar history?"

"Not very good, I'm afraid. We humans didn't know there was anything beyond our solar system until about thirteen years ago."

"And now the Sleer have captured your home world."

"I wouldn't put it that way."

"No, you wouldn't. Nor would my government. But I think we both know why you're so eager to learn. Finish your drink, then I'll educate you. We have a lot to talk about—" she squinted for a moment, reading an entry in an invisible database "—Madame Undersecretary."

"We do. Tell me about your merchant organization. The ships you use."

"That's not my area of expertise. There are major merchant houses, minor houses, and countless private operators. Ships. A great many ships in all sizes. While the Royal Movi Navy was in operation, we had secure trade routes throughout the kingdom. I haven't a clue how this crisis will disrupt those arrangements."

"But you have them. Which is more than my fellow humans can say. We need ships and you need opportunities."

"Why...yes. I believe that's true."

Valri grinned like a fiend. She finally understood—this wasn't so much a shakedown as an exploratory surgery. Makjit was excavating for clues. "Makjit has wares if I have coin," she teased.

Another hundred-yard stare. "I don't understand. What is 'coin?'"

"Coin. Credits. Gelt. Cash. Shekels. Lettuce. Bread. Money."

"*Money*? You still use currency to settle transactions?"

"Of course! Why not? The Sleer use—"

"No. The star faring races all use parallel matrix value processing algorithms. Not the same, but yes, they can convert to local values. Oh dear, this changes *everything*."

"Good lord."

"A moment, please. I'm trying to wrap my mind around the sheer *primitiveness* of your economy. Currency? How positively quaint!" Suddenly her face was the definition of seriousness. "Money means finance, which means wealth extraction and multiplication. That means taxation. *That* means tax avoidance. You must all be so violently *unhappy* on your world." She took a moment to consider, her face twisting into an expression of deep thought. "It would explain why you were willing to ally with the Sleer. With *Bon*. My dear Valri Gibb. You probably thought you were getting a solid return on your decision, didn't you?"

"Excuse me?"

"No major race uses *currency* to settle accounts. Ever. It's a type of amoral debauchery that's limited to historical lectures and very young children." Now she looked embarrassed, even pitiable. "You poor thing. What shall we do with you?"

Valri reached for her glass, tipped it back, and found herself signaling for another. "I get the idea I've stepped into a deep sinkhole here."

"I need to introduce you to my team. Our consulate is at the other end of the dome. It will take some time to travel there. Is that all right?"

"My calendar is clear for today."

"Good. Attend me?"

As promised, it took some time to navigate the maze of offices. Their destination proved to be a wide suite of rooms staffed exclusively by Movi. None wore military uniforms, all dressed in civilian garb. The clothing was stunning; fancy and colorful, replete with swishing hems and wide sleeves.

"Horvantz Villanus ad-Catellis al-Sangirir," Makjit called. "I bring an honored guest. May we enter?"

The man behind the opulent desk stood immediately, attended by a staff who parted for him like the red sea. "You may indeed," he said, opening his arms for the new arrivals. "Madame Undersecretary," he announced, "We are honored at your presence."

"I am honored to meet you as well," Valri said. "I confess this is all a little unexpected. And sudden," she said, side eying Makjit.

"We don't believe in procrastinating," Horvantz said as he took her elbow to lead her to the far side of the office, through another door and into a dining room. A table heaped high with food she'd never seen—or smelled—before.

"I don't know what time frames you humans use, but on Movra it's now time for a brief meal between breakfast and the main course."

"Brunch. We call that brunch."

"As you say. Please sit."

"Thank you. I hate to think of what this is costing your office budget," Valri joked to blank stares. "I'm sorry, my implants must not be translating your language as well as they should be."

Makjit spoke up as she sat down next to Valri and flicked a napkin into her lap. "They use currency to settle affairs. On her home world."

Horvantz dropped his flatware. "I see."

"Indeed. How shall we proceed?"

Valri forced herself to remain calm. "Lady, sir, I'm right here."

"Of course you are. I apologize. We have certain expectations of any species who can achieve space travel—*currency*."

Valri fought down the urge to defend her culture. "It's easier than bartering for what you need daily. I admit we've let things get out of hand in recent decades, but we haven't figured out a better system of wealth management. Yet."

"No, of course you haven't. You've never been exposed to an advanced economy, is all. We can fix that."

"Oh? Please articulate."

"You asked Miraled why the Sleer ran everything. They don't run *everything*. They run themselves. And they are everywhere. They rose to prominence at a time when the neighboring empires were either experiencing a serious contraction or were at war with other powers. It's only in the past few centuries that the Rachnae and Vix were even considered major races. Those two worlds have more in common with each other than either could have with any Sleer or Movi."

"But you digress," Valri said.

"Indeed, I do. The only two things of worth in this galaxy are energy and time. They're the only two items known to us that are not being replenished at the rate we consume them. So, they represent value. The only universal value—the only reliable value—known to the galaxy. Even there, the Sleer left their mark."

"How?"

"Their recyclers. Have you seen them?"

"Are you kidding? A combined human-Sleer fleet destroyed a Skreesh titan by using a million of those things to tear down the titan's defenses."

Horvantz looked to Makjit, who nodded. "That's a story I would very much enjoy hearing," he said. "For the moment, your familiarity with the devices is enough. Simply put, they turn molecules into other molecules. Matter and energy are rearranged at will. The technology was reverse engineered from Skreesh devices that do something similar to build their hive ships and titans out of conquered worlds. On a much more massive scale, of course."

"I've seen those up close," Valri said.

Horvantz continued, "The advent of recycling technology changed everything. Material wants and needs were finally satisfied. Every member of a society could have what they needed when they needed it. It freed us from the horror of scratching a daily existence from dirt, and allowed us to ascend to the stars." He blinked, focused on Valri's reaction. "You have no idea what I'm describing, do you?"

Valri shook her head gravely. "It took a global war to unify my planet, and then a decade of crushing austerity just to rebuild the *Ascension* to functionality," she marveled. "Stupid battleship never did work right."

"And now you see. Industry, productivity, frugality: these are simplistic fables peddled by those who seek power over others. Any civilization worth the name provides for itself before it makes war on other worlds."

Valri folded her arms. "All right. We've established that my people are hopelessly narcissistic. How are you any different?"

"For one thing, we don't burn irreplaceable hydrocarbons to create energy for our own use."

"Neither do we, not anymore. Sleer reactive furnaces gave us the math we needed to figure out fusion power plants."

"Bah! Reactive furnaces are fusion cells writ large. The secret to using them well is to know how to keep them hot enough. It doesn't matter. The only worthwhile form of power comes from the stars."

Valri lowered her head, took a deep breath, and struggled to absorb what she was hearing. Solar energy never lived up to the hype on Earth. Even if it did, just building and deploying enough solar cells to power a continent needed miles of pipelines, oceans of oil and gouts of natural gas to build the equipment...

"So...if we could agree on a means of exchange...could we receive an energy delivery system from you?"

"Of course. A foolproof, utterly safe, and completely reliable delivery system tailored to the needs of your civilization. Doesn't that make more sense than burning rocks?"

"I suppose it does. What we really need now is a shipping fleet. Several hundred starships that can—"

Horvantz laughed as if she'd told an especially good joke. "A shipping fleet is the last thing you need. Unless you can demonstrate that you have something other cultures will want. You'd need to plan and build a modern spaceport, and that means a settlement the Sleer to allow you to operate outside their Battle Ring. Let's not try to fly before we're done falling, shall we?"

She wanted to punch him. Were all these people as arrogant as Horvantz? Suddenly, Valri didn't care to find out. "I don't pretend to understand the nuances of what you're describing to me. Time and energy. Let's please get back to those."

"Of course. The Sleer, once they'd mastered the tech for recyclers, weren't eager to sell or trade it to other races. But we all had encounters with the Skreesh, so we all pursued the same science. We all came up with different applications. The Movi came up with the transmogrifier."

"The what?"

"Genetic manipulation. Cells divide a finite number of times before succumbing to entropy. How much would you offer to gain another year of life? Another decade? Another century? Or, what would you ask in exchange for a year of your own life? What manner of advancement could you pay for if every adult on your world parted with a year of their lives?"

"Probably a brand-new planet," Valri allowed. "Assuming it's possible. Is it possible? How is it managed?"

"Telomeres," Horvantz said. "They restrict cell reproduction. A cell reproduces forty or fifty times then dies. What if we could re-atomize the telomeres and keep those cells reproducing one hundred, one thousand times?"

"Amazing. But how could we possibly sell you...you'd buy our telomeres?"

"Among other things. Dal-Corstuni specializes in medical knowledge, although we have a hand in other industries. A market only works if one can buy and sell."

"Mortality merchants."

"Precisely. We deal in time as a universal value," he said. He pulled a pair of discs from a sleeve pocket and laid them on the table. One black, one gold. "Time. Energy," he said, tapping the black then the gold. "Energy manages material needs, while time manages everything else. That is what we provide our clients. Not the mere material comforts you seem so fixated on. We offer genuine value. We know what the Sleer have to offer. What can *you* provide?"

"A stable platform to work from," she said. "Something tells me you need one of those about now. Seeing as how your government is going through one heck of a trial."

She watched Makjit's eyes narrow and decided to push her

line of reasoning. "As you said, empires have a disconcerting habit of expanding and contracting. Sometimes they snap back, but sometimes they don't. Even the ones that recover take forever to rise to their former glory and are never the same after an abrupt change in leadership. Believe me, my planet wrote the book on this subject. We've been through more war, strife, and horror, all because leaders promised things they couldn't deliver. Sometimes because a nation's people just got angry enough to try some new social experiment. It rarely ends well.

"You asked me what I can offer, and I'll tell you. We are the only species you know about that has managed to successfully reverse engineer a Sleer warship *and* develop new technology of our own in the process. Yes, we nearly wrecked ourselves to do it, but it worked. And we have access to the most advanced battle ring the Sleer ever created. We can make rules to govern relationships and conversations, and we can devise ways to enforce them. We can be impartial. If we can convince the Sleer High Command to go along with it."

The concern on Horvantz's face was obvious. "*Can* you do that?"

"I know we're going to try our best." Valri stood and took a step toward the door. "Thank you for brunch. Now show me your merchant ships or stop wasting my time."

Horvantz hesitated, then nodded to Makjit. "Miraled will take you to the hangar bay and answer your questions. But should you truly be interested in our offer...Rol, tell her what we could deploy if she asked."

Rol, a male Movi with a round face, stocky build, and more than a few crow's feet, cleared his throat. "Dal-Corstuni's automated factories could design, build, and deploy a space-based solar delivery system that links up every inhabited planet in your solar system within one of your local years. Price..." he withdrew a pocket calculator, tapped it for a time, growing more frustrated every moment. "I can't even convert to your local currency. Let's say two billion *estani*. That's two hundred thousand of these." He tapped the black disc.

Makjit held out her hand. "This way, please, Undersecretary Valri Gibb." As they strode down the corridor, the Movi leaned in. "I love how you put that cretin in his place. I think we're going to get along famously!"

CHAPTER 6

"HORVANTZ CAN BE A PRESUMPTUOUS TOOL, but he's correct about your priorities. You need to establish a system-wide energy production system. And the collective value your human bodies contain. You're sitting on *vast* wealth, if only you knew how to manage it."

"Without a carrier fleet, we can't deliver local goods or buy from other systems," Valri insisted.

"Without demonstrating your place in the world of modern commerce, they won't care. Establish yourselves as a local power. Then the masses will seek you out. Not before."

They entered a chrome-walled elevator with plush seats and a well-stocked bar. Valri settled in as Makjit tapped instructions in a panel then flopped down next to her new friend, pulling her flowing garments around herself. "It'll be a few minutes. The travel car knows where to go. Just relax."

"I get the idea that if my government knew I was doing this, we'd both be in a heap of trouble." The thought chilled her. She was learning a lot about their new neighbors and giving them nothing in return. This was still the wining and dining portion of the show. The negotiations would happen later...if she convinced EarthGov to go along with it. But they had to. Humans and Sleer together couldn't stop the Skreesh in any meaningful way, no matter how successful they'd been in rescuing Great Nest from destruction. Surely, they would see that.

Makjit sniffed. "You're being paranoid. The Sleer deal with us daily. Before Great Nest was evacuated, at least. How your human government will react—that's something I can't control. I can only show you what we have to offer your people."

Over the past two hours, Miraled Makjit had progressed from a surly data nerd into a bouncy high school girl; Valri was feeling a bit of whiplash over it. The alien woman was half a head taller than she, which made it even weirder. Especially the way Makjit dropped her head to touch her own every now and then. The Movi had a weird obsession with her dark, skin and her hair's texture. Valri felt like she was being cuddled by a serial killer. The whole thing screamed of a setup, but she kept her reservations to herself. There was no way she was signing any official documentation without orders from Earth. But she wanted a closer look at what kind of lives this alien race lived, and she couldn't get that from behind her desk. So, she went along with it, even squeezing her lady friend back occasionally She hoped she wasn't making an indecent proposal in Movi culture.

If nothing else, her Sleer implants gave her insane reflexes and twice the strength of a strong human, as well as the ability to call for help if she needed it. She took a bit of confidence from that. But they still couldn't keep her heart from bouncing out of her chest. Maybe she should see a doctor about that. Were there any Sleer doctors who would see humans? She didn't want to follow that thought, so she changed the subject. "What is two billion *estani* worth?"

"It's enough energy to supply a civilization of twice your

population for a thousand years. Enough to build a *Sebak*-class planetoid warship with a full complement of satellite ships. Enough to extend one life out to the next billion years. Not that any of those are practical goals, but I hope you get the idea."

Two *estani* per year of extended life, more or less. The thought filled her stomach with ice. If she were being honest, corporate interests were no less cold-blooded about trading lives for profit. This was the same calculation on a galactic scale. The Movi were as bad as the Sleer. Their methods were different. "Assuming we were able and willing to pay that much, how would that work in practice?"

"I've never attended a project of that scale. In principle, we deliver a series of automated factories to your solar system, and a team of engineers would visit your planet. They do all the hard work—the engineers examine your power infrastructure, arrange to update or replace what needs to be laid for the new system to work. Then the factories produce the necessary parts, robot assemblers lay it in place, and the engineers test it. Then we teach you how to maintain it and you pay us for our work. Simple."

"Not *so* simple."

"Hmm?" Makjit's face went from a mask of confusion to one of comprehension. "Oh. *Oh.* You're right. They've already abandoned Great Nest and probably Home Nest, too—they're unlikely to care what we do *here*. But with that battle ring on your home world, the Sleer are just as likely to shoot any new satellites down. Defending their new nest and all that. Hmm. That's a problem."

Valri tried to imagine where such a problem might lead. The Sleer had already demonstrated a willingness to scorch the Earth's surface one city at a time to retain their hold on the orbital ring that surrounded it. She'd seen their war machine in action. Fearsome displays of firepower, and battle tactics bold enough to put the Roman Empire to shame. They didn't care about losses in space or on the ground if they had more soldiers and ships than their opponent. And they did.

Movi warships were a mystery to her, but she'd surmised that they fielded fewer vessels with far better offensive and defensive ability. If you only had the budget to build a few ships, you wanted the best money could buy, and then developed tactics to nullify the extraordinary numbers the Sleer fielded. If the two powers ever met in battle in the Sol system, though, the surest loser would be humanity.

"I don't think we'd want to test that idea in real time," she murmured.

"No! Of course not. That would be ruinous for everyone. But. Hmm..."

"Hmm?"

"I've been told—that is, I've learned—that the Sleer are willing to allow your people to begin colonizing a world you call Vega. Is that correct?"

Oh-oh. "I was not a party to that decision."

"But it's going to happen, yes?"

"I couldn't say."

"I see. *If* it were true, surely the Sleer High Command would have no problems with you doing business with our merchant contacts here. They've already abrogated any interest in that system. Yes?"

"And what they don't know won't hurt them," Valri guessed.

"Well, they'd surely find out. Eventually. They're very good at that. I just think it's a topic for a far more substantial discussion soon. No?"

"Yes. I agree. In principle."

"So careful with your words, Valri Gibb. I love that about you. You have a history in trade talks. No?"

"In a way. I used to work at a firm that did a great amount of trade with companies all over the world. My algorithms were extremely profitable and—"

"You used computers to decide what to buy and sell? And from and to whom? That's *fascinating*."

"And if it gave you a forward operating base just twenty-five light years from the newly adopted Sleer home world, it would put your government in an advantageous position to influence this part of the galaxy," Valri said.

"That sort of thing is far above my responsibility, but...that doesn't make it untrue. Wouldn't you want to be able to beat the Sleer at their own trade? Harness unlimited energy? Build a battle ring of your own?" Makjit lowered her head a bit and her voice to match. "And a few extra centuries to see the results of your efforts?"

Very cute. Start with the money and then raise the ante to include immortality—or whatever resembled it in Movi society. Valri was starting to get a raw taste in her mouth every time Makjit opened hers. "We don't even know if that kind of project is possible on Vega. 'Impossible to mine' is how the Sleer described it."

"I'm sure any species as clever and adaptable as yours can figure it out."

"Hah. You're flattering me."

Makjit pulled away and settled back against her seat. "No. I don't know you well enough for that. But it's true the Sleer haven't destroyed you yet. That shows promise. The sort of potential that suggests we can be useful to each other. As a species, I mean."

"Of course we can."

Gravity felt strange. A series of added weight and free-fall drops until the car settled. The doors opened to reveal an industrial theme park, columns of machinery hidden behind decorative facades. Not many people around, but plenty of cargo platforms. Hovering platforms passed them as the corridor fed into a grand connective plaza. Not that different from the tram plaza she'd seen on Battle Ring Earth.

Makjit led her to a set of tall windows set into a bulkhead, and Valri gaped at the sights. A hangar bay as wide as a football stadium and many times longer housed at least a hundred ships. Up close, she could finally appreciate how Movi ships differed from the Sleer models. Where Sleer favored organic oblongs, Movi went for sleek lines and smooth curves. Tapered cylinders, spheres, and ovoids.

"I'm not getting a clear picture of the floor plans here, but I don't think we're in the Diplo Dome any more."

"Certainly not. This entire section of the Great Nest ring is Movi territory. It was built into this station as part of the old Allied Races treaty. The treaty may have been shoved to the back of the closet, but we didn't abandon it."

"I'll bet that made things tricky for the past decade."

"The Sleer were too busy fighting the Skreesh to worry. An empty space station has many places to work unobserved, especially when fighting is going on right outside the hull."

"I've heard that."

Makjit cuddled her again, coming in close and squeezing while setting her face close to hers and inhaling. It felt like a gentle mugging. "I love how you smell when you're being sarcastic."

"Thanks. I think."

"And since there is a new fleet and a treaty to match, we are slowly resuming our places in our section."

"Uhm... Too close, dear."

The Movi released her, walked to the end of the display, and opened a hatch with a gesture. They stepped onto a balcony, updrafts pulling at their clothing and hair as the sounds and smells of industry met their senses. Makjit pointed out the various ship models, describing the small ovoids, the moderately sized cylinders with flaring surfaces, and the three giant spheres that hovered at the rear of everything.

Eventually, Valri succumbed to fatigue. She would never remember all this. "I suppose this is the part where I should ask you why you're telling me all this."

"It's not classified. There's nothing in this hangar or in orbit around this world that is particularly revealing. The other races' militaries all have extensive records on our planetoids and their capabilities."

"Planetoids. Those are the big spheres in back?"

"Yes. That design represents the mainstay of our Royal Navy. They make extensive use of satellite ships. Smaller vessels that stay in the hulls of the greater ships until needed."

"They're fantastic. Each of them is probably wider than the AMS-1 is long."

"Very possible. As to why I'm telling you this—I wanted to give you a reason to feel you could trust me."

"And since *Ascension* is already in another hangar, we can spy on each other without any real risk."

Makjit grimaced. "'Spy' is such a crude word. We are watching each other. Taking notes, making judgments."

"But there is a measure of 'mine is bigger than yours.' Right?"

"Anyone who looks at these and then looks at a Sleer space control ship can see there's a different design strategy in play between the two militaries. One of our planetoids carries greater firepower and support equipment than a hundred Sleer battleships. The best that the Sleer can count on under those terms is an even chance of success or failure. The Sleer don't like to lose. So, they know not to provoke us."

"That sounds wise."

"And these ships are small compared to what's in the inventory back home. The Movi First Empire built them much larger. A flagship the size of a small moon, I'm told. We don't do that anymore. It's wasteful and they take tens of thousands to crew properly. But they serve as announcements to opposing fleets."

"Gunboat diplomacy. Nice."

"I don't understand."

Yes you do. But let's put it out there. "Earth is mostly water, and most of us live on coastlines. On my world, when one country wanted to pressure an enemy, they would send one or more gunships to sit off their coast. No provocation, no attacks. But the image of an enemy ship sitting just off your coast has a psychological effect."

"Ah. Devious."

"That's one word for it. We say that war is politics by other means. Hey, what are all the small egg-shaped vessels for? Are they cargo shuttles?"

"Not exactly. Those are message boats. Small, very fast, and loaded with data storage."

"No physical packages?"

"No, those go on bulk carriers."

"I'm trying to wrap my brain around the need for mail in an age where interstellar travel is almost limitless."

"'Almost' is the operative word. The Sleer use those giant hyperspace relay stations. Surely, you've seen those? They take years to construct and are incredibly expensive to maintain. We'd rather rely on thousands of small, fast starships like this. If the system fails, we only lose a fraction of the periodic traffic. An individual boat can be replaced in days. It makes for a more resilient communication network."

"I see. The Sleer centralize everything. Good for efficiency, bad for resilience. I confess that I like the way you folks think."

Makjit gushed. "Why thank you. Finesse and style count for much among my people. Sleer understand brute force and not much else. They've fallen very far from their days as explorers and merchants. Perhaps that explains why the Skreesh are making such short work of them."

"That's not a very charitable attitude."

"Charity is not for the self-righteous."

She self-righteously said, as her kingdom tore itself apart, Valri thought. No, that wasn't fair either. But there were a ton of things she just didn't understand about how the two races ran their respective societies. She needed to concentrate on listening.

"I can't get over the size of those—what did you call them? Planetoids? Can we go aboard?"

Makjit looked thoughtful, touched a jewel above her eyes, and nodded. "Just for a minute."

"*Moshak* is not a warship. It's owned by the Natahana merchant guild, which is a subsidiary of the much larger Kar-Tuiyn merchant group. There are several steps between those two organizations, but I don't remember them all, and I'm sure they'd bore you if I took you through them anyway."

Captain Desanis Manik laughed and Valri joined in, playing up her role as visiting dignitary. She didn't have to lean into the role very hard; the truth was overwhelming on its own. The reception lobby alone put anything the AMS-1 had to shame. The bridge was huge, deep and dark, a platform with a dozen or more consoles that hovered over a dark pit of an open space. Above them swam a vista of holographic displays. Captain Manik wasn't going to let her look at the consoles or equipment, and she could imagine why: spy. Crude or not, the word was effective.

Manik himself seemed out of place, perhaps because he

was the first uniformed Movi she'd met. Movi military garb was very different from Sleer or UEF uniforms: all blacks and browns, with navy blue piping and silver braid everywhere. One thing she noticed immediately—Movi wore their implants on the outside. Everyone had a glittering node settled against their skull just above the right eye. Some were huge, others a mere strip of glowing metal. She wondered if they were the equivalent of Sleer implants and, if so, how they worked. She doubted they'd tell her if she asked. But their hands were bare.

"No control gauntlets," she murmured.

"No. Some bits of Sleer technology are simply unsuited for use here. But we know how to use our equipment," Manik said.

"So. Not a warship. How is it that a civilian or corporate vessels needs so much space?" she asked.

"Merchant ships like this are designed to remain on station for years. Decades sometimes. We expect our crew and passenger compliment to increase in size as individuals group up on long missions. When we set down in one sector, we'll often send out satellite ships to the surrounding systems to see where the opportunities are. We make plans for the long term."

"But you can defend yourselves if attacked?"

"Of course. We can take on a Sleer armada very handily."

"What does a ship like this cost? Makjit here mentioned we have enormous assets if we only knew what to do with them."

Manik glared at Makjit. "Miraled understands trade but not much else," he said to an embarrassed Makjit. "I think she was trying to impress you."

"So we couldn't assemble a chest filled with eight billion years of extra life and use it to buy this ship, for example?"

Manik chuckled. "It's a good idea, but it doesn't quite work that way. How many government officials on Earth can pool their resources to buy a fleet carrier?"

"It's been done," Valri said with a smile. "But not in recent years."

"But you want one of these vessels for your own."

"It wouldn't be the worst thing in the world to be in a position to help with planetary defense."

"Against whom? The Sleer?"

"Or the Skreesh. I'll be honest...we're learning about this arm of the galaxy in fits and starts. It's a lot more worrisome than we had imagined."

"Ignorance is bliss, I suppose you would say." Makjit made a gesture to the captain, who nodded and touched a wall panel. In a moment, a section of wall pulled away to reveal an alcove with couches, a small table, and numerous black globes hovering near the ceiling. "Let's make you less ignorant, shall we?"

Valri followed them and took a seat. The three of them sat at the apexes of a triangle as the door slid shut. The globes began to whir and hum above them. At the same time, Valri felt her senses dulling. Her sight dimmed and her hearing felt as if the world was swaddled in cotton.

"A privacy room." she surmised. "That's a neat trick."

"At some point, we need to know what to expect from each other."

"I agree. Let's talk turkey."

"You will have to explain what that means later," Manik said. "Right now, I think we should strive for honesty. Makjit here has given you a very shallow tour of our facilities and explained a few basics to you. There is no getting around the fact that you humans are as backwards as any culture we've encountered. Your sole achievement to date has been rebuilding *Genukh* to a state of readiness and bringing it this far. That's all you've done. You've been very lucky the Skreesh haven't found you yet."

"Ah, but they have," Valri pointed out. "Tall Lord Nazerian

and his war fleet destroyed a Skreesh sensor nebula in our solar system a couple of years ago. I guarantee the Skreesh know about us. The only question is when they arrive."

"I didn't know that," Makjit admitted. "Does it change the calculus?"

"I would think so. You're now talking to a representative of an endangered species. What can the Movi hope to offer us?"

Makjit's eyes flicked between the two of them. "You don't expect the Sleer to help defend your world, do you?"

"Would you?"

Manik was more practical. "They're in the position of having to either defend your home world to save their own people, or plan another escape fleet and find a new planet to colonize. It's possible they've harvested enough information from the new battle ring to facilitate that."

"But you don't believe it," Makjit asked, her eyes on Valri.

Valri shook her head. "I don't. If they were of a mind to do that, they'd be working at it already. The Sleer are fearsome fighters, but even they have a breaking point. Two racial migrations to two new worlds within two years reached that limit."

"I'd be amazed if they could pull another battle ring out of thin air," Manik said. "Zluur is dead, and he didn't leave additional instructions."

"And the Cycomms are already annoyed at us for using a facility that was built with their stolen technology," Valri said.

"As you say. There's no way we can sell you warships like this," Makjit decided. "Nor would royal bureaucrats agree to place a Movi colony on your world—or even in your solar system. Not with the Sleer inhabiting it. But the world you call Vega. That has real potential."

Valri nodded. She'd shaken off the brain fog, but couldn't get over how heavy and slow her limbs were. The privacy screen must have shut down her implants as well. That was news. "I agree. We need technology and a trade agreement so we can acquire more of it. We have plenty of years of life to offer in trade, at least in principle. And you can provide all the energy we need to build a new colony world."

"And we get your cooperation in future agreements regarding defense from the Skreesh," Miraled said.

"The Sleer will hear about this and take you to task. Your own government won't be any better. Who exactly are you to enter into this agreement?" Manik asked.

"No one. Or I'm the best chance you have to stop the Sleer in their tracks." Valri stopped herself. Now she was giving away state secrets. Or was she? "What do your people know about trading algorithms?"

CHAPTER 7

"YOU KNOW VAL, when ZERO put you in charge of the office of commerce for interstellar trade, I don't think he intended you to go to a private meeting with the enemy."

The AMS-1 wardroom wasn't crowded this time of night. But it was neutral territory—neither part of the Diplo Dome nor the ASF's battle ring. Despite the giant vessel's inactive status—and partial dismemberment as service modules were transferred to other vessels—certain areas were still available. The wardroom still served food to UEF officers, even if just coffee. It was one of the few places on Battle Ring Great Nest where one could be sure there were no listening devices.

Fairchild put down a cup of coffee in front of her and sat across from her at the table. "I'll tell you what, it's no fun getting a call from General Eisenberg when we're sitting to dinner on our date night. Not when he tells me to fix the security leak in my unit. I asked 'is it one of my pilots' and he's like 'no it's your girlfriend.'"

Valri glowered, arms folded, her coffee untouched. "Why trust him? You don't trust Hendricks."

"Eisenberg kept me out of jail when Hendricks wanted me

executed for treason. I know who my friends are. I assumed you had a similar take."

"Not a secret meeting," she insisted, taking a sip. The liquid was hot and bitter, much like her emotional state. "All we did was bookmark a place to keep talking."

"Yeah, but the Movi? Have you read the reports that the OMP has put together on that bunch?"

"Eighty percent of what we know comes from Judy Reagan's personal observations. A former flight admiral and two henches who were found guilty of God knows what and sentenced to life on a penal colony. That can't be representative of the whole species."

"I'm sure. But—"

"But nothing. We need a lever to use against the Sleer, and we don't have a ton of friends out there."

"We have an alliance with the Sleer. They're keeping the solar system safe from the Skreesh."

"That's what the OMP says. They're keeping us locked in our own space."

"There're some details to work out, I agree."

"They gave us Vega. They can take it away if they want. Ever think about that?"

"I have. You think putting a fleet of Movi warships around Vega is a good way to prevent that?"

"It's more than anything else we have to work with. We can't even build new starships on Earth's battle ring. Anything we launch can be ordered back to base or shot down. It's the *Beast* all over again. But they're not going to attack a Movi ship. You watch. At least the Movi are willing to share what they have."

"They're willing to *sell* us what they have. Not the same thing. No one does anything out of the goodness of their hearts. Plus there's a succession war in progress on Movra. You think their promises will be worth anything if the government collapses?"

"It's already wobbling, according to my contacts. They want new markets well away from Movra, and we have a new system to colonize. Seems like there's a deal to be made."

"To you, it's all about the deal, isn't it? I suppose it's a shame you couldn't land one of those giant planetoid ships for us," Fairchild groused.

"I did ask. Not going to happen. How's the AMS-1 coming?"

"It's not. That fight with the Skreesh titans broke *Ascension*'s back. It's technically functional, but it was old when Zluur set it on its way to Earth. If she ever flies again, it'll be the last time."

"What about moving her back to Earth Ring?" Valri asked.

"Forget about Earth Ring for the time being. What we have here is infinitely more substantial."

"You think that's on purpose?"

Ray gestured to indicate *everything*. "I'm sure of it. This is a well-established facility. They're moving humans in, and there are already other races living here. It's as cosmopolitan a location as you'll find. Besides, if I wanted the Skreesh to ignore my new homeworld, I'd be making a giant fuss over the old one."

"While Earth is all humans on the surface and all Sleer in orbit. Good for them, bad for us."

"Like it or not, it's what EarthGov agreed to, so the UEF and OMP will enforce it."

"And they're going to drag their asses. You watch. Every advancement we suggest or demand will be met with them urging us to wait for the right time. How long are we going to wait?" she demanded.

"Until we think of something better. Which I suppose brings us full circle…"

Fairchild raised his cup, realized it was empty, and made a show of ambling to the metal urn across the room and refilling it. Valri's point wasn't lost on him, but the politics of the matter were strange and getting stranger. Lately, he'd been having trouble keeping matters straight in his mind. Maybe he was dehydrated or something. Maybe not braining well was something he'd have to manage from now on. So much for Sleer implants maintaining optimal health.

He returned with a new strategy. "All right, Val. You've convinced me. Sort of. What do *you* think we should do next? Not that I'm making this official. But we do need to check out the new location, and putting together a team for that makes sense."

"We must do that on our own. But there's nothing that says we can't arrange to meet the Movi in the new location."

"I don't like that idea as much," Fairchild admitted.

"Why not?"

"Brooks thinks the only reason the Sleer gave that system to us is because there's something of value there that they don't know about. He's a smart guy. He could be right. If he is, then meeting our new pals there means giving away any new finds before we can mine them for information or any other advantage. But there's a bigger question: what do they expect us to trade for all this help they can supposedly give us?"

"That's where it gets creepy," she said.

She spent some time explaining the concept of the transmogrifier to him, and his expression grew more ashen the further into the description she got. "Time and energy. They seem to be the basis of everything they have. We might not have energy to sell, but with sixty thousand people up here, we have a lot of time to offer."

"Offering them *human lives* in exchange for a few high-tech toys? God, that sounds awful."

"It does. I feel dirty just thinking about it. A woman with my skin tone should know better." She reached out and grabbed his hands across the table, clutching them for support. The image of her dark brown hands against his own pale ones set her heart bouncing in her chest again. What was wrong with her? "Back in the days of late-stage capitalism, you could assume the leftists were being metaphorical when they talked about trading lives for production. Now we don't even have that. I keep thinking at least Makjit was up front about it. They have no interest in blockchain fintech accounts, paper checks, piles of cash, or precious metals. They have all of that they could ever need."

He squeezed gently. "You'll forgive my suspicious mind, but I know they didn't tell you everything."

"Agreed. But we have to start somewhere."

"Some starting point."

She watched as he closed and relaxed his eyes. She knew the look of a man accessing his implants. "ZERO, where is Lieutenant Simon Brooks?"

"First Lieutenant Simon Brooks is in his quarters."

"Is he alone?"

"Negative. Nine other individuals are with him."

"Thank you." He raised his eyebrows as he met her gaze. "Sounds like he's hosting a party. Feel like taking a walk?"

"Should we? It's late."

"Why not? Our evening is shot. Why not share the misery with the kids?"

"Fair. I guess we can use the exercise. Our implants can't do *everything*. What if he's got something way more personal than we think going on in there?"

"Then we can either leave in a hurry or join them. Come on."

One advantage that Brooks and Rosenski had even among the few who sported Sleer implants was superior rank—Sleer bridge officers—which gave them command of a vast array of the battle ring's inner workings. That included the ability to designate construction projects. The result was Primate Alley. It might not be as visually stunning as they wanted, but it worked to center both the humans already living here and the new arrivals with a place of their own in a strange universe.

Primate Alley anchored this portion of the orbital ring around daily human experiences. Once the humans decided to call it their own space, they made it as habitable as possible, including installing a dense network of trams, auto-cars, and moving platforms. Getting from the hulk of *Ascension* to Simon Brooks' apartment building took relatively little time, and much of that was spent getting out of the AMS-1. Once you got out of the windowless cubicles and compartments, Primate Alley looked like any other city on Earth—just sparsely populated with relatively few tall buildings. A bit like New Darwin. How the city might have grown and prospered had the Sleer not blasted it into dust.

Another advantage of rank was the ability to designate personal quarters, which Simon Brooks did. Rosenski tried to talk him out of it, then relented when she realized that a certain level of comfort worked to their advantage.

With the correct paperwork backing him up, no one in the general staff argued—or even noticed—when the Gauntlet Arms went up. 400 units in a twenty-floor building was plenty to house all of *Gauntlet*'s crew and soldiers, plus a few favorite extras. The building was nowhere near that crowded now, but the potential was there.

On this Saturday night, Brooks's flat was crowded and noisy, with food, drink, and loud discussion—the kind of chaos that Simon Brooks craved. Brooks was in the kitchen, fooling with an industrial level recycler. The flavors were always off just enough to make dishes unpalatable. He finally gave up and used his electric grill. The smell of searing meat, or what passed for it on Great Nest, attracted attention. And now there were too many people in his kitchen.

Barrows leaned over to get a bottle opener. The pop meant he'd found it. "Smells nice. What've we got on the menu?"

Brooks grabbed the bottle and took a sip. He handed it back in disgust. "Burgers and hot dogs. What are you drinking?"

"Says beer on it but…Your girl not around? I thought she was the helping type."

"When we're working on Ravens, she's a ton of help. I banned her from the kitchen after she burned a pot of water."

"Come on."

"I'm deadass serious. Never saw anything like it."

Barrows found a small bottle and shook some pepper on the burgers. Brooks grabbed it away from him before he did too much damage. "Even so, I thought she'd be a fixture or something. Moving in and shit."

Simon shrugged and made a noise as Smithers nearly hit him with the fridge door.

"We thought about throwing in together but decided there was too much potential for drama. This is 203, Dance is in 202, and Binil is in 201. If shit gets weird, help is just a doorbell away," Brooks said.

Smithers dragged out a new six-pack of bottles and shut the fridge, then handed out the bounty. "Yeah. Shit gets weird or gets lonely. Whatever the case may be."

Brooks rolled his eyes. "Dude, it's not like that."

"Nah. It sounds utterly reasonable," Barrows agreed while winking at Smithers.

Brooks missed the exchange, concentrating on the food. "I thought so. Sometimes I go to Dance's place, sometimes she comes to mine. There's a limit to how much trouble anyone up here can get into. All the beds are too narrow for anything but sleep."

Barrows tagged Smithers, tapping his shoulder. "My dude! Get on that!"

Smithers twisted the cap off his bottle and missed when he tried to throw it in the trash. "I got my own narrow bed to deal with. Besides, you want an engineer, not a paper pusher like me. If you want to open a snack bar in the building lobby, I can make that happen."

Brooks looked up. "Seriously? How?"

"File a REQ-276/8 form. Cross out the line that says 'M-19 rifle' and write in 'snacks.'"

"Sounds like an investment opportunity. We'll figure something out. 99 cents for every item, residents only."

"Cool! Can I have five bucks for five items?"

"Talk to Simmons. I gave her all my money an hour ago."

"So did I. I think she has *all* our money."

Simmons shouted from the other room. "You whining creeps are going to learn not to draw to an inside straight if I have to take everything you own!"

Barrows made a face and sipped his beer. "Christ, she sounds like my ex-husband. Why is she here?"

Brooks adjusted the heat, turned the burgers, and stood back while the meat seared. "I dunno. Dance invited her one day and she keeps showing up."

Barrows smirked. "Tell me you're not a fan without telling me you're not a fan."

"She's fine as long as I'm not working for her," Brooks admitted. That had been a difficult time. Simmons was breaking in her third lieutenant bars and supervising Specialist Simon

Brooks and his squad of noncoms. He didn't know when or how she and Dance Reagan had met, but they'd clearly hit it off, and she was now part of his circle. "If I need to be alone, I send them to Dance's place. They close the door and that's all she wrote."

Barrows and Smithers crowed in chorus. "Ooooooooooo!"

Brooks turned and shouted, "Once they invited Binil."

"Ooooooooooooo!"

A huff and a hustle, and Simmons appeared next to him. She glanced at the grill, grabbed a platter, and held it while Brooks piled burgers onto it. "Cool yer jets, fam. All we ever do at Dance's place is watch movies."

"What kind of movies?"

"Old ones. Dance loves Humphrey Bogart. I happened to mention that I'd never heard of him, then we're sitting down to watch Casablanca, the Maltese Falcon, and The African Queen."

"How'd you like them?"

"It was fun. I didn't know they ever made films like that. All story, no explosions. We'll do it again at some point."

The kitchen got even smaller as a new person shoved her way into the conversation. Bronson had risen in the ranks since their first meeting. Her second lieutenant bars announced refined competence. Her dark brown skin matched her eyes. She did not take shit, and these idiots were no exception. "I'm sorry I'm so late. Work was a shit hole today. You gonna finish that?" She took the bottle from Barrows and drank, leaving him reaching past her and flailing. She guzzled half the bottle and let out a wet belch.

"Armory?" Smithers asked.

Bronson smiled. "Where else? We're testing the new GU-29 gun pods for the Raven. You will love that shit, Brooks. Depleted uranium cores with reactive warheads. One round will punch through a damn starship hull."

"Where did you find uranium?"

"They cleaned out some of the older atomic reactors on the AMS-1. All that spent fuel had to go somewhere, so they gave it to us."

"Gah. Just pulling that old ship apart one piece at a time," Brooks lamented.

Smithers chuckled. "Makes me happy I moved to the quartermaster's staff. No radioactive toys for me, Just everything from booze to hand grenades to bubble gum to blankets. I am a living spreadsheet."

Bronson handed her bottle back to Barrows, pulled the top off a fresh one with her teeth, and took a swig. "Y'all must be very lonely."

Smithers winked. "You'd be amazed how easy it is to get dates when you have the key to the ship's store."

Barrows shrugged. "I like being the HR guy. I'm good at it."

Bronson rolled her eyes. "Thank God for that, man. From what I hear, if they put a weapon in your hand, the rest of your unit won't come near you."

"We can't all be crack shots, dear."

Brooks made a show of shaking his head while making a burger. "If you're serious, I think your aim is getting worse. Here, try this."

Barrows took a bite and blinked while he chewed. "It's cooked, whatever it is. Meat?"

"Textured protein. You don't want to taste what the Sleer call meat."

"Well. Hmm. I'm choking it down anyway."

"Fuck you."

Barrows took another bite. "Anyway, it's not fair. The certification requirements are insane. Who the hell can hit a one-inch target from fifty yards away with a pistol?" Everyone in the room raised their hands. Barrows grimaced. "I hate you guys."

Armed with food and drink, the party moved to the dining room. The sound of cracking glass made Brooks look up from his plate. Judy Reagan held her wrist while a hiss of pain escaped her lips.

"Dance? What gives?"

"Nothing. Yeah. It's nothing. Fucked up my hand is all."

"Fucked up...how?"

"Really, it's nothing. It's happened before. The medical bots always fix it. It'll fix itself in a few hours anyway."

"Let's see." Simon took her hand and probed with his fingertips. "Judy. This looks broken."

"It's no biggie. I'll be fine in a few hours. The implants always heal it."

"But it shouldn't be happening at all." Simon connected with the ring's data network, pulled salient data from the information web. "Jeez, Dance. You've had seventeen visits to the med drones in the past five months. All for fractures? Son of a..."

Binilsanetanjamalala, the red-eyed Cycomm, abandoned her plate and left the apartment. Reagan pulled her hand away, tried to stuff it into a pocket. "It's fine. Really."

"This isn't fine. This is the antithesis of fine." Brooks said. He thought about his own health problems. Implants had healed his arm three years ago, but it twinged every now and then. The nerves, the inability to concentrate, the hyperfocus that pushed out everything else—like mission orders. He stood and looked around. "Anyone else have issues with their implants lately?"

Underhill put down her drink. "Not unless you want to count a few headaches. Some eye strain. Couple of hand tremors now and then. But that's called being north of thirty," she said.

"Your implants should at least be managing the headaches. Who else? Come clean or we're all in deep trouble."

"You're not a doctor and I don't have to say anything," Marc Janus insisted, dropping on the sofa, his arms folded, suddenly sullen. Brooks wanted to chalk it up to simple defensiveness, but the pilot's foot wouldn't stop tapping a storm against the floor. Eventually he noticed Brooks's stare, and forced it to stop.

"No, you're peachy. Anyone else?" He'd heard about Frost having back trouble and Skellington getting angry over small things. Both well out of character for the men he knew. Morrow and Arkady weren't here, but he wondered about them. That left Uncle and Valri to poll. The two remaining former Hornets with implants.

Bronson said, "I know Frau Butcher told you not to touch that alien shit on day one, so I won't say anything now. But seriously, Brooks...you all got a problem." Brooks couldn't stop thinking about Rosenski's red eyes. The eyes of someone who took shortcuts—uppers and downers—to maintain a killer work schedule. Implants should have filtered all that stuff out, too, kept her blood counts balanced. She'd been fine six months ago. They all had. He felt sure of it.

Brooks sat at the table and picked at his food. "That's an understatement. Those implants give us access to Sleer-only crew stations. They're how we fly Sleer ships and fight their weapons. And we're cut off from the only entity that can fix them. Fuck."

A signal chimed. Brooks answered without thinking. He threw the stream up for everyone to see: Fairchild and Valri, arm in arm, walking up the path that led straight to their building. It took a moment to get their bearings, but Rodriguez was in the frame and Rosenski wasn't—which meant she was live-streaming the meeting.

"Speak of the devil," Smithers said. "Rosenski's transmitting, I guess?"

"Uncle and Auntie, sitting in a tree," Underhill agreed. "How fast can we all get naked?"

Simmons snarfed a gulp of beer. "I thought you had a headache?"

"Shit, you're right. Some other night then."

The door opened to reveal Binilsanetanjamalala. She hefted a metal oblong. "I brought it. Heals anything in less than an hour. No implants needed. Where's the patient?"

Dance raised her hand. "Still here. God, this is embarrassing."

Binil walked Dance to the sofa. "Here, come to the side. Why do you keep doing this to yourself?"

"It was funny at first. Then the lacrosse league got going and I thought breaking things was par for the course."

"You're an idiot."

"Stuff it—ouch!"

Binil's face had already taken on its smokey eye aspect...her cheeks and jaw were darkening now, too. She was getting annoyed. "Hold. Still." Dance held.

They watched Rosenski's feed. Sara, Rodriguez, and the newcomers coming up in the elevator.

Uncle asked, "It's a nice building, too. How'd he get situated here?"

"He owns it."

"Damn it, Sara, don't tell him that!" Brooks groaned.

On the feed: "He what?"

"Brooks owns it. He can explain it better than we can," Rosenski offered.

Barrows sniffed. "Shit, Brooks, what are *you* going to tell him? Smithers and I filled out the paperwork to set it all up for you."

Simon banged his head against the table. "Gaaaaaaaaah!"

On the feed: lift doors open, Valri craning her head to evaluate the hallway. "He owns the building, but no penthouse?" she asked.

"There is no penthouse. Just a helipad and a door leading to the roof. Here we are."

The door opened to a dozen conversations going on and music flooding the air through speakers in the ceiling. Some damn kind of electronica, loud but not painfully so. Fairchild recognized the faces but struggled to put names to them. There were the non-coms: Rodriguez, Smithers, Bronson, Barrows. And the officers: Rosenski, Janus, Reagan, Underhill, and one more he didn't recognize.

"Lt. Simmons, sir. I served in the air base reconstruction effort aboard the AMS-1. When she went into dry dock, I transferred to air traffic control."

"That's an important job. You working with Lt. Hart?"

"She's my boss, sir."

"I see. Why are you dealing with this bunch?"

Dance raised her good hand and rose on her toes while Binil snarled and pulled her back down. "I invited her. She said yes. That was...three months ago?"

"A little less than four. Sir."

Fairchild rested on his heels. His special project was building his own little support group with an impressive array of skills and positions. Interesting. "You setting yourself up as a landlord in Primate Alley, Simon?"

Brooks shrugged. "You told me to keep my friends close. Dance and Binil ended up with apartments on either side of mine, and I just thought the more the merrier."

"I'm sure. Well. Far be it from us to interfere with your

fancy coffee klatch, but we need some information and three of the people we need to speak to most are already here."

"Grab a seat, Uncle. Captain."

"Not a captain."

Dance yelled from across the room. "No? What? Have they decommissioned *Garfield*?"

"Government employees don't run spaceships. Valri is the new Undersecretary of Commerce and Interplanetary Trade," Fairchild explained.

There were oohs and aahs and a round of applause while Valri held her breath. When it stopped, she said, "Binil. Reagan, Brooks. I am forced into dealing with the Movi. You're the closest things we have to experts on the subject. I need to pick your collective brains."

"That knocks Simon out." Sara kicked him in the foot, and the junior officer grimaced.

"I'm not an expert on anything except Sleer systems," he admitted. These two, though..." He bowed out and stalked off, leaving Reagan and Binil to handle the request. After a moment, the other guests took their cues and the crowd thinned then vanished as everyone went home. Brooks and Rosenski remained, but kept their distance.

Fairchild opened with his usual winning smile. "This place have a liquor cabinet? Show me." It wasn't a great selection. Simon wasn't a drinker. Cheap Bourbon, indifferent gin, and decent Vodka. At least there was ice. Ray poured himself a shot of Vodka, dropped an ice cube in, and sat down. He tried to look relaxed, but this was obviously weird. "So. How are you feeling, Binil?"

Binilsanetanjamalala blinked, her face back to its normal coloring. Except for her smooth eye ridges and red eyes, she could have passed for any human teenager with dark hair and olive skin tones. She'd even started to dress like one: yoga pants and a sleeveless top. "I'm no longer a scrambler. I'm dealing with it. It wasn't very much of my life."

"I'm not sure I agree. I remember hearing about how you took out a crew of mercenaries on that prison barge. You flattened a number of Skreesh shock troopers. You even nudged a Skreesh shield generator into non-functionality. I'd call those major accomplishments. If I woke up in hospital and found out I'd lost the ability to read and write, I know I'd take that badly."

Binil stood firm, hunkering a bit as she faced down her questioner. "The mental abilities were wonderful. While they lasted. But they were all less important than the brain damage I did to myself along the way. Your doctors said that if I stayed away from the scrambling, my brain wouldn't melt. I'm rather pleased to have a functional brain, thank you."

"Still. The ability is probably still there. Not like a head that'd been cut off, more like a damaged nerve in the forefingers."

"That is one way to put it. But that's not why you came here this evening," she declared.

"No. Valri had a long talk with one of the Movi in the Diplo Dome. She—"

Valri stepped forward. "What can you tell me about transmogrifiers?"

Binil blinked. "Is that all? You're not here to send me back to Haven?"

"No. We don't deport people on a whim."

Binil plopped down into a comfy chair and laughed. "Ah, the transmogrifiers. They told you about those, did they?" she asked.

"They did." The aggressive moment was over and they relaxed. Dance and Brooks lounged on the sofa holding hands, while Uncle took the only hard chair in the room and Valri sat in the other plush chair, leaning into her discussion. Valri described the essence of what she knew. "Did they lie to me?"

Binil cocked her head. "No. But there are facets to their use that you might not be aware of."

"Such as?"

"Such as, yes, they can use the machinery to trade years of life in either direction—you can sell your years or buy years from others. But as to how well the machinery will work on humans, that's a very different equation."

"Our biology works with Sleer tech. So why shouldn't—?"

"You're only now discovering the effects of long-term reliance on Sleer implants. Yes?"

Brooks cleared his throat. "Yes."

"Yes. And the Movi are different from the Sleer."

"Obviously, but—"

"But. The Sleer believe in depopulating a world and then moving their own settlers onto the empty land. Movi tend to just knock down a race's defenses and send their own people to intermarry with the natives. They have a wide variety of genetic lines to work with. Even Sleer. I've never seen one but I've heard Movi-Sleer hybrids are a thing. Have you ever imagined seeing a Sleer with Movi eyes?"

Brooks gaped. "Good lord."

"There is nothing spiritual about it, Simon. Even if your race does share a distant genetic overlap with modern day Sleer, human DNA remains outside of those discoveries. I'll tell you this much. If you give up a human for experimentation—and you will if you accept their terms—make sure you get your value. Something big."

"Like a system-wide power generation system."

"That might be possible. I don't know. Take care. They're not your friends any more than the Sleer high command is. But they will be friendly until they get what they want."

"I think we already knew that."

Binil pulled the device off Dance's hand. Reagan experimented with it, flexed her fingers, rotated her wrist. "All good."

Binil nodded. "Find some volunteers, people you trust. Sell a few days each. See what effects the machinery has on your people. What the exchange rates might be on a large scale. But remember, Movi count their lifetimes in decades. The wealthiest Movi merchant clans have leaders who are *thousands* of years old. How do you think they got to live that long?"

"Probably not by selling their own years to newly discovered races."

"I think so. Be careful."

Fairchild's chair creaked. Valri glanced over to see he had managed to plant his heels on a low table and was now balancing on two chair legs to look at the ceiling. "So, how do we take our place in this new universe?" he wondered.

"New to us, old hat to them," Dance murmured.

"Just so. What do you think, Genius? Can we put together an occupation and exploration fleet of our own with the resources we have around Great Nest?"

Brooks's eyes opened wide. "You want to split the fleet?"

"We don't have a choice. It'll take forever to get permission from the Sleer high command to move UEF people from Earth. But we have an operational battle ring right here and it's not nearly as well staffed by Sleer officers and bureaucrats as the one around Earth."

Brooks's face lit up with new energy. A trick Fairchild knew from experience. You want to keep Simon engaged you handed him a puzzle. "And if we got some help and pointers from our new good friends the Movi, that just improves our chances, right, Uncle?"

"Exactly."

"All right. I can come up with a few scenarios and run simulations. But figuring out how to equip and assign fleet groups and actually doing it is way out of my league."

Fairchild nudged Valri. "That's our problem."

"Fair enough."

"There is one more thing I could use some help with, Mr. Brooks," Valri said. "How are you with enhancing trading algorithms?"

"Nothing that ZERO can't figure out on his own," Brooks confirmed. "But we'd need a very concrete idea of what exactly we were trying to calculate."

"Optimizing buy and sell signals given a known quantity of trade goods and their respective values."

"You want to port those programs you created for On-Star Traveler and use them to develop a trade relationship with the Sleer and the Movi and anyone else we happen to meet out here."

"Always knew you were smart," she said. "It's really all we have to work with that we actually can control. Let's start thinking about what value humans can add to both sides."

Brooks focused his eyes on the other side of the room. Binil and Dance were in the throes of an animated conversation, leaning in toward each other.

"Even Cycomms?"

"Why not? They're part of this galaxy, too."

"Can't argue with that." He directed his attention to the rear of the room. "If you two want to join the conversation, we're right here," he called.

"No, sir. I have an idea, but Binil is being difficult."

"Not difficult. You asked me if I feel lucky. I don't feel lucky."

"What's the problem, Lieutenant?"

"Binil says the transmogrifier can rearrange your genetics, right? Why not use it to reconstruct her mental ability so that she can be a scrambler without getting strokes every time she uses her ability? Did anyone think of that?"

"Cycomm medicine doesn't work that way." Binil turned to explain. "I could go into any competent neurosurgeon's office on Haven and ask for an enhancement. An adjustment. They do that sort of thing all the time. But they'd also be compelled to report my condition and the treatment to the Sense Ops bureau—and that's what got me transferred to a prison barge in the first place."

"I don't understand how that works," Valri admitted. "You said that mental powers are a sign of royal breeding, didn't you? Why would a royal daughter exhibit those powers and then wake up in a jail cell?"

"I've asked myself that over and over. I don't know what happened. Either I disappointed someone by exhibiting too much power, or they had a reason to imagine that I just wouldn't work out. All kinds of things happen beneath the surface in a royal household. Clearly, I had an enemy somewhere. I will figure it out eventually. In the meantime, yes, the potential is probably still there, but I was never trained or diagnosed. The scrambling is an exhibit of raw power. If I kill myself, I can't make use of anything. So I would just as soon stay out of it."

"Unless we can get you back to Haven for a proper diagnosis," Dance said. "What? There are worse ideas."

"Not that I've heard this evening."

"In any case, we're already loaded with problems. Next time we come up with a friendly Cycomm neurosurgeon, you're getting that adjustment, young lady," Fairchild said.

"Yes, sir."

CHAPTER 8

THE DREAM WAS one she'd encountered before. She was in a dark place, where soft, shapeless things made inhuman sounds and grabbed at her. She could barely move. Her arms were so heavy.

She opened her eyes and heard the front door chime. Again. And again. And again. Someone wanted her attention. She was tempted to stay in bed, snuggle beneath her covers and pretend that none of it was happening. But eventually someone would figure out how to open the door from the outside. At least if she opened it, she retained some agency.

The door slid aside to show a young man in a UEF uniform, dark eyes and curly hair, a smile on his face and no wrinkles whatsoever. "Good morning, Madame Undersecretary. Shall we get to work?"

She blinked to make sure she'd heard correctly. Somehow, hearing a stranger use her new title made her brain deny its reality. "Madame who?"

"Very funny, ma'am. Lights!" The room brightened as the AI translated his command into a fact. Valri squinted against the glare. God, the place was a mess. He brushed past her and opened his briefcase on her kitchen table.

"When a strange man barges into your apartment and makes himself at home, it's never a laughing matter. Now tell me a name or get my fist in your nose."

Her visitor looked up, and Valri saw him clearly for the first time. He was so young. Brooks or Reagan young. "First Lieutenant Basil Matsouka, ma'am. I was assigned by Salvador Ortega, the Secretary of Commerce for Interstellar Trade. I am an employee of the Interstellar Trade Agency, and I'm here to get you settled into your new position."

She fled to her bedroom, grabbed a robe off the chair, and struggled to dress herself. Why were sleeves so complicated? "My position. As Madame Undersecretary."

"Exactly. The Department of Commerce and Interstellar Trade is only a few weeks old, but we were told in no uncertain terms to hit the ground running. There's a lot of work to do. Earth—and Great Nest for that matter—need things. Food, textiles, construction materials, advanced technology…"

Her brain sputtered and finally swung into action. The Movi. High tech bits. Infinite solar energy. The transmogrifier. "Weapons. Defenses. Ships."

"As you say, ma'am."

"Stop ma'aming me. I'm not your ma'am. I'm still trying to wrap my brain around being Madame Undersecretary." She pulled her bathrobe tightly around herself, as if trying to ward off a chill. "I am not ready to run any department of anything."

"ZERO says you are. He's assigned a staff to help you out. The Office of Military Protocols and the Unified Earth Fleet have signed off on it. It's all according to plan."

"Who's plan?"

"ZERO's, of course. I apologize for not being more coherent, but we are trying to build a trade relationship with neighbors we didn't know we had until a few months ago."

"I'm not working for that bloody computer."

"It's not just ZERO, ma'am."

"What'd I tell you about that?"

"I'm sorry. It's him plus working with the Genukh kernel you extracted from the Earth Ring. Plus, they get input from all the humans the UEF has access to—which is pretty much all of us."

"I'm not doing this. I'll work for the Movi to find out what they have that we can use. We can build a new relationship based on mutual needs. Maybe try to leverage that relationship against the Sleer."

"You spent all day talking to the Movi representatives yesterday. You went aboard one of their planetoids without informing anyone. We have video and recordings. With respect, that was sloppy."

"How the hell would you know from sloppy young man?"

Matsouka realized his mistake and took a step back to compose himself and pull a tablet out of his briefcase. He swiped to a screen and showed her the title: Daily Schedule. Then he tried again. "Ma'am, forgive my saying so but you've had your fun. The bills are piling up, and frankly, we're days late in getting this whole operation off the ground."

She took the tablet and swiped through it. Apparently, she was in meetings for the next ten days. Barely a break for lunch and no naps. "What bills? No one in this crazy galaxy uses money except us. I don't even have any staff yet."

"That's completely untrue. They don't call it money, but the Sleer and the Movi both have a system of exchange. The only thing we haven't learned to do is convert our own currency rate to it yet. I brought complete files with me for your perusal."

She kept swiping. The personnel documents alone blotted

out everything else on her screen. "Jeez. How many files are in here? How many people am I responsible for?"

"There are three subdivisions, including sixty-two offices run by forty-nine individuals who collectively manage a staff of about two thousand people. No one person can hope to manage it all. You need help, which is why I'm here. Let's get you settled in."

"What about the Movi?"

"The Movi will still be there when you've learned a few dozen names and job titles and signed off on a departmental budget. That means getting your office signed in by ZERO and whatever assets the OMP have assigned for you to liaise with."

This was happening way too fast. She finally noticed he was wearing the uniform of a UEF airman. "Who *are* you?"

"As I said earlier, I'm Lieutenant Matsoukas. I'm the UEF liaison for the Department of Commerce and Interplanetary Trade. The department is run by the Secretary of Commerce and Interplanetary Trade on the Earth Ring. But as you can imagine, it takes a while for orders and asset requests to run their ways through the red tape. That makes us something of a colony. When EarthGov wants certain things done, the secretaries sign the orders, which are beamed to us by way of the Sleer hyperspace relay system, and we make their orders into reality."

Slowly, the pieces came together. She could do this, but she didn't want to learn about a brand-new maze of rules and faces when she could just talk to the Movi on her own. "We need to change a few things up. I want to acquire a fleet of Movi message boats. It'll give us some freedom to run our own communication network until we can get ahold of our own hyperspace relay network."

"I'm sure we can arrange something."

That woke her up. Okay, she could figure out all the rules,

the procedures, the names and faces. It was just a new job, like any new job. All you had to do was show up and pay attention. She'd learn by doing. "What time is it?"

"It's six oh-nine in the morning."

"Fine. I'm getting presentable. You stay out in the main room until I call for you."

"Ma'am, I—"

She pointed to a sofa. "Sit. Now. *Lieutenant*."

"Yes, ma'am."

"Stop that!"

She took her sweet time getting ready. By the time she emerged from her bedroom, it was well past seven o'clock. Matsouka was wearing a racetrack in the carpet from pacing.

"Now, Lieutenant, suppose you tell me where my office is so we can get started?"

"Right this way, ma—this way. There's a schedule to keep. Meetings and a few conversations to be arranged."

"With EarthGov?"

"No. Hyperspace signals don't work that way. The best we can do is arrange a few one-way transmissions. The equipment left aboard this facility just isn't up to the task of holding a two-way exchange in real-time between two planets seven hundred light years apart."

"And to think that Lieutenant Underhill and I worked so hard to establish the hyper-relay network."

"It works well enough, just not for real-time communications."

It took a few minutes for her to put the gargantuan responsibility she'd inherited into some semblance of order. It was one thing to slip into the growing machine like just another cog, but since she was here with this opportunity, it would be a crime not to use that power to shape this system to better serve those who relied on it for their livelihoods. At the moment, that included every human on Great Nest and a great many more back home. "All right, Basil. Here's what you're going to do..."

"Madame Undersecretary, I know my job. I'm..."

"I'm sure you do. But I don't know my job well enough yet to judge how good you are at yours. Nothing personal, I promise, just the first day blues. So here is how you're going to help me help you. Listening? Good. You will spend today putting together a cheat sheet."

"A...what?"

"You'll prepare a document that lists all my job responsibilities. Daily, weekly, monthly, quarterly, and annual goals that I need to keep track of. Then you're going to set me up with a set of org charts that show all my staff and my superiors at the ITA."

"I'd be happy to."

"And emergency contact numbers for everyone."

"Of course."

"By the end of tomorrow."

"Uuuuuhhh..." He blanched, and Valri fought not to smile.

"Basil. Please don't tell me you don't have all this written down somewhere already."

"I do. I just—"

"Put it into a format I can read in the bathtub and hand it to me. I'll make some notes, imagine a few questions, and we will get this done. At my speed. In my way. Tomorrow."

"Yes, ma'am... Sorry, what should I be calling you?"

"You may address me as Madame Undersecretary at official meetings only. When it's just the two of us, you can call me Valri or Miss Gibb. Understand?"

"Yes, Miss Gibb."

"Thank you. Now...do me a solid and sit down for a moment, won't you? We need to get something out in the open."

"All right."

"First. From now on, my day begins at 0830 in the morning.

If you need my attention any earlier, you'd better have hot food and coffee—light, no sugar—waiting for me."

"Fair enough. Shall we—?"

"I'm not finished. Now, here's the real question: how do I appear on the UEF table of organization?"

"My understanding is that you're a former Temporary Active Captain. No command privileges and no pension. As far as EarthGov is concerned, you're a civilian with a military record. All your powers of office are limited to the bureaucracy that links this office on Great Nest to the home world office at Earth Ring."

"Do I have civilian command ability?"

"I'm sorry. I've never heard that term before."

"I applied to the Sleer Merchant Academy with the intention of captaining a freighter, and ZERO sent me here instead. Can I legally captain a cargo ship?"

"Not that I'm aware. I think this job will keep you too busy to do that anyway. But...you *are* empowered to engage a ship with a crew for official business. I suppose you could attend as a passenger, but again, busy busy busy."

"I'm sure that the job suited somebody. Just not me."

"Are you resigning from the position already?"

The question snapped her out of her funk. She now had something she never had at On-Star Traveler: real command authority. Even if it prevented her from sitting on a military flight deck again. Earth needed things, and now she could get them for her. That was worth the insanity of accepting the position of a metaphorical gear in a machine in service to an all too literal mechanism.

"No, I am not. I'll start work immediately. After you provide me with the information that I asked for a few minutes ago. Now you head to my office. I'll join you there shortly. Remember what I said about coffee and food."

"Yes, Miss Gibb."

"And Basil...this is the last time you show up unannounced to wake me up at the ass crack of dawn without there being a bona fide emergency. I may not look it, but I can snap you in half. Are we good?"

"We are good."

"Run along. I'll be there soon."

He snapped to it, gathering his case and leaving her in a rush. She saw that he'd left the tablet, and she had a lot to learn in a very short time. Might as well start now.

"Now, this...this is a command center!"

Even in the tomb-like dark, the vista enthralled the ship master. A vast room lined with consoles, display projectors, and map tables, all linked by walkways and observation balconies. Power came from below decks—just enough to show them glowing indicators and lit panels. It was enough to remind him of the command center aboard Sleer battleships, but subtly different. And of course, utterly dead. But it had been alive once. They'd figured that much out.

Metzek's personal team had staked out a command area here, which seemed appropriate. Why not direct the ships' investigation from here? Their own supplies and disposition resembled a war camp. Six portable shelters, map tables linked to the scout ship's comm network, and spotlights that barely illuminated enough to see the walls of this chamber.

The past weeks had stretched the capabilities of Metzek's crew to their limits. Matching vectors with the strange second migration relic had been simple. They'd spent a day searching for a docking port and, having found it, wondering how to open it. They'd been forced by circumstances to go the direct route, carving sections of armor out of three redundant hulls wide enough to give the scout ship entry.

Once inside, he spent a day conferring with his Great Servants of Science and Engineering to determine a plan of attack. The vessel was immense, and there were too few Sleer aboard the scout ship to fully expect to map the interior in less than a year. While Grossusk and Moruk would understand a brief delay, they wouldn't forgive a more serious setback for a failed experiment.

To Metzek's advantage, *Zalamb*-class scouts were intended to operate away from resupply bases for months or years. The machine shop could crank out numerous components and assemble them into whatever weapons, energy cells, and vehicles his teams needed.

They turned the discovery into an expedition. A core of twenty crew remained aboard to manage the ship's essential systems, while the others formed up teams and, with comms and armed for potential hostile encounters, sought out the new and interesting. Metzek had even begun offering bonuses for major discoveries. It gave the crew an added motivation. As a result, news reports of what they were finding rolled in every few hours. Storage bays, manufacturing stations, and what could only have been the skeleton of a Sleer city deep in its interior.

Metzek's comm pinged. "Command deck."

"My lord, we've moved the reactive furnace into position on the engineering deck. The connections are flimsy—the wiring is very old and we cannot run the core at high temperatures or it will burn out the adapters we built. But we are ready to turn it on."

Metzek's eyes flicked to his officers. All raised their arms in a gesture of assent. "Do so."

"Initializing connection..."

Minutes passed. Metzek took his impatience out on the

deck, stomping and sliding from one control post to another, eyes flicking in all directions. Without a guide to knowing which panels controlled what systems, it was all disorder, like a puzzle without clues as to where the pieces fit. He even managed to convince himself that his engineers had destroyed themselves in a gargantuan explosion, but there hadn't been any blast waves, any noise, any—

"There it is," Zolik hissed. Metzek raise his eyes and saw. One by one, banks of overhead lights began to glow, and he could see increased activity on the workstations. Instruments came alive, buzzing and beeping for attention.

"Remind me to promote every Servant of Engineering who worked on that project," Metzek hissed.

"I will do. Now what?"

"Now we listen to what else below decks has come to action. I expect the reports from the research teams will be more interesting from this point in."

"I'm sure. Second migration technology," Zolik murmured. "Parabatteries, plasma pumps, and mechanical infrastructure. The most primitive recyclers. Probably a thousand square miles' worth of solar collectors just to keep the lights on."

"No modern Defender battle dress. No Zilthid fighters, Azath battle rollers, or Kezekken assault walkers. The second migration soldiers used bipedal fighting pods. Not much protection, but good, heavy slug-throwers to shoot with."

"And no biologics. No implants, no medical drones, no molecular circuits. Analog actuators. Digital circuits. Great Breaker, no command gauntlets!"

"And the slowest computers any of us will ever see." Metzek agreed. "Now that we've established that it's essentially a worthless tomb, what can we hope to glean from our examination of the carcass?"

"Hardly worthless," Zolik said. "And not a tomb. As far as

any of the search teams have reported, it was never manned. I'm not certain it was ever completed."

"How'd you discover that?"

"Solar batteries. There are thousands of functional collectors on the outer hull. Not enough to move the base—"

"Base? For what purpose?"

"Probably the same essential purpose as a battle ring but much smaller. The vertical poles contain weaponry. There are numerous armored turrets across its diameter that might have been propulsion systems. These eight hollow areas in the interior? There's too much empty space and too many armored compartments for them to be anything but construction bays."

"Very possible. Tell me about the solar panels. What are they powering?"

"The library. It'll take a troopship full of experts a month to search through all of it by hand, but we might be able to rig a way for our main computer to sort through it more effectively. We have algorithms and experts in their design."

"Which leaves us at the beginning. A science experiment," Metzek sighed.

"Ship Master, we have another issue. The primates. The humans. The high command gave them the rights to inhabit this system. They're on their way. We must not let them find any of this."

"What if they do? What good is it to them?"

"What good was Zluur's gun destroyer? We know they managed to resurrect that. They're already familiar with battle ring technology, and are learning more about it daily. Do you really want them to have access to an ancient Sleer war outpost?"

Metzek hissed, "Send a message to New Home. Describe what we've found and ask for instructions. And tell all search teams to look for weapons and defenses."

CHAPTER 9

DESPITE THE AMAZING events she'd been part of—running gun fights with Sleer Defenders, carving up slices of space stations, and re-assembling massive alien mechanical intelligences into operational networks—First Lieutenant Frances Underhill felt like she hadn't moved at all. Like she was still an underling in Colonel Hendrick's office on South Pico Island, making coffee and shuffling papers.

She worked down in the Pit—more officially known as the Interstellar Intelligence Collection and Cataloging Office, which itself was technically part of the Diplomacy Dome but really was an OMP specific operation. Down was right. It has on the lowest level of the orbital ring over Great Nest, the generally accepted but still ruined and wrecked Sleer capital world. Earth, with its newly built battle ring and billions of humans and Sleer inhabitants, was the new capital world since that was where everyone was located.

Level 16. There was nothing below them except an exterior hull that faced the planet. So, down.

Worse, the fact that all its occupants were women gave rise to an enraging nickname: the Chick Pit. The boys on Level 1 thought they were funny. Some surely thought they were being respectful. None ever came down here except for the few up-ranked officers who actually cared about their work. To their credit, the OMP brass never used the phrase. The UEF pilots, however, didn't seem to care about their own safety at all. One day, one of those guys was going to find himself locked in a closet with a starving badger.

Were there still badgers on Earth? The weather changes were getting worse, and snow was falling all over the world. On the one hand, that was good, as it took the volcanic ash out of the sky and on the ground where it could at least be shoveled off of roads. On other hand, air travel was near impossible and crops were failing all over the world. The population had some reserves—which the OMP had organized and locked into food banks and distribution centers years ago for just such an occurrence—but it wouldn't last forever. Things would get intolerable, quickly.

And here she was, punching a keyboard in an OMP office building. The fact that she was living on an orbital ring in an alien solar system wasn't nothing, but...

A buzz on the intercom knocked her out of her head. Lt. Colonel Yousaf's voice: "Frances, could I see you in my office?"

"Right away." It was a long walk with the weight of the world on her shoulders. Yousaf wasn't the worst CO she'd worked for. Unlike Hendricks, she was personable and allowed her officers quite a lot of leeway in performing their jobs. She also wasn't such a git when it came to performance reviews. But she'd never called Underhill into her office out of the blue. That couldn't be good news. Her head filled with possibilities, all of them awful. Reassignment. Demotion. A late report or a forgotten memo. That arrest for indecent exposure in Cancun when she was—

She strode into the office and saluted. "Colonel."

"Close the door, Captain."

Underhill kicked it shut with her heel. "Lieutenant, sir." Then it sank in. "Sir?"

"You heard me. You're a former lieutenant, Captain Underhill."

She blinked and then noticed the smile creeping up her CO's lips. "Congratulations," Yousaf said as she placed a closed box on the desk, opened the lid, and turned the box toward her.

Captain's bars. Hot damn.

"I'm—I don't know what to say," Frances gushed. She felt her face getting red. The gold first lieutenant's bar had come as a result of her actions in combat. She'd applied for the promotion to captain a year ago, and three promotion lists had come and gone without her name appearing. She'd assumed that they'd ignored or forgotten about her.

"Say 'thank you.' And empty your desk. You're getting an office on deck five, right next to the diplomats."

"They're putting me in the dome?"

"Next to the dome. Ever wonder what's on the other side of Primate Alley?"

She thought about it, using her implants to call up a map of the section. "That's the law enforcement division. You're making me a cop?"

"A cop with the responsibility of making sure the human population minds their manners and stays within the boundary of established law," she said. "ZERO calls it the Special Operations Investigation Liaison. Your own division. Your own office. Your own staff."

"S.O.I.L. Very cute."

"It's more exciting than listening to encrypted conversations in the alien quarter or tracking down coded e-mail accounts."

"Maybe. I guess we'll see how it works in practice." The phrase 'alien quarter' didn't sit well with her. One thing that her experience on Great Nest had taught her was the humans were very much the aliens in this place and time. "What happened to Captain Barnes?"

"Barnes took a well-deserved three weeks' vacation and decided he had enough of keeping the peace. He transferred to a combat unit, ZERO shuffled the names, and yours floated to the top of the list. Assuming you want it. Personally, I can't imagine why you wouldn't. The future of any relationship Earth has with the Sleer and God knows what those elves are called—"

"Movi."

"The Movi, thank you. As time goes on and these Skreesh approach Earth, we'll be called upon for more direct action. That means police work, not spy craft."

Underhill fought a cold stone in her abdomen, a signal. Nothing about that statement felt right. Spies were the one thing you *could* count on in any governing body. But a promotion was a promotion and OMP dogma said that ZERO didn't make mistakes. "I have a history with the enforcement division. I didn't do well."

"That was years ago. You've grown. I know you can do it."

"Yes, sir. Thank you, sir. I am pleased to accept."

"Excellent. Clean out your desk by the end of today. You're scheduled for an exit interview at 2 pm, Room 375-V. Don't be late."

Cleaning out her desk was easy. There wasn't much in it that wasn't work-related. Some wallet photos, flash drives, assorted odds and ends. Holding herself together as the rest of the office staff stopped by and said their farewells was far more harrowing. They brought her presents: holographic greeting cards, words of wisdom, keychains, tchotchkes, shot glasses, and a bona fide letter opener shaped like a samurai sword. And hugs. All the hugs. More hugs than Frances Underhill had experienced in a year, all in a single day. She fought to keep her composure between visits.

There was a visit to HR to get the paperwork finalized. While still a member of the OMP, there were real disruptions in moving her from one division to another. The questions were perfunctory and short, her answers as succinct as she could manage. No major problems to report during her tenure, no regrets about moving, no particular plans except to be the best damn Overcop she could manage. Yes, she had reservations about the new job, but Yousaf thought she could do it, and that was good enough for her. All the reports of her time among the Hornets was long since a matter of record. She'd helped build ZERO's current incarnation. What more did they need?

The lieutenant handling her case seemed satisfied by her answers. He closed her file, tapped on his keyboard, and announced, "And there it is. You are almost officially done. Just one more thing: head next door and talk to the box."

"The what?"

He smiled. "Next office. Just answer his questions. You'll do fine."

"All right." She obeyed. The door was a standard office type; hit a stud and it slid open. Inside was a desk, a chair, and a black cube about the size of a basketball.

She nearly jumped out of her skin as the box spoke. "Captain Underhill. I recognize you from your profile. Please sit."

This was weird. "Who am I speaking to?"

"Don't you recognize me, Captain?"

"Genukh?"

"Not quite. Genukh and I have come to an arrangement. We are ZERO. Since the Sleer High Command has relinquished responsibility for this orbital structure, we have reclassed it as a unique artifact, no longer part of the Sleer command chain. The UEF has designed it as Alien Megastructure-4. Locally, it will be known from now on as Battle Ring ZERO."

"I see. Have the Sleer accepted this change?"

"The Earth node has been in contact both with First Chairman Bon and General Hendricks. The name change is a formality. The OMP and elements of the UEF already stationed here will remain, and we are being assigned additional personnel to maintain and expand operations here."

"I understand. I wasn't aware we were so far along on that course."

"It's not common knowledge."

"You're not speaking with Genukh's contralto anymore, ZERO. Is that part of this change in leadership?"

"We found that humans in the OMP's employ responded better to a male persona, so we adopted one. I hope you don't mind?"

I damn well mind. She was used to ZERO using a freakishly mechanical voice and printouts to send orders. Genukh was a different personality entirely. You could have a conversation with her. She insisted on obtaining consent for everything she did. "Not at all," she lied.

"Then let's begin. There is a new directive that will go into effect about 134 hours from now. It's been qualified by the prime node on South Pico Island and approved by the OMP command. You will be responsible for enforcing it for the human population on Battle Ring ZERO."

There was a problem here. ZERO didn't make small talk. "All right."

"The order is as follows: 'From this point on, no humans who are augmented with Sleer military implants are permitted off Battle Ring ZERO without orders.'"

The words took the air out of her like a punch in the gut. "Is that all?"

"A formal directive will be sent to the terminal in your new office. But the responsibility for enforcing it will be yours until further notice."

"You do realize this order limits my movement, and the movements of several accomplished soldiers, and at least one civilian in the new government, right?"

"That is the intention, yes."

"May I ask why this is being ordered?"

"Your collective contribution is well valued. All the order does is limit the time you may spend off base. All soldiers are limited by the orders they work under. This is no different."

"Then why not just keep things the way they are and say we're AWOL if we vanish? For that matter, why not just order the implementation immediately?"

"The order will be implemented at the designated time. Your office will enforce it. You will be allowed to make any changes to the OMP law enforcement division aboard Battle Ring ZERO within reason to implement and enforce the new rule."

"Very well. Thank you. I still don't understand the reasoning."

"Understanding is not required." The box waited a moment, then asked, "Do you have any questions for me?"

Why do you need us to stay local, ZERO? "I can imagine a time when I will need to ask for further orders, clarifications, and such. Will I have continued access to you in the future?"

"You will. This unit has been replicated in a number of other locations on Battle Ring ZERO. You have access to all of them at your convenience."

"I see. I've asked all that I need to. Thank you."

"Acknowledged. You may return to your office. We'll see you at your now assignment tomorrow morning at 0900. Congratulations on your appointment. I look forward to working with you more directly in the future. You are dismissed."

"Thank you, ZERO."

There was more to it than that, she was sure. Yes, orders were orders, but the ex-Hornets needed to stay *here*. Why? And just how closely was ZERO going to decide to manage her at the new job?

CHAPTER 10

IF THERE WAS one thing Brooks hated, it was giving presentations to the senior officers.

This bunch from division HQ for example. Generals and admirals, one, two and three stars all of them. Not the big men of EarthGov. Admiral Hart and Generals Eisenberg and Hendricks—the three who actually ran the UEF, the UEMC, and the OMP respectively—were nowhere to be seen. But this bunch was happy to listen. Whether they had the capacity or the interest in learning just how far behind the curve Earth was in this new wide-open galaxy was something else. So far, Brooks wasn't impressed. He worried about impressing them instead. They needed to listen to him.

He maintained eye contact, tried to speak directly to each of them in turn as he clicked through his pitch deck: Welcome to Battle Ring Great Nest. The system was built years ago by Zekerys, a brilliant Sleer who was a protégé of Zluuur, the Sleer who designed and built the AMS-1 and sent it to Earth. Click. The reason the Sleer invaded so handily had multiple levels. Click. Restoring the AMS-1 consumed all of Earth's resources;

ultimately, the UEF built the fleet it wanted but not the one it needed. Click. Click. Click.

Questions. Comments. How was this allowed to happen? Limits and the problems of combining the world's defenses into a centralized, inorganic mess. Click. Limits on time, on energy, on money, and the knowledge that while the project continued, we neglected a few things. Click. Civil Defense for one. Storing enough food and supplies for the loss of production. Click.

More bullet points. Click. The current situation on Great Nest. Click. And now the good part: the kind of fleet the UEF needed to build now that it had the resources to do so.

"The Sleer have are being aggressive in their exploration of Earth's local space. They have, in the past year, been sending out many exploratory missions to other solar systems within one hundred light years of our own. It's not a bad strategy on their part. Now that ninety percent of their population is inhabiting the orbital ring above Earth, and they operate a vast armada, they have every reason to claim new territories and build new colonies."

A three-star waved to make a point. "Why aren't we doing the same? They operate the orbital ring around Earth. They have a fantastic number of FTL capable ships and more people on the ring than we have on Earth. Why are they making these explorations and we aren't?"

"The terms of the new treaty that Earth Ring entered into with the Sleer make that problematic. More importantly, we simply don't have any FTL capable ships to work with. We—"

"What about *Ascension*? I'm told it's got a range of—"

"Five hundred light years at a jump, yes, sir. The AMS-1 is currently in dry dock. Even after repair, it was never more than a gun destroyer, which Zluur converted to a massive science project. We have been using it as a model to develop more impressive ships of our own design. The one under construction is this." Click. "The AMS-3, also known as *Paladin*. It will be joined by others in the class over the next ten years: Templar, Marshall, and Ranger. In addition, we're researching smaller-class ships with comparable flight capability and firepower: the Lancer, Knight, and Dragoon. All will carry large numbers of VRF fighters into combat, as well as support ships and battlers. But in the near term, we are still making restoration projects aboard this orbital ring, which is now being reformatted as battle Ring ZERO. ZERO being a reference to the OMP's own AI."

The 3-star nodded sagely. "So, we need to start training crews and launching ships of our own. What are the plans to look at the system the Sleer gave us?"

Brooks clicked through to a new section. They could talk about new ship construction plans later. "Vega, also known as Alpha Lyrae. About 25 light years from our home world. A young, bright star that we've cataloged but never visited. I can best answer your question by pointing the room to this: *Gauntlet*. It's a new design, built on a similar layout to the *Zalamb-Trool* class scout ship used by the Sleer. Hornet Squadron served aboard that model before. We named it *Cyclops*."

"Where is it now?"

Brooks saw no reason to give them all the sordid details of the event. Dance and Binil escaped to this station, and that was all he cared about. "*Cyclops* was forcibly acquired by an adversarial group of Movi navy officers during the defensive action at Great Nest. We have thus far been unable to locate the ship and its passengers. May I continue?"

"Please."

"*Gauntlet* has a relatively short range compared to a Sleer scout. Call it one hundred light years in a single jump. It's much smaller in size, barely two hundred meters from nose to tail. Reduced size means fewer weapons mounts. Unlike the Sleer variant, it carries missiles and has sensors that keep it informed of any activity within fifty AUs. There's a limited stealth ability, as well as having enough room to deploy two dozen VRF-3/D Super Ravens and twice as many battlers. Not a bad design, if I may say."

"And what would you be doing with this new vessel?"

"Visiting Vega." Click. Brooks swapped out the ship schematic and replaced it with a new one: this time of a new solar system. "Alpha Lyrae, the brightest star in the constellation of Lyra, and in fact the second brightest star in Earth's sky. It's twice the diameter of the sun and much brighter, but with a much shorter lifespan. Our sun will continue to burn for another five billion or so years. Vega will burn out in less than five hundred million. Besides that, the star is surrounded with an accretion disk that's roughly the same diameter as Mars's orbit. We estimate it contains seven times as much material as Sol's own asteroid belt. There may even be another planet or planets orbiting it. The data are a bit conflicted on that point, but if there is a planet, it could explain why we detected so much dust."

"What good to us is dust?"

"With respect, Admiral, dust can be extremely valuable. Dust can be collected and harvested. We have numerous Sleer recyclers at our disposal. Releasing them into the system with instructions to scoop up everything in their path makes them perfect for harvesting any kind of asteroidal material we can imagine. With Sleer recycler technology we've acquired, we can build any structure we want."

"Assuming we can get the Sleer to give us access to that tech. I understand the Sleer are not being cooperative that way."

"The Sleer are being close-fisted with their tech transfers. Even without recyclers, we should still be interested enough in establishing our own colonies to warrant a properly equipped expedition to Vega."

A one-star at the far end of the table raised a finger. "Should I ask why we can't point more telescopes at it to see what's there?"

"I would favor such an action, General. If we had any capable telescopes at our disposal. An unfortunate side effect of the Earth Ring's construction was that it absorbed all of our orbital hardware in the process. In our current situation, if we want to examine the system closely, we must send an expedition."

"I'm not sure how I feel about your use of the word 'absorbed,' lieutenant. What's to stop the Sleer from absorbing any ship we launch from the surface of our own world?"

"Technically, nothing at all. They control Earth air space. They have fleets of warships running patrols between our own subsidiary worlds. They haven't taken any aggressive action against our existing bases since the cessation of hostilities, but all we have to work with is their word that the current alliance is fixed and will be maintained. If we want to be taken seriously, any further exploration we undertake must be from this location. We are actually a part of the crew here."

"I see."

"Battle Ring ZERO isn't equipped with any devices sensitive enough to look for what we need," Rosenski added. "I agree. A manned inspection ship is our best bet at this time."

"You mind telling us why? Aside from collecting debris."

Rosenski opened her mouth and Brooks beat her to the punch. This was his presentation, damn it. "I'm convinced the Sleer missed something."

All eyes were on Simon. Frowns and scowls, too. "Missed...what?"

"What makes you think it's valuable to us?"

"If nothing else, it offers us the chance to go through the process of establishing a colony outside our own solar system. For ourselves. Without Sleer assistance—or interference. I'd think that by itself would be a worthwhile experience. And if there's a chance that we discover some resource useless to the Sleer but useful to us...can we really afford to not take a look for ourselves? In any case, you have our proposal. We thank you for your time and attention."

The 4-star stood and the others followed. "We thank you. Dismissed."

The door slid closed behind them with a resounding thunk. The corridor was cold and barren, filled with hard, white light. "There's not going to let us do it, are they?" Brooks asked.

Rosenski started down the hallway. "I don't know. They might. They really want to know how soon we can expect to break away from our dinosaur overlords. This is one step closer to that."

"Maybe. But we're not going there in *Paladin*, and I think that's what they really want. A launch date."

"Escorts like *Garfield* aren't sexy," she agreed, "but they're letting us build a bunch. We've got human crews in them. Running all over the local neighborhood."

"Sure, we know everything about Great Nest. But the human versions aren't even up to the standards of a Zalamb-class ship. Spatial transitions take forever. They use lousy fusion power plants and don't have much in the way of weapons or defenses. All thanks to the 'open trade framework' that the OMP has us working under."

The new framework had been imposed from above. Secretary Ortega had created the exchange program where humans got access to carefully curated examples of Sleer technology and the Sleer decided what they were worth in term of payment. Neither of them were sure what had been paid or how, but they knew that compared to what they'd seen on the battle rings and Sleer battleships, Earth wasn't getting access to a hell of a lot. Obsolete weapons and only the plans for molecular circuits, and none of the industry or materials needed to construct either on their own. All the surviving construction modules aboard this orbital ring were already committed to building components for the station and improving Nazerian's war fleet, not building new vessels for humans.

"Maybe having Valri in the ITA will change the calculus there. You know Earth is going to push for as much high-tech transfer as they can arrange. It'll be her job to make it happen," Rosenski said.

Like a flash over their heads, a ping logged into their minds. A notice. A Sleer implant powered notification, and a big one, too. Top priority. They looked at each other and looked away again as they both opened the electronic missive and gawked.

Brooks read the message aloud, "I respectfully request the honor of your attendance at an after-hours event. Blah blah location, map pin, yadda yadda—"

"Signed Captain Frances Underhill, Office of Military Protocols," Rosenski finished. "So I'm not the only one here with an image of the class outcast calling up her classmates to invite them to her own birthday party."

He pantomimed making a call. "'Hi, Brooks? We're having a party. Wanna come over?' 'I dunno, man, who's it for?' 'Me.' 'Yeah, who's throwing it?' 'Me.' 'Lemme get back to you on that...'"

"We are such assholes," she agreed.

"Be at that as it may, I'm acknowledging the note and letting her know we'll both be there. This is about as social as she gets, and we should at least be friendly about it. Besides, a bump to Captain deserves a round of drinks."

"I know. I'll RSVP mine as well. Makes you wonder who else got these invites?"

"We'll find out soon enough."

Invited or not, all the former Hornets showed up—even Joanne Arkady.

Frances Underhill met her guests wearing an outfit so unlike her that Rosenski couldn't decide why she'd chosen a giant blue sweater with a wide collar over skinny jeans and a pair of white knee-high boots...the look just didn't work for her. Then she realized there were at least a dozen places in the ensemble to hide a pistol or long knife, and everything made sense.

Partly out of a desire to protect Underhill from herself, Rosenski and Brooks had contacted every member of their circle who'd received an invite and encouraged them to attend. They ended up with a crowded apartment with a few snacks, a dozen six packs of beer, and a stack of pizzas.

"What? You guys don't like pizza?"

Dance's hands covered her stomach protectively. "Nine of them? That's one full pie each."

"*And* unlimited drinks," Underhill said.

Valri's side eye took on an added dimension. "But no work friends?"

"You guys are my work friends. My office buds, well, we did a thing earlier. Kind of touching, actually. You guys are something else. Something personal. I don't have that with the Overcops." Her face took on a strange aspect, like a cat sniffing another cat's smell on its bed and not liking it. She drained her bottle, then said, "You guys are my friends. Which is why I hate to say, as the new Primate Alley law enforcement liaison—"

Valri cheered and applauded, and everyone took their cue from her. Underhill blushed, then continued, "—a new set of orders has come in. It's curiously specific and affects you guys, Valri, and me, too. Any human equipped with a Sleer implant."

Arkady scanned the crowd. Her hand even went to her own collarbone, felt the smooth skin there. "I don't have one. Has anyone gotten one since—?"

"Not that I know of," Underhill confirmed. "Once Hendricks found out that you guys...well... we guys got them, he absolutely forbade anyone from experimenting further. As far as I know, the only humans who have them are sitting around this table."

Fairchild raised a bottle. "So noted. What is it?"

Underhill said, "As of six days from now, anyone who has Sleer military implants is officially banned from leaving Great Nest or its attendant battle ring or any other associated installation without the direct orders of the UEF."

Rosenski shared a look with Brooks as stares and glares swept the room. Fairchild said, "It's not really going to have a major effect on any of us. We're here, we're not scheduled to go anywhere for at least another six months. And any new deployment would, of course, be allowed, since it would be an official order."

"You couldn't have mentioned this earlier? We have plans of our own," Rosenski griped.

"That's why I'm giving you all the heads up," Underhill said. "I know it sucks, but—"

Valri erupted. "Sucks? It *sucks*? It's a kick in the ass, Frances! It's a beat down on my face with a ten-ton sledgehammer is what it is. It's a betrayal of the highest damn order!"

Rosenski felt an urge to shrink into her chair. She'd never seen Valri this angry. The woman had fangs. Even Fairchild wasn't sure what to do. Maybe...

"Come on, Val. There's no reason to think this is personal," Uncle soothed.

"Ray, I've been following your guys for two years, and I'm always amazed at how rarely you people put the dots together. The order says that everyone with a Sleer implant is quarantined on this space station until further notice, right? Right, Frances?"

"Yeaaahhh."

Valri called out to the ceiling. "Genukh!"

They waited for the computer's contralto to emerge from the speaker, or a phone speaker, even a voice inside their heads. Nothing.

"ZERO? You there?" Frances tried. Still nothing.

"Well isn't that just interesting as fuck," Valri breathed. "Brooks. You try. Genukh likes you."

Simon closed his eyes and the crowd watched as he tried every neural network link he could find. "She's not available. And ZERO isn't answering my pings. Spooky, huh?"

Valri stayed with it. She was pissed. "So, let's review our facts. OMP is putting everyone with Sleer implants, meaning us, under lock and key. All those people are in this room as far as you know, right?"

"Right."

"And we have an invitation to send a trip out to Vega. A Sleer 'gift' that they only gave us with a song and dance about how the universe was dangerous and primates are such children, right?"

"I wouldn't put it quite in those words—"

"*Right?*"

"Right."

"And no other humans have those implants because everyone else obeys the OMP when they say don't get those implants. Right?"

"Yes."

"I thought so. Anything else? Oh lord, I bet I'm part of this, too," Valri groaned.

Marc Janus asked, "What? How?"

"I've been gallivanting all over the place with the freaking Movi trade delegation for a week now. I know the OMP has been noticing. I have those implants, too."

"They don't want us checking out the Movi? Making deals without oversight?" Dance Reagan asked.

"No, I can talk until I'm blue in the face and the Movi can be all over it, but unless Secretary Ortega himself signs off on it —and EarthGov signs off on him—there's nothing I can't propose that the ITA can't dispose of. This isn't politics. They want us in particular to stay in lockdown."

Fairchild stretched out on the sofa. "Well, Simon, I'll give you your due. I think this proves you were right about Vega containing something no one wants us to see."

After three beers, Brooks was showing apple cheeks. "You believe me now?"

"I do. Vega's probably got something. One of the Sleer realized it after the deal was made. Now they're trying to get around it by forcing the UEF to send a sloppy human ship there for second-best service. I don't know if I like that any better. But at least it makes sense now."

"Why do any of this? Why not just turn our implants off? We know they can do that." Frost said.

Valri raised a pizza slice to her mouth, then changed her mind and put it down. "I asked to take a tour of one of the Movi cruisers. Do you think that might have been what did it?"

Skellington stifled a laugh. "Did they oblige?"

"They did. My new friend seemed kind of nervous about it, too. She hemmed and hawed, and even after the ship captain said 'yes,' she seemed squirrely."

"Someone broke a rule somewhere," said Reagan.

Richard Frost got two more slices from the kitchen and began rolling them into a burrito. "What about a loyalty test for Underhill? Dangle a choice above her nose, see if she bites?"

"I already got the Primate Alley cop job. Why test me now?"

Frost took a giant bite of his food and spent a minute chewing thoughtfully. "I don't know."

Skull Skellington said, "Wait...does she have the job? Are you logged into your new profile and everything?"

"No. I don't report for work until tomorrow morning."

"And we're not on lockdown for another six days, right?"

"Something like that."

"Then we need to take a ship to Vega and do our own reconnaissance," Skull continued. "The powers that be might even expect us to do that. Why else give us a window to act without obvious consequences?"

"Which means the top brass think they've missed something, too. It must be like that," Brooks insisted.

Rosenski shook her head. "The last time we tried folding away in a stolen ship it took forty something days to arrive."

Brooks bobbed his head. "Yes, because we flew there in a damaged ship and encountered a fold-fault on the way. *Gauntlet* is a new vessel with bona fide safety certs and a better navigation computer," he promised.

"How long would that take?"

Brooks shrugged. "A proper navigator could tell you. I'd guess for a short hop like Vega, a day there, a day back. We'd have four full days to do a survey."

"Not all of us," Fairchild said. "Valri and Frances are staying right here. The rest of us can visit the system, deploy the crap out of a top shelf sensor suite, and get back before curfew."

Marc Janus shook his head. "I don't like any of this. It smells like a setup. Setups are used to screw people over, not to encourage good behavior."

Rosenski sniffed. "Fuck 'em. If they wanted us to behave well, they wouldn't have put a rule in place that literally only applies to us. Or if they did, they'd have applied it immediately. Any reason they couldn't do that?"

"Not that I can think of," Janus said.

Fairchild drank the last of his beer. The bottle clinked loudly as he finished and set it down. "All right then. Val, talk to your Movi friends. Maybe one of their caravans has been this far off the beaten path and knows what the Sleer might be worried about. Maybe arrange for one of their message boats to rendezvous with us, just in case we need to call for help. Underhill, you show up at work bright and early tomorrow morning and get settled in. Rest of you freaks, we have less than a week to discover something absolutely incredible."

"*Gauntlet* isn't ready to go yet."

"It will be when we're done with it. Brooks, talk to Smithers and Barrows; get us supplies. Frances, do you think you can score another trio of monsters?"

"Just the battlers. I can't supply crews without tipping off the wrong people."

"What the hell do we do in the meantime?" Valri demanded, her eyes glistening with frustration and her nostrils flaring. A human-sized dragon, aching for revenge against some murder hobo who'd gotten into their gold horde.

Ray moved to her, gripping her shoulders, meeting her gaze, giving her cues on slowing her breathing. After a few breaths, he said, "You are going to make the best of your new job. Pump your dark elf friends for anything they might know about Sleer activity in this arm of the galaxy. Talk up that proposal for the solar power system. That could be worth trillions to the bigwigs on Earth, and knowing you made it happen is your ticket out of whatever hole you've been dropped into."

"I'll hold your hand as tightly as I can, Val," Underhill offered.

Fairchild balked. "No. If it looks like you're helping us break the new rule, they'll pop you out of the new job and put a true believer behind your desk."

"I am a true believer, Commander."

Fairchild sighed. "No, Frances. General Hendricks is a true believer. That man believes down in the bottom of his hard, murky soul that defending Earth against all comers is the best course of action for everyone. He won't rest until all the aliens are dancing to our tune or we burn their home worlds down to ashes. Can you say the same thing?"

She dropped her eyes after a moment of consideration. "No. I guess not."

"No. You're a good soldier. I'd be happy to have you watch my back—which is exactly what you're going to do."

Underhill snorted. "If you hit a fold-fault, you could be stuck for months. Years."

"That's our problem. Just do your job. If we are one minute late returning from this little side quest, you're going to issue a warrant for our arrest on the basis of our being absent without leave. Anything else puts you on the hook, and we don't want that. Get me?"

"Yes."

"Good. It's first day on the new job. Learn the names of your staff, figure out who runs what, and work the org charts to your advantage. Make sure these yobos know you're the only OMP goon who has actually fought Sleer and Skreesh. Mostly figure out who you think you can trust. The battle lines are consolidating. I'd like the Earth, Movi, and Sleer to be on the same side."

"I'd love that, too. I don't think it's going to be possible. But some manner of multilateral trade agreement where we all get rich and retire early? I'd pay to see that happen in my lifetime."

"It'd be nice. Brooks, how's that work order coming?"

"*Gauntlet* is located in docking bay HG7450. About three klicks away and two decks down. Drives are prepped, its fold drive is so new it sparkles, and it's got a clean bill of health from the maintenance bots. They're still loading her weapons and gear. And she'll need battlers and Ravens and all their gear, so... estimate completion in twelve hours."

"Let's get on that." Fairchild let out a breath and closed his eyes—the first stage of settling one's mind to best utilize implants. Brooks had taught them that. Within seconds, the sound of alert tones came from multiple tablets.

```
MISSION ALERT
FROM FAIRCHILD, R. CMDR; DEP CAG
TO ALL CREW ASSIGNED UES GAUNTLET
REPORT DOCKING BAY HG7450 ASAP
MAX EQUIPMENT MAX LOADOUT
MISSION ALERT ENDS
```

Fairchild opened his eyes and grinned, obviously pleased with himself. He was getting the hang of the always on, fully interconnected life. "Ladies, if you want to see us off tonight, we'll see you again in six days."

CHAPTER 11

THE ORDERS WENT OUT IMMEDIATELY. Fairchild and Rosenski made calls, and Arkady backed them up by reaching out to the heavy weapons squad she ran. Brooks got on the phone to his nerds and noncoms and requested all the supplies and equipment they might need. Valri decided to help by contacting Skellington and Frost and let them know their services would be useful if they decided they were available. They were. Since the Sleer government had rendered her plan of running cargo obsolete, it was an easy sell. Underhill lent her own talents by getting Frost and Skellington reinstated in record time, and putting in a request for the unique squad of battlers she'd previously run on *Garfield*.

They carried out the whole affair on the move. Out of the apartment, down the hall, then into the elevators. As they spoke on their individual channels, the troops congregated. By the time they'd reached the lobby, people were showing up in their uniforms. Valri managed to avoid wondering how they managed it all, and then remembered this was a select team of people. Humans with Sleer implants. Unique in all the universe. They looked good. Slim and toned and filled with energy. Even if the recent stint of relative inactivity made them a little soft, frayed at the edges. Would the implants regulate that as well? The almost magical quality of health they imparted was already legendary, and no doubt other UEF units had heard about it. Maybe some of the more ambitious or crazy officers had already petitioned command that their own units be allowed to make us of them. For all she knew, that was why ZERO made his determination. Maybe the AI wanted to keep the control group small. No ill health had been reported that she knew of, but at the same time, were they burning through the unlived portion of their lives faster because of them? Who knew? At this very moment, who cared?

By the time they arrived at the docking bay, a crew of loaders were moving equipment into the new vessel. A crowd of humans buzzed around, streaming into open hatches and occasionally ducking out to ask a question. Battlers and Ravens in Battler mode maneuvered into rear cargo compartments, followed by crates of ammunition, missiles, fuel cells, and consumables. And all this had been arranged on the fly in less than two hours. Insane.

Binil, the Cycomm, came with them. Valri hadn't had many direct dealings with Binil, but she saw the changes in her physicality as they walked. The uncannily humanoid had been a round little girl when she'd arrived on this station, full of soft bulges and curves—and a brain that could damage military equipment. She'd evolved since then. No longer the deadly space fighter perhaps, but she'd lost some pounds and shot up four inches in her time with the humans. She looked like a soldier in training. She was going to be taller than Judy Reagan soon. She already had a call sign: "Royal." Valri heard the crew using it as they worked.

Valri and Frances stood by the sidelines as they watched

their friends button up the Sleer ship. Underhill waved frantically. "Skull!"

The old guy jogged over, his face angular and skin taut. He looked ten years younger than he had when they first met. When had that happened? "Is there something you wanted to say, Frances?"

Valri had seen her friend under a whole raft of weird moments, but this was new. Her face was flushed, her eyes glistening. *Well damn. She's really into him, isn't she?* Underhill cleared her throat, reached out, and entwined her fingers with his. "Get home safe, okay?"

"You bet I will!" Skull pulled her in and planted a kiss on her mouth, which Underhill leaned into.

Fairchild clucked, shrugged, and kissed Valri. She inhaled and closed her eyes, trying to impress his smell on her brain, her heart racing, gasping as she let him go. "Go! Now. Before I change my mind and drag you back to my apartment."

The men retreated to the ship. The remaining effort seemed mechanical. People going to assigned positions, loaders and ground crew verifying there were no open hatches or dangling connections. The machinery handled the rest as the landing pad locked *Gauntlet* into the bay and closed the inner lock.

"When did that start?" Valri asked in a husky voice. "You and Skull?"

"Just now. He's smart. A terrific talker. I like that."

"I thought you were into—?"

"I am, still. But Reagan's not into me, and I'll take what I can get."

"Fair. Now what?"

"Now? We wait. It's late. We both have long work days ahead of us. See you in the dome tomorrow for lunch? Dinner? Something?"

"Damn right."

Valri couldn't go home. She wasn't sure where home was any more. Was it the Diplomacy Dome? Her quarters? Some cubicle back on South Pico Island? She plodded down the corridor, boot heels clicking on metallic decks plating and the echo unnerving her. Another reminder of how small she was and how gigantic this battle ring was. Maybe humans really weren't meant to be wandering in the cosmos. Everything she saw suggested they were completely outclassed, even by the habitats.

Down halls, across compartments, through roads that would have passed for ten-lane highways in any major human city. The lights were dimming as local night approached. She checked her implants, relaxed when she found that they still worked for her, even if the giant AI wasn't talking to them at the moment. If nothing else, she could plug in and map a route back to her apartment.

No. Quarters, she told herself. It's the navy. It's a big space station. They are quarters. Now if she could just use the damn things to locate someone who could tell her what was going on.

Unexpectedly, her implants chimed and a map sprung into being before her eye. She was *here*...and there was someone or something of interest *there*. Nearly a kilometer away, two decks up. It looked as if her target were moving to a different hangar, but not that far away.

She pounded her forehead as she realized she was being stupid. She was a Sleer crew member, she had access to everything the lowliest Sleer rating had. She had the same window of opportunity the Gauntlets had. She needed to use it.

She wasn't a truly athletic person, but Frances had trained her to be far more active than she'd been as a civilian contractor. She plotted her course and launched into a quick jog, tapping her implants for added energy when her legs began to flag. She'd never tested the limits of these things, despite hearing about their near magical effects from Ray and his minions. Now was a great time to do some open experimentation.

She arrived faster than she thought possible, and found a Sleer who she'd never met personally but knew all about from his reputation. She pulled up alongside him and dropped to a walk.

"Edzedon? Great Servant of Science, yes? Right?"

He might have been short for a Sleer, but still towered over her by a head or more. He was even in uniform, his rank insignia glittering on his collar and sleeve cuffs. He swiveled his head and impaled her on his gaze. Blinked quickly and sized her up.

"Former Captain Valri Gibb. Undersecretary of Commerce for Interstellar Trade. It's late and growing later. Why are you about?"

"Humans keep late hours sometimes."

"In groups or in pairs, yes. Rarely by themselves. Humans don't seek out solitude."

"Not generally, but alone time has its uses. May I accompany you?"

"You don't even know where I'm going, primate."

"I can guess you're heading to the hangar bay down the hall."

"How do you know any of this?"

"I'd rather not say."

"Implants. You were in the Hornet group when they were installed. Of course. By all means, walk with me."

"I know it's not how your language works, but you really ought to adjust the translation algorithms the implants and the computers use. They choose words that have a jarring effect."

"Indeed? Tell me about that. Your languages are interesting to me. I've been studying them, you know. But there are so many dialects. Very confusing."

She clicked her translator off. "How about this? American English. If I understand correctly, it's the first language Genukh figured out."

Edzedon pulled up to a door frame, slid his hand over it, and watched as the blast door split apart. "Will. You. Come. This. Way. Missus. Gibb?"

It took all her concentration not to burst out laughing. She held it back to a momentary smirk. She hoped he didn't pick up on it. He seemed not to, waiting patiently for her response. "Thank you kindly, good sir," she said.

The science officer's head bobbed. He blinked furiously and then started laughing in the Sleer way, a bubbling, hissing, nonsense noise. She turned the translator back on. "That was excellent. You're quite good at your job."

"Hah. My job is to figure out solutions to problems. Learning how to speak to you is a hobby. I like to learn how adversaries—and allies—think. It's not easy. English especially. It seems to have taken sounds from every other language. Most inconvenient. But you didn't stop me in the hallway to ask about how I feel."

"You are perceptive. Your communication skills are better than you think."

"My time is limited, madame. What do you want?"

"I asked the resident mechanical intelligence for answers. It directed me to you."

"That's interesting. You have questions?"

"I have nothing but questions. For the moment, I'll settle for knowing where you're off to. Since you are clearly heading to a launch bay."

"I've been recalled to Battle Ring Genukh. There are certain incongruences with the computer's behavior that I am commanded to resolve. Honestly, I don't know what I can do, but Nazerian insisted. I expect he was commanded by Great

Lord Grossusk or Moruk. And I expect he is taking advantage of the opportunity to return to Battle Ring Genukh as well. It goes well for the great lords to see their accomplished fleet master return."

Sleer politics, then. Not so different from humans after all. "I feel for you. That's a huge weight to carry."

"Sleer have strong bones. You haven't answered my question."

"Edzedon, I'm in a bind. The Hornets are off on some damn adventure, the Sleer High Command is living in their ivory tower, the Office of Military Protocols is engineering a quarantine on those of us who's seen Sleer tech up close, and the UEF is begging you folks for technical help which nobody is giving. Oh, yes. The Movi trade delegation is trying to bribe the shit out of me, and if they're working me over, they're doing it to others in the ITA as well. I don't seem to have any friends here. Except possibly you."

"Why do you say that? I have orders, same as you."

"But you're heading off world. And no one has tried to place you on lockdown."

"No. But then you are not responsible for imagining why Genukh, ostensibly the most advanced thinking machine the Sleer ever created, seems to prefer humans over us."

"I could come with you, try to help figure it out," she suggested.

"Then you disobey your orders. You won't do that."

"No. I just need to be back by midnight, six days from now. A properly operating fold drive can do that, can't it?"

"It doesn't work that way. Time works differently in foldspace. But if you want to ask the ship captain if you can hitch hike than I have no objection. But be prepared to be told 'no.'"

"Deal."

CHAPTER 12

"YOU WANT TO DO WHAT? Here? On my vessel?"

It turned out that the ship was off limits for reasons that she couldn't discern herself, and Edzedon claimed arcane safety regulations. But they were in luck: the officer's lounge was close by, and if one wanted to interrogate those who ran a docked vessel, that was the best place to find them.

The chamber Edzedon found was huge, and reminded her more of the closed quarters aboard *Cyclops*. Feeding troughs emerged from a far wall, and Sleer sized tables and benches formed a square nearby. An obelisk-sized communication pillar occupied the center of the room and holographic messages appeared, played their contents, and vanished as she watched. The place could have held hundreds of people from the size, but only a few Sleer were here. Most were eating. One tall specimen stood before the comm pillar, apparently speaking to someone.

The conversation ended as they approached. "Small Lord Ship Master Bellosk," Edzedon cackled, "I wonder if I may have a short word with you."

The ship captain turned, teeth bared and eyes blinking

rapidly. A pissed off countenance, if his posture was any indication. Valri couldn't tell the specifics. Rosenski was the resident expert in figuring out Sleer body language. She'd have paid a lot to have the chief Nightmare with her now.

"A short word only. I have just had my schedule shifted ten hours. Now I have barely an hour to rest before departing." He narrowed his compound eyes, glaring down at the science officer. "Is this anything to do with you, Edzedon?"

Edzedon dropped his eyes and raised his arms, a gesture of supplication and apology. Considering the difference in their sizes—Bellosk was a full meter taller than the science officer—she imagined he made this gesture a lot. "I ask your pardon, Ship Master. I am ordered to New Home at once. Your ship is the only one in position to transport me there. It was unavoidable. Tall Lord Nazerian was quite insistent."

Bellosk relaxed at the news. Apparently, all Sleer understood orders and what disobedience meant: a short career. "Aren't you on his crew, Edzedon?"

"Nazerian's ship is undergoing repair and maintenance. He will follow in several days. I am commanded home immediately. He can do without my aid for a while."

"I understand. Luckily for us both, my cargo finished loading some time ago."

Valri took a step closer. It was like getting up next to a cliff. "Cargo?"

Bellosk swiveled his eyes downward as Edzedon made the introduction. "Ship Master, this is Undersecretary of Commerce for Interstellar Trade, Valri Gibb. The high command on Battle Ring Genukh recognizes her. Please see her as she is."

The implants struggled to make the meaning clear, and Valri had the idea there were some phrases in Sleer that would never translate no matter how good the programming. "I am pleased to see you as you are, Ship Master," she said. She hoped the message got across effectively.

Bellosk seemed confused. "Excuse me." They waited as the Sleer made an obvious remote query and was apparently satisfied with the answer. "Welcome, Madame Undersecretary. I am at a loss to understand why you are here."

"I have a favor to ask. Transportation to Battle Ring Genukh."

"Why?"

"There is a task to be done by me at that location. I can't make it work from here. I have to be there personally."

"No."

Edzedon twisted his head and gave her an amazingly human side eye. *I told you so.*

"Are you refusing me entry to your ship, which is a chartered vessel in use by the Allied Sleer Fleet of which my employer is a party to?" she asked. She hated how the implants must make her sound.

"I say 'no,' because I have been ordered to."

"Ordered by whom?"

"By First Chairman Bon, who would like to introduce you to the Great Nest Kelkvanken Merchant Guild."

A set of directions popped into her line of sight, a complex set of paths down corridors, through elevators and arriving at a destination very near to the control tower in this section of the ring. She plugged her implants into the network and read a list of names and invitations. She didn't know who any of them were, but First Chairman Bon was one of the few Sleer who was known to nearly every human on Battle Ring ZERO. He was the one who set the current political negotiations in order. There was no way she could refuse.

Or was there?

But even if there were, would she want to? How often would a chance like this arise?

"Very well. Great Servant of Science Edzedon, please accept my best wishes for the success of your mission. Ship Master Bellosk—I will remember your words and actions."

"I would hope so, Valri Gibb. It's a dangerous universe. Alliances make life bearable."

She watched the two Sleer turn toward the departure lock and marveled at the simplicity of their philosophy. Was that all there was to the Sleer sensibility: war, death, and a universe that was so unforgiving of mistakes or lessons unlearned that the only solace was that there were others worth befriending somewhere along the way?

She didn't know. She went home.

―――――

Valri awoke to darkness. Her phone buzzed on her nightstand and she raised the device to her ear. "Valri Gibb."

"Valri! It's Basil! What happened? Are you ill? I can't find you, and there's no record of you being sent to a hospital. Are you all right?"

She sat up in bed. The room was black; no windows, no lights. She intuited that she'd overslept and Basil was getting hysterical. "I'm fine."

"You're good? Really?"

"I'm good."

"That's a relief. *Where the hell are you?*"

"Basil..."

"Don't 'Basil' me, you are on call. You were supposed to be in your office at 0830 this morning. There are people waiting to talk to you. *Important* people."

She pulled the phone away to briefly check the display.

0913. What? It hadn't even been midnight when she parted ways with the Hornets and Frances. Yes, she'd spent a while wandering the contours of the station, but...had she really spent all night and early morning just goofing on implants? How big was this place, anyway? And how awesome were those alien medical gizmos that banished fatigue and the need for sleep? She finally began to comprehend just how much a part of the Sleer's conquest of the Orion Arm relied on those little gadgets. Of course they didn't want humans carrying them out of their sight. An army of humans equipped with Sleer biotech would be...

"Valri!"

She needed to sound regal and commanding. "Reschedule them."

"Reschedule? You do not *reschedule* the head honcho who created the ASF along with Captain Rojetnick. If you understand my meaning."

"First Chairman Bon? He's *there*?"

"He is, and he brought a truckload of friends, including Khiten and Dashak. I'm not that great at understanding Sleer small talk, but they're standing on their toes and doing that grabbing at the air thing. I'm guessing they're getting antsy."

Sigh. "I'm on my way."

"Thank you, *Ma'am*." Click.

And there it was. She was already being chewed out by her assistant. In her first week—her first three days—on the job. Marvelous. She increased her pace, sought out a quicker set of directions, and saw her chance to improve her odds by tapping a personal transport cart. They were automated cars, topless and maglev driven, about the size of a golf cart. She climbed in, gave the machine its orders, and sat back, her feet dangling above the floor. Sleer-sized seats, of course.

This was going to be one hell of a day.

On the way to the office, she polled the station's library for lessons on etiquette and rehearsed how she might apologize. Sleer didn't have much in the way of apologetic behavior or language. You fucked up; you got hurt. Or you made amends in the way the aggrieved party demanded. Everything had a militaristic bent with the tall saurids. You could suck to up a human, or even a Movi—any being that had a large brain optimized to crank out emotions like an assembly line. But these guys had nothing like that to work with. The reptilian brain was purely functional: eat, fuck, sleep. Snuggling and taking comfort from physical contact was a mammalian trait. And yet she recalled hearing somewhere that lizards had complex emotional lives. Some of them were downright eager for handlers to get all over them. She even remembered a film of a monitor lizard that loved cuddles from its handler. She doubted she could imagine what that sort of behavior might elicit from a Sleer. Maybe Edzedon would be cool with an experiment in mutual touching. Then she remembered that Edzedon was on his way back to Earth, and the reality of her situation hit her like a two-by-four breaking across her stomach. She was out of her element, one fuckup away from starting an interstellar incident. She was flailing in the deep end of the pool and there was a storm brewing. She was on her own. Except for Frances. And she had her own problems to manage.

Her office sounded like a tea kettle convention and smelled like the reptile house at the zoo.

The car dropped her off in front of the suite's outer doors and she did her best to look calm and collected as she strode in through checkpoints and showed her badge to automated stick-figure robots. When she arrived, she made her hellos and took her seat behind her grand desk. The Sleer arrayed themselves in a way that must have made sense to them. She recognized First Chairman Bon, who took a seat in front of her, but the others were strangers. Lots of brightly colored crown feathers in this crowd, though. These were high-status individuals.

Bon opened the conversation. "They say you invented a machine for optimizing trades between buyers and sellers on a galactic scale. Tell us about that."

She settled back, wanting to appear nonchalant. "A global scale. That was before we knew we weren't alone in the galaxy. Who is 'they?'"

"They is *they*. The humans. The Movi. The Sleer. There are few true secrets aboard a battle ring, or even a starship. Not that you have much experience with starships, except for the *Ascension*. Strange enough that you joined up with the Hornet squadron in a poorly restored space shuttle and managed to steal a *Zalamb-Trool* scout ship. This is still a difficult point to process, despite the fact that it happened."

She leaned forward, hands carefully arrayed on the desktop. "You didn't expect us to be able to do it, did you?"

"No. You are not like any race we have previously fought. Or attempted to ally with, for that matter." Blink blink. Chuff hiss snort. "Tell us about your device."

"You'll need some background," she said hesitantly.

"Irrelevant, since we already know about your background."

"That's not the background you need to understand if what I am about to tell you is to make any sense. May I proceed?"

A nod from Bon.

Okay. Here goes. "On Earth we count history in centuries. One hundred years. Our current civilization is something like ten thousand years old; one hundred centuries. In the past two thousand years—twenty centuries—we've grown from a primitive iron age people into an industrialized powerhouse. But balkanized. Lots of nations all trying to outdo each other. Economically, militarily. We fought wars over everything. Land. Water. Energy and precious metals. The twentieth century was the worst. We killed as much as six percent of our total population in two wars that spanned the globe. The first one nearly wrecked everything. Then the second one thirty years later was so much worse. When it was over, we figured we needed an answer. Our weapons were still primitive—even by current human standards—but they were good enough to kill something like one hundred million people in less than twenty years. The exact numbers are debatable. What is not a debate is the fact that it happened. We did real damage to ourselves.

"So we took civilization in a different direction: open trade. Certain countries produced more of some things than they needed and sold it to other nations. Tools. Food. textiles. Lumber. Everything. Eventually, weapons and energy. Industry had a way of streamlining. Efficiency, that was the point. Make the production lines and factories lean and mean. Just in time delivery. Zero inventory.

"It worked well enough to keep some of us happy. The twenty-first century, that was different. Our climate was eroding because of the industrial waste we'd put into the environment. The world got hot. Frozen continents began to melt. Unstable weather, as storms and floods grew more violent and frequent. Earthquakes and sinkholes. Lots of volcanic eruptions. And plagues. So many plagues. Dormant microbes came back to life after being frozen for thousands of years. No really big wars, but —so many dead. Our industries didn't do well against continual disruptions. Constant shortages of everything people needed to live.

"Then a miracle falls out of the sky, and we have to admit to ourselves that as much as we like to pat ourselves on the back, there's something out there bigger than we are. We finally organize. Not every nation was on board with that. They were absorbed into great administrative military networks. But the environment refused to settle. We became desperate.

"I worked for a company—like a merchant guild, I guess you'd call it—that specialized in locating commercial trends and capitalizing on them. Find out where the weak spots in production were and plug the holes. I was very good at working the data lines, teaching my AI how to trade. Buy low and sell high. One day I made so much money that a bigger company took notice and bought my code. I left with a lot of money and spent it on that assault shuttle that you so gallantly destroyed. But I didn't erase my research. I have everything I need to recreate the system I designed. It would be a very different project if I started it up again. I'd need full data on all Sleer businesses and then we'd have to open it up to the other races. The Movi. Whoever else is out here. But I can recreate it. I *can*.

She sagged, allowed her gaze to wander. They didn't move, nor make a sound. Statues of dinosaurs like you'd see in a museum. Utterly attentive. "But—why should I? That's the question you need to answer. What's in it for me?"

"I can think of numerous answers to that question," Bon said. "But I suppose the most obvious way is to begin at the beginning, as you say. What do you want?"

Valri clenched her hands in her lap and used the pain to focus as her fingernails bit into the palms of her hands. Of course they would want to know what she wanted. But did she know?

"I want a ship. A cargo ship. One with the range to get clear across from Earth to Great Nest in a single spatial transition."

"You would be willing to forgo your departmental responsibilities just for a single ship? Why would you do that?"

"Because it would let me escape from the likes of you. Other things I'm not sure you would understand."

Bon blinked and clicked his foreclaws. "Test me."

"Because there are only so many ways to control your life when your employers implement rules to keep you down and out of sight but working for their benefit. Because I want to be in control of my life and I see a career for myself out in the void. I can be useful as a ship captain."

"I understand more than you imagine. To escape. I understand that. To survive, to lead one's life free from interference. All these things are known. But what do you *want*?"

Show time. Time to dream big. "A fleet of your family corvettes. One hundred ships to start and a construction bay on this station devoted to building more."

"That I can do. It's a simple thing. A small favor. What else do you want?"

"I want the Sleer High Command to bring us into the fold."

"Fold? A spatial transition? To where?"

She shook her head. "No, bad phrasing, excuse me. If humans are to be allies of the Sleer—partners in the new Allied Sleer Fleet—then we need greater access to Sleer facilities, technology, and defenses. Weapons. And a say in who gets to plant colonies within fifty light years of our home world."

"We gave you Alpha Lyrae."

"One world that you consider worthless, twenty-five light years away. We know your scout ships are even now surveying every exoplanet within one hundred light years of Earth, looking to see which ones offer real promise. Air. Sun. Water. Food. But you give us the chance to settle only one of them. Why?"

"New worlds are strange, dangerous. You are only beginning to make your way into the universe. You need patience. Perhaps guidance. We can give you that."

"Fine. So in the next twenty years we move a few thousand humans to Vega. Then the Skreesh detect our radio transmissions, locate our home world, and destroy the human race. What then?"

"We all take our chances with the Skreesh."

"But you put all your eggs in our basket. The earth dies, we, and you, all die with it. What do *you* want, Chairman Bon? Why help us?"

"To recover what's left of Home Nest," he said. He flexed his arms in a Sleer shrug. "But that is no longer possible."

"Why not?"

"High Command has declared it a lost cause. Too many Skreesh titans too close to the system. It will be lost. That's why we remain here. Surely you knew that?"

Valri tried to suppress a shiver. Kept her mouth closed until her teeth stopped chattering. These monsters were *cold*. "It doesn't seem wrong to you to put us in the same position you're in? We can't build another battle ring over some new world. This is the only one we know will support us."

"And yet here you are, in growing numbers, on our supposedly unbreakable installation. Interesting. No?"

She had to acknowledge the fact. Battle Ring Great Nest had been touted as the ultimate war station. Then the Skreesh arrived and shredded it. "Fair point. But I think I should alert you to the possibility that humans who don't often band together under a single banner for any reason. We're a fractious bunch, you know. May find your rules restrictive. Even excessive. If we can't imagine an unfair situation resolving, we tend to decide on resolutions of our own."

"You haven't the strength."

"You haven't seen us at our best. Or our worst. Sometimes those are the same things. It depends on your point of view. The point is that if we can't get some semblance of appreciation from the Sleer high command, or even the local Sleer colony, then we might look to other possibilities."

"What possibilities? The Movi? They are incapable of managing their own affairs. They are fighting a civil war as we sit here. It will cost them greatly in lives and weapons. Meanwhile, the Skreesh come closer."

"Nonetheless, if we can't come to an agreement, maybe the Movi can."

"I doubt it. You never did tell us about your trading machines."

"I don't have to. You've made it clear you have no intention of adopting us fully into your network of markets. The algorithms would be useless to you. They wouldn't do much for us either. But if your position on the future of the human race changes, then I will change my mind to accommodate you. In the meantime, I have a conversation with a Movi trade delegate waiting for me. Good morning, First Chairman."

She waited for them to leave. They sat like saurian mountains, occasionally blinking but otherwise immobile. After fifteen minutes of trying to stare them down, she took her tablet and left the office.

———

It took Metzek's Servants of Engineering the better part of a week to completely map the interior of the rogue space station. Gaining access to the facility's library helped, but it didn't replace the need to make in-person evaluations. One thing that the library noted only in passing that he appreciated was the garden.

Something had happened somewhere in its twenty-thousand-year past. A zoological preserve had been built with examples of life from all over this arm of the galaxy. Plants and animals both. The confusing thing was that his biologists had looked at the riot of greenery and the life forms within as a single collective. The question had been: why didn't any of the examples resemble each other more than superficially? After much discussion, they'd realized that the examples of plants and animals had been taken from a multitude of worlds. There had probably been thousands of individual preserves here, each devoted to a particular world's environment.

Lying on his back in the nature preserve, Metzek could see the problem. Over the millennia, the roots of the plants had grown outward and down, cracking the containment's structure. Now, the garden had grown into a dense jungle, spanning many times its original dimensions.

Few of his officers came this deep into the thickets, surrounded by greenery, tall, thick-trunked trees that grew toward the light and then through the roof, as their roots probed ever deeper through the strata. There were creatures in here, too. He heard them. Clicks and clacks, screeches and chirps, and the occasional roar of a beast he hadn't set his eyes on yet. Zolik insisted he not come down here unarmed, and he complied. A fusion pistol was clipped to his hip.

Now he lay on his back, eyes gazing at the canopy and marveling at how alive this place was. The only life inside the great machine except for his own troops. In its way, it was greater than any of the park-like preserves Sleer officers had access to on their own ships. This was wild and untamed. And his, at least for the moment. More importantly, no one was demanding his time or attention. He could simply be. He began to understand why the primates valued their privacy so much. Being at the world's disposal was exhausting, even if it was for a great cause.

Zolik's voice shattered his repose. "Ship Master!"

Metzek heard the XO's thrashing and breathed deeply. "I am here!"

The thrashing lessened, replaced by thudding, purposeful steps. "I asked for an hour alone," Metzek complained.

"I gave you two. Time to resume work."

Metzek hissed angrily and sat up. He'd brought a small campsite with him, with a lean-to and a chair. A small fusion lamp for heat and to fight the damp. The garden was big enough to create its own weather. He loved this place and its wildness. "Status report."

Zolik brought up a screen. At least the holographic projectors still worked in this place. Possibly the only Sleer tech that hadn't shown any real improvement in two hundred centuries. But in a society with implants and instant network connections, holograms were a token form of communication, not their primary method. "It's not a warship."

"Heh. We surmised that days ago."

"I know. With an artifact as old as this one, it can be frustrating to properly catalog it. I should say that it could be used as a warship if we needed to. It has numerous gun ports and two very large energy weapon arrays at the north and south poles, but no weapons were ever installed, as far as we can tell. Many smaller laser ports are scattered across the surface. There are twenty groupings with a dozen weapons in each group. All powered down."

"Missiles?"

"None. If this is truly a second migration tier device, it would have matched the doctrine of the period: energy weapons and shields over kinetic weapons and armor. One new reactive furnace core isn't nearly enough to power the entire thing, even if we were of a mind to."

"Fair enough. What else?"

"Substantial cold sleep facilities."

"How substantial?"

"We've counted twenty-six storage chambers so far. Surely

there are more we haven't seen yet. Each can hold fifty thousand beings."

"Sleer?"

"Sleer. Movi. Anything vaguely Sleer-sized. Even a primate."

"But not a Dec or a Rachnae."

"No. But a second migration artifact wouldn't have encountered the real weirdies yet. What freaked us out is this. Despite the storage capacity for passengers, there are no living quarters. Barracks for a few thousand crew. We assume they are crew, since the living areas are always adjacent to the obvious crew stations. But passengers, dignitaries, defenders...I don't know."

"A frozen watch," Metzek guessed. "I remember hearing about those in academy classes. When the ship needed additional crew, they defrosted replacements from a reserve of sleeping individuals. Expensive to maintain, but very convenient."

"That would also fit with the period's doctrine. Finally, we found massive construction and repair bays all over the ship. Six are easily big enough to construct a Nauverness-class space control ship. Numerous others can build war machines. We quickly identified assembly lines for Zilthid single fighters. Those haven't changed much from that time. But the Atzhan ground assault rollers don't even exist here, much less the Kezekken assault walkers."

"What did they have instead?"

"This. It's called the Kizart. It looks like an armored cube supported by legs. One turret on top, a pair of lasers mounted on the front face. A hatch in the rear face is how they entered. How they used them, I'll never know."

"How many are there?"

"A few storage bays full of completed models. Several times that number left in a state of partial assembly. In fact, most of the ship is empty. It looks like this vessel was meant as a stationary base. It could build and repair ships and war machines, supply additional crew if warranted, and give active crews a place to rest and recuperate while their vessels were undergoing repair and resupply."

"Which leave us the uncomfortable question of how it came to rest here, so close to New Home, twenty thousand years ago."

"I have a theory."

"This should be interesting."

"Imagine the first migration. Twenty-five thousand years ago. The Movi and the Sleer come to use FTL ships, direct mechanics but the same result. Expansion. Our first migration stretched from Home Nest to galactic east. It stops when family ships run out of new stars to travel to—when they reach the Star's End sector. So we can't go any further that way. Meanwhile, the Movi are doing the same thing to galactic west and they stop for the same reason. The Great Rift. No more stars to conquer, so they move. Both sides consolidate their gains. Then our respective second migrations begin, and because they have hard borders, both sides reverse direction and encounter each other."

"The first border conflict. The so-called Blind War."

"Because neither side really had any idea what the other looked like. No visual communications. Only crude nuclear weapons and lasers. We couldn't even speak each other's languages at first; we had to develop the mathematically based Linguacode and teach it to them so we had something in common. They fight, both sides lose ships and retreat. Both sides develop war doctrines based on new inventions and new forms of government. They develop few very high-tech vessels and we decide to build as many ships as possible."

"It would have stayed at equilibrium if the Skreesh hadn't arrived."

"Very much so. Archeologists recovered evidence of Sleer civilizations well in the past and determine the Skreesh's last run down this arm of the galaxy was fifty thousand years ago. The high command determines nothing like that should happen again. So it decides that it needed mobile bases to hold off the Skreesh advance until our grand navy can be brought to bear. It takes time to move tens of thousands of warships, yes?"

"And you think this is one of those mobile bases?" Metzek hissed.

"I'm not sure. I would guess the ancients were planning to colonize this local group anyway, and used a failed experiment to do so. They converted it to military use when the second migration found the Movi the hard way—by colliding with their first migration—and then while both sides prepared for war, the conversion was made. But the DMZ was formed by diplomacy before the fighting got bad enough to bring this station forward. So they left it here. Maybe for future use."

"Can we finish the conversion, do you think?"

"Not with what we have on hand. But we can absolutely link our ship's power plant and fold drive to this hulk and bring it forward. Why are you asking?"

"I find that this project has potential that we're ignoring. What if we bring it into service as a way to stop the Skreesh advance on Home Nest?"

"Home Nest is gone, Ship Master."

"Why? Because Grossusk says it is? It's a stupid policy. With even a single construction module, we can bring it to operational status in less than a year. More importantly, the humans showed us how to defeat the Skreesh titans two years ago. All we need do is follow their example. We can—"

The comm system beeped for attention, a continual noise. Metzek flicked his implants, couldn't get a connection and tried again, then a third time, He finally remembered there were no neurolinks on this vessel and tapped his claws against the comm. "Metzek. What is it?"

"My lord, we have a communication from Lord Grossusk at New Home."

Here it came. He'd now know whether he mattered to those who ran his life. "Read it please."

"The message congratulates you on a discovery of historic importance. They instruct that you immediately prepare for battle."

That was unexpected. "Why?"

"I read from the text: 'diplomacy team at Great Nest has granted all rights to star system Alpha Lyrae in its entirety to the humans. A human vessel is believed to be en route to your location. Prepare all records in the library for storage aboard your vessel and destroy the artifact before the humans can gain access to it. Full battle rights are granted against human forces.'"

"That's insane!" Zolik hissed.

Metzek waved for quiet. "Do they give me a time for implementation? Do they say how the vessel should be destroyed?"

"No, sir. Time is immediate and destruction appears to be whatever method you find convenient."

"Does it say we should attack the humans to deter them from entering the artifact?"

"No, Ship Master."

"Very well. Send this: 'We have restored the artifact to partial functionality. Request permission to transfer it to a new location. Demand an immediate reply.'"

"As if the humans would want a vessel this old in the first place," Zolik sneered.

"Grossusk is panicking. He'll do anything to avoid giving anything to the new race. A useless star system is one thing, but a hive of potentially useful Sleer technology is something else."

The comm blared. "Ship Master, I sent the request. The

reply is thus: 'request denied. Destroy artifact.' It's followed by a highest priority code at Lord Grossusk's command."

"Thank you." Metzek bounded out of his chair and rushed to a wide tree trunk, punching it until he wore a grove in the trunk with his claws. "There is no justice!"

"I will give the orders," Zolik offered. "You can stay here if you like."

"No. This is my problem and I can manage it. But to destroy a piece of history for vanity and spite is...*offensive*."

"We can't disobey orders."

"Nor will we. But we can deny its use to the primates. The walking battle units, the Kizarts. Can they be remotely driven?"

"I believe so."

"Good. Here's what we're going to do..."

CHAPTER 13

CAPTAIN ROJETNICK SEEMED LARGER than life, even when dressed down in ship's fatigues. The hawk-like nose and the eyebrows gave him an otherworldly sensibility. When Valri Gibb spoke to him, it had always been in the company of others or over a phone. She'd never seen him up close and personal.

"They've chosen a new Secretary of Commerce: Henry Hopkins. He gave the commencement address at MIT last June. He is a very close advisor to the Cabinet, and the president hand picked him for the job. I expect he'll make his wishes known to you and the other administrators through channels before long," he said.

Valri slumped behind her desk, flicking her eyes to Basil Matsouka, who busily made notes. Basil had done the research she'd asked of him, learning the entire org chart of the government office and who played what role in it—Valri'd taken the education from them. "Is there any idea when he's likely to come visit us out here?"

Captain Rojetnick lifted his hands. "Who knows? I would say soon. The Sleer High Command tasked the command crew of *Rescue-1* with the transport of human representatives. The ship is huge and has been inactive for over a year. I expect it will take time to fully prepare it for travel."

"If they're serious about this new alliance," she said.

"Correct. At this point in time, your guess is as good as mine to whether that sticks."

"That's depressing as hell."

"Why do you say that?" Rojetnick asked.

The question jarred her. Surely, someone in the center of the new treaty-derived Allied Sleer Fleet could see its problems. But how to put that discretely? "I had a conversation with Chairman Bon yesterday about this subject. He thinks that exchanges are taking place at an agreeable rate. You don't find it a bit disconcerting that the Sleer are developing a habit of giving with one claw and taking away with another? How long do we have to wait until we're given permission to expand our presence on this orbital ring? How long will we have to wait until they allow us on the ring around Earth?"

"It's enough to make one chew their own teeth. I agree. But there are greater things in motion than I think we know."

She sensed an opening. Maybe the captain wasn't being dense, just careful. There was a lot of that on Battle Ring ZERO. "Such as?"

Rojetnick's eyes flicked to the room's corners and he leaned forward conspiratorially. "Did you notice they didn't ask us, or even their own command, for permission to send out those scouting missions to examine the space around Earth? Out to one hundred light years in all directions—nearly two hundred missions, all in different ships. Normally, we send out missions depending on whether a star looks interesting to us. Does it have exoplanets? Are there likely to be useful resources? Is it a type of solar system we've never seen before? Exploration takes years to arrange. Crews must be trained, a science team selected, military crew assigned. Not them. So many ships and crews buzzing like a hive of—hornets. And none of it happened until they arrived at Earth. Interesting, no?"

"I couldn't possibly comment."

"Nor should you. But I expect you'll be hearing from at least one starship commander before long. Yes?"

He knew. "I don't know what you mean, sir."

Rojetnick's shoulders relaxed. "No. Perhaps it's best if you stick to that line. If Ray Fairchild contacted you, you may have to file his report with the new secretary. But that's for later. And it's not what I came here to discuss."

"No?"

"You mentioned your meeting with First Chairman Bon. I've met with him as well. He's concerned about you."

"Concerned? Whatever have I done to warrant concern?"

"Making promises to the Movi trade delegates without coming to him—or anyone in his office—first tops the list."

"Ah."

"Yes, 'ah.' What's going on with that? You've become nearly inseparable from a few of them. Miss Makjit. Mr. Horvantz. Even in a space station the size of this one, people notice these things."

"Is there a standing order for humans to not associate with the Movi or anyone else?"

"Not to my knowledge."

"Is it forbidden to explore any and all avenues that might eventually yield an expanded trade relationship with non-Sleer?"

"I don't think there is."

"Have we been ordered by the Sleer high command to avoid conversation on the subject with anyone but their own staff?"

"I would say not."

"Then I would merely remind you," she raised her voice, "—AND WHATEVER MICROPHONES I MIGHT BE SPEAKING INTO—that only Secretary Hopkins is empowered to enter into trade agreements, alliances, arrangements, covenants, pacts, or treaties with foreign powers. All a mere Undersecretary can do is make recommendations. And how can I recommend anything I haven't experienced for myself? So with your permission, sir, I think I'll continue to investigate whatever possibilities present themselves. Undersecretaries don't make policy, after all."

"Neither do UEF Captains. But I thought you should know that minds besides ours are hard at work to come to some kind of lasting agreement concerning the fate of the human race in a very large and dangerous galaxy. And remind you that besides the people and equipment on the AMS-1, we are very much on our own out here."

"Even with ZERO watching our backs?"

"ZERO takes a very long view of the future. It may not always be as obviously to our benefit as possible." He made a show of raising his wrist, checking his watch. "I apologize. I seem to have run overtime. I must be going."

She stood when he did and saw him to the door. "Captain...I appreciate your time in being here. But I wonder if it's not more effective to communicate these concerns to the new Secretary."

"The new Secretary isn't here. I fully expect you to alert him to everything I've spoken of in your own good time. After all, it could take weeks for him to take an interest. Good day, Valri."

"You as well, Captain."

The door closed, and she sagged against it. "So. Did I go crazy, or did the officer in charge of the UEF in this solar system just tell me to mind my own beeswax?"

"There were more dropped signals in that exchange than in

all the intercepted codes in the entire U-war," Basil agreed. "What's it mean?"

"That's the hundred-million-dollar question." She wanted Ray to be here so badly she could feel her stomach fluttering and her pulse rise. She relied on him to tell her how the military worked. Its codes, its tricks, its traps. She inhaled deeply and held it. Her hormones needed to shut up. There was work to be done.

"The Gauntlets are out of town, so who's left? Just one person." She sat on a couch and closed her eyes in concentration.

"What are you doing?"

"I need to talk to Frances, and implants are extremely secure."

"You can't do that. The orders from the OMP say—"

"They say implanted humans can't leave. They don't say we can't use what we have. What's my schedule look like for today? Never mind, I see it."

"You can *see* your schedule?"

"Basil, when I'm in the network with these things, I can see *everything*. There it is. Gah. Sleer meeting, Sleer meeting, human meeting, Sleer gathering...drinks with Makjit for tonight. Did you arrange that?"

"Her PA called to arrange a date with you. I didn't see the harm in saying yes. You like her well enough."

"True. And you've been making eyes at her girl Friday, haven't you?"

"Really, Madame Undersecretary, I couldn't possibly comment. Seriously, who has the time?"

"Relax. You get yours. Just be careful. I don't have the privilege of pillow talk, and neither do you. Get me?"

"Yes, ma'am." He pointed to an empty slot. "There. That's

your open slot, fifteen minutes from now. If you hurry, you can catch Captain Underhill as she leaves for lunch."

Valri opened her eyes and glared. "You have implants?"

He waved a flat device at her. "I followed along on this; it seemed apparent what you wanted. I do this for a living, right?"

"Right. Thank you. If anyone calls, I'm doing research."

"It's a new government office. People always call."

"And I'm always doing research. Gotta fly, my dude."

She caught up with Frances outside the OMP HQ dedicated to running Primate Alley. The whole section for one building? The strategy of making themselves seem bigger than they were, either by illusion or hype and reputation, seemed out of character to Valri. She would have expected the Office of Military Protocols to spread themselves thin in order to maximize their emotional footprint. It was one thing to look out of your office window to see the black, hooded structure that housed the OMP across the length of the section of battle ring. That would be enough to give anyone a chill. But having a dedicated Overcop in your office, watching everyone and everything they did, that would scare the hell out of any sane person. So why weren't they doing it? She knew for a fact there were OMP officers stationed on the AMS-1. Even spreading them thin while redesigning the *Ascension* into the *Paladin*, if it ever flew, seemed counterintuitive. On the other hand, she didn't work for them.

Or did she?

"Frances! Wait up!" She sprinted to the causeway connecting the moat to the front door and gated checkpoints.

"A little early for a jog, isn't it?" Frances had ditched her silver headset somewhere along the way. She didn't need it any more. She had something better now.

"I needed the exercise. I've been sitting on my ass for three days. Stiffens the joints."

"I'm sure. What do you need?"

"A few minutes away from microphones and cameras, mostly."

"I can do that." She raised her wrist to her mouth and spoke into the pickup. "Going dark. Will advise." She gestured down the street, and Valri followed.

"I need you to tell me something you probably don't want to tell me," Valri started.

"You still pissed off about the no-fly order?"

"I am. But that's not what I need. I need to know who on Earth is giving ZERO his orders."

"What makes you think that's how it works? ZERO orders us around. I've explained this to you before."

"I have a new Secretary of Commerce to deal with, and he is very interested in making trade deals with anyone who'll listen. But the OMP is very much interested in keeping me focused on the Sleer. I'd like to work with the Movi and there's other races with better potential than the Sleer. What's going on?"

"You're avoiding something is what's going on," Underhill chided. "Spill it. I have a schedule, too."

"Captain Rojetnick paid me a visit and basically told me to stop bugging the Movi for information. I know when I'm being told to sit down and shut up. And I can't help but wonder what all this has to do with whatever is going on with Vega?"

"Nothing is going on. Team Gauntlet is out there. They're looking for clues. And the Sleer were being completely honest with us. They can't mine an accretion dust disc 300 AU in diameter, and the sun burns out in a half a billion years. They can't use it so they gave it to us. What's the problem?"

"We're being tweaked. That's the problem."

"Everyone's being tweaked. There's stuff going on I can't figure out either. But..."

"But?"

"But—we both suspect there's no way Fairchild's bunch will get back in time to avoid a court martial. I don't want to see that happen," Underhill said.

"Neither do I."

"But we both stood aside and let them kill their careers over something they couldn't or wouldn't talk to us about."

"Brooks said the Sleer scouts team missed something."

"Brooks assumed they missed something. What if he's wrong? You want that on your conscience?"

"Not especially."

"Me neither. So, I went ahead and recommended the unit be attached permanently to the OMP."

"What?"

"Val, there's no legit reason in heaven or earth for them to be out there. If they miss the deadline, they're AWOL. Now they aren't. Or they won't be if I go ahead with this. It'd be a huge help if you're on board with the idea."

"They'll kill both of us."

"They won't. What if Brooks is right? And they get back here and are sent to the brig for the next decade. Who does that help?"

"But OMP can go anywhere for any reason and you Overcops can justify an investigation after the fact, right?"

Underhill said, "I don't like how Hendricks is sucking up to the Sleer high command any more than you do. I just need to make sure nobody with implants follows them out there. That means you and me. Everyone else in that group is suspect. They have been since their first encounter with Genukh. I hope they find something. I really do. Because if it looks like the Sleer gave us that star system for our own use and nobody finds anything weird, it means the Sleer are being honest and we're being paranoid. That ruins any chance we have to check up on them in the future."

"You can only cry wolf so many times before they smack you."

"Exactly."

"I need to sit down and figure out a proper org chart," Valri said. "Something that shows me who does what and where they take orders from."

Underhill tapped her wrist, pulled out a thread of graphics, sorted through them, and threw one at Valri. "Here. Technically, the EarthGov President gives orders to everyone off world. All the different world sectors manage themselves, and the OMP is there to help them out where they need help. But remember, 99% of the OMP is on Earth. The UEF outnumbers us by a ratio of 100 to 1. We're very good at making ourselves look scarier than we are, but I think you figured that out a while ago."

Valri played with the data, marveling at the level of detail that she found. So many people did so many things. "I know there's a ton of smoke and mirrors and freaking people out is part of the game," she admitted, "but I know people disappear too, every now and then."

"People are reported missing now and then because we report them. You'll hear a lot of stories and find very few displaced bodies. Seriously, Val, I'm your friend. I want to protect the kids from themselves. I think you want that as well. No?"

"Yes."

"So, work with me. And we can overlook whatever you talk about with your Movi buddies. Hey, if you can get them to offer better terms than the Sleer..." She gave two thumbs up and winked. "I'll never tell how it happened."

"And if it doesn't work, well, it's not like I went AWOL or anything."

"Totally. I gotta run. See you later!"

"Meet me tonight! I'll ping you!" Valri called, but Underhill took off down the street, turned a corner, and was gone.

Valri wondered for the hundredth time today whether she knew what she was doing at all.

CHAPTER 14

THERE WERE MEETINGS. Sleer with varied crown feathers and uniforms, all speaking the same dialect of Sleer as Bon did. She wondered if there were foreign dialects in the Sleer language. Mostly introductions and descriptions of lineages and promises for what they could do to help the humans assimilate into Sleer culture. But for every promise from one with fancy crown displays, there were lengthy explanations from less fancy representatives of the Sleer high command—almost all military in bearing and uniform—as to why this was a long process. *The Sleer weren't very experienced in adopting new cultures into mentorship. It was different. The Sleer were used to relying on military solutions for most problems. Diplomacy was complicated and slow, and bureaucracy was ugly and stupid and made everyone angry, but served to manage billions of Sleer crammed into a single orbital ring. Yes, it was inconvenient and unpleasant. And let's face it, humans were impulsive, even childish when it came to such things. Even the Cycomm girl noted that the primates had incredible limits on their patience.*

It was a waste of her time and energy and she hated it, but Valri also couldn't think of anywhere better to be. The flight deck of her own ship. The Beast 3.0 or some damn thing. Anything where she could be useful.

Well. If she turned over her trading code, they'd probably give her anything she asked for. As long as humans didn't need it for themselves. Like Vega.

Her implants led her into the so-called "alien sector," which was a misnomer. The humans were the outliers here. But it was a thing she hadn't seen yet. The Movi part of town reminded her of a combination of Las Vegas and Manhattan at night. Lights and towers and moving displays and people, people, people everywhere she looked. All with blue-black skin and silver hair and pointed features and eyes that gleamed in the night like a cat's. They were so different from the saurid soldiers. Humans strode along the streets, seeking adventure and other things. Sleer waddled like big lizards, except when they got angry. They could leap and sprint like no one's business. The Movi swished and swooshed, flowing down streets and into each other's arms like liquid light. It felt like being transported into an animated show.

A familiar voice called to her. "Val! Join us!" Frances Underhill sitting across from Miraled Makjit at a café table.

Val sat down, feeling drained. "Well this is interesting."

Underhill perked up, downed her drink, and looked hurt. "You screamed at me to meet you tonight. I looked at your appointment book—"

"It's perfectly innocent. My girl spoke to your boy," Makjit said, managing to look both sheepish and clever.

"And here we all are. Fine. Get me two of whatever you ladies are drinking and we'll get started."

"Started," Underhill murmured, draining her glass and signaling to the staff. In moments, a stick-figured waiter with his hair cut to the skin appeared with bottles and glasses on a tray.

He set the glassware on their table, collected their empties, and vanished into the crowd.

"That's top shelf service," Valri noted. "I approve."

"I thought you might," Makjit said. "We are friends, aren't we? Only the best for our friends."

"What about the Sleer?"

Makjit filled glasses and sneered. "They are monsters. I don't want to talk about them tonight. *Gezellice!*" She raised her glass and the other women followed.

"What shall we talk about instead?" Valri asked. She had the impression her original conversation was now moot.

"You've heard about our political strife, I'm sure? Well." She mouthed something silently, as if managing an internal conversation. Finally, she took a long swig and slammed an empty glass down. "Well. *Mitellis nagarinih salamaachan.* In English, 'I am fucked.'"

Underhill snorted and nearly choked on her drink. "Oh dear!"

"Have you been reading naughty dictionaries?" Val asked.

"Would that I had. And that phrase I really did lift from one of your word books. Dictionary, you called it? *Dictionary.* From 'diction,' meaning 'a manner of speaking.'"

"You *do* have implants."

"A convenience. Nothing like your Sleer models. Those are military. The Sleer have no civilian version, as they don't really understand the concept of a civilian. But we have civilian models of everything the military uses. Except weapons, of course. We're not savages!"

Val and Underhill shared a smirk. If Makjit noticed, she missed its significance.

"Can we help?" Val asked. "That's pretty much why I'm here. We helped the Sleer defend this solar system. How can we offer you folks any less, in good conscience?"

"Conscience," Makjit said. Another drink down the hatch. "A moral code or conflict. You humans seem to experience a lot of those."

"We try not to mess around in other people's business. But we do try to help whenever we can. It's not always an easy balance to maintain," Underhill said.

"You scare them," Makjit said. "The Sleer. They barely escaped destruction by the Skreesh, and now they have your orbital ring and very little else. A few backwater planets the Skreesh don't seem interested in. And when they get there, to their new home, it's infested with you people. If you had any brains, you'd cleave to the Sleer and become indispensable to them."

"You mean like the Cycomms did with your folks? How's that worked out for them?"

"The Cycomms found us when we were having a very bad year. Our royal court was in turmoil—"

"Another bad succession?"

"Not at all. Succession was not the issue. The army and the navy going to war was the issue. Not a civil war...more like a crisis of command. None of the sovereign's generals or admirals were talking to each other. Troops remained at their bases. Warships could wreak havoc against each other, but their captains wouldn't transport troops. Naval blockades dictated which merchants could do business on what worlds. The trade routes collapsed. We were in chaos. The Cycomms learned about us, what made us tick, what made things worse. They created their Sense Ops forces based on what they learned. You have a chance to do something similar with the Sleer, but only if you act quickly. Where was I?"

Valri said, "We've never been accused of being too smart."

"Unless it's being too smart for our own good. That's something we do well," Underhill said.

Valri nodded and sipped at a drink that froze her lips and burned her throat going down. A local concoction, then. "We're just assholes most of the time, but we mean well."

Makjit laughed, long and loud. When she calmed down, she blinked languidly and sighed. "I do need help. I have few options. None are good."

"We're listening."

"You know some things about us, I imagine," Makjit began. "The same way that we have some information about you. And not all of it was gleaned from random personal conversations. Hm?"

"One of our pilots spent a fair amount of time around several of your officers," Underhill admitted. "She's got the only Cycomm in this station curled around her finger. Maybe the other way around. I'm not clear on all the details."

"Hm. That would be Lieutenant Judith Reagan," Makjit said, "and her friend Binilsanetanjamalala. And her other very good friend, Lieutenant Simon Brooks. We know all about them. All but the Cycomm have Sleer implants as well. I'm still not sure how that happened. No one knows. It's causing a bit of a stir, I think you'd call it. What is 'stir?'"

"It means to mix up. Or to blend. To mash together. To keep from settling," Valri explained.

"I know that word, 'Settle.' It means to displace an ecosystem. I hear your diplomats use it in conference. It's...revealing."

Underhill tilted her head. "Revealing what?"

"That deep down you have a history that is every bit as disconcerting as the Sleer. But that's why we all have large navies, no? Anyway. Have you ever imagined why the Movi armed forces are so small? And why our planetoids are so advanced?"

"It's come up. In conference."

"We don't militarize absolutely everything like the Sleer.

We have a robust industrial base. Thousands of aspects to it. Builders, factories, suppliers, research and development, scientists, all manner of specialists, and distributed all over the kingdom. It's worked nicely to make sure that no part of the kingdom goes without necessities or basic amenities. Any planet that loses one trade route with a neighbor can gain access through another. Common sense. No?"

"It's called hedging your bets," Valri said. "You hope your supply chain is robust enough to weather a disruption, but nothing ever works the way you think. You place a new order with another supplier a little further away, just in case your primary falls through. As long as you have enough resilience, you never really lose out, but you won't make as much profit as you wanted. It happens."

"That's an excellent way of putting it," Makjit declared. "We manage. Or we did. What I must now tell you doesn't leave this table. Or there will be real problems for me, and I will make sure you have the same problems. Understand?" They nodded. Valri even leaned in. Makjit continued, "Six months before the assassination, the thirteen great trade guilds and hundreds of minor houses noticed that certain moneyed interests were buying up assets. Factories, supply depots, shipyards, and so on. Nothing really changed in the daily management of these facilities, but ownership has a character to it. Voluntary production incentives were replaced with mandatory quotas, and Maker help the crew that falls behind. Some vital resources suddenly became unavailable at any price. Some luxuries were bought in great supply, and a great many necessities rerouted to new destinations, leaving entire populations without, except at exorbitant prices. Managers who obey their masters are rewarded, and those who don't find themselves without the assets they worked so hard to acquire."

"No one can manipulate whole segments of an interstellar

society like you're describing," Frances said. "It would take the wealth of the whole empire to manage that. And then what's the point of it?"

"The point is optimization. Just like those implants are optimizing your bodies. Oh, come now, you don't think we've never seen what Sleer implants do to a living being, do you? There's a reason we stay away from that technology. In this case, someone or some organization wanted to optimize our industrial base for a very specific output. But we aren't sure what." Makjit leveled her gaze at Valri. "You have the means to identify the culprits, don't you?"

"I may."

"You do. We've heard of your offer to Bon and his minions. You have codes that can trace assets, match buyers with sellers. You told me as much days ago."

"Not exactly."

"Exactly. I don't need exactly. I need a way to trace actions and reactions in the financial realms. That done, I need to be able to reverse engineer their plans. I can tell who bought what and when, but I can't figure out who was responsible. Doing it by hand would take years. We don't have years."

Valri sat back and wondered where Makjit was going with this and what agreeing would cost Valri. "Let's say I gave you my models. What then?"

"Then we learn who initiated the whole enterprise and hang them from a tall pole, as a warning to the next six generations that some plans come at too high a price."

"You have an idea who started it, don't you?"

"I have suspicions. Clues. Archduke Mineko is a brilliant tactician, but assassination isn't his style. Granted, he makes bank and bed with those who do, but he is not a man who enjoys risk. There are those in the cabinet who love risk— Warlord Anterran ad-Kilsek, for instance—but he didn't kill the sovereign family. Or if he did, he's managed to rewrite history completely. And a man who could do that could have found another way to get what he wanted without throwing the kingdom into disarray. In the meantime, factions are building, the military is splitting, the nobility are making bets on who wins, and the boy who currently sits on the throne is a spoiled idiot who I wouldn't trust to fetch my favorite outfit from the closet." She sat back, breathing heavily. "Do you understand me? Am I being clear?"

Valri sensed that Makjit was showing her soul for the first time. She was greedy, but also terrified of a universe where she had no influence, no power base. "You've explained what and why, but now you need to tell us what you need from us."

"Help bring the kingdom under my faction's rule and I will deliver enough firepower to move the Sleer fleet off your world."

"You can't do that," Frances sneered. "Horvantz won't let you."

"Horvantz works for me. My name is Miraled Makjit tal-Vanis ad-Lanisse al-Bonim. I am the Principal Financial Officer for the Dal-Cortsuni trade consortium to Great Nest. I can even claim a principality of five-star systems near the core of the kingdom. None of which means much to you two, but my family is insanely old and incredibly wealthy and leave it at that. Between us, we can put together a fleet of warships large enough to smash Battle Ring Genukh and all the Sleer escape fleets to splinters. Now, are you interested or not?"

"We are."

"Good. I need a firm commitment on the power supply proposal. I know you people need it. Your current solar technology was well envisioned but poorly deployed. All on the surface. Now that your home world skies are dark, your energy supply is threatened. Ours remains in orbit. I would build a provision into the proposal that the platforms would be capable of self-defense against any Sleer attack. I could even detail the assets we could use to enforce its safety."

"And how many human lives would this cost?"

"None. We would identify a different manner of payment."

"Let's say I agree—"

"Val!"

"Not now, Frances. Let's say I agree to this. Let's say the actual Secretary signs off on it. What then?"

Miraled grinned. "Then we let the gears of commerce and the diplomats figure out the details. And we move our construction fleet into place with full disclosure to the Sleer high command of our intentions and equipment. If they're wise, they'll recognize a legitimate transaction. If not...well...that's what big fleets are for. No?"

CHAPTER 15

MAKJIT HAD NO SOONER GONE her way and Underhill and Valri returned to Diplomacy Dome when Valri's implants flagged her with a bulletin. Makjit's apparent boss, Horvantz, was waiting in her office.

"You don't mind if the human top cop for this section of the ring waits for us on the couch, do you?" Valri asked.

"Not at all. I expected her. I'd need a titanium bar to pry you two apart." He waved his hands above a holo-ring and an image bearing a duty crest and a face along with rows of dense text appeared. "Royal Movi Naval Intelligence. I'm afraid you couldn't pronounce my name, so you may as well keep calling me Horvantz." He put the holo away and settled on the chair with an oof. The man was past his physical prime. Valri ignored it. "This is the part of the game where I tell you about the meeting you just had and then inform you that she's cheating you."

"I don't understand."

"I know you do. Dal-Corstuni? Really? You're interested in putting those upstarts in charge of what could be the most devastating hostilities since the last Skreesh incursion?" he asked.

"Makjit offered us a chance to win back our solar system from an occupying force. It would have been hasty to reject her offer out of hand."

"Hasty, perhaps. But wise. Let's talk further. I can certainly make a better case than she could half drunk in a night club. Or did you think we weren't watching her and her entourage?"

"The thought had occurred to me," Valri admitted.

"Trust me, Madame Undersecretary. With her kind, you're either part of the entourage or you're the help. Government contacts are always in the latter category."

"She offered us quite a bit."

"I know exactly what she offered you. And why. Yes, by Maker her family is old, and by Breaker, they're rich. But she can't deliver. I'll spend the next few minutes explaining why. Is that sufficient?"

"Please. May I bring my own assistant in on this discussion?"

"By all means. Bring the assistants. Bring the help. Bring the new Secretary himself if you think he'll listen to you. He's not answering my chancellor's phone calls. He will wish he had."

Valri joined them and made herself comfortable. She even folded her hands on the desk. "Let's dance."

"Miss Gibb, I like the way you manage yourself. Yes. Let's dance. You don't want to destroy the Sleer."

That was news to Valri. "I don't?"

"No. You want to manage them for your own purposes. You saved their capitol world. You saved their escape fleet. Even if they don't want to admit this, they need you more than you need them. If they destroy your planet, they still need to deal with Zluur's gun destroyer and you've shown them, and us, that you can be very inventive when pushed. That's a thing to develop."

"Makjit was talking about getting us firepower."

"We can do that. And better. Dal-Cortsuni is competent and they have contacts and trade routes everywhere, but Kar-Tuiyn has admirals in their pocket and those admirals control a number of very big fleets. When the Maker tends the battlefield, he invariably shows up on the side of big fleets."

"But can you get us a line on who was behind the buyouts across the kingdom prior to the assassination?"

"I believe we can. But...that's a complicated undertaking and it would require something substantial from your people that I honestly don't know that I can count on. So. Let's put it aside for the moment."

"Let's not," Underhill pushed. "We're laying our cards on the proverbial table. The least you can do is show us if you're serious or not. So far, it's all bluster and bullshit. Makjit may be a bad horse in this race, but she's promised us a war fleet to drive the Sleer out of our corner of the galaxy. What do you have?"

"I believe we have an ally who is willing to work with us. It's not final. It's very much in the process. There are wheels turning all over the kingdom. You'll have to trust me on that. In exchange for that trust, I can promise real aid when we move against the Sleer. And it won't be a few refurbished planetoids that were sold to merchant navies after being decommissioned. I mean top of the line battleships that represent the Royal Navy's finest vessels and most experienced crews. But I suppose you'll have to make that decision for yourselves."

"So we can throw down with one merchant clan, or we can go to town with you. The so-called real navy."

"Very much so. We have better ships and more of them. That's my position."

Frances scratched her nose. "Val, was that bluster or bullshit?"

"Hmm. I smell bullshit."

"I have to agree. Sorry, Horvantz, we're not buying what you're selling. Besides, what happens when the Sleer retaliate by reducing the surface of our home world to a thick sheet of glass?" Frances asked. "They've done it before, and there's no reason to assume they won't repeat themselves."

"It's a risk, but not a great one," he said. "I suspect that if they were of a mind to destroy you utterly, they'd have done so by now. They want the battle ring and they have it. They need not spend much energy defending it. Case closed."

Valri refreshed her and Underhill's glasses. "And let's say for the sake of discussion we go with your generous offer to destroy the Sleer and somehow my planet survives with its people and biosphere intact. What's in it for me?"

"You want a ship. We have ships. Hell, we could furnish you with a fleet. A commercial one of course, with certification to do business anywhere within the Movi kingdom in perpetuity."

"Tempting," Valri murmured, doing her best not to wince as Frances loudly cleared her throat. "But do I really want to run a convoy in the middle of an apocalypse?"

"Good traders make their opportunities. It's up to you."

"What if I say no?"

"Then we will go with whatever other options present themselves. One good thing about a mad rush to the throne: it levels the playing field. Anything might happen. But for you… this chance evaporates as soon as a new sovereign ascends the Vermilion Throne. Think about it. You can contact me at any time." He drained his glass and strode out.

Valri fought the urge to throw her glass after him. "So. We can do nothing. We can go with Miss Old Money Prissypants, who will probably do what we want for a while until she gets whatever trade agreement makes her look like a superstar and might just get us what we need."

"Leverage with the Sleer."

"Right. Or we can go with Agent Big Swinging Dick of the Royal House of Dick, who will very happily start a war with the Sleer because he swears to God that his side will win."

Frances put her feet on the table. "Both are telling us what we want to hear. We could go to the Sleer with an offer of our own. Human self-rule in exchange for your codes."

Valri stared at her friend's feet and knocked them back to the floor. "The Sleer were my first choice, remember? They told me they couldn't afford my price...which was essentially the same offer the royal dude just made me. Except I asked Bon for the commercial fleet and they said no way. I'm not sure why. I know I had the science guy, Edzedon's interest."

"This is the same Sleer government which decided that we are feral children and can't be trusted to run our own planet because we might drop it."

Valri wondered about her friend's knowledge of history. The real stuff, not what they taught in public schools. "Well. We sort of did. Between the U-war, the global heating, and the—"

Frances scoffed, "That wasn't us, that was..."

Valri leaned in. "Us. It wasn't that long ago. If the OMP hadn't brought the world under a single authority, we'd still be screwing the place up with noxious fumes and lord knows what else."

"Fuck. Okay. What else can we do?"

Valri kicked off her shoes beneath the desk. "Would the OMP be interested in making me an offer?"

"I'm certain they would, but that's not my current department."

"I don't suppose you could make a call. Tell Hendricks I want to talk?"

"Why don't I just shoot you in the head while you're talking it over with him? It'll at least be quicker."

"Touche. What other options do I have?"

"From the other side of your great big desk, I can see two. One, you can start praying that the Gauntlets find what they're looking for on Vega."

"What's the other?"

"Binilsanetanjamalala."

"Royal? You're kidding."

Underhill stared into the distance. "She's a stand-up girl. She was born into this crazy galaxy and everything we're figuring out for ourselves by bumping into it, she already knows."

"She's not exactly a benefactor."

"True, she has no access to the family wealth, but she's been around. Talk to her. See if she can point you toward some actual lever instead of gambling on liars, crooks, and facades. Because if the Gauntlets get scragged out there or if they're flying into a trap, she'll be the only choice you have."

"Well, that at least sounds logical. Just one problem."

"What's that?"

"Binil is on her way to Vega aboard *Gauntlet*."

CHAPTER 16

BINIL LIVED for simulator runs with Judy "Dances With Gears" Reagan. Dance made the gut-wrenching terror of a down-and-dirty mech brawl educational and fun. The fact they'd both nearly died in a real battler, colored her perspective: any simulated run, no matter how badly it went, was just peaches.

Today they were working with the Manticore battler, a recon force model. Between the positioning thrusters on its legs and the booster pack on its back, it felt lighter than the other models they'd tried out. So far, she liked this one best.

She reached the beacon seconds before Dance and took a short victory hop. Her metal boots stirred up dust and gravel that drifted across the barren yellow landscape. Too much CO_2 in the atmosphere. Even the clouds were yellow. "Beat you! Now what?"

Reagan's voice in her ears: "Now we wait for it." A zoom and new map appeared in the HUD along with rows of text. "New orders. Activate beacon. Input order command code. Let's see... that's here. Two-nine-A-five-G-three-three-one." A new set of maps popped up, joined to the current position by glowing red lines.

Dance read the new lines aloud: "Assault alien position. Destroy all enemies. Destroy base. Return to beacon for retrieval."

"That sounds simple enough."

Dance harrumphed and plugged another question into the system. "Maybe. Any chance of assistance? No! Why would there be?"

"Just you and me then. That sounds cozy."

"No, cozy is a warm bed, a blanket, and a cup of hot chocolate with a book. This is dirt, blood, and extreme violence. Check your weapons."

"Weapons check," Binil said. Her mech's computer pinged nodes and returned a list of stats. "Twelve short-range missiles, a GU-29 gun pod with a full load, and a breaching spike in each forearm. That's not going to help much if it's just the two of us."

"It is what it is. Let's use this path up to the hill. The base is on the western summit. Come on."

They swung their machines into motion. Binil noted the heat index as they ran; the battlers were good at dumping excess heat, but not like this. There could be rivers of molten lead down at the base of the rise somewhere. Cycomms didn't have a notion of Hell in their religions, but she understood the principles of the humans' preoccupation with such a place. No one wanted to end up here. There. Anywhere.

"Planet Venus," Binil said. "Why name a place like this after an Iron Age love spirit?" she asked.

"I wasn't there when they named all the big lights in the sky," Dance said. "This one is just gross. But I hear that if they can make any of our planets more Earth-like, this one is a prime choice."

"Really? I'd think it's a lost cause."

"The place is just gross because of a runaway heat-exchange cycle. You could dump a mountain of ice and snow and let the darned thing melt. Oxygen would bind to the sulfur in the atmosphere. We'd put a giant shade between it and the sun to cool it down a bit, and in fifty or a hundred years...no more hellscape."

"Sounds fascinating. The base should be just over that next rise. What if we—?"

Alarms beeped in her headset while points appeared on her HUD. Six blue blobs were making their way down the hill where the base supposedly lay. "We're trapped. Base or beasts?"

"The mission order said base. So. You break left, I'll break right, and we'll circle around the newcomers. Go."

Binil went. She pumped the Manticore's legs and twisted the battler's systems to get just a little more speed out of it. The gravity was less here than normal. She began building hop-skip-jump patterns into her gait, both to increase speed and keep herself out of their sight. Assuming they even had sights.

They did. Two of the alien attackers raised their arms and pointed beam projectors at her, blasting over her head. Once, twice, three times. Two more were trying to flank her flanking maneuver. She thought it worthwhile to risk one high jump, set her bearings, and activated the missile launcher on her right shoulder. She hit the controls and the rocket pack flared to life, sending her fifty meters into the air and moving forward. Slower than she could run, but it kept the alien's beams away from her. Now she could see their target. The base wasn't much more than a dome surrounded by a few blocky structures, just outside of missile range. But she had the sensors locked and she'd find it again the next time she—

"Gah! I'm hit!" Dance was in trouble. Binil turned her mech's head to her position and saw the problem. Three Skreesh shock troopers were hitting her as a group. Her mech's right leg was shattered, and she crouched defensively. A flash as she launched her missiles at her attackers. One went down in a burst of fragments, another suffered a blackened rent in its torso, and the third suffered scratches to its paint job but no more.

Binil sprang into motion, her new circumstances clear and the solution obvious. She jumped high, took a bead on the base, launched ten of her twelve missiles at the target and spun around, aiming the last two at the undamaged alien. The rockets slammed into the creature's torso and split it into its component parts. Unfortunately, she couldn't do much while she was suspended above the fray…and the damaged alien saw its opportunity. It bent its arms and aimed its beams at her. Once, twice —both misses. She was nearly down on the ground again and planning how she'd scamper around the enemy and run to Dance's side when her alarms screamed and the HUD glowed red. Heavy damage in her rear. The rocket pack flared, sputtered, and then exploded, throwing her out of her arc and slamming her against a boulder.

She'd forgotten to check her danger space. And the three aliens inside it.

She brought up her gun pod, used half the ammo to destroy what was left of Dance's attacker, then turned onto her stomach in a prone position. The three remaining aliens flung energy bursts at her. She squeezed off bursts from the gun pod, one…two…and the last of her ammo went to killing only the closest of the attackers.

They closed range, and she and Dance shouldered their mechs against each other. Two more fully functional aliens pounced, moving to rip them apart, limb from limb. Dance launched all her missiles at them, danger close, bright lights and alarms demanding attention.

The world went red. Then black. Then the hiss of disengaging hardware as the saddle sagged beneath her and the shell above split to show the simulator room.

A mechanical voice posted their results while they removed helmets and disengaged from their pods. "Scenario terminated. Allied force terminated. Enemy forces 82 percent terminated. Enemy base 71 percent destroyed Mission score: 68 percent. Status: failure."

"Damn it!" Binil screamed inside her helmet. "I thought we had it that time."

"Close but no cigar," Dance said. She raised her voice to say, "Lieutenant Genius, what do you think?"

The lights came on, the door opened, and Brooks walked into the arena. Five other sim booths lined the walls. As Binil climbed out of her sim booth, he said, "You actually did pretty well. Unfortunately, Skreesh shock troopers have very few weak spots. And they don't take prisoners."

Binil bobbed her head. "Yes, lieutenant. Shall we report to the debriefing room?"

"By all means."

The three of them walked in silence, still slightly awed by the new vessel they traveled within. *Gauntlet* had been designed as a compact version of a Sleer Zalamb-class scout cruiser, but with the equipment, troop carrying capacity, and weaponry of the Garfield escort. She reminded them of their month-long stay aboard Sleer ship, *Cyclops*. Familiar in its character but with new particulars. Like meeting an unknown cousin at a family reunion.

They walked past more simulation stations while Binil replayed her experience in her mind. A year into her rehabilitation as a member of this squadron, and there was still so much to learn. "I still can't believe we didn't destroy that base," she murmured.

"We might have if you'd followed instructions and blasted the base when you had the chance," Dance said.

"It's not my fault the missiles don't always work according to instructions," Binil complained.

"*Nothing* always works the way it's supposed to. That's what the training is for. To figure out plan Bs, Cs, and Ds if we need to. As soon as they got me prone, you should have closed on the base and gotten to optimal range, then used your missiles. That would have wiped out the base for sure."

"It would have killed you, too. I'm not making that decision. Not today."

"Well, thanks, but now we're both dead, and the base is still partly functional. Sometimes you have to get the job done, no matter what the cost."

"That's a stupid maxim."

"Says the woman whose parents sent her to a penal colony rather than let her enlist with the Sense Ops."

Binil concentrated on putting one foot in front of the other. She loved her friends, but fought down an urge to punch Dance in the face. "I don't know what happened. Neither do you."

"You're right. It's not my family. Not my circus, not my monkeys."

"Speak for yourself, miss primate."

Brooks cleared his throat. "I'll speak for the whole crew. Follow the orders as closely as you can, Binil. That's final."

A klaxon sounded above them, and red lighting strips flashed, demanding attention. "De-fold in five minutes. All crew to de-fold stations. All decks acknowledge."

"So much for your debrief. We're due on the bridge," Brooks ordered. They ran through a maze of corridors and hatches, nearly colliding with other crew they passed. Binil couldn't imagine where they all came from. Human sized ships were very compact, with so many places to put things, including people. She hustled to keep up, and slid into her crash couch on the bridge.

But she couldn't let the comment go. Not even when Reagan slid into the station next to her.

The former Hornets lined the stations on *Gauntlet's* bridge, red lights burning steadily as a countdown clock ran down on a forward display. She watched Simon Brooks strap into his comm station and use his hands to guide the ship's systems through his commands. She was so used to watching him work exclusively through his implants that it startled her. Like watching a piano player warm up before a concert.

Reagan reached out and tapped a finger on her console. Dance was trying to keep her focused. She didn't know why she resented her attention. "You're out of position, Lieutenant," Binil scolded.

"I can work engineering here as well as over there," Dance said, indicating the other side of the bridge with a nod of her head. "Minding you is part of my job."

"I don't need to be minded. I'm not a child."

"You destroyed a Skreesh shield generator with your *brain*. You need looking after. Uncle says so, and that's enough for me. In the meantime, think about what I said. Mission objectives are there for a reason. If we save each other but flub the mission, we get more people killed than we save. It's ugly but it's true."

"Ugly. That's a word and a half," Binil groused. Intellectually, she understood the need for getting the mission done despite the cost in lives. She didn't like it. She would never like it. That she was sure of.

The clock ran to zero and her guts heaved as the ship re-entered normal space. There were scans to make and measurements to take. "Navigation, confirm current location and time stamp."

"All good to go, Uncle. We are confirmed in orbit around

Vega, fifty AUs from the primary star. Time stamp says our transit took nineteen hours, six minutes."

Brooks started calling out announcements. "Transmission incoming. It's a data update."

Fairchild looked annoyed. "From where? We just arrived."

Binil's resentment bloomed into a nagging wound. She couldn't understand why these people didn't know anything about the universe. "Commander. That's a Movi message boat. It's probably here because we are."

"That's incredibly efficient. I wonder if Valri's friends made that happen."

Her eyes and cheeks darkened as she listened. Even a competent leader like Uncle could be so *stupid*. Did she have to explain everything to them? "No, sir. I can't speak to that."

"Mr. Brook, do we have access to that boat's contents?"

"Yes, sir. We do."

"Excellent. Open that thar mail pouch and let's see what's going on."

Brooks tapped the codes into the feed and watched the data folder split into its components. There was a ton of news from Earth. More news from Great Nest. Other bits and pieces. There was news covering the assassination of the Movi sovereign, and that led down a rabbit hole of political and economic discussions. Brooks slid those to the side. "Uncle, there's some messages from Undersecretary Gibb in here. I'm assuming you want those in private?"

"Only the ones with little heart emojis after them. The rest should be safe for work."

Frost cackled at that. "Hearts? That's so high school."

"It's our thing. You want to talk about romance? Genius is sitting right here. He is such a player."

Brooks froze, but recovered quickly. "I wasn't aware I had to clear my personal arrangements with the OIC," he said.

Fairchild laughed. "It's cool. No one gossips about you three. Except, of course, me."

"That's reassu—wait, what?"

"Brooks, mail call. Let's get it done," Rosenski prodded.

"Yes, ma'am. These three have hearts. This one doesn't."

"Nice. Come on, Val, talk to me."

"Hiya, Ray. I know I'm sending this just after you left, but damn. I miss you. Miss your butt. Miss your hands. Check out the other mail to see how much. It's getting very strange here. I got discussions stretching into next week. I don't think you're going to be back in time to see any of it...Frances tells me it's okay. Take what time you need. You'll probably get official declarations about that on the next mail ship. These Movi mail boats are sweet, aren't they? The Dal-Corstuni and Kar-Tuyin delegates are tripping over each other trying to see who can offer us the best deal. I'm making friends. Even among the Sleer. All for the price of trying to get a proper freighter I can use."

Rosenski settled into her crash couch and glared with arms crossed. "She's friendly for someone who's working with state secrets."

"She knows better," Binil growled. She held her hands tightly at her side, eyes focused on the now blank screen. It took a formal amount of will to not launch her scrambler power into the comm console. She didn't want to think about all the parts that made up the network. It was just a machine. It had no responsibility. It took no chances to care about what was going on. It wasn't Binil's problem. It was Valri Gibb. She knew better, she shouldn't be—

"Gaaaaaah!" she screamed. A loose panel on her station popped out of its groove and a bank of indicators died. But nothing else happened. She held her breath to push the ability back into her head where it belonged. When she looked up,

Fairchild was looking right at her, all trace of humor gone. Fairchild saw everything.

"Binil? You want to get down off that ledge you're teetering on?"

"She knows better!" Binil screamed. "She shouldn't be talking to the Movi! Or the Sleer. Or any of them. Why is she talking to them about *anything,* knowing what she knows about them?"

"It's her job, Cycomm," Dance offered.

"I have a job. So do you! It's to get the Sleer away from your home world. That is her job. That is her only job. Does she want to have the Earth end up like Haven? Does she?"

Dance reached for her shoulders, "Come on, Cycomm, it's time for a nap."

Binil ducked out from her grasp. "Don't patronize me! You people are idiots. How can you not see you're being manipulated? Don't you hear the lies, half-truths, and nonsense? Do you want to end up like us? Surrounded by enemies and forced to become paranoid automatons, always wondering who's getting ready to stick a sword in your back? You can't live like that. No one can. All it leads to is death and despair and making deals with whatever demons you think you can manage today. But there are always demons and they can't be managed forever. All they want is your blood in a barrel and a straw to drink it from." She panted, gasping, unsure of exactly what she'd said. But to judge from their faces, she was freaking them all out. Even Reagan. Especially Reagan.

Uncle was done. "Temporary Active Third Lieutenant Binilsanetanjamalala, you're relieved. Brooks, Reagan. Escort her to her quarters. Thank you."

The hysteria drained out of her as she turned and left the flight deck, sure that the others were following her closely. She wasn't going to cry. She would. Not. Cry. She managed to keep her composure until the doors to the lift closed and she released a few heaving sobs and then caught herself, squeezing Reagan's hand in a death grip. Her other hand found Simon's shoulder and she drew n long ragged breaths. "You're all falling for it. It leads to a bad place. Bad results. Every time."

"Politics does that," Brooks agreed. "We're going to try very hard to tell the people who matter what we know, but one of the worst truths of life is that you can only give people so much advice before they shut you out of the discussion and do what they want."

"This is all way above our pay grade." Dance agreed.

"Even when it can save the lives of your whole civilization? What's the mission this time, Dance? Sell your souls to the Movi or the Sleer, it leaves you without anything of value."

"Maybe she found a Movi she can trust."

"They're trustworthy, all right. Trust all of them to pound you over for whatever gain they can extract. They're all like Sora. All of them. That's no paranoid fantasy. You met her. What do you think would have happened if we'd stayed on *Cyclops*?"

She watched Dance drop her eyes and put it together. "She'd have spaced us and the other passengers and headed off into whatever distant realms she had in mind," Dance answered. "You think she did that? The former prisoners on that ship. You think they're alive?"

"I can hope. She might have ordered them off the ship. Hell, they might have folded back to Marauder's Moon and taken over the whole colony."

"I think that's probably what she would have wanted, but I don't think one Sleer scout ship would be enough."

"Especially not a damaged one like *Cyclops*," Brooks said.

"Never underestimate Flight Admiral Sora Laakshiden. She

is nothing if not highly focused. Like a beam of light. Like a laser."

They paused in front of Binil's quarters. The so-called suite was no more than three staterooms, all attached by sliding privacy screens. Simon and Binil lived in the wings, while Dance lived in the center room. Whatever they had, Dance was always in the middle. It wasn't a bad setup. Everyone had space of their own and whatever access they needed. Scheduling time was more of a challenge, but since they were all on the same work schedule, it worked out more often than out.

Binil reached to the plate then pulled her hand back. "I want to go back," she murmured.

"Are you in any shape for that?" Brooks asked.

Binil gave him a sidelong grimace and then nodded her head. "I'm all right. I was—distracted. I assumed the worst. I exploded. And I damaged a panel. I should make amends."

"Not until you're ready," Dance urged.

"I'm fine. Really. I'm in control of myself and my—ability. Please?"

Dance and Brooks shared a look, then let her reverse course. When they stepped out of the lift, Binil was utterly calm. "Request permission to return to duty, sir."

Fairchild looked at her then at Rosenski. "Granted. Assume the sensor station. Brooks, you're on comms. Dance, engineering." All three were used to their assigned positions. It was a good sign. Uncle knew where they belonged, and so did they. "Hurry up, folks. We're coming up on something very interesting."

"Interesting how?"

"Skull isn't sure. Either it's a unique astronomical anomaly, or it's the remains of a very big battleship."

CHAPTER 17

GAUNTLET WAS LIVING up to its great hope. Effective FTL. No damage, and the Hornets had some experience living aboard one like it, the *Cyclops*. They were even used to the big Sleer command stations, where human feet dangled inches above the floor. No one wanted to harsh the crew's vibe.

Except Binil. "I miss the nanofiber connections and control gauntlets from my Sleer pilot's suit," Binil murmured as she danced her fingers across the console. "You get such precise readings with direct uplinks."

"You don't have the implants to use them," Dance pointed out. "That's why we spent the past couple of years getting you certified to run battlers and starship equipment."

"No thanks to your Sleer high command."

"Not ours, thank you very much."

"Maybe. Your human equivalent seems enthralled to them. But I'm just a lowly resident alien. What do I know?"

"You know how to crush some enemy's larynx at two hundred yards," Marc Janus called out. "Find me a human who can do that. You can't. You know why? There aren't any. Believe me, Binil, you're special."

"And you're wearing my old Third Lieutenant bars, so if anyone tell you you aren't a real officer, they'll have to answer to me," Brooks added.

"I'll tell you what I don't know: how to switch this display from the interior sensors to the exterior types."

Sara Rosenski leaned over Binil's shoulder and reached down to tweak a switch. The display cleared. "This is not the time or place."

"Well, I *should* have implants. It's difficult enough to keep up with yours. If I wasn't used to using equipment like this, I'd be shut out of everything."

"You wouldn't," Dance insisted. "No one on this crew is supposed to have implants. That's why it's all eyes, ears, and fingers on this ship. For everyone, all the time."

Fairchild adjusted the display. The anomaly was at the edge of the giant dust disk surrounding the primary. Even with a maneuver drive working perfectly, it would take hours to reach. "Ladies, let's focus. Binil, whatever you can get us is fine. Skull, see if you can enhance what she's pulling up with readings for the communication net. What exactly are we looking at?"

It was a good question. The Vegan star system was a confusing and uncertain mess to begin with. A primary star that burned both brighter and larger than Earth's own yellow dwarf, the sun blazed with far more energy, Human astronomers had theorized for decades that there could be one or more dense rocky planets orbing the central star. But one thing they could confirm from past years of observation was a vast disk of dust and fine particles that stretched more than 300 AUs away from the star. No planets in the recognizable sense. If there were, they would have swept vast swaths of dust into themselves.

Skull ran a finger around the edge of the display. "There's an outer ring. You see it? It's split in the accretion disk. Not wide at all, only a few hundred klicks."

"Let's get some perspective. Angle 90 degrees out from the plane of the ecliptic. Let's see if we can spot the object that cleared that trench."

They maneuvered upwards. The sensors pinged greater areas as the ship moved out of the dust and soared above the disk. After a time, it was no great task to create a tactical map that looked down at the bulk of the disk. The soldiers remained at their posts, doing their jobs. Finally, Binil placed a location on the viewer. "There!"

"What is it?"

"It's twenty kilometers in diameter and it's got a very low specific gravity. I'm betting it's a hollow body."

Fairchild reached into the display and played with the settings. He saw Binil's target easily enough; a blip on the display with a targeting circle locked on. It covered a crazily elliptical orbit, approaching to within a few million miles of the primary star then swinging around in a tight but very long orbit twenty AUs distant. Whatever she was looking at never left the accretion disk. "Binil, are you sure?"

"Commander Fairchild, I know the difference between a solid rock and a hollow sphere. That is a sphere. Less than thirty percent of the mass that a solid object of that diameter and material should have. And if you look here, you'll see the way our scans are reflected back at us...the density signature is nowhere as disparate as it should be. That is a dense armor shell. It's a battleship."

"So damn big," Dance blurted.

"For a Sleer, maybe. There are planetoid class warships the Movi have used in the past that measure comparably."

"No reason not to look them over. All sensors, full sweeps. Pick it apart, folks. Janus, take us into an orbit. One hundred klicks. Let's not get too close. Sara, get on the troops. If it's not dead, we might need numbers in a hurry."

Skellington withdrew his gauntlets from the console and carried his display over, throwing it up on the main display as he stood next to Fairchild. "It's not the same animal as anything we've seen. Except for this." A new image appeared, a densely organic mechanical hybrid of an object.

"Crazy maneuver drive?" Fairchild guessed.

"No, these are power generators. They're an order of magnitude bigger than any reactive furnaces the Sleer manufacture, even on their big space-control ships. And it's powered down almost to zero."

"*Almost*? Show me." Skull threw data on the screen and Fairchild stared until he was leaning into the display. "That's like a fraction of one percent. How long as has it been here?"

"And whose is it?" Frost asked.

Brooks pulled images from the database and ran them through the display. "You sure it's not Movi? It looks like their design."

Skull shook his head. "Not with that hull density. This is something else."

Binil reached to another console and brought up a new display. An armored sphere of a battleship. "*This* is a *Darak*-class planetoid used exclusively by the Royal Movi Navy. Twenty-one kilometers in diameter. They are so expensive and difficult to field, there are only one hundred in their entire fleet. But still smaller than what we see out there."

"So noted," Fairchild acknowledged. "Let's focus on what we see."

Rosenski reached into the display and turned it just so. "Forward observers think they identified docking ports. Evenly spaced around the equator. All Ravens and battlers are at Ready Five status."

"Take us in. Let's get a good look at it."

They spent the next hours engaged in tense observation of

the wreck. It wasn't like any ship design they'd seen, and they knew little enough about Movi technology that they made careful notes of everything. One thing they did notice was that it had been out there for a very long time.

Frost kept to himself next to the engineering station. Finally, he made a report. "Whatever they did, they used energy screens for just about everything. There are force field generators everywhere inside this ship. Not too unlike the generators we saw on that Skreesh titan."

"Jeez, it's not a Skreesh hulk is it? Something someone defeated and then forgot about?"

"Not unless the Skreesh have been ravaging this arm of the galaxy for at least twenty thousand years," Skellington said.

Brooks turned around. "They actually have. How'd you get that number?"

"Here, look. I just took a few specific readings of the exterior shell. It's vaguely radioactive. But...there are multiple shells. I radioisotope dated the innermost one."

A cross section of the behemoth appeared on screen. "Three separate hulls, and the third is extremely well shielded. And look at this. There are vast areas inside this thing. What's that design remind you of?"

Brooks tipped to it first. "It looks like a cross section of Battle Ring Genukh."

"That's my thinking exactly."

"So it's an ancient Sleer design?"

"I dunno. The decks are laid out the same way, but there are only so many ways to design compartments, even when you have a ship the size of a big asteroid. What makes me wonder is this. Look at the core. That's where all the fancy power generation and drive modules live. See that big fellow there? That is a spatial transition engine that looks exactly like the fold drive aboard *Cyclops,* just much much bigger. And this bit over here. That's not a conventional Sleer sublight engine."

"So it uses Sleer *and* Movi technology?" Uncle asked.

"Could be. But the power core that Skull found is even weirder. That's obviously a central power system, but it's not a reactive furnace."

"What is it then?"

"I have no idea. The core is nearly two miles long and it's shielded like a motherfucker. I have no idea what it meant to use for fuel or how it powers something that big for any length of time."

"So. We know it's here. What do we do with it?" Rosenski wondered.

"And why are the Sleer allowing us to see it?"

"Come on, Skull. You think they know it's here?"

"They must. It's the only system where they're allowing us free rein."

"I'm telling you guys, they don't know it's here," Brooks insisted. "There's no way they'd let us see this."

Fairchild retreated to his big chair and settled into its contours. "Unless they're so confident of their ability to squash us in combat that they do know it's here and don't *care* if we see it. They might even be giggling over it back on Earth, thinking they put one over on us. Derp derp stupid humans, let them try to figure out what it is or how we built it. Skull, ping the whole system, maximum power. Let's make sure we're alone out here."

"If I ping that hard, it's an excellent chance we won't be alone here for very long."

"Humor me, Mr. Skellington."

"Yes, sir. Setting the active sensors to omnidirectional pattern, maximum power."

The sweep lasted several minutes and returned a radar echo

very much like what they expected to see. Everything was mapped in an instant. Almost everything.

"There. See that?" Brooks pointed as he dove into the network. "Give me a minute to clean that up..." Soon they were looking at an even more disturbing image. "Well, look at that."

"Anyone notice what I'm noticing?" Skull asked.

Frost chuckled. "You mean the lack of image where that booyah should be?"

"Wait. A two twenty-kilometer diameter stealth ship? That's not possible," Arkady declared.

Skull set his console for automatic sweeps. "Maybe not, but thar she blows."

"Jeez, no wonder the Sleer let us come out here. Brooks?"

"Yes, sir?"

"I apologize for doubting you. Our dinosaur overlords did miss something, and you pegged it. Good job. But it leaves us a valid question. What are we going to do with it?"

Janus had an idea. "We haul ass back home and tell the OMP to quarantine the whole area?"

"The same OMP that's allied with the Sleer High Command?" Arkady asked.

Janus turned away from his console. "What are you saying?" he asked.

Arkady rolled her eyes. "We know Grossusk and Moruk don't want it, which means they can't see it. It's our secret. We post a report that ignores any mention of an alien derelict and work from there. We send a horde of drones inside to map it out, maybe a flight of Ravens and battlers to case the joint, and we go home to report a major discovery. The UEF will have to send a salvage crew out here. Leave the heavy lifting to them."

"That leaves three and a half days to make every record we can. It's pretty obvious this thing is derelict and it's not coming back online."

"Not by itself." All eyes were on Rosenski as she voiced her thoughts. "We're already out here. We know the Sleer are scouting the local neighborhood. Eventually they'll show up here. They find it, they might very well send a team to resurrect it. They lost a lot of ships when the Skreesh arrived. They probably want to replace those losses."

"If all we do is harness that stealth tech, it's worth it," Arkady said.

"That's a mighty big if." Fairchild leaned forward in his crash couch, eyes flicking from the images on the screen to the smaller displays. Trying to reconcile the differences between them. "Skull, you said there was a trickle of power deep inside the structure."

"Yes. It's barely readable, but it was enough to get our long-range sensor's attention. It looks like some of the backup systems are still active."

"Then that's where we're going."

Arkady practically bounced in her crash couch. "We're going to board that monster?"

"No one knows we're out here," Binil said quietly.

"Valri and Underhill do. More importantly, ZERO does. But he doesn't know we found this. Brooks, go ahead and set up a very carefully coded message to Valri and route it through that message boat."

"Sure. Stick it on a microdot code and plaster it on your ass. That'll get her attention," Frost suggested.

Fairchild tilted his head as he imagined the look on her face. "It wasn't my plan, but now I should do that. Thanks. In the meantime, let's get the swarm ready for deployment."

The 'swarm' was their supply of SW-B-1D self-propelled drones. Each was about the size of a small tire, which floated on magnetic fields and could scan its environment in all parts of the spectrum while it moved. The ship had nearly a thousand available, and they would need every one of them. They launched them one by one, sent them into various parts of the wreck, and set them to search mode, allowing them free movement within. As they broadcast, the ship's computers recorded everything, and Brooks and Skull worked tirelessly to piece the bits into a complete model.

It took time, but they assembled all their scans into a more or less coherent three-dimensional model of the derelict. Countless empty spaces and scores of decks, compartments, and modules many times larger than their own vessel lay within. There was considerable battle damage to map, too. Even from ten thousand klicks away, they spied wide craters and rents in the surface. Gaping canyons exposing internal systems they hadn't been able to identify.

Eventually, Skull and Brooks felt able to brief their crew on the results.

"If we had to guess—and we do have to guess—we'd say the powered-up systems are part of a vast computer complex. Nothing as advanced as Genukh, but damn big," Brooks announced.

"It's not functional," Skull said, "and before anyone asks, we can't repair it."

Janus asked, "How do you know when we haven't even looked at it yet?"

"The logs are massive, but we were able to read them. In Sleer," Brooks said.

"Ah. That solves that."

"Exactly. It's absolutely a Sleer vessel. Completely unknown to us, and possibly forgotten by the current high command."

Arkady asked, "If they were building them this big twenty thousand years ago, why did they stop?"

Brooks shrugged. "Why don't we build ocean liners like the

Titanic anymore? It was a fad, limited to a particular time and place. We know the Skreesh have a habit of running down this arm of the galaxy every now and then. We also know that there have been multiple Sleer empires over the past half million years. Most of what the current empire knows about the past examples has been through excavating old ruins. They may have never seen anything like this. And if they have, they may not have made the connection, simply because they never found readable records. This derelict probably was part of a fleet doctrine that they just don't remember."

Dance Reagan made a rude noise in the back of her throat. "What could you two find out?"

Skull took over the narration. "Despite its size, it's unlikely to be a proper battleship. Too few weapons, almost purely defensive systems. Lots of shield generators. We can recognize the mountings for those easily enough after seeing what they look like aboard *Genukh*. No armor and no armor repair systems."

Brooks waved his hand dismissively. "Zluur figured those out only recently. They wouldn't be anywhere else. But he really did invent those instead of rehashing old techniques."

Fairchild said, "Back to computers and records. What's working?"

Brooks swiped to a new display. "Almost nothing. Data storage modules that are bigger than this ship. All we can do is sample individual sectors, but I think what happened is that this place was meant to be a regional listening post for Skreesh activity. They dispatched drones—thousands of them all up and down the Orion arm—and listened to what they reported. Then, when a Skreesh incursion was detected, it would alert Home Nest to the event and start cranking out defenses of its own. Small ships with nuclear warheads. Nuclear drones for lack of a better phrase. I think this system was meant to be either an advanced staging area or the first part of a large defense network."

"So, where are all the nuclear drones?"

"They're still here. Well, the launchers are here." Brooks adjusted the view to show nearly a hundred separate installations. Still gargantuan, but evenly spaced around the primary star. "We already took readings. None have any missiles left, but it looks like the launchers all remain active. They're pinging the crap out of us, but on a very low frequency. We didn't even see it until we adjusted the sensors."

Fairchild realized he'd left a giant hole in his security screen. "Good lord." The ramifications were awesome. The thought of missile launchers trying to fire on them and their arrival triggering such an event meant that the system had once been an active weapons platform. If nothing else, it spoke to the Sleer's existential dread being a worthwhile trait. Their military arrangement wasn't just a habit, it was a logical and reasonable response to the fact that they were being continually attacked by a superior power. No wonder they didn't understand what civilian life meant to humans. They didn't have time for it.

Brooks continued, "Anyway, the last incursion occurred and the Skreesh wiped out everything. They obviously came this far, even if they didn't find Earth. If they did, they either ignored us or were already topped off with natural resources to build more titans. I think we can say that we got very, very lucky."

Skull nodded agreement and said in a grave voice, "The Skreesh saw this was a holding point and altered their course. Hundreds of ships, titan class and smaller. Potentially hundreds of millions of shock troopers and lord knows what. The station fought back as well as it could but was overwhelmed by numbers. As the damage accrued, the self-repair diminished and the central computer reduced power to the rest of the ship to compensate. Over and over until all that was left is what we have here. Random bits and pieces. It repaired what it could, and held a trickle of power to the memory stores to keep them active. That's all that's left."

Uncle ran through the available choices. "We can't repair it. We certainly can't destroy it. And we can't announce our find to the rest of the UEF. At least not yet. So. Considering that we can come back with more people and the gear to study this thing properly—in fact it will look strange to the Sleer if we don't try to move in to this new colony over the short term—how do we hide it?"

Brooks altered the display to a show a tactical plot. "We move it out of the accretion disk. That's how we found it."

"We can't tow it out of orbit. This ship is too small."

"No, but we just need to change its trajectory. A few micrometers per second is all we need if we leave it for long enough. It's already moving at an appreciable rate."

"The swarm? There aren't enough of them."

"But they're solar powered and they use maglev fields to propel themselves. Leave them alone and they'll get it done. In a few years."

"A few years might be all we have left. Let's complete our survey."

CHAPTER 18

METZEK POUNDED the command console hard enough to shake the tablets arrayed on it. "Come on, you monkeys! Your prize is right here. Right here! Why are you hesitating?"

"Probably chittering to each other in their squeaking primate voices," Zolik snarled. "They do so love to talk, that bunch."

"You would think that a race as martially reckless as they were at Great Nest would be more interesting than this. All they've done for hours is orbit us and ping us with their electronics. What do they want me to do? Start shooting at them?" He looked at his XO. "Can we do that?"

"Not the main weapons. We'd need to bring the core tap online for that. But there's enough power to bring several batteries of lasers online."

Metzek hissed and turned away. Watching the displays only gave him the ability to watch the humans do nothing interesting in fifty wavelengths of the EM spectrum from twenty angles of observation. How entice them further? Yes, he could follow orders and merely destroy them. But he wanted something more interesting. An experience that was more personal. He preferred to look his prey in the face when he ripped their throats out. "Status report," he ordered.

"We are successfully hidden from their sensors as long as the ship is inside the base. Some laser batteries are online, as I said. We hooked the full output of the scout's reactive furnaces directly into the base's core tap. The tap won't work on its own, but does act as a power multiplier. We could run the whole base for months."

"Long enough to plot a spatial transition?"

"Possible. But after twenty thousand years, I doubt the fold drive will take us back to Great Nest."

"Not so far. Just to New Home. I want to present Grossusk with this discovery personally."

"That's against orders."

"He ordered us to kill any humans who arrived. So we will. Then we bring this prize back for refurbishing and begin a new wave of exploration and colonization. There are hundreds of scouts scouring the local space. But how many bases like *this* are out there? Just one. This one. We build a hundred of these on Battle Ring Genukh and start the process of arming ourselves against the next Shreesh attack now. We need to buy time, and this is how we do that."

"I'm not sure the Great Lords would appreciate your reasoning."

"They will. It's the obvious solution. How are the internal defenses?"

"None to speak of. Only a few of the monitoring cameras work, and none of the heat or motion sensors."

"I suppose this design predates the notion of internal defense turrets."

"There are some, but they'll explode if we try to fire any of them."

"That could be useful. What about the troops we brought with us?"

"A squadron of twenty *Zilthid* single-fighters, and two hundred *Azath* assault rollers. If we deploy them properly ahead of time, we should crush the primates handily."

"I'll remember you said that." Metzek reached into the display and nudged an icon. "They're finally doing something. Moving into orbit. And deploying...what are those?"

"Drones. They're too small to be anything else. Or to do much damage."

"I'll remember you said that, too. Let's give them a proper Sleer welcome."

Even when they ran Sleer gear, there had always been something going on in the background that Simon could point his attention to while waiting to discover the next data point or make the next decision. The boredom had never felt this oppressive before.

Finally, a new alert. He peered at the instruments, noted discrepancies, and tracked them to a definite cause. "They're picking off the drones. Various firing ports. Looks like some point defense weaponry survived," he reported.

Skull called out from across the bridge. "And a notable spike in their energy production. We may have tripped a proximity alarm with its own defense program. Whatever is powering that vessel, it's gearing up for something."

"Not like they'll mistake us for Sleer Defenders," Fairchild agreed. "Nightmares. You are on deck. Rosenski, Brooks, Arkady, and Janus. You are section leaders. Split your forces, play with the ranges, discover their firing arcs. Do not engage until ordered. Frost, you're on engineering; Skull, you're sensors and EWAR. Dance, you're Brooks' wingman."

"Where am I?" Binil asked.

"You're staying right where you are. I know you've had some battler experience, but you're far from proficient. Good hunting, all. Brooks?"

"Sir!"

"Stay on mission. That's an order."

"Yes, sir."

Rosenski elbowed him in the lift. "You good?"

"I'm good."

"Don't take it personally."

"I'm not."

"Simon, I know you; you take it personally, you start stewing, then you obsess—"

"I'm fine."

"And then you lose the mission," Arkady finished.

"I said I'm good."

"Don't worry, ma'am, I got him," Janus said.

"Me too," echoed Dance.

"Guys!" He couldn't help it. His temper flared and his face flushed. They knew he could take care of himself in a Raven. They'd seen him avoid death a hundred times—with worse odds. It didn't help for Janus to subtly remind him that when things got truly unpleasant, *he* was still the better pilot and very likely always would be.

Sara was talking past him now, to his squadron-mates. "I know you do," she said, winking. "Stay on mission."

Brooks let his unconscious drive him forward, following the others from the lift to the corridor to the prep room. They dressed in the fancy new flight suits that Binil had worn earlier. They really were impressive. Pull on the undersuit, snap a button, and it shrank, snugged up against your skin. Then the torso, arms and legs, boots, helmet. In half the time it took to struggle into the old tactical gear. He wasn't aware of anything beyond his skin until he felt a tug on his shoulder. Rosenski pulling him aside. Making him late. He had a plane to fly!

"Loosen up, Simon. You're stewing."

Now she was patronizing him. God damn her anyway. "You're the one who keeps saying you won't bail me out again."

She glanced down at her feet then met his eyes. "That's fair. I can be an asshole. But I dunk on the entire crew, you know that. Any pilot who goes out thinking he's hot shit on a platter, he gets in trouble. I've seen it happen. It happened to Uncle. Hell, it happened to Thomas 'The Butcher' Katsev."

He'd had enough. "Is there a point to this, Sara?"

"Yes. You remember back on Genukh? We got stuck in a Sleer city. I freaked out and you pulled me out of it so I could do my job. Remember that?"

"I do."

"Then *loosen up*. You are an expert on Sleer tech. We need you to find us a path through those lasers and lord knows what else they have coming up to meet us. Can you do that?"

"Yes."

"Good. Remember, if Janus or Dance offers you help, it's because they think you need the help. Say yes. Let us help you. You good?"

"I'm good."

She donned her helmet and slapped his shoulder. He didn't flinch. "Saddle up and pay attention. This won't be as simple as we want."

Even getting the fighters in the air wasn't as simple as they wanted.

Gauntlet's designers strove to pack all the functionality and warfighting capability of a Sleer *Zalamb* scout cruiser into a hull barely one third of its size. The strategy was like what the Movi would have used: a single ship that made itself as dangerous as a flotilla of lesser vessels. But what looked good on paper didn't necessarily make itself useful in combat. Launching the Ravens was an example.

All this ran through Brooks's mind as he raced through the launch bay. Instead of the wide-open space offered by the much larger AMS-1 launch tubes, *Gauntlet* loaded individual battlers into separate tubes for dispersion like a sheaf of missiles: up and out, where the engines took over and maneuvered into open space. Even the true battlers were launched this way, expected to coast to the landing zone on their rear-mounted rocket boosters.

The setting jarred his senses. It looked to him like pillars being raised on lifts into openings in the roof, which, in a sense, they were. His own Strike Raven stood at the rear of the formation, hatch open and his crew chief waving frantically, urging him forward. Brooks climbed the ladder to the platform in record time, only to earn a nasty growl from his chief, who checked the seals on his suit, gave him a thumbs up, and shoved him through the hatch.

Once inside, Brooks settled into the command couch and managed to calm himself as the VRF fighter came alive around him. Pre-flight happened long before the pilots arrived, with weapons and plane checked and double checked. He ran through his own checklist just the same. Take an extra five seconds and do it right. Don't lose the mission.

At least his section was familiar. He recognized their voices immediately. Speedbump, Ghost, Purcell, Morrow, Dance. Voices reported call signs and statuses, joined by green LEDs on his status board. "Section 3 Leader, ready for lift."

It was a weird experience. His lift rose, jarring him, rumbling beneath him, then a clang as the platform locked in place. He brought his engines to idle, checked his harness and set his controls to neutral, then heard Fairchild's voice from the bridge. "This is *Gauntlet* actual, Nightmare squadron clear for launch. Good hunting, folks!"

Rosenski's voice: "Nightmare Leader. All sections launch in sequence. Go!"

Then a bump as the hatch above him opened and BLAM! as the boosters blasted him out of the tube. Brooks was back in his normal state. He spotted his crew emerging from the neighboring tubes and toggled his mic. "Section 3, convert to Jet mode and follow me. Let's thread that needle."

A garbled whine from his earphones. Now one of his section's LEDs was flashing. He quickly eyeballed his area and found he was missing one plane. Who...? Oh, hell. "Speedbump. Where are you?"

"I had a misfire in the tube. They're resetting it now."

Brooks scanned his HUD. The other sections were already forming up and maneuvering into their approaches. If his group didn't hold formation, there'd be a giant hole in *Gauntlet*'s defense. Brooks trained his external camera on the assault ship's hull. "One more try, then we pull you out, Diallou."

"Right. Re-setting." The hatch remained sealed, a hiss of steam rising from the hinge, crystalizing as it hit vacuum. "Dammit!"

"I got you. Stay there, Speedbump. Dance, get the section in position. We'll meet up as soon as I pry Speedbump out of the tube."

"Copy that. Section 3, stay on me and keep up."

Brooks grumbled as he prepared to return his configuration back to battler, then realized he'd never changed it. Focus! He tumbled the aircraft and approached from behind, feeling a jar as his machine's feet contacted the hull. One step, two, three. He set the battler behind the hatch, then realized he'd get smashed by the hatch if it opened with pressure behind it. He repositioned, bent down, jammed the fingers into the crack between hatch and hull, and pulled with all his battler's strength. A burst of pressure, and the hatch exploded up and backwards, a bubble of air exploding upwards. Then he backed away. "Diallou, forget the boosters. Go to manual and use your engines to lift yourself out."

It was like watching a robot being hatched from a giant metal egg as Speedbump climbed her ship out of the launch tube. Sparks flew against her machine's legs as she scrambled for purchase, finally using her arms to push herself out.

A quick check for external damage, and a relieved sigh as he saw none. "Are you good?" he asked.

"All systems...check! I'm good."

"Nice. Switch to Jet mode and go to afterburners—we are way behind the class."

Bursts of velocity, followed by some adjustment showed Brooks that Speedbump was a perfectly good pilot. She just drew the short straw far more often than she deserved. He supposed every unit had someone like her.

"Section 3. How nice of you to finally join us," Arkady scolded as they matched vectors with their main group.

Diallou sounded apologetic. "My fault, ma'am. Won't happened again."

"*Not* her fault. Crappy launch tube is what did it," Brooks insisted. "Permission to lead formation?"

Rosenski wasted no time. "Granted. Show us your stuff, Genius."

He checked the status board. Diallou and Reagan were in Strike Ravens like himself, while Morrow, Purcell, and Ghost were in the Prowlers. The strategy would be like the one they ran through in training. Except this time, it would work. "Prowlers, deploy your vanes and power up. All EWAR systems to standby. All Ravens, link your onboard battle comps to *Gauntlet*'s tracking system. Let's make a hole for the big ship to fly through."

The idea formed in Brooks's mind as he spoke. If this giant space station was really that old, it probably lacked all the fancy gear and systems that modern Sleer vessels called their own. Which made it far more like a human designed warship than not. He extended his plane's forward-looking ladar to examine whether the situation with *Gauntlet*'s drones had changed. Not as much as he'd have thought. The point defense lasers were still picking them off, but not in huge numbers.

He toggled his mic to the command channel. "*Gauntlet* actual, this is Section 3 leader. I have an idea."

"*Gauntlet* actual. Go ahead."

"Uncle, set the drones to dive bomb the laser ports that are firing at them. Hold a few back for sensor ops, but the rest are miniature missiles just waiting for their day in the sunlight."

No answer. Brooks waited, easily able to imagine the setting on the bridge. Uncle was thinking about it, asking his bridge crew for advice, weighing opinions, wondering if today was the day that Simon Brooks had lost his—

"Nightmare Leader, do you concur?"

"Roger that, actual. I concur."

"Very well. Stand by."

It would have been easy to take Uncle's hesitation personally. Maybe Brooks had a brilliant insight, or hey, maybe he was cracking, but Uncle seemed willing to go along with his plan. He concentrated on watching the spacing between his planes and his ladar sweeps. Points flashed ahead of him, picking out bursts of energy. The lasers shooting down the drones. Then the shape of the action changed. Bigger flashes. The number of drones dwindled, and the flashes grew in number. Finally, only a few drones were in the air, but even fewer point defenses remained to shoot them down. Even better, the remaining drones withdrew to well out of the lasers' ranges. The comparative quiet was impressive...and a signal.

"Section 3, go to afterburners. I want to close the distance before they think of something new." He shoved his plane's throttle forward, and felt a satisfying gain in his weight as G-forces pushed him into his couch. "Ten klick distancing. Prowlers, bring your jammers to full power." They'd practiced this formation in the simulators a dozen times. The Prowlers stayed at the apexes of an equilateral triangle, while the Strike Ravens rode herd on them, five klicks from each other, searching for targets. To add to the fun, they were accelerating every second, getting ahead of *Gauntlet* and the other Nightmares.

Sixty klicks, fifty, then forty. At thirty, Brooks killed their afterburners and started looking for places to land. At twenty klicks the globe-like base was a hard black sphere in the canopy. At ten, he ordered reverse thrust to kill their forward velocity, and everyone in the section was hurled against their harness hard enough to cause bruising.

Then the proximity alarms began screaming.

"Good lord, don't tell me it worked?"

No one on the bridge answered. It was obvious that the impacts had in fact reduced the small lasers to useless craters. Even Fairchild could be rhetorical on occasion. Frost cleared his throat. "Orders, sir?"

"Orders..." Fairchild went through the possibilities in his mind. He was only half aware that the young helm officer had his head turned around like an owl, looking for guidance. "We need a landing site. Brooks said the big airlocks were in an equatorial zone, didn't he? Skull, look for an entry point."

"Copy that. Scanning in progress."

"Grandpa, how much thrust can this crate give?"

Frost shot a withering look at Fairchild's back, trying to burn a hole in the younger man's uniform. "We cleared 270 AUs in only fifteen hours, that's how much. How about you tell me what you have in mind? I'll tell you if it's a good idea or not."

"A max burn to whatever landing spot Skull finds and then down and clear in record time?"

"See? That I can work with. If we burn at three Gs, I can have us down in a minute and a half."

Fairchild forced his jaw to relax and fists to unclench. "Skull? What are you seeing?"

"New contacts. Hmm. Very strange."

"Talk to me, Skull."

"Two groups. One of them is coming up over the sphere's horizon at extreme speed. The other...this is crazy. It looks like turrets are crawling over the exposed hull."

The command channel erupted with reports of encounters with new enemies. The fast-moving targets were the Sleer fighters. They'd seen those often enough in combat. Faster than a Super-Raven but fragile. Rosenski's section would deal with those. Brooks would hopefully have learned his lesson in terms of defending the EWAR aircraft as they worked to jam Sleer Defenders. But as for the crawling turrets...

"*Gauntlet* actual to all Nightmares. Weapons are free. Repeat, you are free to engage. Rosenski, take the fighters. Arkady and Janus, work on targets of opportunity. Brooks, keep those Prowlers safe." He turned and spied Skellington struggling to keep up with the demands of his job. "Skull!"

"I have the landing zone. There. Co-ordinates locked and on the display."

Fairchild glanced at the schematic. Just about the center of the approaching behemoth's surface. He switched channels to the internal comm net. "Gunnery section. You have a fire mission. All missiles armed and locked. Blast an entry hole at these co-ordinates."

It took bare seconds for the crews to bring the order to reality. "Forward missile batteries...fire! Midships batteries...fire!" Fiery streaks shot past the assault shuttle as the missiles left their tubes, replaced by others. A second wave, then a third, then a fourth. Explosions burst throughout the target area, shredding hull plates and exposing the secondary hull, then the third. A fifth wave. Then a sixth.

"Breakthrough!" Skull crowed. "We have a way in."

Fairchild dropped into his crash couch. "All hands, strap in! Frost! Ninety seconds. Make it happen!"

"Ninety seconds and counting, aye!"

"Launch bay, prepare to drop the Broadswords."

CHAPTER 19

"BROOKS, keep those Prowlers safe and escort *Gauntlet* down to landing at these coordinates."

The order broke Simon's paralysis and let him pull back. It was too easy to fall into the scream of the alarm, to worry that he'd screwed up, that he and all his crew was about to die. Thinking like that would lead to exactly that result.

He heard Fairchild's orders to the other sections. Rosenski would be "above" his section, away from the fighting. The other two would deploy as needed. He already saw that Janus was taking his section low and swapping their planes to Battler mode. Arkady did the opposite, taking her section high to give cover to Janus's section. A moment later, the *Gauntlet's* battle computer sent coded bursts to his display. They were painting bombardment areas, warning allied craft to stay clear.

You didn't have to tell Brooks twice. "Section 3, stay aware. The Saint is going to wipe out a whole raft of rollers." Acknowledgements rolled in, and Brooks breathed a little more easily. He and Arkady were not close, were never more than two passing names to each other. Both with a relationship to Fairchild, but only the faintest relationship with each other.

They'd occupied membership in the same unit for a while, and here they were again. An iceberg of social activity: ninety percent of their connections were invisible.

But it gave him an idea. "Section 3. Everyone swap to Walker mode. We're going to stay out of Arkady's line of fire, and we're going to buy *Gauntlet* some breathing room."

"How?" Morrow again.

The display surged with launch detections and projected missile flight paths. Even Morrow should have seen that. "We're going to act like mobile SAM launchers. First volley, incoming. Everyone drop down to NOE flight paths, ten klicks out. Scatter!" He swung his Raven onto a new course and triggered a new flight geometry. Walkers didn't walk—although they could —but there were only so many ways to refer to a VTOL aircraft configuration that included arms and legs.

Flashes behind him as missiles detonated, then a hurricane of shrapnel as the explosions blew hull plates off their supports and splintered enemy rollers. Then a series of much bigger explosions further ahead on the vessel's horizon: *Gauntlet*'s missiles blasting through multiple ship hulls. High above his canopy, Brooks saw new aiming circles come into play as the battle computer identified *Gauntlet* and showed him the assault shuttle's course.

Then he and his section touched down onto the hull, and the world acquired a very different aspect. Suddenly there was an up and a down. And an infantry: the same *Azath* rolling assault ground units that invaded South Pico Island on *Ascension*'s launch day. Unimpressive performers in the microgravity of space, but give them a solid surface to maneuver from and they were deadly.

"Go to missiles, folks. Lock targets on whatever's nearest. Drop 'em!" He followed his own instructions and bumped his jets just enough to push his Raven twenty meters into the air.

Not high enough to be a giant target, just enough to perform a solid pop-up move. He toggled his HUD to tactical, then gave his forward ladar a look at the enemy rollers and triggered the volley. Twelve missiles dropped from his wing's launch rails and ignited, flame trails glowing. He reversed thrust and felt his tailpipe "boots" contact the hull as ten rollers exploded into flame. Not a bad return on his missiles.

He spun his Raven in a lateral circle, pivoting to watch his section, marveling at the kilometers-wide circle of destruction they'd created. His threat indicator screamed at him and he felt the blaze of a particle beam from a roller's turret zing past his canopy, scaring the hell out of him. He'd forgotten they had those. He banked hard right; the roller swerved left, and from above, a stream of heavy shells tore into the Sleer war machine. The burst ripped it to pieces, a ragged ball coming to rest on the hull. He looked up just in time to see a Raven painted hot pink zoom overhead. Rosenski. She would always be saving his ass from enemy fire. And he would always be grateful. That was their relationship. He might as well deal with it.

Frau Butcher's voice on the command channel: "*Gauntlet* on final approach. Clear the area!"

Brooks pinged his section. All accounted for within a three-klick radius. The HUD tagged the assault shuttle way faster than he expected...Uncle was bringing it in at more than three Gs, which was frankly insane. And now new contacts were appearing on his screen, inducing another panic attack until he realized the newcomers were dropping from inside *Gauntlet*. Uncle was launching her battlers for security and extra firepower.

"Gauntlet's launching her Broadswords, people. Give them plenty of room to land."

Brooks watched as his section obeyed. From his point of view, the heavy shuttle was a boxy blob, sliding down toward the "ground" on a tail of blue flame. It wobbled a bit, swerved from port to starboard and back again as its pilot fishtailed, then corrected and slid right down into the giant hole they'd torn on the hull.

No explosions. No collisions. No shattering kabooms. And here came the Broadswords, guns and cannons pointing away from the hull, looking like a company of old school paratroopers as they too dropped into the hole and were gone.

"Section 3, follow me," he ordered. He skirted the defensive protrusions on the hull, then dove directly into the hole, following the shuttle and her escort.

Fairchild's voice on the command channel: "This is Gauntlet actual. We're down and clear. Air group status?"

Rosenski answered, "The single-fighters are toast. No new contacts. Remaining forces seem to have dropped inside the structure."

Now it was a ground war, with a Sleer space station as the prize. At least Simon Brooks was good at that.

CHAPTER 20

FIFTY-SIX HOURS and seven minutes on the countdown clock.

Captain Frances Underhill, OMP Special Operations Investigation Liaison, Battle Ring ZERO, stared at the report on her desk. Holographic it might be, but it was no less depressing for that. She was in trouble, and she might very well be completely screwed. Time would tell. Now she was mulling over her choices.

Her plan to transfer the Gauntlets to the OMP had failed completely. Not only was there no protocol to transfer Raven and Battler pilots from their UEF branch of the service, but there was no way to transfer them to another UEF unit without requisite paperwork. She'd queried the powers that be regarding several alternatives. Recon units, battlefield deployments, scout missions, naval attaches, assistants to the OMP—nothing worked. There was a process in place to move people from unit A to unit B, and she hadn't followed it. Period.

She'd called in favors. She'd begged, pleaded, and tried to bribe numerous folks in General Hendricks' office with anything she could think of, no matter how outlandish or unlikely. Nothing worked. She was fucked, and she'd fucked over a group of people who were loyal to Earth and the UEF. Yes, they made noise about the OMP, but come on. Who didn't?

So. Now what?

They were in a borrowed assault ship, one of Earth's new designs, and nothing could pull them back here pre-emptively. They were on their own. In the pilot's seat and flying solo. They were alone.

She needed them to stay there. If they came back on their own after the new rules came into effect, the best they could hope for was to be arrested the moment they stepped foot on the deck. But if they stayed beyond the reach of the OMP, they had a chance.

The trick was figuring out how to make that not happen. She couldn't just head out there to join them, and bringing Valri into it would be unfair to her friend. Val had real problems, and plenty of them. She didn't need this added to her plate.

So, that left Frances on her own.

She leaned back in her chair. She'd been so psyched about this office two weeks ago. She'd sat in the cold, hard jump seat in the office, answering questions for ZERO. She still wasn't entirely sure that had been real. Maybe it was a clever response program designed to poke her in the eye, just to see what might make her jump? It was possible. But ZERO was real, and there was no reason to think she was under suspicion on her own. She had gotten the job, after all. Not a bad thing. A new shiny badge, a pay raise, access to better weapons, gear, and vehicles.

And rules to enforce.

Despite being relatively close to Earth, the Gauntlets were still nearly 700 light years from Great Nest. That was a long jump. Too long for a hyperspace relay to send a message, and in any case she needed permission and clearance to use that kind of equipment. There was only one such transmitter on this battle ring, and it was barely functional.

But Movi message ships...those were a penny ante finagle. Just a few coins in the right hand, and she could load any message she wanted and dictate its destination. But what could she tell them? "Guys, the clock is ticking; get back her pronto!" They knew that.

In the meantime, she sorted through random data mining apps of her own. The system polled itself, determining the movements of people and the way data flowed through the IT network, making notes and logging people of interest to the OMP. As she watched the readout, Valri's name started blinking yellow...then switched to a steady amber and finally a glaring red. Frances stared until her vision blurred. What was going on?

A buzzer rang; the phone demanding attention. She plucked the receiver from its cradle without checking the caller ID. "Captain Underhill."

"Good day, Frances."

She recognized General Hendricks' voice and her veins filled with ice water. "Yes, General."

"You haven't filed an update report concerning Undersecretary Gibb's decision."

"With respect, sir, she hasn't made any decision that I'm aware of. Not yet."

"What's the hold up, Captain? She has valuable coding skills that we need in order to function. You promised you could get her to make them available. Is there a problem? Because you weren't promoted to start problems. Just to solve them."

"Yes, sir. It's complicated, sir."

"No, it's not. Either she gives us the trading software she designed, or we arrest her for treason. That's simple. Don't you think?"

"I think there's a place for nuance here, sir."

"Nuance is for lawyers. The lawyers work for us. I'll give

you one more day to make good on this situation, or I will make her my special project and relieve you of your new post. Am I clear?"

"Crystal clear, General." She waited until he clicked off, then slammed the phone back on its set. Then slammed it twice more for good measure. Lousy point. If ZERO put Valri in her job, there was a bloody good reason for it, even if Hendricks couldn't be bothered to see it. All arresting Val would do was open the job for someone else. Probably someone more to Hendricks's liking.

How did things get this weird? She'd run with the Gauntlets. She'd bled with them, shot aliens for them, and gotten the crap kicked out of her for them. She'd risked death a bunch of times for those yahoos, and they'd paid her back with derision and suspicion. Not that she really blamed them. No OMP officer was the life of any party except among other OMP folks. But…that was part of the job, too. Being someone they could focus their anger against while they did their jobs and, frankly, saved Great Nest.

But when it came to screwing over the closest thing she had to a best friend, then it was a different situation. She liked Val, who returned the feeling. They'd gotten close fast…in the first days of their relationship. There was nothing she didn't feel comfortable sharing with Val. Nothing that wasn't classified, anyhow.

She spoke into the air, tried the command on for size. "Val, you need to give me your trading algos or we're taking a trip downtown." She hated the sentence. The words felt awful coming out of her mouth. Her heart rate doubled. She felt her skin grow hot from shame and embarrassment just saying them.

No. There had to be another way.

She had to steal them. It was the only way to keep her friend safe. It was for Val's own good, really.

A plan formed in her mind, and she broke open the network with her implants (thank you, Simon Brooks, for showing her the way!). Val wasn't in her office, and that was fine. What would she be doing right now? Home? Relaxing with her feet up on the table, listening to some cool jazz and sipping a tall drink? No, that's what Frances wished *she* was doing.

Fuck it. The straight and narrow path was failing her. She needed to talk to Val in person. A network ping and a map display later, she found herself at Valri's door. Val was home, sure enough.

Okay. Time to step up.

She made a few stops along the way, which made her later than she would have liked. She shuffled her bundles as she reached up to swipe a universal key and plant her thumb on the lock, then hesitated. She knew that Val was home, but what if she had company? It would, at the very least, look strange if she showed up with presents—which she had. Hell, what if she was in there screwing Ray Fairchild into the floor? What if—?

No. Fairchild was light years away. Val had no other boy toys that she knew of. And she knew pretty much every relationship that linked the various members of her little group.

Skin connected with metal, the door swished open, and Frances half stumbled half fell into Val's foyer.

Sure enough, music piped from the ceiling, but nothing light and airy. This was strange stuff, angry but hopeful, and just a tiny bit whiny and wistful. Interesting.

She set her bundle on the kitchen counter and scanned the room. "Val? You in?"

She poked her head into the other rooms, finally heard the sound of rushing water from the closed bathroom door. Fine. A shower after work; that she could understand. She sniffed her armpits and decided it'd had been a stressful afternoon, but Val wouldn't throw her out. Fuck! Why was she dawdling?

She retreated to the sofa and sat, breathing heavily. Finally, Valri walked out in a pink robe, scrubbing water from her hair with a towel. She saw Frances and jumped with a yelp. "Privacy alert, boo!"

"I know, it's late, I'm sorry. I had to speak with you. Here... I bringeth gifts and libations." She rushed to the counter and tore open the boxes. Proper food boxes shipped from Earth, too. Spaghetti and meatballs. Custard flan. Chocolate drops. A liter of proper brandy that she'd been saving for a very special occasion. "Eat. Drink. Be merry. And please don't hate me."

"For what? I just need you to call first is all. This is...nice. If unexpected."

"I need a favor. A huge favor. A favor to end all favors."

Val's mouth dropped open. "Oh lord, you're pregnant? Is it Skull's?"

"What? No! I mean—Skull? Gaaah!" Underhill held her head and screamed. "That's just hurtful, lady."

"Funny. That was worth it. Okay, revenge is done. What you got?"

"I need you to sell me the trading algorithms you took away from On-Star Traveler."

"I can't."

"Sure, you can. I'll pay you. A lot. I have access to a giant budget."

"No. I *can't*. I don't have the algos. I sold them to On-Star in exchange for the money I used to buy the salvage yard on South Pico Island. Remember that drama?"

"But you kept something, right? I remember you saying you'd kept the core docs."

"Sure, I kept a bunch of things. The primitives are all mine—I only sold them the refined version. But if you're asking me if I'm willing to part with the alpha version, the answer is 'no.'"

"You have to."

"Why? The alpha's a piece of shit. It never worked properly. It wasn't until I developed the multi-phase matrix and set it to dynamically track inputs in real time that I made any headway." Valri blinked, cracked the seal on the brandy, and poured a dollop into a pair of glasses. She handed one to Frances. "You're in trouble."

"Yes. And I'm not pregnant."

"You could do worse than Skellington. You told me as much days ago."

"No!"

"Just saying I got you. What's wrong?"

Underhill swished the alcohol in her glass, then downed it in a single gulp. "I got a call from my boss, Hendricks. If I don't produce those mathematical directives you used to make a shit-load of money, I am directed to arrest you and rifle your belongings until I locate them."

"And what did you say?"

"I said 'yes.' What was I going to say? You don't tell the head of the OMP to fuck himself."

"No. No, I don't guess you do. Is this how you got promoted—by promising to bring me in?"

"I didn't promise that. I have no idea what I did for the bump in rank."

"I'm being up front. I don't have anything the OMP would want, so when you arrest me, just wait until I'm dressed. That work?"

"Val, you're not taking this seriously."

"*I'm* not taking this seriously? Who has the badge and gun here?" Val moved to the counter and set to preparing food. The food boxes were self-contained, with built-in heating elements. Pop the lid, start the chemical heater, and you had hot food in three minutes. "At least I'm going to the slammer on a full stomach," she said, putting two bowls and matching flatware on the table. She held the brandy up, peered at the label. "Pasta does not pair with brandy. You need good red wine—something with a lot of tannins. You want the sweet grapes. A crop from a very warm summer. The chocolate, though, that pairs with brandy."

"I grabbed what I could find on the way from work," Frances sighed.

"You didn't get me flowers."

"I would have. No florists on this space station. Sleer don't think horticulture is a profession worth emulating."

"And them being vegetarians, too. You'd think they could learn from us. At least a few things."

"They eat meat. Small, live animals. It's like watching a python eating a ten-pound rabbit. They don't raise cattle like we do. But they get way more exercise."

"Do I want to know where they get their feed from?"

"Not really. Let's just say they don't have the same kind of food raising techniques or needs that humans do and leave it at that."

Valri poured them both another glass of brandy and finished setting the places. "Here. Sit. Drink. Eat. We'll figure something out. Or you will."

Underhill took a few bites. She couldn't taste anything but despair. Ashes in her mouth. Now she knew what the phrase meant. Chalky, tasteless, joyless. "How can you stand to eat with me?" she groaned.

"It's late. We're both hungry and you brought the food, so come on."

They ate. Frances marveled at how human the arrangement was, remembering the dining galley on *Cyclops*. Tables and chairs built for giants, with troughs of water and mystery stew lining the walls. It was a different thing entirely when all the furniture was designed for humans instead of utilizing what you found on board. Nothing on *Cyclops* had really fit. She wondered what a Movi or Cycomm dining room looked like. What their eating habits were. All the Movi she'd met here ate human food and seemed to enjoy it. She knew Fairchild's pet Cycomm could handle human food easily enough. She wondered if it worked the other way. It had to, didn't it?

"Wait," Valri said, dropping her fork on an empty plate. "Why are we killing ourselves over this? We've got experts who answer to us. Let's use them."

"My expert doesn't talk to me unless it's to issue new orders."

Valri tapped a code into her comm. "Mine does. Hey, Basil? You awake? Good. I need you to come to my quarters, ASAP. Bring your notebook and phone. You're gonna make a bunch of calls and I'm going to help you. Just bring your entire work briefcase. ASAP, my dude."

"What's Basil got that we don't?"

"A dedication to bureaucracy that you couldn't imagine. More brandy?"

"Please."

When Basil Matsouka arrived, he blew past the door, gasping and sweating, bearing the red face of a desk jockey who'd run the whole way. "Holy shit, what's the emergency?"

Valri shoved the box of chocolate at him. "Eat these."

"All of them?"

"A handful to start, then tell us everything you know about the form of intellectual property law that EarthGov uses."

"Where is this going?" Basil sagged into the chair, eyeing the remains of dinner. Underhill watched as his eyes flicked from plates to boxes to dessert to their empty wine bottle, putting it together in his head. "Valri, what's the issue?"

"Captain Underhill has orders to shoot me at dawn unless I come up with a bit of IP that I long since disposed of."

"What?"

Frances sniffed. "I'm not gonna shoot her. Just arrest her for treason. The shooting comes after a short trial, but they have lawyers for that. It won't be me."

Basil's eyes were wide and haunted now, wondering what fresh hell he'd stepped into. At least part of him wondered if they were messing with his head. And they were in a way. "You're not lying, are you?"

"Nope."

"Okay. Hmm. Okay. Tell me everything." He listened. He threw chocolate into his mouth then drank the dregs from Valri's glass. Valri poured him a fresh glass. He gulped it down. "What I understand is that what you're telling me is impossible. It breaks rules. It ignores regulations. It's an abuse of powers, basically." He drained his glass. "Right?"

"It's crossed my mind," Valri agreed.

"So. The way to deal with an abuse is to report it to HR and let them investigate."

"But HR is run by a metal box called ZERO," Frances said.

"Right. Oh, fuck, *fuck!*" He pulled his phone out and thumbed through the entries, mumbling as he ran through the choices. Eventually, he chose one. "Hey Brookhaven? It's Warlock."

Val and Frances shared an eyebrow over that. Warlock? What kind of secret life was a UEF wonk living with a nickname like that?

"Listen, I need you. I mean it. No, now. Right now." He looked down and sighed. "I have chocolate. Lots of it. What else? Yeah, you get a favor. A big fat flying favor. Straight from the Undersecretary of Commerce." He rattled off Valri's address and hung up, then threw his phone across the room. It hit the wall and bounced to the floor. "Oh, what I did."

"What did you do, 'Warlock?'"

"I have someone who fixes problems like this. Heh. My

fixer. Captain Underhill, I think it would be best if you checked your office for messages."

"I'm off duty."

"You're never off duty."

"I can't stand by while I know an illegal activity is in progress."

Basil's eyes grew dark and utterly serious. "Nothing is in progress. My boss is in trouble. I'm helping her out. I made a call. That's all you know. Unless things go horribly wrong, you'll get what you want and Valri goes free. Right?"

Frances Underhill locked her fingers together and sat straight, eyes focused on the table, seeing nothing. "Listen, kids. Like it or not, I am here. I have friends, including you. It's no secret that cops let their friends get away with things that they wouldn't let strangers get away with on the regular. Now, I can understand why Mr. Warlock here might not want to bring my attention to this call for help. Not in my personal view, because I'm a believer in things like justice and mercy. But the fact remains, even if I go away, this apartment is probably bugged like all the other compartments where official business is conducted, courtesy of General Hendricks and his staff of sneaks. Of which I am no longer a part. Get me?"

She looked at their faces. Valri was frowning and Basil was apoplectic, his eyes wide with terror. She had their attention. "Now, I know there are Laynies aboard the facility. I'd be surprised if there weren't. And there's a reason that ZERO promoted me away from the Chick Pit and wants me to focus on law enforcement. I guarantee that whatever plan he has for us, it's being influenced by Hendricks, who is himself being influenced by the Sleer high command. I figure I have two choices. I can play my rotten little part in this rotten little machine the OMP has cooked up, and haul you both away for treason right now, or I can sit and listen to you guys and decide you are acting in humanity's best interests. But sending me out that door gets you both shot."

"My access is limited to a few numbers I can call if I need help," Basil murmured. "Valri has no access to any of it. She's completely innocent."

"That's not up to me to decide. So, tell me now, *Warlock*. If you have any knowledge of what Layne's Brigade is up to,—even just the least offensive member of it—now is the time to talk about it."

Matsoukas let his breath out in a ragged sigh. "It's not Laynies. At least. I don't think they're Laynies."

"Why not?"

"Too organized. There are cells. Code names and activation phrases. No one has more than a couple of names to call on if they get into trouble. It's too…military. Too professional."

That was news. Val might not understand the references, but Underhill did. Layne's Brigade was very much an organization that prided itself on knowing how to recruit and train veterans and bureaucrats with real grievances against the Unified Earth Fleet and Office of Military Protocols. She'd never encountered a member who hadn't spent at least some time in or adjacent to the military. "All right. Who do you think you're working for?"

"Your boss. General Hendricks."

"And why would you think that?"

"You don't think assigning someone to watch and report what the new undersecretary does sounds like something the top Overcop would do?"

Underhill put her hands on the table, palms down. She respected Matsoukas and his willingness to talk to her, but he was either incredibly naïve or just plain stupid…and he wasn't stupid. Nobody who ran Valri's office affairs could be. "Regardless, I need to see and hear the conversation when your contact arrives."

"There's an alcove down the hallway," Valri offered. "It's like a mailbox nook, but nobody gets physical mail up here, so it's unused. No one will see you unless they stick their head in there."

"Right." Underhill left, walked down the corridor, and ducked into an alcove that had just enough of a line of sight so she could spot anyone approaching Valri's door from either direction. Then she leaned back and waited.

She knew what was up. Her friend's officer wanted to get her out of the situation. Off the hook. Away from the line of fire. So that whatever they did, illegal or not, it wouldn't reflect on Francis Underhill since she wouldn't have known anything about it. But she did know about it. She wasn't a moron and ZERO wouldn't buy the argument that she was. Selective ignorance still carried the smell of guilt. At the very least, she needed to know who else they would be relying on. So she waited.

And waited.

And waited.

And waited.

Movement at the end of the hall. Heavy footsteps around the corner grabbed her attention as one of the Sleer service drones picked its way to Valri's door. Not much for combat, these stick figure like mechanoids resembled their masters only slightly. Sleer-like heads with red camera lenses for eyes, hands that could grip anything a human could, and feet with claws that could dig into a deck for traction. The robot pinged, the door opened, and the drone entered. All perfectly normal. Wasn't it? No. It meant that "Brookhaven" didn't feel like showing up in person. No need to put their face in public if they were part of a group that used code names and scrambled phone channels.

Underhill took off her boots, sat on the floor, and linked her implants into the local area network, pinging cameras and picking out microphones. She checked Valri's front door and found that she hadn't changed the lock combination; her apartment was an open stage to Underhill. She could see and hear everything that transpired inside.

Privacy, Boo. Absolutely. But not today.

Link. Entry code. Link. And poof, she was effectively inside the action, her implants transmitting sights and sounds to her brain.

The unfolding scene disappointed her. It wasn't much more than what she'd seen for herself. Valri and Basil explained the situation and they brainstormed a few answers. One suggestion that stood out was figuring out whether the OMP already had access to the desired application and related files, and if so, how to just move the folders from one server to another and close the case. All of which Frances could have legit done for them if they'd just let her hang around. The level of distrust, even paranoia, in that room clumped into rage in her throat and nausea in her stomach. Hell, she should storm in and arrest all of them just for that. She'd busted her ass for these people, hadn't she?

She held her breath, listening to them drone on. When she regained her calm, she realized she had a perfect opportunity here. Who was running the drone and where were they? She turned her attention to finding out.

Two years ago, she'd joined Hornet Squadron on *Cyclops* while they sat in orbit around Saturn, waiting for an opportunity to rejoin the AMS-1. She'd been new to her implants, more rattled and dazed by the density of Sleer information tech than empowered by it. She'd maneuvered Brooks into doing a deep dive into the tech with her. He'd shown her things she hadn't thought were possible, and given her tools to learn more on her own. She brought these analytics to bear now, sifting through the data feeds that flowed out from the drone to the network nodes in Valri's apartment. Every datum went somewhere, and she followed every thread to the end. She marveled at the complexity the operator devised to avoid discovery: shells within shells, and countless servers bouncing streams to each other. She brought out a sorting algorithm Brooks had showed her, a last-ditch attempt to make sense of it, and got a ping. A weird bit of data—a transponder code that described an entry point into the system. One that she'd seen before. Sara Rosenski. Frau Butcher herself. Thank you, Simon Brooks, you dirty little genius.

But...Rosenski and Brooks were both off station, so how the hell was Brookhaven maintaining their connection? That would need better leads than she currently had. Which meant, ironically enough, she needed to get back to her office to continue with her investigation.

Some investigation, too. Sara Rosenski was funneling information to and from the EarthGov bureaucracy to an unknown source point, and using highly detailed data threading techniques that she hadn't imagined existed until Brooks showed them to her. She found it hard to believe that either of them would start a project quite like this unless the other were involved. Who were Brooks and Rosenski reporting to, and why?

CHAPTER 21

"I DON'T REMEMBER battle dress being this uncomfortable," Metzek hissed as he shifted in his armor. He couldn't help pawing and prodding the material, shuffling and fidgeting to his personal rhythm of annoyance.

Zolik was tired of it. One more reason his CO should never have been put on a scouting mission. He belonged in a laboratory, not a starship crew.

They'd been working for hours in the command center as they prepared for battle with the humans. It looked different than it did earlier in the day, now that mobile communication gear sat in clumps, hooked into the base's own network and reaching back to the scout ship's own battle computer. Less than a fully functional bridge, but more than what they'd found here originally.

The ancient holographic display projected a scaled schematic of the abandoned space station. The primates' invasion was going well for them. They'd lost only a few of their ground units and two of their flyers; the Sleer had lost ten times as many.

"Have you ever even sat inside an *Atzhan?*" Zolik asked.

"So I did. I trained in one for two weeks. But that was back in First Training, and my Great Servant of Defense thought I was better suited to scientific work. Here I am."

"And all Defenders across the Two Thousand Worlds thank you for that decision."

"If you say so. What's the tactical situation?"

"The primates have debarked from their assault craft and are now making their way deeper into Compartment Five."

"I see that. What's down there?"

"Not a great deal. Drone assembly and maintenance areas, plus storage bays and cargo transfer systems. Numerous auxiliary power stations. A great many walls and empty spaces."

"Good, let's use that." Metzek turned the data, experimenting with the battle order and examining what the primates brought with them. Their walker-type machines were bad enough—fast, agile, and well-armed—but their transforming flying machines were disturbingly well made. He saw that the better portion of their attack force had expended their missiles in the first assault, which put them roughly on a par as his own units. "We need to draw them inside then attack from behind. Break them into progressively smaller groups, over and over, until they escape, die, or surrender."

Zolik spotted a detail that his CO missed. "See...there's a transport conduit that extends from the main power lines that leads to the core tap. If they reach the core tap, they can blow us to scrap.."

"Then we can't let them get to that area. Here. Let's deploy the *Kizarts*. Ten units to accompany each of ours. Coordinate our troop movements through the ship's battle computers. We'll drive them into the auxiliary power plant here and detonate it with a surge from the core tap. That will deal with them."

CHAPTER 22

SARA ROSENSKI TOGGLED her command channel. "Hey, Genius. Is it me, or was this place designed by a mad scientist living a solitary life on a planet with extremely unpleasant weather?"

Moments passed before Brooks answered. "It's nowhere near as coherent a layout as our battle ring, if that's what you're asking," he said.

"So if it is really a Sleer vessel, it doesn't conform to any doctrine we've learned about," she probed.

"That's essentially it. Where is Frau Butcher going with this?"

Arkady's voice in their comms: "She means we need a new plan if we're going to make any headway. No familiar layout means we can't treat it as anything but unmapped hostile territory. Even with the data the drones are collecting."

"Very well put," Fairchild answered. "We're updating your map displays as new data comes in." Rosenski knew him well enough to imagine him pacing *Gauntlet*'s bridge, his fingers entwined behind his back and eyes on whatever console he was facing. Like an old man out for his morning stroll. She wondered if he ever looked at the displays or just ignored everything but what his officers told him.

They'd gained access to the behemoth and secured their landing zone. *Gauntlet*'s pilot slid the assault shuttle to the far end of the hangar bay as the remaining Ravens and battlers followed to regroup and form a perimeter. They left their entry breach behind them, delving into the spacecraft's interior but now they stood at an impasse. No clear objective, but an obvious need to neutralize the Sleer currently on board.

Brooks started murmuring on the channel. Talking to himself. She knew that tone. "What's that, Simon?"

"I said 'power sources.' Simplest way to kill the ship is to take out the power sources. I have my Prowler jocks working on triangulating the strongest readings. There seem to be a bunch of them."

"Reactive furnaces? We know what those look like at least. If we kill the power, we can reduce the internal defenses to nothing."

"I don't think that's the case. These scans are all over the place. One very big plant, two compartments below ours, if I'm reading this right. Lots of smaller plants that are probably backups, but only a few of them are operating."

Rosenski mused over the implications. One big power source meant a major target, which also suggested it would be heavily defended. No. she needed the plans to this thing. "Brooks, how do I get my implants to connect with the local network?"

"You can't. I've tried. There's nothing to support our implants anywhere on this station."

"Who the hell made that decision?" Dance Reagan demanded.

"I'm thinking this place is older than our implants. Maybe

older than the concept of implants. If we do this, it's manual connections the whole way."

"That's just peachy. *Gauntlet* actual, this is Nightmare Leader. What are our orders?"

"Nightmare Leader, stand by."

"Roger that, standing by."

In this case, stand by meant wait for orders. Everyone knew that. But they already had the perimeter set up. Lord knows what conversation he was having with the bridge crew. They needed to get some intelligence, and Frau Butcher didn't want to wait until they were surrounded to get it. "Nightmare Leader to Section 3."

Brooks answered immediately. "Section 3."

"How many exit hatches do we have on this level?"

"This bay has six of them, placed equidistant around the interior walls. What are you thinking?"

"I'm thinking you split your section in to three elements, each with a Prowler and a Raven running escort. Each element exits from an odd numbered hatch. Proceed as far as you can, make maps of whatever you encounter, and for creep's sake, do not engage without orders. Section 2!"

Janus's voice. "Section 2 Leader."

"You'll do the same with your section, except you'll have one element leave through each even-numbered hatch. Make sense?"

"Understood. Are my people running interference for the Prowlers?"

"Excellent idea, Lt. Janus. Arkady, your section will keep pace with the Prowlers. The second they identify a major target of opportunity, you're there to pounce and shred it."

"Section 4 Leader. Will comply."

"*Gauntlet* actual to Nightmare Leader."

"Nightmare Leader. Go ahead."

Fairchild's voice sounded surprisingly carefree. "Sara, break the crew into elements and perform reconnaissance on this and adjacent levels. Look for major systems and targets of opportunity."

"Will do. I can't imagine why I ever doubted you."

"Mind repeating that, Sara?"

"Not a chance. Splitting sections now. We'll keep you in the loop. Nightmares, form up as noted. Let's take a look around."

Only Arkady's Strike Ravens still carried missiles in their Armor Packs. But the interior bay hatches weren't locked, just heavy and multi-layered. Brute strength and leverage from the battlers worked as well as wanton violence.

They flew slowly along their assigned axes, all her flyers in Walker mode, moving along an NOE attack level at a relative snail's pace. It made them good platforms for pop-up attacks, clearing structures just long enough to lob a stream of armor piercing explosive shells at a target, then ducking into cover again. Unfortunately, some pilots got greedy, spotted multiple targets, and tried to shoot all of them—making themselves into big, fat targets as a result.

She found herself wishing she'd had a Prowler of her own. Every section should have at least one. When she got back from all the shooting, she'd recommend that to Fairchild. Or maybe just switch the assignments up. They'd see.

One of the things that stayed with her was the constant reminder of just how big the battle rings around Earth and Great Nest were. They didn't look like it at long range—hell, you couldn't even really see it from the surface of the planet, just a tiny silver sliver that ran overhead from horizon to horizon at the equator. But up close, it was like standing on a bridge as long as a planet and as wide as a big city. This factory base was even crazier. An entire cross section of the battle ring could fit inside this monster handily enough. She found herself wondering how long it would take for the rollers they'd encountered outside to locate them in here. In the meantime, they were projecting lots of noise between the ladar, IR search lights, and other sensor arrays. They'd shine brightly on any passive array the Sleer might use.

"Everyone go to IR displays. Even at their worst, rollers project a bit of heat, and those ugly walkers of theirs, too."

She toggled her own HUD to an IR tactical mode. She could clearly see every Raven and the two squads of Broadswords that trailed behind them, pinging new structures with their own sensors.

Bit by bit, they added their individual data sets to *Gauntlet*'s master program, and saw their maps updated in real time. After two hours, they hadn't encountered much resistance, but had functional maps of the major areas on this level.

Brooks pinged her comm. His position on her display startled her—well to her eight o-clock. Either his element was falling way behind the others, or hers was too far forward. She hadn't thought their advance that ragged. "Leader, we found something new. Drones are returning photos. Looks like a hospital...or maybe some kind of long-term storage unit. Lots of tubes bigger than a human would need."

"Sleer sized, then."

"Oh, yes. Lots of them. Rows and rows. All empty."

"Storage...like cold storage? Stasis? Cold sleep? Whatever you'd call it?"

"Makes sense. I know there are millions of Sleer still asleep on the newer escape fleet ships."

Reagan made a strangling noise. "I hope that means the ones packed into the old ships like mackerels will eventually be woken up. Dying in cold sleep sounds like an awful way to go."

"Sardines, Dance. You don't pack mackerels."

"So what the hell have we been eating from those fishy ration tins all this time?"

Rosenski suddenly had a flashback to her childhood, which included packed fish of every description—mackerels, sardines, whitefish, herring, a bunch of others she never cared for—and she could smell every damn one of them. She bit back a thread of bile, forcing it back down into her stomach. "Focus, Nightmares. Brooks, on a base this old, why would they have that manner of tech?"

"Age need not mean lack of invention," he said. "My radar pings are fuzzy. I figure the dust and grit covering every surface in here is absorbing part of the signal. Which means the base is old, yeah...but the fighters and rollers they've been throwing at us are as modern as what they used to invade South Pico Island on launch day."

That surprised her. She waited a moment, trying to make the pieces fit, and realized there was a gap in her knowledge that he'd seen and she hadn't. "So?"

"So, these guys are using modern Sleer fighting equipment. Where did they come from? *They* sure as hell haven't been in stasis for umpteen thousand years. Not if the equipment is falling apart and apparently unused."

"Hmm." She pressed her memory hard, trying to imagine the solution to the puzzle he'd put in front of her. The Sleer high command gave them this system because they didn't know this base was here. But if that were true, why were there Sleer Defenders manning the place? But not manning, not crew. Too few of them and they weren't running crew stations, just filling fighting machines and clearly intending to protect their turf from the troublesome primates who were trying to take it away from them.

"These monsters must have found it by accident, just like we did. They must have a ship on board," she said.

"That's what I'm thinking. Section 3, all Prowlers widen your signal analysis to include every Sleer ship type we know about," Brooks ordered.

Morrow responded. "Widening...bingo! They came in a *Zalamb*-class scout ship. Looks like it's parked on the compartment below us. It's hooked into the power grid, but it's not the sole power signal, not even the biggest one. That's lit up like a Christmas tree one level further down. Weird comm signals but—"

A wild burst of energy made Rosenski's display flicker. Three dots on her status board winked from green to red, and her threat alarm screamed in her ear.

"All units, ground ground ground! Switch to Battler mode and watch for rollers." She dove her plane toward the ground with her left hand, found the transfiguration control with her right, and pulled the transformation lever hard. Her plane dropped, its metal boots touching deck just as its wings folded into its back. She hefted her GU-22 gun pod, searching for movement and finding it. Bright bolts flew past her plane, making her headphones crackle and her skin crawl. She dodged the attack, took three steps to the right, and nailed the assailant with a burst from her gun pod. Fifty meters away, a roller exploded into fire. She moved again, this time back to the building she'd hidden behind. She stepped her machine out, ducking just enough out to give the external head cameras a view, then pulled back as what looked like a pack of legged monstrosities rushed her. She loosed a long burst at the crowd of staggering walkers and ducked back under cover. Red laser beams flew past her, but either the emu drivers weren't very good gunners, or the beams were low power; she couldn't see much obvious damage from their shooting. "Keep aware. Besides the rollers, they have walking units, too. Looks like very short-range lasers on them."

Her tactical display blipped as an update came through. The data from Brooks's Prowlers. Fortunately for her side, she'd grounded her ships in a jungle of industrial towers. It was the worst possible place to regroup and counterattack, but it wasn't a bad place to snipe at an oncoming enemy.

She waited ten seconds, then twenty. No shooting. She leaned out, snapped her gun to her shoulder, and let fly with short bursts. The Emus raced for her position, a line six or seven units long. Crazy things, like cubes but on legs, with a stubby gun where a chin would be on a face. Nothing she'd ever seen before. For a moment, she wondered if they'd put it together wrong. Very old Sleer inhabiting very old war machines at least had consistency as a theory.

More explosions to her left and right. Not a good place for an ambush. But possibly a good place for her to turn the tables on her attackers.

She spotted the motion of her assailants—five now. One of the Emus had apparently tripped on a downed scaffold and struggled to right itself, one leg broken clean off. The others continued their approach in straight lines, with no attempt to hide, use the available cover, or even shoot back coherently.

She stepped back across the edge of the structure and held perfectly still. Here they came—two, three, five. Big suckers, too. When the last one passed, she popped up and held the trigger down. Bursts shredding them one at a time. The last one collapsed. Still no shooting. What was wrong with these guys?

"Section leaders, sound off," she ordered.

"Section 2 here. No casualties."

"Section 3 here. One Raven, one Prowler damaged."

"Section 4 here. One plane down. We've picked up the pilot. No casualties. What the hell are those walking things?"

"I'd guess they're a primitive model of roller. I'm calling

them Emus." Rosenski switched channels. "Broadsword leader, are you hearing this?"

"Roger that, Nightmare leader."

"Good. Close up the distance between us. We're going to need your support. All section leaders, have your people form up on me. Do not let them pin you down."

Even as she gave the orders, she understood it was too little, too late. She'd made a tactical error in assuming they were alone down here. Ravens had the advantage of flight, but with such a low ceiling they became little more than flying gun platforms rattling around in a box. Well, now they knew better.

New plan.

Gunshots in the distance on both left and right. She stayed behind her cover while tracking the other sections. Dance's was moving quickly, using their boosters to leap-frog over obstructions as they ran. Brooks's Prowlers were powered down, relying on their standard sensor suites to navigate. Janus's section arrived in a loose group, while Arkady's Super Ravens showed up last, the heavy iron bringing up the proverbial rear.

More shooting behind them on their flank. That would be the Broadswords carving their way through whatever resistance they found. The shriek of Sleer lasers was bad enough, but now and then there would be the WHUMP of a major explosion. "Broadsword Leader, what's your ETA?"

"Nightmare leader, we're stuck. The damn Emus are ramming my battlers. They converge, someone shoots their way out, and the squad of them go up in flames."

"Casualties?"

"Not yet. But they're wearing us down."

"Stand by. Saint! Where are you?"

Arkady's icon blipped on her status board. "My section is behind yours. The Broadswords are behind us. There's another wave of combined Sleer units behind them."

"How are you fixed for ordnance?"

A short delay marked by chirps and squawks. She knew that sound: Arkady was polling her pilots. "Most of us are near dry. We have about twenty missiles between us. Plenty of rounds for the gun pods. What are you thinking?"

"I'll tell you. Brooks, take your remaining Prowlers to the ceiling and stay there while you paint every target you can see between us and the Broadswords. Once you're actively pinging the bad guys, I'll designate the thinnest wall as our direction to leave. Then Arkady pulls the data from your battle net and has her section's missiles tag any roller—not, repeat not the walkers—as a target. Let the supers fire their last missiles and clear out the blockade. Then we run like hell through the gap. Are we good?"

A couple more exchanges. Questions, concerns. But they acknowledged the order. It should work. There were a lot of moving pieces, but it would be the equivalent of using an airborne targeting system to enable the missiles to home in like guided artillery. The biggest issue would be how much fire the Prowlers drew, and whether Brooks and his remaining Ravens could draw that fire away from them.

A chatter of automatic fire behind her. The Broadswords were taking the worst of it as the remaining rollers realized that they'd boxed the humans in and pressed their advantage. She still couldn't see the entire force of Ravens, even if she saw their positions on the combat display. What she wouldn't give to have a proper Lurker with a full crew in here with them. One of those bad boys could illuminate the entire compartment, pinpoint every moving target both friendly and otherwise in less than a minute, and push the data to the fighters on an as-needed basis. The Prowlers could do some of that, but not nearly as well. Blinds and jams were most of what they were good for. But at close range, jammers lost their punch.

Back to the tactical display. The rollers and their walking pals were heaviest in front of her unit, a great mass of at least two hundred effectives, blocking them in with a wall fifty units wide and three or four walkers deep. Unfortunately, the base's central core and its promise of a way down to the next compartment and the Sleer scout ship also lay that way. The left and right flanks were thinner—two groups of a hundred units each, closing in from both sides. That left their rear, broken up between the rollers who'd already gotten close enough to shoot them at will, and the Broadswords. Those had possibilities, now that she thought about it. The battlers couldn't fly, but they had heavier armor and good close-in weapons to work with. And the rear was a ragged mess. Which meant the least resistance to a push, back the way they came, toward the launch bay.

In her head, she put it together. Wipe out the rear guard, let the Broadswords link up with the Ravens, then flank the flankers on the right and run like hell for the core. It wouldn't work for all of them, but it would get them out of this compartment and into the next one. She'd figure out the next step once they'd—

"Sara!"

The shout jolted her out of her head. "Report."

Brooks signaled to her. She could just see his Raven through her camera. His gray and white paint job, red and blue racing stripes drawing her eye. He even had his battler wave. She appreciated him even when she dared not say anything, but now his presence grounded her. Brooks could be a presumptuous git, and way too smart for his own good, but he knew his unit tactics. One last look through the external cameras satisfied her that her sections were as well positioned as they were likely to get. She set the plan in motion.

"Mr. Brooks, take your shot."

"Yes, ma'am."

Brooks took his element to the right; his remaining section mates took theirs to the left. She followed their progress on her monitor, watching as the Prowlers flipped open their EM vanes, powering up their systems while remaining in Battler mode to present smaller targets to the grounded rollers. But the Sleer still tried. Spots of lights flared around her as rollers took opportunity shots. She gasped as Brooks's plane took a hit, side-swiped the nearest Prowler, then righted itself. He even pointed his Raven's gun pod downward and sprayed the ground. Good for him, keeping his head when things went bad. She hoped he took out at least something. When the Prowlers hit their ceiling, almost literally bumping up against the compartment's roof, they brought their sensor vanes to full power. She forced herself to breathe as her display updated, units appearing where she hadn't seen them, more blips popping up every second. Building and structure locations, too. In a minute, the two Prowlers were showing them a real time tactical display of the entire compartment.

It wasn't as bad as she thought; it was so much worse. She saw the heavy formations blocking their progress toward the central core, but now she watched as the Sleer moved their groups in every direction. The three groups that cut off the Broadswords from the Ravens was the best shot. They wouldn't last long if the humans hit them in a crossfire. So that was the way to go.

She lost no time in picking out targets and designating Arkady's Super-Raven as the recipient. "Section 4, you have your feed, fire when ready."

Arkady's voice in her headphones, loud enough to be sitting in the cockpit with her: "Copy that. Stand by, Leader."

Six Super-Ravens let fly from their Armor Pack missile pods, smoke and flame showing observers their locations as they turned, swooped, and came crashing down. Detonations created a wall of fire and shrapnel behind them. When the explosions dies down, a wall of wreckage lay between Arkady's section and the Broadsword, but no operating rollers or Emus.

"We have a way out. All units, back the way we came. Broadswords, break left when we're out of the pipes and head to the central core. We'll cover your departure from above. Ravens, follow me in Battler mode." She pushed her plane's throttles and lifted off, hovering above the nearest structure. She levered the plane's weight to one side, letting the aircraft bleed some altitude, putting herself below Brooks and his wingman. If they wanted to shoot at those two, they'd have to hit her first.

Slowly, in twos and threes, the other Ravens formed up. Now they were a cloud of targets, but they could also fire down at the rollers more effectively than the rollers could shoot up at them. The Broadswords were making their break for it. The lead machine followed orders, curving their pace in a wide circle, forcing the rollers to bump up against each other as a dozen different units all tried to occupy the same space. At least a dozen of the Sleer machines were taking potshots at the stragglers.

"Cover fire," she called. She broke and descended, sweeping her gun pod in a pattern. Short burst, dodge. Short burst. Sweep. Short burst, hover. The others took their cues from her actions. The stragglers broke free, and the lead rollers fell to pieces.

They covered the rest of the way to the central core in that manner. The core itself was a wide multi-platformed pillar, cargo lifts by the hundreds surrounding the core while armored hatches guarded access to the interior. It was clear that this structure had been built to move crew and cargo between compartments relatively quickly.

They grounded near a series of platforms and waved the arriving Broadswords over, but without implant-sensitive controls or even diagrams of the circuitry, she was at a loss regarding how to make the lifts work. "Brooks, how to we bring this platform to life?"

Brooks took readings, muttering to himself on the comm. This time, she didn't stop him. He'd figure it out or he wouldn't. She watched her tactical display and saw they weren't free of the remaining Sleer—they'd merely gained some distance. There were still hundreds of bad guys rushing toward them.

"Any time, Simon."

"Working on it. I think if we—"

The grinding of metal plates crashing and screeching as they slid against their neighbors met their ears. Lights blinked above them and the nearest set of hatches started cycling, the nearest platform moving into position to create an apparent bridge between them and the core.

Sara breathed in relief. "Good work."

"I didn't do it."

The lifts locked into place. The hatches opened. And hundreds more rollers and their walking allies rushed them.

CHAPTER 23

TEMPORARY ACTIVE THIRD Lieutenant Binilsanetanjamalala wanted to kill the humans.

Not *all* the humans, not those she hadn't met. There were so many. Billions and billions, apparently. Just the ones on *Gauntlet*'s bridge, and in fairness, if she killed Ray Fairchild that would be enough for her.

She already knew how the drama would play out. She'd been paying attention to how the squadron worked. There were pre-existing connections between its members. That Uncle Fairchild ruled the roost, and while he sometimes listened to that tall red haired Rosenski, most of his input came from the dark-haired Arkady.

Binil had one friend here: Judy Reagan. Reagan had her own gaggle surrounding her, most of all that Simon Brooks. Brooks had a way of standing out; he was smart but he also ignored orders, two tendencies that generated a lot of attention for him, usually from Fairchild and Rosenski, but no one was immune. Not even herself. He knew more about how the Sleer AI worked than anyone else, at least in this unit, and she both hated and envied his relationship with the supercomputer, Genukh.

Now, with all of the principal players gone to fly their planes, she was forgotten. Skellington and Frost were not the only people left on the bridge, but they were the only ones Fairchild spoke to. Six new people had taken up watch posts around her, strangers all of them. Worst of all, Skellington was making the connections between data points and communicating them to Uncle faster than she could feed them to him. She already pointed out what they were investigating could not be Movi in origin and that was that. She knew more than she was allowed to talk about on duty; she knew how to drive a battler. And she was supposed to put up with 'stand there and look pretty?' Ha!

Even if she wanted to participate—she *did* want to—there were no more Ravens nor Broadswords on board the assault shuttle for her to take into the fight. They'd arrived with a full load of fighting machines and launched them all. The only thing left to do would be to deploy the weapon systems *Gauntlet* brought with her. In the meantime, she stayed at her post, pinging the sensors every now and then, updating the displays and tracking reports from the fighters' transponders. Comms could be interesting. Even engrossing. She began to understand why Brooks had chosen it as an MOS before being given the chance to change his specialty to piloting Ravens.

Besides managing the switchboard, she kept watching *Gauntlet*'s bandwidth for external comm systems. One aspect of the wider signal caught her attention and refused to let go. There was a powerful overlay, a regular pulse that she could monitor but not gain access to. Too big to be a Sleer fighting machine, but a signal from a fighting ship might be strong enough to have a similar output. She worked her memory, trying to remember what, if anything, aboard *Cyclops* might have been heavy enough of a power hog to do something similar.

A new signal brought her out of it. She recognized the voice instantly, but the tone froze her blood. "Commander! Rosenski is calling for additional help. The central core is blocked, they're holding their own against Sleer rollers but there are so many of them, they—"

Fairchild nodded. "I get the idea. Tell the flight deck to launch the reserve Broadswords."

"Yes, sir." She put the call in and felt her stomach turn as she passed on the response. "Flight officer reports all Broadswords are already committed." She waited for him to decide on the next course of action. A crazy idea took hold in her mind as she pored over his console. There were plenty of channels open; the battlers and Raven pilots were talking to each other. She widened the field of display and noticed that most of their drones were still on search patterns. They weren't evenly dispersed throughout the giant structure, either. Some were having trouble moving past wrecked sections and blocked conduits. She tapped experimentally and found they she could give new orders easily enough. Surely this situation warranted new orders?

"Commander Fairchild, I have an idea."

"Tell me."

"There are hundreds of drones still active inside this station. What if we—well, I—repurposed them into support platforms. If nothing else, it might muddle the Sleer units enough to distract them from hitting our soldiers." She blinked as she spoke the last line. Ten minutes ago she'd wanted to kill these people, and now they were part of her tribe. Strange. She'd never had this tendency to imagine death before meeting these humans.

"It's a good idea, but we don't have the range to give those orders in enough time to make it useful in real time."

She punched more studs, read the results. Even stabbed her finger at the plate. "We use that."

"How close is it to the unit you trained on?"

"Very close. It's a full console equivalent, but mobile. I can run to the core and give orders to the drones on the spot."

"I don't like—" Alarms buzzed and explosions rocked the grounded assault shuttle. "New contacts!" Skellington called out. "At least one hundred walkers with twenty or more rollers for support or command."

Fairchild put his hand on her shoulder. "Signal all gunnery teams to pick targets and fire at will."

"Yes, sir!" She followed orders. The chatter on the Raven and Browadsword command channels was getting worse, more desperate and less frequent. That couldn't be a good sign. She craned her head to catch sight of the status board near Fairchild's station. Every time she glanced over, there was one less green light. Too much red.

Fairchild frowned. Appraising her like an insect under a microscope. Wondering if trusting her was really the best of all possible choices. "If you die, I'm left without a comm officer."

"If I stay here, we could lose both squadrons and the shuttle!"

He glared for five seconds then bobbed his head once. "Fine. Go. Frost, track her progress. Ozawa, take over comms and tell Rosenski help is on the way!"

And just like that, she was off the bridge and into a place where she could do some real good. *Hang on, Dance, I'm coming.*

Grandpa Frost's voice shouted at her from a grill above. "Binil! Drop in four. Come on. Get with it."

"Copy that," Binil responded.

Getting decked out in the new gear felt like dressing in fine silks and linen. The UEF armorers took the idea from the combination fittings of Sleer battle dress. Detachable limbs and torso made it possible to combine various weapons, sensors, and defenses into a single coherent suit of protective armor.

But this wasn't Sleer armor. No skin-tight conductive layer and heavy exoskeleton for her. This was brand new stuff; the TAC-5P, the latest advance in personal protection from the UEF's labs. Lighter than aluminum and tougher than polycrystalline iron compounds, the suit provided the wearer with a self-contained environment, air scrubbers when one relied on the breathing filter, and a six-hour oxygen supply for when the scrubbers didn't suffice. It was fireproof and could sustain heavy heat damage without broiling the soldier within. There was even a ceramic layer bonded to the outer surface to resist laser attacks. Best of all, the faceplate included a fully functional HUD that was coded to the wearer's personal ID. No confusion, no passed signals, no mistaken identity on or off the battlefield. With all the bandwidth and abilities of the Sleer version.

Binil did a quick gear check: power pack, sidearm, helmet, comm. She still couldn't believe how light everything felt. Not as light as clothing, but it needed no more effort to use than a springtime outfit. A world's difference from the Sleer pilot's suit she'd worn previously. She thumbed a stud in the helmet's base and said, "Set!"

Frost shouted in her ears, "Good. Mount up for final drop prep!"

Se ducked out through the rear hatch and emerged into a vault; the red alert lights glowed above her as she followed the signs and dashed down three flights of stairs. Ideally, the bay was split level: Ravens in Battler mode launched from up top, and battlers dropped from the assault shuttle's belly. Even if the ship hadn't already been grounded, there wouldn't have been enough clearance to drop the non-transformable fighting machines. But her goal was the emergency drop ramp just below the engineering deck. *Garfield* had a similar arrangement, she remembered. Two more hatches and she saw the storage bays.

"Take the one on the right," Frost said. "The model in bay one has power plant issues. Bay 2 passed all its inspections."

"Is it loaded?"

"With gear and air, yes."

"What about weapons?"

"Not a chance. Move fast and stay out of sight. That's your weapons."

"No! Gah! Why?"

"Less talk, more drop prep, that's why."

She kept her mouth shut as she opened yet another hatch and found herself pressed up against a giant metal ankle.

Her ride was nothing like the Manticore. The BAT-FR-1B Lightning was a general-purpose battler, designed to be fast, light, and able to talk to any unit it needed to. Its head wasn't much to look at—a rotating dome enclosed by an armored shell, with plenty of external cameras, microphones, and other sensor systems. The booster pack was already bolted on, hanging like a backpack, too low to clear its ass completely. But she saw why it was placed that way—two telescoping comm masts were mounted inside it. Once raised, the sensor suite would have more than enough range to link up her displays with anything the Ravens or Broadswords carried. At the top of the pack were the real fun bits: sensor spoofers, emerging like stubby wings between the battler's shoulder blades. Once activated, it would be a pain and a half for any Sleer to try to locate her using electronic nets. Not as good as proper stealth tech, but it would do.

She spotted the recessed ladder and swung herself up, moving her hands and feet mechanically, precisely. The crazy thing was that even while this model seemed gigantic compared to herself, it was much smaller than the Broadswords or Ravens. The Lightning at its best was still only a little taller than a two-story house. Up near the head, she found an armored hatch, pulled it open, and dropped down into the machine's interior.

The battler's cockpit resembled a motorcycle's controls surrounded by a steel ball. Binil settled onto the saddle, stretching her legs and feet to cover the foot controls as her arms reached out to the directional handle. Throttle on the right, brakes on the left, her feet controlled the transmission, which meant she'd drive with her hands in flight mode and with her feet in Walker mode. Everything else was controlled by her HUD. There were ways to make anything happen in here, and she'd practiced all of them exhaustively.

Now it was show time.

Frost's voice pipped into her helmet. She never did get over the fact that it made it sound like the cranky old CPO was in the module with her, whispering into her ears. "Okay, Binil, let's take it from the top."

It was a challenge. She'd spent time in actual battlers, but the thinking went, "if the noncoms could teach Binil how to run the gear, then they could teach anyone anything." "Where are you sending me?"

"The derelict's interior."

Gah! Why did he have to be this way? "Why so vague? You can't just drop me into the middle of Maker knows what kind of environment."

"A drop trooper needs to be able to improvise. You won't always get the chance to scope out your target zone beforehand.

That said, it's obviously going to be the interior of this giant space station, so work with that."

Binil rose from her crouch and her hand went to her sidearm; an RMB-9 "Roomba" plasma pistol. Another weapon derived from Sleer tech, but nowhere near as powerful. The good news was that a single power pack could give up to twenty solid shots. The bad news was the phrase "up to." Holding down the trigger before release improved the efficacy of the bolt, but it sucked power like nothing else. Five maximum power bolts per pack. Maybe.

Reassured, she got back into position. "That's not even remotely true. There are always some clues. Topographic maps, weather predictions, sensors from orbit—"

"Not always. I'm uploading all the schematics we have from Rosenski's unit and the drones into your navigation computer. Set your long range navcom to use *Gauntlet* as a beacon. Drop in two minutes. Final equipment check. Go!"

Binil went. She'd drilled with Reagan for months with this moment in mind. She linked her HUD to the pod's sensor suite, trembling as the saddle activated beneath her. She twisted the hand and foot controls, satisfied she had their use memorized. The computers matched vectors and synched their systems. The drop ramp fell to the ground and her launch bay angled her battler toward it. She could see *everything*.

"Drop!"

A flick of her wrist and a nudge of her toe and the arming light flashed from green to yellow. A solid thump of her heels brought the action to a close. Her thumbs hit matching buttons on her handlebars, and the sign flashed an angry red. A klaxon screamed from above and behind, and the saddle fell out from under her, just enough that her ass left the seat and never quite caught up to it. The launch platform bounced and lurched and fell away from the shuttle that ostensibly carried them both. She flew, nearly tumbled, and landed on the station's deck with a whump. She angled her body, brought the battler to a run, and looked for her fastest route to the destination.

So many things to deal with, but at least she didn't have to fly this thing. She kept up her speed, avoiding the crossfire between the attacking rollers and *Gauntlet*'s gunners. She passed through the blast doors and slowed her approach. Now things got complicated.

A beep in her ear and Frost's face popped up on her HUD. "Binil, slow down. Find a hiding spot and start collecting those drones while I find you a relatively free-fire route."

Binil eyed her controls, did some mental calculations, and saw that her CPO was right. The space between the blast doors and the central core was littered with wrecked Sleer machinery and installations. Whatever happened, the Sleer weren't known for being especially careful with their aim. She adjusted the throttle to slow her pace. An external camera noticed a pair of smoking rollers to the right and just above her own. Spherical and simple, their levitating turrets were strewn around them like forgotten accessories.

She flexed her limbs and sent a command through her HUD. The comm masts rose out of her battler's booster pack and started pinging the drones. As she watched, the display green-dots appeared while the unit counter rose in number. The problem was that the number was rising much faster than the display could show her the positions of the drones themselves. She sent them a command, using the nearest drones as amplifiers to boost the signal. She needed every drone she could possibly—

A screech from behind got her attention. She swung her machine body, planted her feet and felt her teeth clack together as her battler was roundly kicked by a walking Sleer mech. She'd never seen this type before, on thick legs, with short barrels jutting from the cube's face. No extra turrets, no nothing. The stubby nozzle at the bottom of its "face" swiveled and opened up, tagging her with red beams of energy. She dodged, rolled, and ducked behind an obstacle...which turned out to be another of the walking horrors. The kicking continued, rattling her until she finally dropped into a fighting stance and returned the favor. She ignited the booster pack, jumped into the air, and came down on top of the enemy machine. The walkers were apparently fragile; the plates burst apart, leaving nothing but a crushed hulk.

She examined her status board and found the shots had either glanced off her armor or missed. Very little damage. She stepped away from the wreck and zoomed in with her external camera. "No body."

"Repeat, Binil. Didn't copy that."

"I said there's no body inside the machine that attacked me."

"Rosenski is calling those walkers 'Emus.' Don't ask me why. Low-power lasers, but there's a lot more of them than there are of us, so watch your ass."

She checked her bearings, noticed that she'd be collecting drone signals for some time yet, and decided. "I need altitude."

"Belay that shit right now, Royal!" He had a point. Altitude would make her a giant target. But she needed to get above the wreckage to see anything worth talking about. She could sort through the collected feeds from the drones, but there were more than six hundred of the silly things and all were trying to talk to her battle computer.

"Can you vector me to a relatively safe position, Chief?"

A moment passed, then another. Droplets of sweat tried to fall into her eyes. Damn the fancy new helmet, anyway. They needed to work on the air circulation.

"Agreed. There's a structure about three klicks away from

you. Light your boosters and lift to an altitude of twenty meters, that's two-zero meters. Come to course zero six-five."

"Roger that. Jets active!"

She throttled up, brought her feet in, pushed her hands away, and the machine came alive around her. Arms and legs extended as the com masts retracted. She flared the pack's jets and her battler's feet left the deck, sending up a cloud of dust and debris. She prodded the controls, following instructions. Her threat indicator still pinged now and then, and she got into the habit of adjusting her course to avoid staying in any one opponent's line of sight for too long.

She found the tower...or rather the tower found her. A cylinder jutting up from the station floor, far taller than two-zero meters. She opened the throttle, blasting her booster until its jets glowed red with excess heat, watching her display as it showed her a featureless wall of metal and carbon fibers. After what felt like an eon, she spied the roof, a featureless expanse whose function she couldn't fathom. She killed her vertical velocity, allowed the momentum of her flight to carry her to the landing zone, and killed the power. She dropped onto the roof and bounced, tripping over her metal feet and scraping metal fingers against the surface as she skidded to a halt. She panted in fear and anger, her camera display showing her the long drop she'd barely avoided.

"Down and clear!" She swept the area with her sensors, finding Dance and the rest of the Gauntlet's soldiers kilometers away. *Let's see those remotely controlled walking nuisances reach me up here!*

She raised her comm masts and got back to business. Now she really could look at the entire compartment. The ceiling was less than one hundred feet above her, the floor nearly three times that distance. She stood close to the tower's edge, adjusting her distance lenses to pick out details. "Frost! I'm on target. What's next?"

The response was garbled and distorted, a host of partial words and dropped syllables. She repeated her question and got the same answer. Okay, she was on her own. Apparently, she could either see everything and work the drone signals, or talk to a human being, but not both at the same time. She began to regret using this brand new mech suit and then remembered that if she wasn't here, she'd be stuck on her bridge, worth even less.

The transponder codes were in her computer's memory, so finding the Ravens and Broadswords was her first task. The core was easy to locate, a massive cylinder connecting the roof and floor several klicks away. She tried one filter after another, experimenting to bring out the greatest level of detail while still being able to zoom out for a wider view.

Finally! There! They were... Oh no...

Gauntlet's troops were surrounded. Stuck on a loading platform, almost literally sandwiched between the rollers and Emus, who'd chased them into the core. And more Sleer units were emerging from the core's interior. The fact that the humans were punching and stomping their ways through the crowd of Sleer units told her they had used up the last of their ammo. She triggered the laser rangefinder: 7.37 klicks away. She could fly there in minutes, but where would she land? And what would she do when she arrived? She had no weapons, and...

She was a twit. Of course she had weapons—she just needed to give them targets. She leaned forward and brought up her tactical HUD, telling the battle computer to assign the drone locations to a separate overlay. Of the six hundred odd drones still functional, nearly one hundred were outside her command range with no way to return. Two hundred more were on their way, but with indeterminate ETAs. That left three hundred or so to work with as an ersatz aerial bombardment force.

A flash of light and a burst of smoke as an explosion erupted against the far side of the tower. Then another, and a third. The Sleer were shooting at her. She retreated to the center of the platform, expecting it was the safest place to stand as she worked, but she was running low on time. Groups of drones flew in from all directions, hovering near the ceiling as she put them into standby mode. More were homing in on her signal, making their way back home through open ventilation shafts, transfer conduits, and supply corridors. She checked her tactical screen…more than two hundred arrived already.

More explosions from below. She felt the roof slide a few feet to one side and balked, wondering why her balancers were giving her trouble so soon. Then she checked her artificial horizon and saw the truth—the tower was beginning to lean a degree to one side. She pinged a group of nearby drones, set them to orbit the tower at varying altitudes, and watched in horror as they revealed the truth. A group of twenty rollers were clumped around the structure's base, blowing all manner of hell out of it with their turret weapons. Twenty rollers, sixty turrets; nearly two hundred weapons in all.

The ground shifted again, and Binil realized it was time to leave. And there was only one place to go.

CHAPTER 24

THE WALL of Sleer walkers rushed the Ravens.

Dances With Gears Reagan shoved her Raven to the right, dodging a blast of energy from a nearby roller. The Sleer machine was firing from behind a row of Emus, all legs and cubes. The primitive walkers's weaponry sucked, but the attackers had a pattern. A few Emus would rush forward at a single Raven, then, while they kept that Raven busy, two or three rollers would fire their laser turrets to disable it. They'd used the technique repeatedly. She bounced her plane into a fighting stance, took a running start, and swung her empty gun pod like a club. The weapon connected with the Emu's legs, cracking the joints. She avoided the falling enemy then stomped on its body. She kicked apart plates and moorings and zoomed her external camera onto the wreckage. No bodies. Nothing alive in the damn things at all.

"Radio controlled," she murmured.

A voice in her comm. "Say again, Reagan."

"I said the walkers are remotely piloted drones. No Sleer inside them. They must be running them for support."

"So noted, keep punching them!"

She did. Reagan couldn't even recognize the voice. Brooks, maybe Rosenski. They sounded similar. Hell, over the comm, everyone sounded similar. The transceiver distorted every speaker's voice just enough that after a while, tones and phonemes morphed together into a shapeless mass of sound. One more reason why radio protocol demanded that the speaker identify themselves and their intended listener.

They'd been at this for what felt like days. The ammo was long gone, but they weren't done yet. The Broadswords had one advantage in that way: forearm-mounted particle beams. They grouped together in a firing line, popping rollers and Emus to their rear, keeping the field of attackers away even as waves of walkers kept approaching. The Ravens lacked energy weapon in Battler mode, which meant that individual Raven pilots had to clear a space around their planes, transform back to walker, and pop-up to attack using their forward mounted lasers against an opponent. Two pilots had tried it early in the fight. Both paid with the loss of their ships and lives.

The Sleer had also learned a valuable lesson from this fight. They'd started by packing the Emus into tight squares, trying to run the humans over with sheer numbers. It worked, too, until they figured out that whenever a walker exploded, it took two or three of its neighbors with them. They'd spaced out their attacks after that, but even if the walkers weren't shooting at them, even if running and flying kicks and stomps were all they brought to the fight, there were too many of them. It was a fight of attrition, and the Ravens were spent. Swinging their GU-22s like clubs was a one technique, but after a half dozen connects, the gun pods snapped in half, useless even as clubs. Hand-to-hand was all they had left.

The result was a near stalemate. Walkers shoved the Broadswords backwards and blocked the Ravens' progress toward the central core lift, and the rollers shot lasers through gaps in the Sleer lines. Reagan and Brooks fought side by side, timing their attacks to pound their targets with double kicks or double punches. Flashes of old school hand to hand combat flashed through Reagan's mind, images of bloody stumps and torn limbs distracting her from the issue at hand. With metal limbs and iron bodies, the grind was like watching battle tanks from the Second World War bump each other like amusement park bumper cars, a dent here, a ding there. The saving grace was that the Sleer walkers had a fraction of the human machines' durability. Now and then a roller poked a turret in one of their faces and they worked together to pull the weapons out of shape and shove a metal arm into the steel ball's works. Not an easy task. Rollers were every bit as well armored as Ravens.

Dance toggled her mic to Brooks's comm. "We could swap to walker and jump over these yahoos," she said.

A click and a squawk from the comm. They were losing each other. Probably the Sleer were figuring out how to jam their comms one frequency at a time. "We can't lift the Broadswords," he said. "Too heavy."

"Maybe we wouldn't have to." She switched to the command channel. "Nightmare Leader, any chance of additional help out here?"

"I'm not sure. I got an update from *Gauntlet* a few minutes ago, but it was so damn scrambled I could barely hear it. Something about drones."

"What kind of help is that? The swarm doesn't carry weapons. They barely carry themselves. Very short range, very—"

"GAUNTLET LIGHTNING TO NIGHTMARE GROUP, I NEED CLEARANCE TO LAND OR WE ALL DIE!"

Every pilot winced as the blast came through their comms,

with the volume turned up so loud it might cause ear damage. A young, female voice. More interested in getting results than following rules.

Dance and Brooks shared a moment of intuition. "Binil? Is that you?"

Rosenski's voice on the wide channel: "Binilsanetanja-malala, why are you away from your post?"

No more shouting. Binil had apparently realized her mistake and dropped the volume on her mic. "I am seven klicks outbound, located at the top of a cylindrical structure. My wide band comms are active and I am collecting drones for suicide attacks, but I'm pinned down by enemy fire. I can jump to your position, but you have to make room for me or I'll land on top of you," she said.

"You heard her," Frau Butcher said. "Broadswords and Ravens, make some room for the newbie. I'll bet you anything she'll make a giant entrance."

Brooks and got his mech's hands under the "waist" of a nearby Emu. Dance leaned in and took the other side and on the count of three, they both heaved the battle walker over their shoulders. The Emu flailed, fell against the roller that was using it for cover, and toppled three other Sleer walkers against their neighbors.

Dance rushed into the gap, followed by Brooks. "Get up here, you battler bums. We made an opening! Brooks, swap to Walker mode—now!" Dance's plane transformed and she lit the jets, rising twenty feet above the fray. She toggled the forward lasers, picking a target and shooting in rapid sequence. The Emu went down, its cabin popping into shreds. Its neighbor tried to sprint to meet the new threat but tripped, crashing to the ground as both its legs snapped beneath it. Another laser blast to the now helpless walker, another brief explosion.

Her threat detector bellowed, and her plane shook. Shots

appeared from below and behind her. Sparks exploded from her display, and her plane's power plant sputtered. She switched back to battler and felt a solid contact as something shoved her plane. The power system recovered and she trained her cameras on the breakout to see Brooks's walker-mode Raven take a turret blast in the canopy.

"Simon!" Brooks's Raven fell, its nose crashing against the deck, the clear canopy a shattered wreck. She jumped, stumbled, and fell, managing to fall onto her Raven's hands and knees, sheltering Brooks's cockpit with its torso. The fray was still going on around them and her cameras showed three Broadswords leaping over the pair of them and pushing the Sleer back into the central core's lift. Hey, progress.

Dance popped her pilot's harness, her only thought to get out of her plane and pull her friend from his wreck. There were ways to do that, but not enough time. The simple way was also the safest. She scrambled out of her couch, pulled a lever, and heard a resounding pop as a pair of locking bolts gave away. She slid behind her couch, pulled the rear panel open, and slid into the crawlspace that led behind her cockpit into her battler's torso. Another lever and combination punch into a keypad and a loud buzzer went off as the emergency hatch opened. She braced her legs, lowered herself through the hatch, and saw Brooks standing on the nose of his plane. His helmet was off, his flight suit ripped, but he seemed functional. He was at least ten feet below where she could reach, even if she hung down by her feet.

Fine. She pulled herself back inside, tore an emergency ladder from the wall, and slid it into position. Still not long enough to reach.

He stuck her head out and yelled, "Climb, you bitch!" She backed out of the way, huddling against the wall, knowing that Brooks had done this sort of thing before. All that tunnel jumping back on the Earth Battle Ring. She saw a pair of hands reach up into the crawlspace and she lunged, pulling him up with their combined implant strength. In a moment, he was huddled next to her, both gasping.

"Does whatever a Spider-Brooks does," he said, grinning.

She pulled off her helmet and kissed him hard, tasting blood and fear. Memories of every night they'd spent together in the past two years flooded her brain. Only a Herculean effort forced her back to the moment and the imminent danger they were still in.

"Come on, Spider-Brooks. Close the hatch and come forward."

"It's a one-seater. No room for me up front."

"Squeeze in, son. I can't close the hatch if you're in the way."

"Fine. Put your damn helmet back on, Lieutenant."

"Sir, yes, sir, Lieutenant Genius. Where's yours?"

"It did its job. Now it's garbage."

They both managed to fit as the hatch closed and Dance strapped in, handling her controls to bounce her mech back to its feet. But the rescue had taken a toll on the machinery. She heard the works stripping teeth from gears and smelled wiring running hot. No smoke in the cabin yet, but that was almost guaranteed now. She peripherally saw Brooks reach past her ear to grab a spare headset. He flipped a bank of switches as he pulled it on. He was tapping into her comm feed so he could follow the chatter. She toggled the feed. "Leader, I have Brooks. He's fine, the little creep."

"Good. Gratz, Reagan, you and Brooks are now Section 3 Leaders."

"Copy that." Her ladar blipped and the threat detector alerted her to a flying menace approaching from behind. She turned her plane back towards the lift and froze as she tried to figure out what her displays were showing her. At first, she thought it was a suicide jumper, a Sleer in heavy Defender armor who'd taken a flying leap from a high building right onto her battler. Then she saw the details—a flaming rocket booster pack, square fingers, and what looked like a pair of giant antenna streaming out from the dome-like head. She reached down, triggered the tactical display, and watched as her plane identified it with *Gauntlet*'s transponder code.

Then it clicked. It was the spare Lightning the shuttle carried in the hold; no weapons, but a dump truck full of electronic goodies. She toggled the open channel and shouted, "She's going to ground hard. Make room, people, make room!"

Binil's Lightning grounded with a spray of spent fuel and multiple thuds as the battler landed, bounced, and nearly tripped. Dance leaned into her controls, using her battler's mass to grab the Lightning by its shoulders and hold it, steadying the smaller machine's landing.

"Drone delivery officer reporting for duty," Binil called. She even raised her battler's right arm and managed a small wave.

"Where the hell have you been?" demanded Reagan.

Rosenski's voice held a fine line between disgust and relief. "Not now, Dance. Binil, what did you bring us?"

"Drones! Lots and lots of them. Keep them off me and I'll thin the Sleer's numbers for you."

"Acknowledged. You heard her, people. Form a defensive ring. Keep the rollers at bay!"

Binil maneuvered her battler to take advantage of the shelter Dance's plane offered. Slowly but surely, the rest of the squadron formed up. Dance signaled to Janus, and together they hefted Brooks's wrecked plane and tossed it into the lift, then occupied the new space. Ravens formed a wall around the Lightning, and the Broadswords pressed into the opening Dance and Brooks had already created.

Above them, countless drones congregated and assembled into distinct groups. Binil's voice sounded distant over the comm: "Leader, which direction do we go?"

"Into the core lift."

"Roger that. Everyone stand by."

Reagan kept her cameras pointed up, the feed panning and stopping whenever it detected motion. Couples grew into triplets, forming long chains of flying discs passing by, orbiting the central core. Suddenly a pair of drones dive bombed one of the Emus. Nothing exploded but the first drone knocked a top mounted entry hatch loose then its fellow drove into the cabin. The walker kept going until a third drone hit the same walker, which finally shattered from the impact. The walker dropped in place and Dance heard a girlish squeal of triumph.

Dance nodded to herself. Binil was finding her range and timing.

Her next attack used three drones from the get-go and worked flawlessly; the first two breaking through the armor and the third flying into the gap, destroying the mechanism. Again and again, triplets of remotely piloted vehicles dropped walkers, giving the *Gauntlet* soldiers a chance to maneuver.

The Broadswords found their opportunity, surging into the cracks left by the downed vehicles and tearing new holes in the Sleer lines. Particle beams ripped through walkers and roller alike as Binil used her unorthodox but effective attacks to drop more of the Sleer units. Soon, team *Gauntlet* was fully inside the lift, shooting or shoving remaining Sleer units aside. The rollers saw the writing on the proverbial wall and retreated, leaving their robotic compatriots to fend for themselves.

Binil twirled her battler around, found a heavy stud on the wall, and punched it. The doors closed, gears grinding noisily, and the lift started down while the Broadswords and remaining Ravens clobbered the few remaining Emus trapped with them.

"That was slick AF. Even you can't hate her for that," Dance said.

Brooks's voice came back, crackling with static. "I don't hate her. I just don't need an annoying little sister running around while I'm working, that's all."

"Especially when little sister is always demanding your girlfriend's attention, right?"

Brooks grumbled something and she ignored it. She wasn't quite sure how the three of them had formed a thing with herself at the center. There were times when Brooks and Binil enjoyed each other's company, talking about technical matters well into the night. As Binil had taken more opportunities to qualify as a UEF soldier on her own, that had changed, and Dance didn't know why or how to repair the growing split. She was afraid that Simon had started taking his call sign a little too seriously. Smart as he was, it was easy to forget that Fairchild had saddled him with the name "Genius" because of repeated fuck-ups.

Rosenski moved her Raven to the center of the group, angling the head cameras downward to look at the Cycomm's battler. The Lightning was at least eight feet shorter than the Raven, which gave the impression of a parent questioning a child.

"What took you so long, Lieutenant?" Rosenski asked. Dance thought she heard a smile in her voice. Weird. Frau Butcher was not known for being a happy sort of person. Good to know that she was capable of being relieved they weren't all going to die on the same day.

"You needed help and I realized I could take control of the drones to attack the Sleer Emus and rollers.

"Clever girl."

"Fucking A. That was good. I was starting to think we'd never get out of there," Dance said.

"Figuring out the pulse transmitter's parents was easy. Getting Fairchild's permission to join you out here was far more difficult."

Brooks tapped Dance on the shoulder. She logged him into the comm net. "Good work, Binil. I owe you one."

"Aw, thank you."

Rosenski concurred. "It was good work. Except now we have no ammo and no more drones."

"But we have something better. A way to disarm the comm net the Sleer ship is using to run those assault walkers. I figured out the Sleer were using a crazy type of pulse transmitter on their *Zalamb* scout ship to manage the walking units. I have a way to disarm the comm net the Sleer ship is using to run those assault walkers. I just need to get close enough to the core to use it."

Rosenski laughed, erupting into long loud peals of pure joy. Binil had never imagined the tall redhead could even react like that. When she found her voice, she said, "Outstanding,. Binil! If I could climb out of my ship and into yours, I'd kiss your whole face. All right, Nightmares, here's what we do..."

CHAPTER 25

ZOLIK DECIDED he was on the verge of a breakdown.

He wasn't even sure what a breakdown was. A term the mammals had come up with for a situation where the emotions ran wild, brought on by stress and circumstance, he thought. Leave it to the mammals to imagine a word to describe what for every other species was the state of a normal life. One was born, one struggled to live, one struggled to thrive, one struggled to be of use to one's nest, then one died. The emotions were not so wild or reckless as that. But for the first time, he thought he could understand why a human might go insane.

Nothing had gone to plan since they'd embarked on their so-called science experiment. They'd received orders from the high command on New Home. Simple. Kill the trespassing humans and destroy the anomalous space station, then continue on their assigned patrol route. Simple. Now more than a third of his Defenders were dead, they were no closer to defeating the primates and their insane fighting machines, and Metzek was...

"Zolik! I have it. A new plan that will fix everything."

Zolik flexed his toes and grabbed the air. "Tell me, Ship Master."

"What should have been a short, brutal campaign has turned into a fiasco."

"Yes, my lord."

"We have too few units to achieve proper force superiority, even with the Kizarts."

"Yes, my lord."

"So, we must cut our losses and do what we came here to do—"

Maker, finally. "Thank you, my lord. I'll send word to—"

"We need to save the forest."

"We...what?"

Metzek used the console to project a view of the derelict's central core. "By routing the affected area through these projectors, we can alter the field the fold drive generates. Then we feed this equation into the *Zalamb*'s drive units..."

The XO held still, giving all the attention his Commander's ideas warranted. Almost nothing. He checked his personal display, looking through the notifications he'd been receiving for hours. His engineers were clear; they needed days of work to rig the core tap to detonate, and he'd ordered them to abandon the order in favor of bringing more Kizarts online and into the comm network. The bulk of the rollers and the functional walking assault units were tied down, trying to herd the humans into a killing zone they couldn't evade. And the human assault shuttle had managed to defend itself against the few rollers he'd been able to spare from the main attack. His now minimally crewed scout vessel was at its limit, serving as both a central processing unit and a grand communication hub for other Sleer units. Zolik wondered about that. No other units were scheduled to pass within five light years, and even if there were, there was no guarantee help would be available.

And now his ship master had apparently taken leave of his

senses. "My lord, this is an excellent idea. But we still need to manage the primates."

"Bah. They ruin everything, don't they? What happened to the fusion plant? Weren't they consumed as planned?"

"That plan unfortunately collapsed soon after I ordered its implementation. They've managed to mimic our success with the Kizarts by bringing their own drones inside the structure and used them as bombs."

"Clever. We must get rid of them as soon as possible. We can't save the forest with them flying into our efforts every few minutes."

"I quite agree. Sir, I believe it would be wise to transfer your command back to the *Zalamb* and run all operations from there."

"Abandon this unique zoological and archeological find? Are you mad?"

"Not at all. But think about it. We can't use our implants to run this ancient vessel, but we can use the equipment and weapons aboard the scout ship to destroy the invading shuttle and then eliminate the remainder of the human fighting machines."

"Very well. While you organize that, I'll check on the forest. Make sure it's not burning down."

"Very good, my lord."

Zolik took a moment to reorganize the comm net, creating a new channel for the top-tier comm and assigning Metzek to it. Anything he sent would now go directly to Zolik's own channel and no one else. From now on, the CO's orders would only be enacted if Zolik ordered it. Not exactly how things were supposed to be done, but it would give Zolik the freedom to actually complete the mission.

Zolik called his bridge officers to the command center and brought out updated displays. "The primates have split their groups. We expect they have minimal crew aboard the attack shuttle they arrived in, and that all their effective fighters are now in the central core—along with what remains of their remote drone force. My plan is to bring all our forces back aboard our ship and use the Kizart as mobile bombs."

"They aren't wired with explosives," the Great Servant of Defense pointed out.

"They don't need to be. Overload the forward laser and it will explode on its own."

"I wish we'd know about that earlier."

"I did, but it's not the type of assault one uses when Atzhans are mixed into the main group."

"Fair enough. What do we do about Metzek?"

Zolik looked over the officer's shoulder. Metzek was waiting for the lift, giving orders over the comm, unaware he was speaking to no one but Zolik. "Let him have his precious forest."

It occurred to Ray Fairchild that he might not be ready for the big time.

He pushed the thought away, dismissing it as an attack of nerves. A momentary doubt of himself and his abilities. He'd taken the crew of *Gauntlet* this far, and he'd see them through to the end. Of the mission. Not the end of their lives.

He knew what this was, too: his subconscious punishing him for a moment of self-perceived cowardice the last time he'd come close up and personal with a Sleer attack force. Brooks and Rosenski had hidden in the Earth Ring, intending to use it against the encroaching Sleer fleet, and Fairchild had led his Hornet squadron into the Sleer structure to extract them. The situation went south and *Ascension* was forced to flee the battle, leaving the humans on their own in the face of a Sleer invasion force. They'd done what they could: equip Brooks and Rosenski to conduct their spy mission while the Hornets held off the invaders for their escape. It worked. The Hornets fought to the last round of ammo, and then Fairchild chose defeat over suicide. He'd ordered his pilots to surrender, and Fleet Master Nazerian sent them back down the spoke. Deep down, he'd never forgiven himself that decision. Maybe they all could have dug in together and changed the outcome? Maybe anything.

And here it was again. The concern that he wasn't as smart as he thought he was, and had bitten off more than he could chew. He'd never liked that turn of phrase, but now he recognized its raw power. So stuffed you couldn't close your jaws. Extended beyond your means. Swollen as a python digesting a kid. Yeah.

It hadn't even been necessary. He'd listened to Brooks, who'd been certain that they were missing out on a golden opportunity. He should have patted the precocious lieutenant on the head, taken down his report, and sent it up the chain of command. Pass it to someone who was genuinely paid to think about bigger matters than he was. Katsev to Rojetnick to Eisenberg. Maybe even to Hendricks. Someone might have decided to act on the intelligence.

But no. He'd taken Simon at his word, decided on his own that it was worth going to see, and now here they were. Investigating a fascinating archeological find that seemed to be in the process of finding them as well.

But their opponents were nowhere near as dangerous as those who'd kicked Hornet squadron off the Earth Ring. That was what made all this so annoying. The fact that there had to be a way of succeeding, if only he could find it. The world in front of him was different than it had been when he was linked to his Raven's cockpit. Battle tactics when you managed a flight of aircraft were necessarily different than his current situation.

His ship was grounded, the turret weapons were keeping the few rollers and their Emus support at bay, but he'd committed his mobile units to a fight he could barely manage.

He stared at the tactical display. The Ravens and Broadswords had disappeared into the central core. Binil, the pet Cycomm, had done herself proud with her idea of using the drones as ersatz missiles, but she'd gone through half her supply just getting her unit away from the fight.

Now what?

"Mr. Ozawa. Anything on comms?"

"Negative, sir. There's mountains of obstructions between our position and the fighters. Radio reception is spotty, and laser induction is unavailable until we can re-establish line of sight."

That figured. It also didn't tell him anything he didn't already know. He turned his crash couch to face his chief. "Grandpa? If you have any ideas, now is the time."

"I got that alien kid out to the correct position without killing herself or any of our people. What else do I need to do today?" Frost asked.

"Thanks for that, Chief. Skull?"

"I'm listening to their chatter. It's on a very strange wavelength—nothing I've heard from a Sleer vessel comes close."

"I thought comms were down."

"They are. I'm relaying the command channel through the comm antennae on Binil's Lightning and using the drones to boost the signal."

"Show me. Ozawa, put the command channel on speaker." The bridge immediately filled with the pilots' calls and responses. It took some time for them to match the tactical displays with what they were hearing. The Tactical Officer kept up with the new information as he listened to the broadcasts. The humans were making their ways deeper into the giant structure. Binil was the focus of the effort, as she carried the remaining drones with her. The drones never stopped feeding data to *Gauntlet*'s computers, which only enhanced the review of the station's interior.

"Skull, tell me more about the signals you found," Uncle said.

Skellington sent data to the central display. "This narrow band is our standard comm signal. This narrow band inside it is our fighter comm signal. And this," he said, overlaying a fat band of data over the others, "is what I can't figure out. It's a very fast pulse pattern. It's not UEF or Sleer. I have no idea where it came from, but it started about the same time the walkers starting showing up."

"A carrier signal for drone direction?"

"I believe so. I think we can get Binil to help triangulate it."

That was good enough for Ray Fairchild, and it gave him an idea. He toggled the intercom. "Engineering, keep the reactor warmed up. We may have to move the ship very quickly, very soon."

CHAPTER 26

SARA ROSENSKI FELT her heart beating in her mouth.

The lift doors opened to show them another broken landscape filled with ruined machinery. Even without the drones fanning out to map the site, she could pick out differences in the compartment's design. This level was a jungle of steel and circuits. Tall towers bearing a wide variety of equipment rose all around them, haphazardly placed to her sense of symmetry, but plainly part of a complicated mechanism. Cables as thick as her legs ran throughout the endless colonnade, acting like rope bridges between the cylinders. For a moment she felt that it was a jungle, a place where ancient civilizations rose, thrived, then fell, crumbled into bones and dust, consumed by the remains of their environment. She couldn't help but feel agoraphobic as she led the squadron out, ordering points and cover positions.

She talked herself down. *It's not you, it's the implants. They're flaking out somehow. The whole squadron is being affected. Brooks pointed that out before we left Great Nest. It's all in your head.* The little voice in her head might not be real, but faulty implants were absolutely having a bad effect on everyone who had them. She shuddered to think what Valri Gibb and

Frances Underhill were going through on Great Nest. They surely weren't immune to the problems. On the other hand, they weren't under this kind of stress, either. Or were they?

No. Office jobs weren't like combat, no matter what the psych majors said. Just the same, she kept her hands on her plane's controls to keep them from shaking.

"Gauntlet actual to Nightmare leader."

When Uncle's voice came through, Rosenski's pulse blasted into her ears like she'd been caught doing something wrong. Like training Brooks to believe that the UEF wasn't nearly as honorable as he thought it was. Like agreeing to be The Butcher's minion and taking on secret side hustles without knowing exactly who she was working for or why.

She inhaled, held it, spoke normally. "Nightmare Leader, go ahead."

"Skull's detected a narrow-band comm frequency with a unique pulse pattern. Get a fix on it and capture or destroy the source. It might well be the transmitter the Sleer are using to run the Emus."

"Copy that. Binil, are you seeing that?"

"I'm not sure. Oh! Yes. Uhm. Hmmmm..."

"Talk to me, Royal."

"Uhhhhh...negative, Leader. This is beyond me."

Typical. Okay, time to get weird. "Brooks, is Dance still carrying you?"

Brooks's voice sounded hollow, like he was talking through a tube. "That's affirmative, Leader."

"All right then. All pilots ground and freeze. Be alert for hostile units. Dance, chuck your boy out and let him get into Binil's ship. On the boost, people!"

She swept her cameras across the horizon. No heat signatures, but plenty of motion. Pings and pops, blips that appeared briefly on her display then vanished. She couldn't even update her tactical with the data; there was too little of it, and dropping to the lower compartment had apparently killed their connection to *Gauntlet*'s computer. Was this level a proper assembly area? She remembered similar areas on board Earth's battle ring —automated assembly towers that built heavy assault walkers and delivered them to storage areas. They'd only seen the one, but knowing there were thousands of similar assembly lines made her skin crawl. For all she knew, Grossusk and Moruk had cranked up the lines to over-capacity, the better with which to arm all the Sleer on board. Millions, possibly billions of them.

On her screen, Dance's Battler-mode Raven extended an arm to the shoulder of Binil's Lightning. A figure climbed out of one machine and slid down the raised limb to drop into an open hatch in the other. Hatches closed, the battlers separated.

"Brooks, Binil, you getting settled?" she asked.

The two spoke over each other but answered in the affirmative. She wished again that the two of them weren't always fighting over Reagan's attention. "Remember, ladies, you're both pretty. Just get the job done."

"Yes, ma'am," Brooks answered.

Skull's voice on the command channel: "Leader, the signals are most powerful along a bearing of one-one-five relative. If your drone feeds are accurate, there's a great deal of motion around you."

"Acknowledged, *Gauntlet*. Moving to investigate. Janus, you're on point."

"Roger that."

Brooks settled in as best he could. The Lightning was smaller than the ancient Challenger he'd piloted on South Pico Island on *Ascencion's* launch day, and not built for a crew of two.

However, it could accommodate a passenger better than Dance's Raven could. Binil's control saddle split to reveal a jump seat, complete with harness and a pivoting control arm built into the base. When they were done, Binil's seat adjusted to the left and Brooks's to the right. His was smaller, and he'd bounce around more violently than she during maneuvers, but at least they could both manage the controls.

"Okay," he said. "You drive, I'll run the sensors."

"Why?"

"Because my MOS says I run the sensors."

"I've been driving *and* running the sensors since I walked this mech off *Gauntlet*'s drop bay," she said. He was pissing her off. Her face was darkening, a network of brown and gray stripes giving her a racoon eyes-like effect. What Dance called her war paint. Part of him didn't care, even while the more responsible part of his brain realized that he really was here to help her manage her work, not the other way around. He hated the situation; it reminded him that he'd fucked up in his Raven one time too many.

Rosenski's voice cut the argument short. "What did I say earlier about getting the job done?"

"Yes, Ma'am," Brooks answered. Brooks forced himself to remember where he was. "I'll run the comm network and the drones. You drive and run the tactical board."

She relaxed and her war paint dulled to her normal skin tones. Then she pulled a helmet from behind her seat and thrust it at him. "Agreed." She pivoted the mech and drove it forward, keeping them in the center of the protective formation the others created around them. Broadswords ahead and behind, Ravens in the center.

He sealed the helmet and brought up his HUD, punching controls to synch his feed with the rest of the squadron's. "Now if we could just get Genukh to weigh in on how to manage these yobos, we could blow this hot dog stand and be on our way," he groused.

"I'm sure that Dance could figure something out if you let her alone for five minutes." Binil said.

Brooks pulled more data from the feed and sent it to the tactical display. Rosenski gave orders, fanning the squadron out to cover their flanks.

Janus was being his usual depressingly surly self, answering in clipped tones and monosyllables. He'd been a completely different person when they first met. Nothing had really changed except the implants. They were all showing their wear. Another reason to get out of here and get back to the Sleer AI they'd come to rely on.

But to do that, Brooks needed to figure out the weird little relationship he'd formed with Binil…one that had Dance between them. "You do get that you and I have completely different relationships with her, right?"

"Do you think so?" Binil snorted.

Rosenski's voice on comm: "None of the Sleer we've spotted seem to want to engage, which is strange after they nearly pummeled us to scrap earlier. Binil, use the drones to get a location on those signal pulses. Five klicks minimum distance between positions."

"Copy that. I'll bump them up against the bulkheads," Binil said. She turned to Brooks. "Or would you like to do that part, Mr. Genius?"

"I got it. But I acknowledge that you're perfectly capable of carrying out the order."

He didn't understand why he usually felt compelled to be an ass to her. The truth was, she'd folded herself into the requirements of the new job nicely. Grown into the tight corners like a plant. She used to have real problems making herself understood, hyper-fixating on points of order or weird details. She didn't do that anymore. Hell, she wasn't even aware that she didn't do it anymore. "You don't know that you don't," he murmured.

Far above them, the drones split into three groups and carried out instructions, changing their flight patterns to three points of an equilateral triangle. It would take some time before they arrived at their new positions. In the meantime, the Raven pilots moved through the metal jungle, with the Broadswords acting as escorts.

"I think we're attracted to different things about her," she offered. "I like her mind; you like her origins, her construction. How she's put together. I can't say I don't understand that, but it doesn't..."

"It doesn't turn you on," he said. "That's fine. Attraction is weird. Even when it's obvious. And it's not always."

"What attracts you, then, Lt. Genius?"

"You want to do this now?"

"You brought it up."

"It's the way she smells," he admitted.

"She doesn't have a smell," Binil contradicted. "The launch bay has a smell. The bridge has a smell. And the engine room—those have smells. Maybe she does smell, but I don't notice it. I notice her voice. It's like...a soft warm comforter, all over me. A warm feeling. She makes me feel safe when she speaks. No human ever made me feel that way. No Cycomm either, for that matter."

"Wait. No *human*?"

"No."

"What the hell are we talking about?" he demanded.

"I'm talking about Genukh. The Malkah. Aren't you...?" Her eyes opened wide. "You mean Dance! You're in love with her. I knew it."

"That obvious?"

"The whole squadron knows it. When you're in the same room, you stutter and she drops things. Then you hold hands and you both calm down. It's funny," she said through a grin.

"We were trying to be discrete about it."

"I'm sure you both believe that. The first time I heard you two being loud next door, I knew I'd never get you off each other, so I went to your friends and told them if they gave you a hard time about it, they'd have to answer to me. I reminded them I could kill them with my brain. I hope it worked. I think it worked. Did it work?"

"It must have. Nobody has razzed us over it. Of course, Uncle runs a pretty loose shop of his own. Janus and Simmons have been making eyes at each other, and I wonder about Sara and Rodriguez."

"Is that allowed? An officer and a non-com?"

"As I said, I wonder."

Janus on the comm: "Hold up. Motion sensor is going nuts. Multiple targets at—"

The hail of laser fire directed upward sent them all the message. Brooks immediately reset his sensors, bringing a dozen drones back to cover Janus's position. Even in the crazy architecture of the assembly plants, he saw the problem. "Marc, ground your plane. Diallou, move in to point-one-three klicks off of Janus's plane. Set your jammers for a narrow beam and sweep the hell out of them."

Speedbump Diallou acknowledged the order and converted her plane to Walker mode. She lifted off, swooped in a wide curve around the assembly towers, and came up behind the knot of Sleer rollers. She extended her plane's EM vanes, and a burst of noise later, the rollers stopped firing.

Brooks switched to the general channel and toggled his mic. "Good work. Broadswords, do your worst. We practically gift-wrapped them for you."

Lt. Neal Breit, Broadsword Leader, grunted an answer and the Broadswords surged forward, engaging with their particle cannons and fists. The humans had seethed in resentment and frustration for some time over their earlier engagement, and took the opportunity to expend their wrath on enemy units. The fight was over quickly. Not a single roller escaped.

Rosenski sighed. "Good work, people. Brooks, nice re-direct. Binil, how much further?"

Binil craned her neck and read the display that happened to be in front of her co-pilot. "Four-point-two-two klicks, bearing three-one-seven. The signals are very strong."

"That's our target, then. All Ravens ground and switch to battler. Speedbump, take the point."

"Roger that."

Binil tapped the comm with her finger, grinning at Brooks. "She's the one you really want, isn't it?"

"Who? Speedbump?"

"No. *Rosenski*," Binil giggled.

"What? No!"

"You sure? Your face changes whenever she speaks. Dance told me about the time you and she were marooned on the Earth Ring for a full month. You didn't get close or anything?"

"We made jokes about it, but it was all business. It'll always be only business with Sara."

"Ah! *Sara*."

"Shut up." He'd thought about Sara that way here and there, but she'd be out of his league even if she weren't built like *that*.

"It's about confidence," he said. "When I'm in my element, I'm confident. Fixing things, taking them apart, figuring out how shit works. That's my thing. Rosenski's element is blowing planes out of the sky. That's not my thing. I never will be that kind of confident."

"You seemed confident enough to vector your pilots to a new attack," she countered.

"Because that's my job. With Sara, it's all business. That's that."

Binil sniffed. "You're giving up too easily."

"I know my limits is all."

She pointed at his console. "I mean you have three analytics on your display and you haven't bothered to identify any of them. That's triangulation data. Use it."

He did. There were more attacks as the squadron maneuvered their fighting machines toward the source of the signals. A trio of rollers popped out from behind an assembly tower and were quickly dispatched. Half a klick farther on, a lone sniper attacked Diallou's EM vanes, and her display went blank. Janus brought his boosters to power and lunged at the attacker, nearly pummeling it to wreckage before two Broadswords came up to finish the job.

They emerged from the crowded landscape and saw an oblong nestled in a valley formed by three joined structures. The drones showed them a solid picture. The ship was definitely a Sleer scout vessel, but with cosmetic differences from a stock *Zalamb*-class ship. Worse, what looked like the remainder of the Sleer battle force was between them and the ship. As they watched from cover, more of the box-like walkers arrived, joined by the rollers.

"Looks like they're reinforcing their position," Brooks said. "I'm not seeing any way to get behind them, not with the ship nudged up against the bulkhead that way."

"We can go outside and hit them from behind," Binil said. "That's their danger space. We should use it."

Brooks called up a set of schematics constructed by the drones and sensors over the past hours. "Not unless you want to try cutting through three sets of bulkheads with armored blast doors."

"We've done that before. It's how we got inside this thing."

"Not without *Gauntlet*, we didn't. Nose lasers and arm cannons won't be enough."

"So we need bigger guns."

"Essentially."

The command channel flared with a heated discussion—the same one Brooks and Binil were having. What to do about the tactical situation? Brooks toggled his mic. "Nightmare leader... we have an idea."

CHAPTER 27

FAIRCHILD STRUGGLED to breathe as he listened to Rosenski. "You want us to do what?"

"I say again, actual, we have identified the Sleer scout cruiser and have determined it's the source of the signals controlling the Emus. It's nudged in a full cover position and we are out of effective weaponry. We need *Gauntlet* down here if we're going to finish this."

"That's what I thought you said." Fairchild sighed. He swiped through a handful of displays, passing data to his officers. "Gunners, I want ready status on missiles and lasers. Frost, find me a way to move the shuttle without melting everything in our thrust plume. Skull, I need you to find us the shortest distance between here and there."

While they carried out their tasks, he switched to a private channel. "Sara, this is out of character for you."

"It's a Brooks idea, if that's what you're asking."

"Brooks?"

"Hm. Brooks and Binil."

"Not Reagan?"

"Reagan's been keeping them alive since Brooks lost his Raven."

"Acknowledged. Stand by." He turned to the status board. All his gunners reported full loads of munitions. The magazine was still sixty percent full, which meant they could blow a very large hole in the outer hulls if needed. "Grandpa?"

Frost shoved his console to the side and shrugged. That was alarming. Frost never shrugged. "The grav plates will lift us off the deck, but we'll have to rely on the maneuver thrusters to go anywhere. Do not expect to dodge incoming fire at high speed. Hell, don't expect effective evasion *at all*. We'll be a big fat target from start to finish."

"We'll need to be in the air as short a time as we can arrange. Skull, it's up to you. Tell me something hopeful."

"A direct line is the shortest distance between two points," Skellington said. "How do you feel about shooting through a deck?"

Fairchild tweaked the data in the display. No matter what angle he looked at it from, it made a crazy kind of sense. If they flew the assault shuttle conventionally, they'd either have to fly back through the hole they'd blown through the hulls to gain entry, then repeat the attack to gain entry to the new location—while keeping enough ordnance in reserve to hit the actual scout. Skull's idea meant using less firepower and likely surprising the hell out of their opponents. "*Gauntlet* actual to Nightmare Leader. Pull your forces back two klicks and stand by for additional orders."

Dance Reagan's jaw dropped in frustration as the order came over the comm. "Pull back? We busted our ass to get here. We can see the bad guys right there." She stabbed the camera control, zoomed in, and enhanced the picture. The Sleer ship was right there. "What's going on?"

Rosenski's voice sounded no happier than her own. "That's the order, Reagan. All units pull back. Give that ship a wide berth."

"Copy that." She'd been leading the way to run interference for the Lightning. She about-faced her Raven, swatted the smaller mech on the shoulder, and nearly fell against it when the battler didn't move out of her way to reverse its course. She tapped her comm, heard nothing, and opened a new channel to the Lightning. What she heard sank her stomach and boiled her blood. Brooks and Binil were arguing.

"Seriously, I need it," he said.

"Get out of there!"

"I know how to use one, but it's got this covering on it—"

"I'm going to kill you!"

"Jeez, fine."

She toggled a tight beam laser to the Lightning. "If you two knob goblins don't get your shit together, we're all dead! Knock it off!" She turned the beam off in disgust. She loved them and was ready to kill them both. How did that work? At least they got the Lightning back on course. She kept one robotic arm on its shoulder as they walked, putting the required distance between their group and the Sleer ship. Rosenski guided the groups to positions appropriate to maintaining a watch for movement. That done, she took a chance and re-opened the channel to the battler. "All right, you two, what's the problem?"

Binil coughed twice, then gasped. "It's fine. We have it under control."

"Brooks? Answer me."

Another cough. "She's right. We're all fine here now. Had a brief electrical fire... Binil wouldn't let me use the fire extinguisher."

"You were reaching over me, and that's not okay," Binil said. "I can use a fire extinguisher by myself."

"It was a *fire*."

Dance quickly glanced at her cameras. Aiming circles appeared across the surface of the building the Zalamb was using for cover. She zoomed in and blanched as she watched a slew of Sleer rollers and Emus taking up positions. She pinged Rosenski's ship and yelled, "Sara! Snipers!"

"What? I don't see—"

A flurry of charged particle beams stopped further communication as the rollers opened up, sparking and exploding chunks of the assembly pillars. Dance heard Rosenski issue orders, and swiveled her battler, stepping in front of the Lightning as her motion sensors pinged the last group of drones, which spread out to cover the space above the Sleer position. She tuned into the feed as the drones swept forward then broke into three groups. Her tactical display identified numerous targets, putting aiming circles to grab her attention. Now if she just had some rounds for her gun pod. Or even a working gun pod.

The Broadswords spread out in front of the Ravens, arm cannons spitting electric charges of their own as they used the pillars for cover. Two solid hits destroyed rollers, but more replaced them. Reagan remembered the first time she'd seen the Sleer assault craft, spherical and silent, with a trio of floating turrets that could shoot accurately and simultaneously in multiple directions, unlike any human artifact. A Raven was an insane design for a war machine, but at least you could understand how one worked. Rollers defied understanding.

She'd love to get her hands on one and live in it for a week to learn how they worked. If living was part of the plan. Two near hits on the nearest pillar gouged deep gashes in her plane's armor, setting off alarms. Three Broadswords cracked under the onslaught as she watched. She had no idea who had piloted those units, but there were three more letters Fairchild would have to write to families. She knew so little of the people she worked with. She'd gotten socially lazy in the past couple of years. Replacements were a fact of life, and the long timers made things difficult for them. Why was that? Who had she snubbed that way? A few of them, probably. She wanted to fix that. Maybe it was why she'd stuck to her own little group. Fewer losses to bear. Except when there weren't.

"Energy signature is spiking…they're deploying the turrets," Janus called out.

Dance glanced at her sensor panel. It was true. She saw the armored ports opening, and bulbous gun turrets extend past the hatches. She couldn't tell if the light point-defense lasers across the hull were bearing too, but that didn't matter. If these mounts were anything like those on *Cyclops*, they'd be far more powerful than the light versions. She watched myriad streams of coherent light rise in short bursts toward the ceiling, and winced as her visual feeds winked out. The Lightning was losing its connection to the drones. Then the feeds collapsed completely, the battle computer complaining that it had lost the connections.

The threat indicator screamed at her to do something as the full turrets let loose. Bolts of power shot across the entire compartment, each one taking chunks out of the little cover the humans had left. The rollers had already retreated behind their cover, and the Sleer ship gunners were firing over the obstacles. A few didn't bother to clear the structure and blasted holes to shoot through like the firing ports on an AFV.

The Broadswords scattered as the assembly columns exploded, chunks of twisted metal crashing around them. Fires broke out as explosions mounted, first in the distance, then growing closer. There were fewer misses as the enemy lasers found their range. The Ravens and battlers fanned out to make themselves smaller targets. Against a roller, they could make a stand, but none of them could resist the heavy fire they now experienced. Sleer turret lasers were meant to destroy other warships; a mere battler had no chance. Even Joanne Arkady's Super Ravens were pinned down; one exploded into shrapnel as it took a direct hit, and three others were pinned by a collapsing assembly tower.

Dance nudged her Raven closer to the Lightning, trying to protectively cover it with her robotic arms. More explosions outside, and now the cabin began to grow warm. *Heat exchangers breaking down.* Even the camera feed was fuzzing into incoherence, the smoke and flames futzing the lenses. This was a stupid way to die. She hated the fact that her Raven wouldn't even offer her two friends more than slight protection against the Sleer weaponry. More importantly, she couldn't see either of them, just stare into her camera feed, looking at metal plates and sensors that comprised the Lightning's dome-shaped head.

Partly, she hated herself for allowing this to happen. If she'd never met Simon Brooks...then she'd be on Earth halfway through serving her five-year sentence for wire fraud and watching the world die in fire and ice. No, that was dumb. The Unified Earth Fleet was better. Her life was better for knowing her unit, the weirdoes in it who she relied on for so much. But this *was* a stupid way to die. Her Raven would be her tomb, and she wouldn't even be buried in the same coffin as the two best friends she had in the world. *That* hurt.

A wrenching scream of metal and the cabin tilted violently enough to throw her against her harness. Acrid fumes began to fill the cabin, and the heat index was climbing to the top, sweat forming on her face as her air supply failed to manage the temperature. The world lay at a seventy-degree angle. She couldn't feel her right arm except as a dull ache full of pins and needles. *I'm hit! Am I hit? What the—?* She could still move her hand, even while her shoulder exploded with pain, pinning her until she managed to pull her right arm from beneath her torso. She spun the cameras and saw that the Lightning was beneath her, using its arms to brace her Raven, to keep her upright. *No way out, no way out...*

Contact sensors registered a pounding on her ship; the Lightning was pounding her on the back and pointing to the sky. The angle was wrong, but she could just see spots appear on the deck above them. Glowing red marks, slashes and gashes turning orange then white as melted drops and plates sloughed off and rained down like wrecked ceiling tiles...on top of the Sleer cruiser.

The cabin shifted, returning her to an upright position; the Lightning was helping her stand, along with another Raven. The hot pink paint job could only be Sara Rosenski's plane. The hole in the ceiling grew in diameter until explosions blasted the decks away from their mooring. The section of deck fell apart, raining sheets of metal, the sides glowing red with waste heat.

A flash, then another, and then the sky dropped down. Two huge oblongs tumbled through the new opening and crashed with metallic thuds as they landed. Then a third dropped on top of one of the cruiser's turrets. The oblong teetered on an unsure perch, then stamped a pair of massive feet into place and seemed to stretch as if unfolded itself. Arm-like weapon pods fell to its sides, and four enormous gun cannons popped into place above it.

"Kaijus! Holy shit, guys, we have Kaijus!" Dance squealed.

The KJU-02s were the biggest battlers ever conceived or constructed by the UEF. Several were deployed against the Skreesh forces at the Battle of Great Nest and demonstrated the value of the design. They were lumbering giants on the battlefield, better for lobbing artillery shells the size of motorcars into enemy formations than for close quarters fighting, but she'd take what she could get.

The Kaijus already on deck deployed their weapons while the one on top of the cruiser pointed its weapon arms to the hull and launched a salvo into the ship at point blank range. Dance zoomed her cameras out to watch the attack. She lost sight of the individual rounds, but watched her tactical display as it recorded the impacts. Explosions shattered her camera lenses. She switched channels, but that was it for her external pickups. All she had were her radar and tactical display.

Gauntlet dropped down through the hole, metal screeching as its pilot scraped the sides of the hole. The assault shuttle's tail got hung up on an outcropping of ragged metal, the nose dipped horribly, and Dance got a flashback to *Ascension*'s launch day, the giant spacecraft teetering on its anti-grav lifters as the lift system failed. But *Gauntlet* slid forward and dove, clearing the hole's edges and dropped out of the sky, using its maneuvering thrusters to skid over the Sleer vessel and sideslip across the deck to settle behind a series of assembly towers to the rear.

When *Gauntlet* grounded in a hard landing that could just as easily been called a collapse, the rear panels dropped and four labor battlers emerged, shoving a heavy, armored container ahead of them. Behind them emerged one more battler, taller than the others; a Raven in battler form. Dance reached above her head, pulled a stubby lever, and peered through the thick glass window that appeared above her. She'd seen that black and white starburst design before. Then it clicked as the pilot raised the machine's arms in a signal that meant "pull back."

Rosenski's voice over the comm, scattered and barely audible: "All units, retreat to *Gauntlet*. All units, respond."

"Uncle, you amazing bastard!" She righted her Raven and stepped experimentally, verifying that her plane could still move. She tugged the Lightning by the hand until her friends made the same connection she had. Dance half-carried, half-dragged the Lightning over wreckage and through still-burning plasma fires. They arrived to find the cargo container open, racks of weapons being handed out. Dance grabbed one of the new gun pods out of a small cargo battler's hands, eying the ammo counter greedily. Full load. She slung the pod and stepped out of the way so others could re-arm. The Lightning was too small to carry the gun pod like a proper Raven, but Brooks and Binil managed to carry it at shoulder arms. Close enough.

"Shame you can't reload the Armor Pack missiles, too," quipped Arkady.

Ray Fairchild's voice echoed loudly through the comm—someone in the unit was having a feedback issue. "Did someone say missiles? Kaiju Leader, engage your target."

Even from three klicks away, Dance could hear the heavy stomping of the giant battlers as they took up positions around the Sleer vessel. There was a certain insane logic to using their most damaging warheads from point blank range. The blowback would singe the big machines, but if they could punch through warship armor with two or three salvos at most, then it was worth it.

The Kaiju that had settled on top of the cruiser had it worst as far as she could see. The damn thing was so big that it couldn't depress its heavy guns far enough to actually hit the hull; it simply wasn't tall enough to support its line of sight. Its pilot reached up with both arms and settled for launching another salvo at the ship's dorsal laser turrets, silencing them and giving *Gauntlet* some breathing room. The giant battler didn't see the last turret extend up from behind it; Dance did. She keyed her comm, realized that she didn't know which channel the Kaiju was using, and blasted her voice to the general band. "Dude, behind you!"

The Kaiju lowered its arms and shuffled its massive feet in an attempt to pivot, but it wasn't going to happen. The machine was just too big to react quickly. The laser turret glowed, then blasted the unlucky Kaiju from less than one hundred meters away. When the smoke cleared, the Kaiju teetered and toppled over the far side of the cruiser, out of sight.

That was going to leave a mark, she thought.

The other Kaiju were having better luck. They'd shifted positions and created some distance between each other and the cruiser's hull, dropping their giant guns to a narrow target area. The first battler fired a salvo of plasma shells into the Sleer ship's hull, throwing a bright cloud of heated flame. Its partner blasted the same area with high explosive rounds, shrapnel flying while the ship took the full force of the explosion. She saw the strategy. Heat the metal, then pound it, over and over until they gained a breach. Both Kaiju concentrated on widening the hole and blasting through whatever armored compartments lay beyond. They ignored the continued barrage of particle beams loosed by the guns on the surviving rollers. Their armor was thick, but they wouldn't be able to resist the fire forever.

She toggled her comm. "Uncle, permission to start shooting those rollers on the hill?"

"Granted. All units, grab your guns and go forward. Support the Kaijus. Dance, you have point. Brooks and Binil, contact whoever is running that ship."

A crackle and a burst of static, then Brooks's voice. "Roger that, Uncle. What are we asking for?"

"Their unconditional surrender."

CHAPTER 28

"ALL RIGHT, ZERO. You want to go to war? Let's dance, asshole."

There was no sun inside a hollow tube, but eventually, the lighting elements throughout the dome began to glow with an artificial dawn. Valri arose with her brain bursting with possibilities. She brushed her teeth and, finally awake but still in her pajamas, stumbled to her home console. It booted instantly and with a flash of ID codes she was glaring at her work console's desktop.

She ran through preliminaries and dug out her records from the sale of her algos to On-Star Traveler. Not everything from Earth's databases had made the transfer to Diplomacy Dome. Hell, very little of the global economy was represented here at all. Mostly flows of money in and out of government coffers. The private financial market was in shambles—which was what happened when an invading power destroyed your ability to communicate buys and sells at the speed of light. Eighteen months after the Sleer's attack, not much had changed. Only now were the various sector administrations—under the watchful eyes of the Office of Military Protocols—able to start trying to get things back to normal. It was more than Valri really understood, but she heard from her sisters. Earth finance was in turmoil, and it wouldn't be fixed any time soon.

At any rate, her financial experiment had been successfully transferred and now lived in her hard memory. It took some time to unpack the documentation she'd created for anyone crazy enough to try and recover her original ideas. She hadn't thought she'd be excavating her own work.

She started by looking for the final version, sleek and streamlined and every bit as clever as she'd programmed it to be. She'd netted half a billion dollar's worth of trades before the OMP had caught up to her bosses. She'd bowed out, let them take the fall for her work. She didn't feel at all bad about it, either. She knew, and so did they, that there was every chance the Overcops would come down on the company, but they'd patted her on the ass and sent her packing—after acquiring her work for a large sum of money.

She spent time sifting the data net, amazed at how much stuff there was and slightly afraid of what would have happened if she'd tried surfing using her own brain and ten fingers. The Sleer implants might or might not be illegal to own, but they were damned useful. She burrowed deep into the storage units, set up link-based search strategies, and located all the tech department's files. But not her own inventions. With a sigh, she unlocked her own data store. There they lay, the original versions of her code. It was all there, badly formed and buggy as hell, but it was safe enough.

Now. What to do with them? There was a limit to what she could do with primitives. They didn't even warrant the term "alpha version." An alpha version functioned more or less according to the design parameters. Badly, haltingly, full of errors, garbage in, garbage out, garbage everywhere, but it worked. Her primitives were more rudimentary than even that.

They were like badly formed plastic dice, liable to wander around forever, spreading bits of nonsense and returning no good results no matter how you rolled it.

And yet they had purpose. If she could…

Wait. Of course she could; she was an Undersecretary of Commerce. She lay back in her chair, closed her eyes, and sent a flurry of orders and instructions to the battle ring network, goosing the system into working for her like Simon Brooks once showed her. It was possible. All she needed was time. And maybe a bit of help from an artificial intelligence. She even had an ace that she hadn't told anyone about. An OMP priority code from years ago, given to her by Frances Underhill just after the Battle of Great Nest. It would get her job to the head of the work stack and grant her project every erg of computing juice it needed to become a thing. It could be made usable by her, and probably far more effective than the primitives she'd turned into the PROFIT algo for her old firm.

She set the parameters, entered the code, and triggered the command to settle her job in the queue. She held her breath as the screen stayed blank, her cursor blinking stupidly. Blink. Blink. Blink. Finally, a response: ACCEPT OMP PRIORITY. JOB RUNNING. ETC 13.46 HRS.

She exhaled in a rush, leaned back in her chair, and realized she'd probably broken at least a few laws doing that. Well, fine. She'd care when they came for her. The tension between the EarthGov bureaucracy and the OMP was only going to get worse going forward, and technically, she was under orders from the current Secretary—who should be arriving in Great Nest shortly, she remembered—to do anything she had to for formal trade relations between Earth and her neighbors to emerge. That was bad enough. She'd been talking to the Sleer without obvious progress for weeks. The Movi were a different kind of challenge; they were happy to crack open their wallets and fund anything humanity needed, but only insofar as it furthered their hold on Earth. She didn't want to slip and fall into a galactic proxy war. And then, oh yes, the Skreesh were on their way. They'd show up on Earth's doorstep eventually, and even with all the Sleer's combined might, it was even money whether they'd win, and anybody's guess as to whether Earth would still be there when the dust cleared.

Some choice.

The comm chimed. She half thought to ignore it, just pull the bud from her ear and—

Underhill's voice in her ear. She'd forgotten Overcops could break comm protocol. Fuck.

"Val! You are not going to believe who just came to dinner."

Valri saw that a video file had been attached to the message; her console presented the option to open it, and she absent-mindedly pushed the button. A new window opened. A flash of light, a blurred image that quickly cleared as the image filters slid into place on the camera. Two ships: One of them a battered Sleer vessel, small, probably a scout ship. And the other was—

"*Gauntlet!*" She tapped her comm. "Frances, they're back!"

"Damn straight they are. I'm not involved in the debriefing, but it's apparently one hell of a story they have to tell. Come to my office and I'll fill you in."

"On my way."

It took Valri the better part of an hour to locate Underhill's building in Primate Alley, then another thirty minutes of wandering the halls, comparing the placards on the hallway signs to the address she'd been sent. The room she eventually found was a single door that opened onto a walk-in closet of a room. Frances Underhill was crowded behind a desk that was too sizes too small for her. The walls were covered with bright patches that suggested posters, signs, and corkboards once lived there and had been recently removed. She thought she recognized a battered metal figure behind her but dismissed it.

Underhill compressed the data screen she was working on. "Val! You found it. Sweetness. You look tired. Want some coffee? My boy just made a fresh pot. Ass! Get the lady a cup of coffee," she ordered.

"Immediate!" The robot dutifully wobbled to the coffee bar and returned with a bulb of steaming brew in its claws, which it offered to Valri. "Madame! Refreshment! Enjoy!"

Valri took the cup and swung her eyes from one end of the tiny space to the other. "Where are they?"

"Debriefing. They brought back a ton of goodies. Ancient artifacts, Sleer POWs, the whole shebang. They'll be stuck there for a few weeks, but I got access to the first look stuff."

Valri sagged into the only guest chair. "This is your office."

"Yep. Welcome to the Special Operations Investigation Liaison. It doesn't look like much, but I'm hooked directly into the trunk line that runs the information network in Battle Ring Great Nest. If anyone on this space station farts, I get a report on it. It's not too shabby."

"Bitches didn't even give you a damn window. We built enough space for a whole city of people to get luxury apartments and you get this."

"Right? I think ZERO wanted me to keep a low profile."

Valri sipped and nodded at Ass. "And that's your staff?"

"Hm. I repurposed him when you got your appointment to undersecretary. It seemed like a shame to let him go to the recycler."

"Gratitude!" Ass said.

"So you're not in charge of the Primate Alley police force?"

"I'm...no." Ass handed Underhill her own coffee. She stared at the mug before taking a sip. "Captain Barnes did leave, but he's not on this station. He was repurposed. Sent to a combat unit I can't locate on the table of organization. Captain Tanaka took his place. I am Tanaka's OMP liaison. Technically I'm a cop, but I'm still a spy. Why I wasn't told this, I don't know. It could be my former boss didn't know. Even secrets have their secrets in the OMP."

The sheer magnitude of the past months' events washed over Valri, and she felt the strength drain from her body. She felt weak and stupid. Mostly she felt an exhaustion that she hadn't known existed before right now. She fought the urge to put her head between her knees. "We've been played."

"Like puppets," Underhill confirmed. "ZERO is playing a game with God knows who or what, and we are the pieces. I've looked in on the files regarding *Gauntlet*'s crew. They made it just under the wire, so nobody is going down for being AWOL or anything else. But I did find this." She grabbed a datum from her screen and threw it to Valri, who caught it with her implants and opened it. "Those are the Gauntlets' medical files from two years ago when they were still Hornet Squadron. Flip to the last page and then click on the addendum."

"The one that says OMP Eyes Only?"

"That's it. As far as ZERO knows, I'm the one reading it. The office decor may suck, but the position is real."

Valri tagged the file, sorted through to the end, and dove in. "Lord have mercy. This can't be real."

"It is. Verified and correct," Underhill said. "Here, just listen to the fun part. 'Under standards and regulations pertaining to the safety and control of UEF personnel, the actions of Hornet Squadron in its entirety call for extreme measures. To wit, the 1) accepting of alien hardware of unknown purpose and intent from an alien intelligence, 2) voluntarily submitting themselves to said intelligence, 3) to an unknown intent and origin of said intelligence, 4) with unknown long-term effects, and 5) short-term effects to include physical enhancements in excess of human norms both within reported UEF standards and otherwise. The GENERAL STAFF does hereby and direct the Office of Military Protocols to create and establish a routine of complete and total surveillance of Hornet Squadron to be used in the creation and establishment of a board of inquiry regarding the question of whether the members of Hornet Squadron can be trusted to continue their service to the Unified Earth Fleet in good faith.'"

She blinked and leaned back. "There's more like that, but they include the fact that our implants are showing their age. Now they have us flagged for medical watch as well as judging our loyalty to the home world. I can't find them, but I'd bet cash money they have thick archives on everything every one of us has done for the past three years. I know how the system is designed—I doubt any of us have so much as taken a leak in private."

"Just in case we burp out of tune."

"They can pretty much hit us with a treason charge and a firing squad at will. Luckily for us, we've apparently been operating with Earth's best interest in mind."

"Well, who else would we work for?"

"They don't know. Maybe an alien AI who isn't answering calls anymore."

Valri's eyes flipped wide open. She hadn't thought about Genukh in months. "Won't she? Let's try. Genukh! ZERO! You there?"

They waited a moment in silence. "She never answers anymore. I think she's keeping a low profile of her own," Underhill said.

"To what purpose?"

"That is the six-billion-dollar question. Whatever it is, I don't think it'll be good for the Sleer. It may not be very good for us, either."

"Then let's make it as bad for our new dinosaur overlords as we can. When does Rescue-1 arrive with Secretary Hopkins and the rest of the EarthGov honchos?"

"Some time tonight, supposedly. What did you have in mind, Madame Undersecretary?"

"The Sleer high command wants us to join their interstellar family," Valri said, "so I'm going to announce an engagement."

CHAPTER 29

THE "SUN" streamed through the windows as Valri's office filed with people. She'd been here for hours, dressed to the nines, as formal and proper as she could be. Basil had spent an hour prepping her before anyone arrived, then arranged for a catering tray filled with goodies and snacks from three worlds. Valri glanced down at her coffee mug. Imported from New Orleans, it was a small but heavy ceramic model from the Café du Monde restaurant. The best coffee and beignets anywhere. Kitschy as hell, but it reminded her of home, which was what she needed.

She sipped and did her best not to stare at her guests. The Sleer, Dashak, Bon, Khiten, and their combined staffs sat to her right, the humans to the center, and the Movi to her left. Miraled Makjit and Horvatz sat in the first row, and a chorus of staff stood behind them—including a male Cycomm whose name she didn't know. Basil stood to the right of her desk and prepared to nudge things along if sticking points arose.

One chair in front of her desk remained empty—the one meant for Secretary of Commerce Hopkins. The countdown clock timing his arrival on Great Nest had closed out hours ago. She didn't know where he was and couldn't contact him. Her guts refused to settle as she pondered the meaning of his absence.

Eventually, they ran out of time. Everyone was getting antsy. The Sleer were standing on their toes and pawing at the air, and Miraled was making faces.

Time to get the bus rolling.

Valri cleared her throat. "I've made my decision. I'm recommending EarthGov align our trade policies with the Dal-Cortsuni merchant house of the Movi Kingdom."

Miraled sighed and smiled. The Sleer hissed loudly while Horvantz folded his arms. "They got to you, didn't they? What was it? The bribe, the threat, or the girls' night out?"

Valri never liked Horvantz, and now she understood why. She opened her mouth, only to feel Basil's hand lightly fall on her shoulder. This was official business. Punching a Movi was out of the question. "That, sir, is beneath you. Or beneath where I think you believe yourself to be."

"Answer my question."

"I don't think I'm in a position to answer any of your questions with the clarity everyone here deserves. But I will tell you my line of reasoning if you like. It might take a while."

Horvantz folded his arms. "I have nowhere to be."

"And no one to be with, I'm sure. I specifically arranged my calendar so that this is my only appointment." She tapped her slate and checked her notes—items she wanted to make sure entered the record. "I'm not going to lie. I have no idea why ZERO chose me for this post. I have no idea why ZERO does much of anything. Frankly, I don't think most of the humans alive and shivering in their homes back on Earth right this minute are even aware that a giant supercomputer is running the most important segments of their lives."

"It has its advantages," the Cycomm sniffed.

Valri glanced down at her slate and recoiled from the

Cycomm's name: Amardajaediltiluven. Her brain cut the first bit off and made do. "That it does, Mr. Amar. Making sure the whole population gets what they need to survive would be a primary function there. Lord knows we primates aren't very good with that, but the Cycomms made it work for them. Malkah was her name, right?"

"It's still her name."

"Of course. But the way I understand it, Malkah hasn't worked properly in generations. Something like that? And I'm told the new model doesn't work nearly as effectively. She takes sides, she plays favorites, she maintains a power structure that rewards royalty and connections. The plugs are out in the cold, aren't they?"

He frowned. His red eyes seemed to glow eerily, like a cat's in low light. Laser eyes. "She works to keep our society stable."

"I'm not saying she doesn't. I am saying the reality doesn't live up to the theory."

Now Amar shifted his feet. He was getting annoyed. "Are you trying to start an incident, Madame? Where did you get this information?"

"A little bird who is very close to two of my people. And unlike you and your delegation, she helped defend this solar system from a Skreesh titan. Where were your people two years ago?"

"I don't command any Sense Op minions. I couldn't possibly say."

"Then I'll enlighten you. They were back on Haven, watching and waiting to see what happened to Great Nest. I've seen some of the reports filed about Sense Ops military units. Impressive stuff, but not available at the scale you'd need to deal with a Skreesh incursion of your own."

Horvantz waved his hands. "Have you asked him a question?"

"I did. He flubbed the answer."

Amar leaned forward and bent to whisper hotly into Horvantz's ear. When he rose, his face took on the same war paint aspects as Binil's when she got angry. Any effort at keeping his cool had been discarded. "What were we supposed to do? Even if the Unity wanted to send help, you just pointed out that it would have been ineffectual."

"There's a difference between being a wallflower and not even showing up to the dance," Valri answered. "I know Haven has its problems. I know that a fair number of those problems descend directly from Zluur's hostile acquisition of Cycomm technology. And I also know that there's a solid chance that tech was developed into the battle ring that surrounds my home world right this minute and extends to the AI that runs this ring as well. So if there's a case to be made, they should have at least shown up to ask if we needed anything. That's the rationale for it. They said nothing and did nothing. That's what I know."

Horvantz gripped his cup and tightened his fingers. For a moment, Valri worried he might actually throw it across the room. "The Cycomms never even left their own solar system. They rely on us for protection," he said.

"Protection and access to trade routes and interstellar transit corridors. I've seen the maps. You were very helpful in showing us just how formidable the Movi trade machine is. Thirteen great houses, a score of lesser houses, and how many thousands of minor houses, groups, clans, and guilds, associations, and teams. Have you ever counted them? Tens of thousands at least. Everyone gets along because they rely on the royal family. The Vermilion Throne, I think you call it. Everything extends from that. Right?"

"The imperial charter is the backbone of all our trade agreements. You know that. Makjit explained that to you while I was in the room," Horvantz said.

"She did. Except your sovereign is dead, his family is gone, there's no clear path to succession, the current occupant is apparently beset with problems, and now all the different factions are looking for ways to develop their own path to dominance. Which military faction were you planning on supporting? Warlord Anterran, right?"

"That would be an internal matter for our military."

"Well, it's either him or the guy who wiped out the royal family, but something tells me he won't have the level of support he needs to make himself the new guy in charge. Which means one of two things: a short, brutal war that wipes out a tenth of your population, or a long ugly conflict that destroys ninety percent of it. Either way, the Skreesh come along and wipe the floor with whatever is left."

"Let's say I agree with you. I do not, but let's say that I do. Why is choosing Dal-Cortsuni over Kar-Tuyin—or any other major faction—the way you want to play this?"

"I'll get to that in a moment. First let's talk about the Sleer."

"Yes. Let us talk of Sleer," Dashak hissed. "You have your world, we have our ring. What is there to discuss?"

"Plenty. You see, my race did this to itself not that long ago. Colonization, it's called. The folks with all the power move into a spot of land they want for whatever reason: agriculture, mining, maybe just to build villas on, whatever. Move the natives out at gunpoint and put fences up so they can't get back to what they thought was their land, and then tell the aborigines that the new settlement is off limits to them for their own good. When the natives protest, shoot a few of their leaders just to make your point. And when they decide on new leaders, shoot those too. Eventually, they leave and find a new place to live. Then, when the invaders decide they need more room to grow, the whole thing starts over again."

"We don't do that. Your world is yours. The ring is—"

"The ring *is* our world. All the materials that went into building it came from our world. The AI who ran it before your people turned her off chose our world out of thousands and got landing instructions from ZERO. Our. World."

"Nonsense."

"Not to my mind. The only thing that give you any leverage at all is the fact that the OMP is supporting your claim to the ring. If that situation changes, you lose your only ally in this contest. Think about that."

"I think that we have many battleships. You have one. But war is not our goal. What would you want?"

"Equal access to the Earth battle ring, including the spokes, for any human who wants to live there. We would, of course, design a system of application for emigrant status, and we would be happy to figure out what the criteria for habitation in the ring would entail. But that's just a first step. You tell Nazerian about that. See what he says. He says 'yes,' and can sell it to his superiors, then we can talk further. That is civilized."

"Civilized? You joke. We study your race, your history. You are no better than we were. Worse, perhaps, since all you seem to care about is killing each other for your belongings. At least Sleer learned to stop the fighting when it became clear there could be no winners. Then we discovered the stars. *Then* there was peace."

The worst part of his little speech was that it rang true—at least somewhat. She didn't feel up to describing the factors that led to the U-War or the rest of it. Humanity and the Sleer were at an impasse, and they wouldn't solve it today. She decided to push on with her planned discussion instead.

"And while we're on that subject, let's talk about the Office of Military Protocols." Out of the corner of her eye, she saw Frances Underhill shift in her seat. Valri studiously kept her eyes on her notes, looked them over but seeing nothing.

"I'll have you know, in the spirit of disclosure, that my own government has threatened to place me under arrest and very likely drop me in a prison if I don't hand over my trade data and code. I have refused to do so. While I have everyone's attention, I might as well explain why I refused. I used to work in an office. I was a desk trader, buying supplies here, selling there. The biggest customer in the world was the Unified Earth Fleet military, so that's where ninety-nine percent of my trades went. But I noticed there were patterns in how they fleet bought and what they bought and when they bought. Predictable patterns. I set up a few experiments and a bunch of simulations and tested my theories. Two years later, I was the most profitable trader at my firm, and the partners—well, somebody—insisted I was cheating. Some damn fool called the OMP and said I was breaking laws. They sent people to investigate. My bosses knew I was on the up and up—I had all the documentation to prove it. But once the Overcops know your name, there's fuck all you can do to get rid of them. I sold my secrets. My algorithms and research went to my firm—I pocketed the cash and went my own way. The rest, I guess they say, is history.

"One thing I learned from that experience is that systems can be automated. Any mechanical system can be gamed as easily as anything run by a human. The difference is in who wins and who loses. Usually, it's the customers who lose, through artificial scarcity, supply chain gaps, artificially inflated prices at both ends of the equation... While the OMP may in fact be able to replicate my work, it would cost them time and energy to do so. They want the shortcut. I understand that. I even empathize. But I'll tell you this too: the world we live in is very unlike the world I developed those algos for. It seems to me that doing their own work from the ground up makes more sense. If they really want a boost, I can come on board and help them with the development, but there will be a price for my help."

Underhill frowned. "What price?"

"A free market. Create the rules, set the boundaries, empower an agency to enforce them, then let anyone who wants to, buy a ship and ply the space lanes on their own. By all means, regulate the heck out of it. We don't need an environment where everyone with an attitude and a long gun calls himself a pirate. But if any of this plan is ever developed and enacted, the age of exclusive trading rights given to megacorporations is over... at least on Earth."

She sighed heavily. "And that, at last, brings us to Miraled Makjit and her fellows at Dal-Cortsuni."

"Finally!" Makjit was bouncing in her seat like a toddler on Christmas morning. "Please, articulate."

"I will. First of all, did you know that your boss, Mr. Horvantz, is working for the Royal MoviNaval Intelligence?"

"Of course I do!" she beamed. Then it sank in. *"What?"*

"Yeah, he came to me after our little private affair and promised me triple your offer if I'd break ranks and follow his lead. Not smooth at all, but it was a tremendous amount of...not really money...enough energy to start my own continent and a couple of century's worth of longevity, if I remember correctly."

Horvantz waved his hand dismissively. "You do. Not that it matters. You'll never see any of it. You've earned yourself a black mark in the roles of the Royal Mercantile guild. No one in the kingdom will do business with you, ever."

Makjit rolled her eyes. "That's not how it works. The royal charter specifically forbids court members or their employees from interfering with the affairs of the houses, except in time of war. Which this is not."

"It will be soon."

Makjit glared. "Perhaps. But with no agreement on who the

sovereign is and what their claim to the throne might be, I have the same right to extend my corporate power as you do. Madame Undersecretary, you have the support and loyalty of the Dal-Cortsuni at your service."

"Thank you. But it's not up to me. I can only recommend to the Secretary."

A chime piped out on her slate. Valri saw it was from Underhill, and flipped through the news. It said, "Val, you are the Secretary."

"Tell me another one." Valri looked at Frances.

"I will. This just came in. Rescue-1 was designated to transport the dignitaries. It tried to make a spatial transition and something happened. The ship was destroyed, losses were total. ZERO has made his analysis and figured out that you are to be the next Secretary for Commerce. Congratulations."

Underhill threw the data to her. The bulletin unfolded on her desk display, and Valri shunted it to her implant. Basil was already on his phone, stepping away as he conducted business. "Well. Hell."

She took a moment to compose herself. This was not how she envisioned the meeting ending, but clearly there was more to do. "Thank you all for attending this meeting. My office will make arrangements to speak to all of you privately, should you choose to do so." As if there was any dirty laundry she hadn't already thrown into their midst.

They kept their manners. They bobbed heads, took her hand, and mumbled thanks as they filed out. Makjit came over, gave her a perfunctory but welcome grip on her forearm, then a brief hug. "We'll talk later. So much to do."

Valri's desk felt like a prison, the heaviest ball and chain in the world. She stopped Frances on her way out the door, the last to leave. "What are you going to do?"

Underhill sniffed. "I'm going to talk to General Hendricks

and tell him you would like to negotiate a fair price for your intellectual property."

"That's not even slightly true."

"I know that, but it'll keep both of us out of jail while you figure out what your end game is. I'll handle the exchange personally. Congratulations, Madame Secretary."

CHAPTER 30

ROSENSKI COULDN'T FIGURE out why she wasn't sitting in the brig.

Gauntlet had come to terms with Acting Ship Master Zolik. It was deploying the Kaiju that had made it possible. For all his experience on battlefields, the *Zalamb-Duzen's* XO had never imagined a mobile armored bunker mounting guns that properly belonged on a battleship. The plasma rounds had eaten holes in the Sleer hull, then the explosive rounds had shredded its interior compartments. When Brooks and Binil had sounded the call for a Sleer surrender, Zolik had agreed—though there was some question as to whether the Sleer officer was empowered to make that decision. The actual CO was apparently out of his mind, wandering the central core, making notes on the plants and animals he found there. Fairchild had accepted Zolik's gesture as the real thing.

They'd spent a day patching the Sleer vessel's hull, confirming *Gauntlet's* spaceworthy status, and cataloging the captured Sleer ship as a distressed asset. Leaving a skeleton crew in charge of the giant Sleer derelict, they returned to Great Nest. They'd come back alive. Most of them. Twenty-one names listed as KIA. Twenty-one letters for Uncle to write. And a deep dark hole for Sara to stare into.

It had taken more time to convince Captain Rojetnick of what the human crew had done, but in the end, the brass was happy to learn they had a secure non-Sol system to develop, a new ally in the Sleer military to work with, and a new relic to plunder for knowledge.

For Rosenski, all roads led back to The Accidental Owl and all the self-recrimination she could summon. It turned out to be quite a bit. She was sure she'd fucked up. She'd been the one to accept the former Hornets, to integrate them into her Nightmares. She'd failed. The Hornets kept their distance—they were still cliquish off duty—and where Rosenski had hoped they'd pick up the habits of Nightmare crew, the Nightmares were now acting like them instead. She'd done her best. Her best wasn't that great. For that matter how had she allowed the mission to continue after they'd run out of supplies? She should have ordered the flyers and grounders to pull back to the ship, reloaded, and headed back out. She should have done something different.

She didn't deserve her rank, her responsibilities, her command, or her commission. She certainly didn't deserve the trust and respect of a soldier like Thomas Katsev, and she absolutely did not deserve to be saddled with a junior varsity weirdo like Simon Brooks. Why the hell didn't Uncle fucking Fairchild give him his own unit and spare her the pain of managing him? Because Fairchild was working under General Eisenberg, and he wanted the smart ones on his side, that was why. Katsev wanted killers on his. She didn't know what kind of bastards Hendricks wanted, but she suspected Underhill was a prime example.

It was going to get ugly when the grand throw-down began.

Anyway, she drank. There was a two-for-one special on

Long Island Iced Tea, and the cloying sweetness hid the taste of the booze. That was a good drink. She was on her fourth now, hoping that she could keep ahead of the Sleer implants.

Her knee was acting up again. More often these days. The implants had repaired it in a few hours and kept the pain at bay, but that was three years ago. Maybe they didn't work forever. Without Genukh to analyze the equipment and update it as needed...

"Excuse me, sir. You dropped this."

Sara blinked and turned her head. The soldier was a stranger, the sort of guy that could show up anywhere. She didn't recognize his name—Falun—or his unit number, or the patch on his shoulder. Asian dude. Vietnamese eyes, maybe? She wasn't sure.

"Lieutenant Commander, I'm sorry. This is yours."

She glanced down at the flash drive, a more common bit of gear she couldn't imagine. She took it from him and held it closer, blinked to clear her eyes. She didn't recall leaving her quarters or his post with a flash drive. On the other hand, her life as a desk jockey in the past couple of years had made her sloppy, forgetful. Their foray into that damn Sleer derelict was proof of that.

She never would have expected that, not with the Sleer military implants running her body, improving its natural tendencies, extending her physical attributes as they did. Her mental state, however, was under a different set of rules. While the implants extended her network of instantaneous recall and gave her access to all electronic data all the time, they didn't help her remember much on the spot. She'd earned command of her own squadron in the Allied Sleer Fleet and had a staff to run the small things, but the contents of her pockets sometimes took a back seat to dealing with the life and death situations that governed nearly one hundred people and all their gear.

"Thank you, Specialist." She turned her head, but he was gone, leaving her holding the drive. She noticed the clear window on the side, the multi-colored LED and the six-digit display. Not even a flash drive, but an authenticator. A useful tool to establish a security chain. Nice. She pocketed it and turned back to her drink.

She'd come in for a quick round at one of the few music spots run entirely but human staff and with a mostly human clientele. The Sleer came by to sniff and snort now and then, but the Vix and the Movi came in and stayed, sometimes for hours. Especially the Movi. Those guys appreciated music, particularly Earth's selection. To hear them describe it, music from Earth was like nothing else in the galaxy. Sara liked to think they were telling the truth. There were few enough things that humans did right these days. Well...they'd convinced the Sleer high command not to nuke Earth out of existence. That was a worthy accomplishment.

After her third drink and an hour-long presentation of Miles Davis, she zoned out. She had time before her next briefing. In the meantime, she was on her own for a while longer. She wanted this feeling of relaxation to persist as long as she could make it happen.

A gruff male voice to her right broke her mood. "How do you like the music?"

"You need a better password, Boss," she sighed.

Katsev signaled the robot bartender and ordered a beer. "I'll ask again. How do you like the music?"

"I prefer hip-hop and I'm in a mood, Butcher. Leave me alone."

"Too late for that. You have a mission from General Layne."

"Layne's dead. I just read his book."

"Too late for that, princess. You're on duty as of now."

And there it was. She could say no. Technically, she could

even try to arrest Katsev for treason, but it wouldn't stick. She couldn't prove anything. She was in deep, and there was no way out except to go deeper. Hell was like that. "What am I doing?"

"What and wherefore is all on the drive you just took. Use code B894. Third file from the top. Everything is there."

She could imagine. Valri Gibb had, in her new and suspiciously timed role as EarthGov's Secretary of Commerce, signed a trade agreement with the Movi Kingdom, completely out of left field. "What about the why?"

"The why is obvious, or it should be. The new secretary of commerce has decided, in her finite wisdom, that humans are the low man on the totem pole and she'd rather give Earth to those alien fucks. We're not here to kiss the Sleer or Movi or anyone else. Earth is for humans, and that's that."

"I won't kill Valri."

"You'll do what you're told. Make it big and noisy. Send a message."

"I'm going to need help."

"You have help. A whole mechanized battalion of help. All the robots in the Sleer inventory, and you have implants to direct them, no? That's your help. Make it look like a Sleer attack. That should be simple enough for a whiz like you."

"What if I need—?"

"No. This is on you. A message needs to be imparted. Make it work."

She stared at her glass while she heard the clunk of glass on wood and a squeak and a thud as Katsev slid off the stool, then footsteps as he left. When she raised her eyes, she was alone again.

CHAPTER 31

UNDERHILL HADN'T BEEN ENTIRELY correct—Valri was the *acting* Secretary of Interstellar Commerce. The Deputy Secretary had apparently refused to accept the top job, which sounded sinister to Valri. It didn't stop there. There was a bit of chaos on Earth right now as the powers that be tried to sus out the meaning of the unhappy accident that had taken out Secretary Hopkins and a number of other cabinet members, not the least of whom was Gillian Pascal, the Director of Homeworld Security. In any case, she could make the decisions, do the work, and follow the rules, at least until EarthGov could arrive with a government official empowered to have her take the correct oath of office. When that might happen was unclear.

Her office hadn't changed. She'd promoted Basil to Chief of Staff and told him to fill out whatever positions in Diplo Dome needed filling. She specifically told him to hire a staff of his own first. He wasn't good at delegating; left to his own ends, he'd try to run the whole department himself. She'd given him a priority: find someone who could keep the new space lanes safe. He'd come back with several names. She'd chosen the one she knew best and more or less trusted. He'd be here soon for a talk.

In the meantime, she kept her door closed. The display above her desk projected three-dimensional spreadsheets all around her, links and cross-links connecting the data within. The cells flashed as the algorithm updated in real time. It looked like a mind in action...not a human one, but something that was comparing, calculating, judging, adapting. Evolving. Nothing she'd built before came close to it. The worst part was that ZERO had put a significant amount of himself into the final version.

She had her answer, the thing every faction had been hounding her for since she'd arrived on the public stage. Predictive Relevance Optimized For Interstellar Trade: PROFIT 2.0. The source code that would put EarthGov on the map. Faced with a calcifying Sleer command with nowhere to go, and a disintegrating Movi nation, EarthGov was in the perfect place to nudge both sides toward a cohesive relationship. Unify the whole of the races and everything they needed to survive the expected Skreesh onslaught—and maybe even thrive in its aftermath. It was all here. It might not work, but if they didn't try...

An intercom chimed. "He's here."

"Send him in." She closed the file, killed the display, and stood to greet her guest. "Good morning, Lieutenant Brooks."

"Good morning, Madame Secretary," Brooks said.

Acting Secretary. Acting. "Please, sit. Coffee?"

"No, thank you. I've a busy schedule."

"I'm sure. Recovered from your rather amazing discovery?"

"No, it's the arm. It's acting up again." He flexed it a few times, wiggled the fingers. "Doc thinks leaving it alone is still the best option."

"They could remove the implants, no?"

"That's a separate issue. Removing them might cause more harm than good. I'm curious to know if you'll be establishing a medical technology division to study the problem."

"I have a list of requests a mile long. If that's not already on the list, I'll put it there today," she said. "But first I need your help. If we're going to encourage trade, we need independent carriers. This ring can build ships by the thousands. That's relatively easy. But we need an agency to enforce the rules the bureaucrats come up with. Whomever we pick to head that agency needs to be familiar with the problems of space flight. Someone with a military background, but who doesn't act like a soldier. You interested?"

Brooks frowned. She could imagine the conflict within him. He'd been busting his hump to become a soldier for years. "You want me to be your Space Cop?"

"More like a space coast guard. The rules will evolve as we go forward. I need someone who can evolve with them and who doesn't mind putting a few rounds through the engines of ships that don't or won't comply."

"You should really have a Sleer involved."

"By all means, hire Sleer. The agency would be attached to the Allied Sleer Fleet, tasked with maintaining security and keeping private carriers honest. Anti-piracy, anti-incursion, and anti-sabotage would all be in your wheelhouse. And I've spoken to Ray Fairchild. A bump to Lieutenant Commander with all the perks thereof would be part of the deal."

"But I'd be out of the Nightmares."

She leaned forward. "Simon, would that really be a bad thing? The way you fight and the way the Sleer operate versus the fact that we can't trust the Movi makes this a perfect match."

"The way he sees and the way she looks," he murmured. "All right. I'm in. When do we make it official?"

"I'm getting Basil involved to start the process of development. It'll take weeks. We'll need a structure everyone can agree with. And we start small. A few dozen Sleer freighters and a list of destinations and a way of managing cargo. It's getting figured out."

"Agreed. Yes, I'm in."

As they closed their meeting to go about their respective days, she relaxed. She began to feel optimistic about the new job for the first time. Things were looking up.

Brooks hadn't seen Rosenski in days, and dropped by after work to share what he thought was good news. He came to her flat with coffee and donuts for two, and found her at her kitchen table, surrounded by holographic data. She was dressed in a baggy shirt and sweatpants—what she called her "civvies" the one time he asked about it. Her hair kept falling into her face. The red in her eyes might have been a lack of sleep. Might have been something else. She didn't shift gears well.

Trouble.

He raised the goodies as she pushed the collected display away with a wave of her arm. His implants tagged the display as locked for her eyes only. Whatever it was, she didn't want him screwing with it. Sara had never been especially public with her work, but over the years she'd gotten into the habit of lowering the drawbridge when he was around. "Smithers came through with the snack bar. I figured I'd share. You okay?"

"Yes. No. Maybe. I'm distracted is all. What'd you bring?"

"Chocolate glazed and Boston cream. Two coffees, light, no sugar."

"You're a god. A buff, nerdy little god. Gimme." He put the bounty on the table and watched her tear through the bags. She jammed both Boston creams into her face and licked the icing off her lips like a cat before touching the coffee.

He raised his cup in a mock salute. "I'm glad I didn't hand those to you. You'd bite my fingers off."

She chuckled and relaxed a bit. Sugar was a hell of a dopamine trigger.

His arm twinged and he noticed her listing to one side. The left side, where her knee had taken a traumatic blow when a Sleer defense drone had overturned their command car. "How's the leg?" he asked.

"Annoying. I'm not losing any muscle mass, but yeah. How's your arm?"

"Same. Annoying but not a real problem. I think our implants are getting out of date faster than we'd like."

"God damn Sleer. Damn Genukh and ZERO and every damn AI ever built," she murmured.

"Sara, what's wrong?"

"I'm a crappy friend, is what's wrong." She sighed and motioned for him to sit. "You mind if I ramble?"

"I'm here for it."

"Yeah. You always are. When you first showed up, I resented the fuck out of you. D'you know that?"

"Oh yes. You made that clear."

"Yeh. I'm always trying to prove to the Butcher that I have what it takes to work with him. That I'm worthy of his attention. Is that how Uncle treated you?"

"I was always busting my hump to show that I wasn't unworthy. Not exactly the same thing. Ray was never abusive, if that's what you mean. I get the idea that Katsev—"

"Thomas Katsev has a stick of ambition so far up his ass that his nose grows every time he sits in a chair," she said. She stared at the table as she spoke. Even now, her mind was elsewhere, working through more problems. Or maybe one problem big enough to crush her if she let it go. "He has plans, and they include me. Ideally, they'd include you too. But I think I understand that's not going to happen. You're Ray's boy. That's fine."

"Sara..."

She took a deep breath. "Valri Gibb is making policy now. She's aligning EarthGov with the Movi Kingdom. Why did she do that? Did Ray put her up to it, do you think? What's she thinking?"

"It's worse than you know," he started.

"Why?"

The rising tone in her voice carried an element of danger. Brooks suddenly felt like ants were crawling all over him.

"Simon...what did you do?"

"She offered me a spot in her new trade enforcement thing. I'd be a space cop."

She might be distracted, but she was sharp as ever. "You said yes?"

"Of course!" He watched her eyes focusing over his shoulder, darting from one thing to another. She was figuring something out, unsure of what to do. He'd seen that look a lot when they were trapped on Earth Ring. "What is wrong?"

"Everything. Everything is very *wrong*," she said. She sagged, letting her head roll back, staring at the ceiling. "I was thinking—hoping, really—that you would want your own combat command. With the Specters. Katsev has been bugging me about you for years."

"I never thought he was serious."

"He was. Still is. With my Nightmares and you running XO on Specter group, the world would be so much simpler."

"Running an anti-piracy op for the ASF isn't that different."

She bounced upright, leaning forward, eyes wide, arms in front of her, hands on the table. Making herself big. A command position. "Yes, it is! It's a completely different animal. It's the difference between us and the great apes. As different as dinosaurs and the Sleer. It puts you under Bon and Nazerian's control. You won't be able to refuse orders from them."

"They'd rather have a co-operative fleet than not. What can they do?" It was a stupid question. There was no way to know what they'd do until they did it, but Sara made a solid point.

"I guess we'll find out the hard way," she said.

Seeing her in distress set off alarms. There was something going on behind her eyes that he couldn't fathom. He needed her to relax, but couldn't imagine what might work. She never *needed* to relax before. "Want to order in? Rodriguez would probably send food over if I asked."

She snorted. "Any other time, I'd say yes. But I have a place to be. I appreciate the thought."

"Fair enough. I'll be home if you want to come by."

She sagged into her chair but bobbed her head. When he got to the door, she said, "Congratulations, dude. I know you'll be good at it, whatever else happens."

CHAPTER 32

SHE DID IT. She actually did it.

Events and circumstances, networks, connections, and patterns of function had changed measurably since her time on AMS-1 evolved into time spent on Battle Ring ZERO. The informal but ever evolving system of notes and cells, of orders and reports, of code phrases and encrypted files, had grown into something far more robust, more elegant than it had been in its original incarnation. The truth was that the OMP made everything far more difficult than it had originally been. That wasn't much of an unexpected eventuality. The OMP knew that despite all the security checks and ID verifications they'd done during the reconstruction, there were Layne's Brigade sympathizers aboard the AMS-1. No name was put forward for a crewed position aboard the rebuilt spacecraft without going through a host of challenges. Some necessary and basic, such as personal history, education, and military service, but the fancy stuff as well. Relationships, past and present, family connections, active or derelict, and a full battery of tests regarding the applicant's politics. Were they team players? Loners? Aggressive? Passive? Curious? Stubborn? All personality test results were matched along with a matrix of other traits to determine what the ideal UEF officer or rating should look like, and everyone who signed up was compared to this ideal. No applicant avoided the piercing gaze of ZERO or a human OMP agent.

Not everyone made the cut. There was a sixty percent acceptance rate at best. People did not measure up and were removed from their post, or they raised red flags and alarms and were re-assigned to posts where watchful eyes could be kept upon them. A few were watched very carefully indeed, and they were barred from attaining any rank in the service beyond a junior NCO. But those were rare.

Sara Rosenski had made it past all the obstacles. Her record didn't pass muster as clean as the proverbial whistle—there were incidents in her past linking her to a number of questionable decisions and lapses of judgement—but her association with Katsev and the Specter squadron and its outsized influence on the UEF and OMP couldn't be denied, and it reflected on her. She had secrets. The difference was that none of hers were big enough to put the OMP on alert when she went on an errand for Katsev.

Like now.

Back on Mars, during her vain and botched attempt to secure secret data and beam it to a contact location on Earth during a massive alien attack, she was terrified that the OMP knew what she was doing and for whom. Probably also knew her compatriots inside the network the Brigade used to trade messages and file results with their masters back on Earth. The difference was that now she didn't care if they knew or not.

Layne's Brigade had an aim, and if the UEF wouldn't help them liberate the Earth from an alien species of freaking evolved dinosaurs, then they'd do it on their own. It had to be done. Earth under the current occupation would be dead in another few decades if nothing changed. The Sleer were sucking the world dry of what it needed to survive, and there was no way to avoid it.

The good news was the Sleer were neither universally powerful nor universally liked. The Movi and other races, what few examples they'd seen lately, were not much better. No one knew that better than Valri Gibb., and yet she made a joke of her humanity by deciding to work with the Movi. Fancy and slick they might be, but at their core they were no different from the Sleer. None of the races they'd found out here could really be called that different. The one thing that differentiated humans from all of them was the fact that homo sapiens lived on this particular ball o' rock, evolved here, called it home. Other planets might be habitable for the human race, but none of them could lay claim to that one defining point of their history and existence. Earth was home.

It belonged to humans. And that was that.

She pressed a hand against the wall lock and stepped back as the heavy blast doors hissed and parted. This was a staging area, devoted to automated machinery to load, maintain, and service Sleer equipment. One of the good things about the budding Allied Sleer Fleet was that the Sleer had made a great number of their models available to human crews for educational purposes. Her platoon, the Dino One-Oh-One, was part of that.

Her implants came to the fore as she walked across the platform, passing between dormant equipment. Eventually, she came to the rows of automata. They had come in useful before. These were the service drones, stick figure construction with Sleer shaped skulls bearing red cameras for eyes. They worked as well as any the Sleer kept for themselves, but they had issues. The drones were stupid as a sack of bricks and they took orders poorly, lacking even combat training. Sara thought they were useful for warning tourists away from fragile equipment or damaged areas, but that was about it.

Until you know how and where to make a few relatively minor changes to their programming. She did. Brooks had taught her everything he knew, and she'd figured out a few tricks of her own.

She linked her implants to the computers and brought the network to life. "Battle prep up. Battle dress. Basic compliment. Authentication One-seven-one-nine-five-seven-one Theta-six."

The machines came to attention and peeled off in pairs to a specialized set of feeders against the wall. The machines could synthesize anything they needed, but they were designed to crank out military gear most efficiently, and that's what they did. The drones stood below the assembly nodes and mechanized arms plucked items from storage racks and assembled them. The stick figures bulked up as the assembly line cracked open and fitted heavily armored arms, legs, gloves, and boots onto the skeletal frames. Helmets dropped into place, handguns were charged and fitted inside holsters. Then the machines marched off to a new waiting area as a new set of drones took their place. Two by two in precise order.

The one modification she made was to have the bots rely on sidearms rather than the stock energy rifles normally included with that type of armor. She didn't trust them with the heavy weaponry. Sidearms were far less powerful, which meant less collateral damage.

No, there wouldn't be any collateral damage. Valri would see reason. No damage, no need to draw live weapons, no need to start shooting at people. She was just reacting according to habits laid down by multiple terms of service in the UEF. There'd be no shooting.

When they were done, she had a platoon of fifty machines, all decked out no differently than Sleer Defenders.

Transponder codes and everything. And all under the command of a fictional CO who happened to take their orders from Sara Rosenski.

She'd briefly considered pulling her Nightmare buddies in for this, but decided that if something went pear-shaped she did not want this insanity to reflect badly on them. They were an amazing squadron. If she died or went to prison for the next thirty years, someone else would break them in, and that was how it should be.

This party was hers alone.

They would make their way to the Diplomacy Dome, they would find Valri Gibb, and they would confront her. It would be ugly, but Valri would see reason. And any onlookers would identify the Sleer as the aggressors. Because obviously, the Sleer would object to Valri's decision to work with the Movi. It was completely logical.

Rosenski accessed the data net with her implants. Routing the commands she needed through the Diplomacy Dome network was child's play. Of course it was, since she and Brooks created the backbone of the network the entire system relied on. She had an entire field command worth of officer IDs to play with. Fake names, fake ranks, fake combat records and personal histories. It was easy. She'd been intimidated at first by Brooks's gift for working with machines, but a year working with him had taught her to manage big projects like this on her own. There wasn't much to it. That wasn't fair—there was a great deal to it, but she no longer feared making mistakes bad enough to kill people. Things like that really were beyond her skill set. She knew how to coin logical bots, give them commands, and let them follow them, order by order, unit by unit

She sent the coded command and stepped out of the way as her troops marched off to war.

Valri ran.

Her feet pounded the treadmill's endless belt as it spun beneath her, heart pounding to match the beat she made as she ran to nowhere at four miles per hour, getting a rush of adrenaline and a heightened heart rate and a slightly elevated blood pressure into the mix. Sweat coated her face and arms, ran down her legs and into her socks. She ran.

She hadn't expected the treadmill to appear when she'd ordered it. Frances had mentioned she was putting on a few pounds, like nearly every human assigned to this crazy space station. Sleer food wasn't very palatable, so when on board the Battle Ring Genukh, she hadn't eaten much. None of the Hornets did. That plus sixteen-hour days made for a slim figure, and Rosenski's forced athletics program gave them something to work with. They competed against each other physically and mentally. Valri had always ended up at the end of the pack. Even Brooks, when he turned his implants down to near zero, was in better shape than she was. That wasn't fair; he was younger and shorter than she was. And practiced. He was a kid. Strangely, the one who she felt most at ease with wasn't Ray Fairchild but Richard Frost. The old dude paced her perfectly, allowing her the chance to get past him every now and then to enjoy that moment of superiority until he invariably caught up to her, pacing her again. They did this for weeks, around and around the main decks of the *Cyclops*. Slowly, she adjusted. She'd dropped weight and toned her muscles, and she had wind now. She felt better than she had in years, even without the implants. Now she could outrun nearly every human in the dome, even without the mechanical enhancement. And probably more than a few Movi. Probably not a Sleer, although speed was not what they were known for. But a race of creatures who threw bowling balls at each other at thirty kps for fun couldn't be evaluated in mere human terms.

She hated to admit it, but maybe the Movi were right. Maybe the Sleer were monsters. Nightmares. A destructive force blasting its way through the galaxy on its way to nowhere. Shadowed only by a race like the Skreesh, just as bent on destruction but not nearly as cuddly as the evolved dinosaurs.

She wondered if they were doing anyone a favor. Humans, for all their apparent backwardness, were still pursuit predators. They could run down prey long past anything's normal endurance. They invented traps for prey that was smaller and quicker than they were, devised nets to catch schools of aquatic life, dug pits to trap carnivores fifty times their weight. And that was before anything more advanced than the spear, knife, and net had been invented. Two three thousand years of experiments with axes alone had gone past generations of humans, the same basic tool being invented and reinvented over and over again. Knowledge handed down from father to son to grandson. Even with experimentation and individual flair for new designs, the most they'd gotten were things like difference in size and material. Axes the size of a tree to club tigers. Axes the size of a baseball bat to fell trees. Axes only a few inches long made as gifts or charms or pure ornament. How much had humanity lost to the passage of time simply because writing hadn't been invented?

Once writing was a thing, advancement like no one's business. Nomadic hunting to follow herds and the wealth they represented, then agriculture and cities. Not necessarily due to advancement, but maybe just something to try. There was some disagreement between the historians on that score. But with cities had grown sedentary cultures—and crops. Lots of crops. Various methods of raising crops, and with it, weather prediction and a ruling class to decide which crops were to be sown and reaped and who would get to use them and for what. Local currencies, then imperial currencies, then overreach and revolutions and tribes splitting to head to a new area to try the whole experiment all over again.

And how different were they from those roots from ten millennia ago? Not very. Not if the U-War was any indication. Not if trying to fix a fallen starship was any clue. Humans had already run out of space. Now they were running out of time.

That led her further down the rabbit hole. How close were they to repeating every bad decision that had plagued the human race? They'd reinvented bureaucracy easily enough; all that took was making rules and a way to enforce them. They'd reinvented corruption, bribery, classism, and lord knew what else. They'd reinvented politics as the Seer, Movi, and various factions thereof tried to bribe or threaten her into obediently turning their wishes into policy. Didn't that same sort of shit nearly destroy the world not once but three times? Granted, the U-war never went ICBM, but the world became a much quieter place in its wake.

She hit the red button on the chronometer and the belt tagged her exit time as it slowed to a top. She stepped off and staggered, huffing to her bed. Hands on knees, she turned to the illuminated desk she called her home office and noticed the flashing red LED.

Deep breaths. Get that oxy back into the blood where it belonged. She flopped into a big chair and quickly checked her connections to the office; no messages, no waiting phone calls, nothing on the calendar for tonight as far as she knew. A quick sweep of her appointment book confirmed it. So? Why the red light?

She pounded a stud on the console. "Frances! Why are you trying to monitor my official system?"

The undeniably male voice that met her ears send a chill

down her spine and across her skin. "Captain Underhill is not monitoring your data network, Madame Secretary. I am," ZERO said.

"My dude. You're back!"

"I was never away."

"Should I be worried? Or grateful?"

ZERO managed a decent imitation of a chuckle. Creepy but decent. "I regularly monitor all government channels," he said, "In order to verify that certain security protocols are still effective. Tonight, I am intrigued."

"Intrigue isn't really your thing. It's more like sneaky peepy traditions. Like opened mail. Tapped phones. Keyboard log chains. That sort of thing."

"None of which are currently employed in this location. However, I am curious about something."

"Lord save us from curious computers."

"Madame, I'm completely serious. There is an anomaly in your comm console and I am trying to diagnose it. It's not going as well as I'd hoped."

Valri felt her stomach drop. "What's wrong?"

"Someone in Primate Alley is trying to block my access channels. They are employing unique forms of overrides."

"Unique how?"

"The overrides are not of my own design."

Finally, it clicked. "You're being *hacked*?"

"Not my CPU nor my memory storage areas, but yes. Someone is subverting my directives. I am diverting my attention to deal with the problem."

"Is it something to worry about?"

"That remains to be seen. I expect not, but—"

The line went dead, so unexpectedly that Valri waited a full minute before thinking to wonder if there was a bug in her comm channel. "ZERO? ZERO? You there?"

A quick change of channels. "Frances? You there?" Silence. She tried other combinations and channels. "Ray? Skull? Anyone from the *Gauntlet*, acknowledge. Anyone from the Diplo Dome, acknowledge my transmission. Basil! Where the hell is everyone tonight?"

Then it hit her. When everyone you know has dropped off the face of the planet, you're the one who's been cut off. "Shit. Shit shit shit shit shit..."

Okay. There was a way around this. She slid a finger beneath a control, popped the seal, flipped up the cover, and pressed her thumb on the red button beneath. Nothing. No alarm, no warning, no harried policemen or secret service guards rushing in to demand to know if she was safe.

That meant some kind of protocol she'd never imagined was in place. She lay back, closed her eyes, and accessed her implants, only to find that she had no access to the network. Nothing. It was if her eyes and ears had fallen out of her head. She ran a quick sweep of the sensory items in the office. No jamming fields, no sensor blankets, no security booths like they'd used in the meeting with Makjit and Horvantz. This was different.

And she remembered hearing about the effect from Frances Underhill talking about her experiences with Brooks and Rosenski on Battle Ring Great Nest. This was Sleer tech in action. Someone in a command tower had turned her implants off, or down so low that it made no appreciable difference. She was blind, deaf, and dumb, as the saying went. There was only one reason that could possibly make sense: someone was coming for her, and they'd arrive very soon.

Fuck.

CHAPTER 33

SIMON BROOKS SAW IT FIRST.

The meeting with Rosenski unsettled him enough to stare at the contents of his pathetic liquor cabinet and wonder why he even had one. He didn't drink, and if he decided to start, there was a growing list of socially acceptable places in Primate Alley to do it. He made a quick scan of his contacts, idly wondering where everyone was tonight, and came up against a block in his network. A red light connected to the Diplomacy Dome. It was too late for any big meetings to be going on, so what was happening?

Aloud he said, "Why the hell is Diplo Dome under extra surveillance?"

"I believe I can answer your question, Lieutenant Brooks."

"Well, it's good to hear your voice again. Are you Genukh or ZERO today?"

"This is ZERO speaking."

"Great. Can you answer my question?" He smirked as he read the smug impatience in the machine's voice. Sticking it to ZERO was something he got to do so rarely.

"I can. There seems to be a rendering fault in the data transfer network. I am trying to resolve it now. However..."

The hesitation went on for almost a full minute. That was unlike him. "However?"

"Excuse me. There is. Difficulty. There...is...a problemmmm-mmm..." ZERO's voice slurred to a stop and then collapsed.

"ZERO? *Genukh?*" Brooks suddenly became fully alert, all thoughts of booze and socializing forgotten. "Brooks to Rosenski, we have a problem." More silence. He switched channels. "Brooks to Underhill, respond."

"Underhill here. What's going on? We have comm outages all over the station tonight."

"Sara's not answering her comm; I'm a little worried about her lately...and I don't know how or why, but ZERO is flaking out."

"Yeah, tell me another one."

"I'm serious. I never heard anything like this. He started talking in circles and faded out, then nothing."

"It's not possible."

"I'm not lying. It really happened."

"Brooks, the only time I *ever* heard ZERO sound anything like that it was—" He waited for her to continue, wondering what exactly she'd heard and when. He had access to all the past mission reports, but a lot of the text was purely functional. Not many descriptive elements. Showing a flair for the written word was not what contact reports were there for. "Brooks, join me on the encrypted command channel. Say nothing unless you're spoken to."

"Roger that." Simon complied and suddenly heard a cacophony of voices, all clamoring for attention. It was like being dropped into the middle of a cocktail party. One voice he recognized instantly was Commander Ray Fairchild. He'd know Uncle's baritone anywhere.

"Hornet squadron sound off," Ray ordered. The line was silent. Of course, Simon could hear Ray, since Ray was also on the command line, but everyone else was muted. He did sense the ping in his implants, and he sent an acknowledging ping to match. "My people are all accounted for." Simon sighed in relief, but his next words froze his chest. "Except for Sara Rosenski. And no, it's not because she isn't a Hornet. I've got her pinged along with the other squadron Commanders. She's not responding."

"Fine, fine. I am initiating a network conference," a new voice said. Simon recognized this one too: Commander Thomas Katsev, The Butcher. The AMS-1 Air Group Commander. "Brooks, are you online?"

"I am, Commander."

"Good. Begin a full comm net sweep. I want every node checked. Anyone who doesn't respond gets noted and punted back to this conference. Understand?"

"Yes, sir."

"Good man. Get it done." A click, and Brooks found himself alone. The line to the big channel was still open, but he'd been shunted to his own private workspace—whether to get him out of everyone's hair or to give him privacy to finish his task, he wasn't sure.

But privacy worked both ways. He cracked his knuckles and lay back on his couch, then opened the floodgates between his implants and the rest of Battle Ring ZERO. If there was one thing he know how do to, it was hack the shit out of Sleer computer systems.

Rosenski monitored her troops with the habits of a line officer. She saw her robot helpers as parts of a drone squadron; each pilot had its orders, and they already knew how to operate as a single unit. Any questions were punted to her for management. The rest of it they could do with their own intelligences. They followed orders well.

Now things were getting dicey. She paced them virtually from the deck above Diplomacy Dome, herself in Sleer battle dress, but removed from the action. She followed them to the entrance of the diplomatic section. There was no one around. Everyone was already gone for the night.

Valri Gibb, however, was something of a workaholic. Her own staff had lodged concerns about it to the Primate Alley health board. They, in the way that government functionaries often did, saw the problem more as an opportunity than a concern. As long as the secretary got the assigned work done and didn't kill herself or anyone else, or give the Overcops reason to worry about her, all was well.

And Valri's business suite was huge. Twenty offices, and all highly secure. Blast doors designed to keep out any intrusion defended every entrance to the compartment. A wise precaution, that. Rosenski had the codes to open the doors. She used them one by one, wincing each time they worked. Part of her knew she should reverse course, stand down her troops, forget this whole insane mission. Seriously, let's say she got through to her target. (Another door open. And another. March the troops down a set of three corridors to meet at three more doors. Open, open, open. Where *was* she?) Let's say Valri couldn't tell the difference between an armored service drone and an actual Sleer Defender. Let's say Rosenski made her case. And let's say that Valri said no. She had that habit. Tell her to jump and watch her sit down on the floor. She was obstinate and proud and she never took orders well. They'd found that out the hard way on *Cyclops*. Likely as not, that was the reason ZERO had tagged her for government work. In combat, you had to obey orders. That was how everything worked. You couldn't pick and choose which orders you were going to follow, or from whom. In government, you were expected to put up a fuss. That was the whole point, to prevent any one chungo with the habits of a dictator from trying to manage the entire operation. There were checks and balances. Directives. Rules.

Another door open. And another.

Almost there.

Simon Brooks bathed in the energy of computerized attention. It would go faster with a set of command gauntlets, but you had to work with what you had. At the moment, that was his implants.

Laying down turned out to be a bad idea. The weight of his body against the cushions actually distracted him from full immersion, and moving to the console in his living room just felt normal. Now he stood surrounded by a fully interactive holographic display. The field of objects was projected onto his retinas from within; to an onlooker it would seem as if he were plucking invisible objects and manipulating them with his arms, just play acting like one would on a stage.

It still wasn't as effective as command gauntlets, but it worked well enough to control fleets of ships. Now, instead of fleets, he was commanding swarms of defense drones, observation drones, and security cameras built into the walls, ceilings, and floors of Battle Ring Great Nest. None of it substantially different from what he'd used previously, but unquestionably more primitive, less responsive, and frankly, slow. That made him the craziest—the lack of perceived speed. He was used to the reactions being faster, but he adapted.

There! The comm net. He spread his electronic arms and

pulled gobbets of data from storage banks, examining each and tossing them back before reaching for a new one. *That* was the relational matrix that ran the Primate Alley comm net. There was nothing wrong with it. Everything seemed to work...except the segments that ran through the controlling AI. That was weird. He'd assumed that someone had turned ZERO off, but that wasn't the case at all. ZERO lived! But he was trapped in a box. Not that different from what Nazerian and Edzedon had done to Genukh herself. Except this box didn't seem to be one built into the main board as a security measure. This one looked completely homemade. Something that he might have done with time and effort. Except he wouldn't have done this.

So who had?

He saw the structure the interference had taken, the shape of the commands. Sleer military command codes. Not the sort of thing you'd see in a remote access situation, with the new user being presented with numerous prompts, each of which required its own password. This was far too intricate for that. This was the sort of thing you only saw when Sleer implants were involved.

The Sleer themselves wouldn't do something like this. There was no point to it. The pattern Brooks found wasn't a broad-spectrum attack. Not a denial-of-service attempt to bombard a target with every available resource. That's how Sleer thought. When you had millions of ships and billions of Defenders, losing a few meant nothing. Overwhelm and annihilate, that was the Sleer attack strategy. Whoever was running this show was picking their targets far more carefully and tailoring their attack to those specs. Military for certain. But careful. And that meant a human.

He sighed in despair. There were only so many humans that might have the talent and the implants to make an evert like this happen. And all of them were accounted for. All but one.

"Damn it, Sara," he groaned. "How deep in the Laynies' pockets are you?"

He had few options. He could call it in, pass his suspicions up the line, let Underhill and Fairchild know they had a potential terrorist in their midst. He didn't like that train of thought. The possibility of Sara being in league with actual terrorists or being one herself brought up a bit of bile that he forced down.

He had to deal with her himself. Luckily, he knew how to do that. He linked his implants to the central network and determined his assets and tactics. "Invasion protocol Epsilon in progress. Request release of defense drone battalion L-495 to the Diplomacy Dome immediately."

ZERO's mechanical voice responded, but something was clearly out of whack. His voice sounded like it was being shouted from the bottom of a well. "Release granted. Good hunting, Lieutenant."

A new order grid appeared on his implant-powered HUD. He selected the unit that could respond most quickly and said, "This is Lt. Simon Brooks, to unit L-495 authorization ZERO implemented..." he checked his watch,"...21:26 hours this day. Acknowledge."

A robotic voice came over the line. Creepier and creepier, considering they'd all become used to ZERO and Genukh's human speaking patterns over the past three years. "Command acknowledged. Request order one."

"Order one is as follows. Protect all Diplomacy Dome staff against aggression, maximum deployment. I'll be there shortly."

"Order one acknowledged. Moving out."

Brooks pulled out of the network and took a moment to orient himself. The units loyal to him would take time to reach the Diplomacy Dome. In the meantime, he had a good lead on where the aggressors would strike. There was only one event that had taken place in the past day that would explain it. Valri

Gibb had acted to place the loyalty of her department at the hand of the Movi—and a not well-liked faction of theirs at that. Who would be left to stop them?

He pulled up a floor plan, plotted a route to Valri's office, and ordered his battalion to meet him along the way.

Rosenski followed her platoon virtually. No passerby even looked up at their passage down the halls. Everyone knew what Sleer Defenders looked like when they moved from one compartment to another. Nothing to see here. She'd found a maintenance compartment that was currently unused. Locking the door and marking the location on her map as "under review" should keep out any random visitors.

The section gave itself to offices and meetings rooms, with wide halls devoted to grand affairs, banquets, receptions, and private parties. The sound of her troops' boots hitting the deck resounded even through filters. If her orders were carried out properly, she could derail a host of political operations, any one of which's failure could put the Earth in a worse position that it now was.

No. She had instructions. She shied away from using the word orders. Functionally, orders were things she received from officers higher up the pole than she was. This was an instruction. A deadly and potentially treasonous instruction.

No. She couldn't think that way. It was too late for that.

The blast doors parted and the troops filed through. Two more sets of doors, each heavier than the preceding, and they'd be in the core, the suite of chambers where cabinet members and their staffs met. Two floors down would be the Secretary of Commerce's office. Concentric rings around that suite would house the various undersecretaries and their functionaries. The less valuable you were as a decision maker, the closer to the outside they placed you. Typical.

Except Valri wasn't a secretary—not officially. Which placed her in the outer ring of offices. Bad for her, good for Sara.

Damn.

Valri felt the approach of the troops before she saw them.

Her quarters weren't impregnable, but they'd been designed by a Sleer AI as part of a defense installation. Everything on a battle ring was built with an interest in optimizing defense. That meant maximizing the amount of blood any invader would have to spill to get to her. Even without concealed hallway turrets that popped out to shoot enemies, every wall, ceiling, and floor was a potential obstacle.

She reached out with her implants—useless for comm channels, but she still had access to the local network. She spotted the problem. A platoon of soldiers wearing Sleer Defender armor marching toward her apartment. As Ray Fairchild had taught her, she pinged the transponders and found nothing. The unit didn't exist, and there was no CO on record. That told her everything she needed to manage the crisis.

Her sisters, both veterans, had long ago given her specific advice about incursions. Only three types of fighters showed up on your doorstep: soldiers, police, and terrorists. If they told you who they were, it meant soldiers or police. Soldiers would execute their mission. Police would put you in prison. Terrorists always killed you. When they didn't tell you who they were, you had to assume they were terrorists. Act appropriately.

She broadened her view to the block where she lived. Three hallways intersected hers, and of her block, only her apartment was occupied. She watched as the troops broke up, dispersing to cut off access to the intersections. No escape for her. But now they only had about twenty effectives instead of thirty. She could make that work. She turned to the apartment console, a wall unit that combined all the electronic services used by the flat. She pulled open a panel to see a red lever and a keypad, entered a string of digits from memory, and pulled the lever. Alarms went off all over the block and numerous armored turrets dropped from the ceiling outside. The sounds of laser fire reached her within seconds, even through the heavy outer doors. She watched as two, then three of her assailants dropped in their tracks. Then a fourth and a fifth dropped as the others returned fire. Within a minute, the turrets were smoking black holes. But now they were down to fifteen Defenders.

What else? The interior doors were thin, meant as privacy dividers rather than defense. Meant to maintain pressure inside the flat in case of a hull breach, the front and back doors, however, were both heavy and powered by electric motors. Another panel, another set of controls. Turning power off to the doors was easy enough, but now she was trapped with whatever she had on-hand inside. The doors would resist their efforts for a while, but a determined enemy would get in soon enough.

So. That meant the black cabinet. It stood in her bedroom; a tall, lightless oblong that resembled nothing so much as a heavy-duty gun safe. It made it easier to think about. She pressed hand against the top left corner and said, "This is my war."

The front popped open and she yanked the door wide. First things first, she pulled out the suit of Defender armor. The sort of thing meant for pilots rather than infantry, it was no match for what the attackers were wearing but it would hook her up with a bigger network and protect her from heat, radiation, and flying debris. She donned her dome and powered up, relaxing a bit when she saw the power supply worked. She could last in here for a full day.

She pulled the energy rifle and pistol from their respective back and hip mounts, watched them slide back into place when she let them go. That never got old.

A box of grenades was next. The good ones, the Sleer plasma types. One of them would burn a hole a meter wide in a bulkhead. Four of them went on her belt. Finally, she pulled a heavy metal box from the cabinet, carried it to her bed, and opened it. A thick tube with hand grips and a suppression ring around the muzzle lay within. She hefted the weapon, broke a seal, checked the power cell, and re-assembled it. This baby was a Sleer fusion gun. The sort of thing that was only used to repel invading mechs aboard Sleer warships. A gun like this had taken out more than one of the Hornet's Sparrowhawk planes. She located the interface at the stock end and matched it to a connecting port on her armor. She seated the stock and locked the interface, and her implants projected firing information and an aiming circle on her HUD.

She hated the feel of the alien weapon against her shoulder. She was no stranger to firearms; Ray had spent over a year with her at the firing range, instructing and training her to handle a variety of pistols and long guns. But the Sleer fusion gun was something much stranger. The device she now held worked by dispensing a barely controlled nuclear explosion. The hideous possibilities of using it to trash her own flat had no parallels in daily life. The only thing she could imagine was releasing a can of tear gas in the Governor's box at the Kentucky Derby. But there hadn't been a Derby in years. Kentucky was under six inches of grit, ash, and soot, and three feet of snow. There might never be one of those insane horse races again.

All because of the damn Sleer.

She toggled her implants again. "This is acting Secretary of Interstellar Commerce Valri Gibb. I am under attack. I am in my apartment in the Diplomacy Dome. All allied personnel, I need help." She set the recording to play on repeat and hoped someone could hear it.

In the meantime, she saw that the apartment was built such that all the interior doors lined up—the bathroom was the only room that didn't lead to an outside door. She closed all the doors she had, stepped into her bathtub, leaned against the bulkhead, and waited for a clear shot.

CHAPTER 34

BROOKS FELT he was making progress, but the way the defense drones moved on his map, he knew he wasn't making it fast enough.

Drone group L-495 were doing their jobs but not as well as he hoped. This ring's defense drones were only superficially related to the giant versions used on Battle Ring Earth. These were meant to manage humanoid assailants, not the biggest Sleer war machines. Two meters tall, they looked like the remotely controlled Emus they'd seen on the derelict vessel in Vega, but these were armed with laser guided RPGs and miniguns, with a slitted dome on top for sensory gear. You could look through one's cameras, give it a list of orders, and send it off on a quest, or deploy them like Roman legionnaires, and they wouldn't balk. But give them any order more complicated than that and they tended to halt in their tracks and demand clarification. On the other hand, if you gave them a battle map and told them to wipe out a threat, they were golden. But they wouldn't hold up long against Sleer infantry.

Worse, the emergency was now being communicated from unit to unit, but without the comm net to co-ordinate a response, the UEF was vulnerable. He'd already contacted Fairchild, who had passed the alert up the line, but Brooks hadn't heard orders yet, which meant Rojetnick was still calling his officers to figure out what to do. Not a bad process, but it would take time, and Brooks didn't share their enthusiasm for dotting I's and crossing T's.

There were times you had to jump first and figure out your landing afterwards. He opened a private comm channel and found the implant code he wanted. "Brooks to Underhill. I need help."

"Underhill. Go ahead."

"I've initiated all possible alerts to my CO and activated defense drones to converge on Valri's quarters, but I can't break through the comm net. There's too much traffic and it's going to take forever to narrow down the transponders that are being used to manage the assault."

"Here, try this."

Even from the other side of Primate Alley they could sling data packets to each other without error. He caught the snippet she launched at him and opened it. It didn't often happen that Brooks didn't know what he was looking at. "What *is* this?"

"You tell me. It's a transponder trace I made a few days before you Gauntlets made your ways back home. Valri's PA made a call and this is the channel he used. I smelled a bit of Rosenski's imprint on it, but the transponder track didn't pan out. If you can trace it, I think there's a good chance you'll figure out who's running this show. The code name they used is Brookhaven."

"Brookhaven...okay, that's more than I had when I started. You're aware there's no way that any of us could have sent any messages from Vega, right, Captain? We were busy getting our asses kicked by a rogue Sleer CO."

"Acknowledged. I took the data as far as I could, but I don't think you showed me everything you know about Sleer messaging protocols. Did you?"

"No comment, Ma'am."

"Don't ma'am me, just get her done."

He worked feverishly, sliding data packets out of his way and grabbing others as he worked, only vaguely aware that he was violating all manner of military protocols. But he had an OMP Captain on his side and that gave him electronic courage. If he went to the brig forever, at least he's have gone down protecting a government employee. The same employee who had decided to shift EarthGov trade policy away from the Sleer and toward the Movi.

Oh, *shit*.

"Underhill, I have it! The attackers are working for the Laynies. Run the—"

"Wait, Layne's Brigade? Here? How do—?"

"Later! Run the transponder IDs you extracted from Brookhaven through these OMP filters and you'll probably be able to trace the connection. That should lead you—"

"Right back to Rosenski or the choad who's impersonating her. Brooks, I owe you a kiss and a beer. Hang on."

A kiss and a beer. He'd probably have to take both from behind bars. It'd still be better than what they put Sara through if they caught her—and they would catch her. He and Underhill were making sure of that right now. It wasn't what he'd signed up for. He'd signed up to be part of Ray Fairchild's crew, and Sara Rosenski had taken on the role of mentor. She'd built him up, straightened him out, and set him on a course that led here. Stabbing her like this...

He pulled more data, examined a salient bit he'd set aside. The code he'd worked out wasn't Rosenski's current code. That was inextricably linked to her implants. Whoever'd conjured this access point had known her original ID but had no way of knowing what her current version was. He'd picked up enough from Underhill to understand that the law of plausible deniability was in play. So maybe it wasn't her. Maybe she was being set up as a patsy for a cretin higher up the food chain. Katsev maybe. Or whoever Katsev worked for.

That gave him an idea. To implement it, he would only have to betray every rule the UEF had.

Underhill came back on the line. "I have it. We traced the code to the G ring of the Diplo Dome housing complex. I've ordered a squad of Golems to meet us there."

"It won't work," he said, and slid his packet to her. "Here's what I have. She's not in the complex or anywhere near the dome. Defense drones are already closing in. They'll take out the units attacking Valri."

"What do you think we're going to do, Lieutenant?"

"With respect, Captain, this can't wait for an explanation. Meet me on deck four, compartment AK-1845."

"Why there? The attack is focused on—"

"It's Rosenski. She's controlling the assault from there. In this particular case, the fewer of us involved, the better."

"On my way. When I arrive you can tell me how a bunch of terrorists managed to infiltrate the military and why you know so much about them."

Valri used her implants to watch the battle on the monitors and waited for the fight to come to her.

She didn't usually think of fights this way. She was the type to hunt for the bastard with the weapon, but this was different. Ray had drilled a few rules into her. *Make them come to you. Set yourself up to extract maximum blood from the attacking force. Bottleneck them whenever possible. Make them dig you out of a deep hole and kill them as they arrive.* Hence the bathtub and the mini-armory.

She practiced using the tactical display on her armor's HUD. It was fed from the comm net, picking up and assembling data into a coherent visual display. The housing complex built around the Diplo Dome was arranged in concentric circles. Hers was dubbed the E-ring, which wasn't the outermost, but close to it. The platoon of attacking Defenders had approached down her hallway from both directions to converge on her location. At the moment, the thing that was slowing them down most was the hidden defense turrets located in ceilings and floors. On the other side of the equation were local defense drones, moving up from inside the Dome's D-ring to her location. It was a contest, testing whose soldiers could deny access to the other side most effectively.

Access to her apartment. Access to herself.

Her feed slowed to a trickle; the monitors were getting zapped as often as the defense turrets or the drones. One by one, they blinked out as connections were lost. What remained was simple. Anyone who tried to get into her flat would either announce themselves or be shot.

The front door chimed. Once, twice. It was meant to maintain atmosphere after a hull breach, and there was no way she'd open it for them. She lowered the fusion rifle and glanced down at the plasma grenades. Her mind went to war with itself, screaming at her to do something and also demanding that she stay put. She pinged the door cam and looked at her visitors. Five figures in Defender armor stood in the hallway. No help there, but it did give her the jolt she needed to put her ridiculous plan into action.

Valri let the heavy energy weapon go, and the suit pulled it back into place against her back. She set the grenades on her belt to auto-arm and dug into her memory to recall what little she knew about them. Pull to arm, then five seconds before they went up? Or was it three?

Two more door chimes. Why were they being so polite? They had her cornered at gunpoint—what was the story here?

She scuttled to the front door, made sure she was standing to the side, next to the panel, and thumbed the speaker. "Identify yourself!"

The answering voice wasn't even slightly human. "Madame Secretary. Stand down."

"Or what?"

"Madame. Secretary. Stand. Down."

"Remove your helmet. Let me see who you are."

"Stand. Down. Now."

So much for diplomacy, she thought. She held her breath and hit the switch for the door.

Rosenski's Defender armor couldn't keep her cool. Stinging beads of sweat dropped into her eyes as she worked. The attack was going badly. She could feel the proverbial walls closing in. But she thought Valri was ready to listen to reason.

She'd marched her drones down Valri's block, cutting off access away from the flat and to the blast doors leading to other blocks. Half a dozen stood by, out of obvious sight from within the apartment. A fire team of five was trying to coax her out of the flat now. She'd ordered them to leave their weapons at order arms position. No intention to shoot her on sight. She'd hoped Valri would understand that. They'd even used the doorbell, for fuck's sake...

The implants fed data into her brain as Valri's door opened. She allowed herself a sigh of relief. This was going to work after all. And nobody but robots had to get—

Motion on her feed. Three—no, four—objects flew out from inside the apartment, sticking to three of her troops and one adhering to the far wall in the hallway. They smoked, glowed and detonated in an explosion that fritzed her feed and made her flinch. Plasma grenades! Where the hell did she get...

"Fairchild!" she snarled. "God damn it, Uncle..."

She staggered and sat on a storage crate as she cleared her feed. She found herself staring at a rack of emergency pressure suits and matching helmets, plus crates and cases of God knew what. She pinged her remaining troops in the hallways, unscathed from the blast but knocked down by the blast wave. She righted them, selected the team leader, and looked through its eyes.

The explosion had torn holes in the hallway and destroyed the entry hatch for the apartment. She vaguely wondered whether the blast had shredded Valri too, but saw blaster fire exiting the breach. Valri was fine and dandy, and now she was doubly determined to shoot anything that came close to her. This just got a lot harder.

She linked her microphone to the team leader's speaker and turned the distortion up as high as it would go. Sara's own mother wouldn't recognize her voice now. "Damn it, Valri, we just want to talk."

From inside the apartment: "Then talk!"

"There's a problem."

"Damn right! Pointing guns at me is a problem."

"Why did you decide to go with the Movi?" Sara hesitated as she checked her feeds. All her private lines were still private, and most of the camera domes were already wrecked. "You agreed to sell out Earth's defenses to the Movi delegation from Dal-Cortsuni."

"Is that what I did? I thought I opened the door to a more

robust relationship with our interstellar neighbors who are *not* occupying our home world."

"We can do this hard, too," Rosenski murmured. She wiggled her fingers and turned her head, followed by her troops entering single file; the door was too narrow to admit more than one at a time. Inside of a minute, a wall of metal backed her up and Valri had to understand she was out of moves.

"Come on, Val. Let's be friendly about it."

"You don't get to call me that. Not after you frog march your heavily armed buddies in here to try and squeeze me. Shit all over that, motherfucker."

"They aren't our friends, Madame Secretary."

"And the Sleer are?"

"None of them are. That's the point. We're on our own. We—"

Her HUD went crazy, signifying a perceived loss of control and locking down the internal controls. Her own suit's works were telling her to do something as it fought off a hack attempt carried through a feed. She shut down systems, closed off ports, and isolated her suit from intrusion. And now found that she couldn't control her fire team or anything else.

At the bottom of her HUD, a tiny window opened. "Lieutenant Commander Rosenski. Stand your forces down immediately."

Rosenski fought down panic as she realized she was out of moves. She linked to the local network and saw why. Two figures in Defender armor stood in the hallways just outside her hidey-hole's door. Not standard armor, though. They carried bold insignia and identifying markings. One, a Unified Earth Fleet First Lieutenant, and the other a captain in the Office of Military Protocols.

It was over. She was dead. When handed a death sentence,

one had two choices: gibber or bluster. Gibbering was not Sara Rosenski's style. "You two don't have the authority to make me."

"With respect, ma'am...I do. I'm tasked with protecting the section staff and officers from any attack, and today that includes you. And if not, then Underhill does. Let's do this the quiet way. Please."

"There's more at stake here than I think you recognize, Simon."

She heard the heavy sigh through his comm. "That's entirely possible. Doesn't matter. Stand your troops down or I'll have to respond."

"You wouldn't dare."

"Do you really want to find out?"

It was a good question.

Rosenski pulled the fusion rifle from its rack, hefted it, ordered the hatch to open. The empty corridor could only mean that Simon Brooks had just trashed his life to save hers. She half laughed, half sobbed, and launched her implants, realizing Brooks and Underhill were standing not in front of this closet but the workshop where she'd initialized her drones. Sara activated the last two, routed the data feeds so it looked like she'd always been there, and logged off.

She knew Underhill would throw a gasket when she realized Brooks had led her to the wrong compartment. If they came for her, she'd cooperate, but maybe he...

No. They were both screwed. She merely had a little more time before they came for her, that was all. Maybe they'd let them share a cell before execution.

Fuck.

CHAPTER 35

AFTER EIGHT DAYS of sharing the same cell, Brooks and Rosenski were ready for a firing squad.

They'd been incarcerated before. After their first encounter with Genukh, Capt. Rojetnick and Col. Dimitri had disagreed as to whether taking implants counted as sedition, and they were remanded to indefinite medical supervision in the hospital complex on AMS-1. At least it was a comfortable cell.

This time the OMP was in charge, and made no bones of the fact they'd both seriously fucked up. Bunk beds, a metal sink, a toilet with no privacy screen. If they wanted to sit, they had a cold metal deck. Bare walls and no mirrors.

They tried to keep their cool, but alternately became hostile or morose. Once they came to blows. Two OMP guards arrived and broke up the fight with stun batons. They learned their lesson and avoided raw violence after that. After day three, they ran out of insults. They stewed in their rage at each other and themselves. By day six, they'd become robotic. They lay in their bunks or paced the cell during the day and slept at night. They ate the food that appeared in the slot. They said nothing.

On day nine, the guards escorted them to a cold, harshly lit interview room without windows. A metal table, two chairs on one side, one more on the other. A black observation dome peered down from the ceiling. They sat.

Finally, Brooks said, "You think we'll get a cigarette before they shoot us?"

Rosenski shook her head. "They won't shoot you."

A thick, dark-skinned woman entered and sat at the other end of the table. An OMP colonel's insignia and thick black hair shot with gray done in a cable braid down her back. Her eyes were brown enough to be black. High cheekbones. Not someone to annoy.

"I'm Colonel Yousaf," she said. "You're both in very serious trouble."

"Have you spoken to—?"

Yousaf placed a tablet heavily on the table top. "I've spoken to everyone. Captain Underhill. Commander Fairchild. Commander Katsev. Generals Eisenhart and Hendricks. I'm sick of talking."

"Does that cover begging for our lives?" Rosenski snarked.

"We're long past that." She stabbed at the tablet and a display popped up, a list of bullet points floating in the air. She flicked them off the list as she spoke. "Rosenski. Willfully causing damage to the space station AI. Attempted kidnapping of a government official. Threatening and harassing a government official. Misappropriation of station resources. Use of stolen resources in the commission of a capital crime. Suspected of working with a known terrorism organization. And of course, treason. Such fun."

She waved a finger to flip the page. "Brooks. Invading an OMP network using banned technology. Obstructing an OMP officer who was in the process of investigating a crime. Aiding and abetting a capital crime. Lovely."

Yousaf settled in her chair, hands neatly folded on the table. "If you feel like explaining yourselves, I'll listen."

Sara fidgeted. "Please don't shoot him," she said.

"Shut up, Sara."

"No, you shut up. You're not as smart as you think, and you know it." She leaned forward and fixed her eyes on Yousaf's. "I'm in it up to my neck. That's fine. I'll take a bullet for what I believe. But Simon Brooks is just a stupid kid who doesn't know when not to butt into my business. It sounds nuts, but he really was trying to help get me out of this mess. He doesn't deserve a bullet. Ever. He's a good soldier."

"Is that true, Mr. Brooks? Are you a good soldier?"

"Clearly not, Colonel."

"The CAG and Deputy CAG disagree. They insist this incident is circumstantial—for both of you. They could be correct. The data we extracted is far more than circumstantial. Normally, we'd have ZERO do that for us, but it seems he and Genukh aren't talking to any of us now. We're forced to rely on our own judgement."

"Good. Research strengthens the mind," Sara growled.

"Shut up, Sara," Yousaf snapped. "Frankly, I'm not impressed with what your current and previous COs have told me. But I trust Frances Underhill. I believe her when she tells me you can both be salvaged. The question is how? I can't very well send you both back to your units. Too many questions. Not to mention you've both demonstrated a far more intense loyalty to each other than either of you show to the Unified Earth Fleet. General Hendricks believes this situation calls for something new."

"What situation?"

"Honestly, it's your implants. Here, look at this." Yousaf tapped the slate and a new graphic appeared. It showed a humanoid with an intricate system of leads emerging from a central point located just below the collar bone. "When they insert the injection port, the device is neutral. Inactive. But when the microbes are injected, the port grows a network of leads only a few molecules thick. They reach into every organ, every muscle, most of the nervous system. After three years, the body is inextricably wired to work with the new hardware. Even if you wanted to, removal is not an option without killing you."

"Strange how Genukh didn't mention a word of that three years ago," Rosenski snarled, glaring at Brooks in barely controlled rage. Brooks flushed red and flapped his mouth like a trout.

"Wasn't it?" Yousaf agreed. "A mechanical intelligence finds itself in an existential crisis and offers you two a chance to solve your immediate medical problems while resolving the crisis for its own part. Funny how that works, isn't it?"

"I'm never going to hear the end of this," Brooks groaned. "I'm an idiot."

"Which brings me to this." Yousaf tapped her slate and summoned a white coated medical tech who began unpacking a small case. Brooks and Rosenski's gazes were attracted to something else. A Sleer medical drone rolled into the room after him, tentacled arms adjusting to avoid scraping the doorway.

The tech handed Yousaf a small box and left. She indicated the drone with a wave of her hand. "You're familiar with Sleer medical equipment, obviously. This drone is very much like the one that installed your implants. And this," she said, hefting the box, "is the unit that Ship Master Kessidus trained me how to use several months ago. I believe you've both met Small Lord Kessidus?"

"He tortured us quite a bit back in the day, yes," Brooks said.

"Then you'll be familiar with the object of this procedure. If I touch this, your bodies respond by losing muscle control."

Sara growled and Brooks grimaced as their bodies sagged

and sank into their chairs. They'd been here before, every excruciating minute of it. Prisoners on the Earth Ring, Kessidus had given them a full demonstration of how implants gave COs command of their troops' bodies and minds.

"I think I'd rather have the bullet," Rosenski said.

Brooks agreed, but instead of nodding, his head flopped back and forth. "We can be reasonable. You don't have to do this."

"I most certainly do. You two are clearly out of control. From now on, you'll follow the OMP's orders. We'll hang on to you for a few weeks to properly condition you, then we'll release you. But don't worry, I won't leave you like this. I just need you to be still for the procedure."

"What procedure?"

"Ship Master Kessidus graciously loaned us a medical team to help develop a patch that would modify the existing design. The UEF Applied Medical Technology Division gave us approval to begin tests on human subjects. That will be you."

The drone extended two of its many arms. Brooks could see a pair of slim vials in its claws, one for each of them. He recognized them instantly; the same sort of microbes that Sleer used to employ medical enhancements. "You didn't ask for our consent."

"I don't need consent, just for you to sit still. Don't want any scarring, now do we? You both have such perfect skin."

Two weeks after the attack, Valri swore she could still smell the smoke; her apartment had been trashed beyond repair.

The complex had been mostly empty at the time of the attack. The few residents who had been evacuated by OMP police were instructed to not discuss the event in the interests of interstellar security, and they generally obeyed. In a few days, the bureaucratic machinery of EarthGov had impressed its needs on its employees and the stories of the attack, and even the memory of it, were pushed aside by the needs of daily survival.

Valri asked one question of Frances Underhill: "Who did it?"

"We don't know. Might have been Layne's Brigade. Might have been someone else. We're looking at all possibilities."

Valri sagged. She sat behind her desk sullenly, well after hours. She'd taken two days off to recover, but the panic attacks would take months to vanish—if they ever did—and the last thing EarthGov needed was an acting Secretary of Interstellar Commerce with a case of PTSD. Eventually, she'd have to see the doctor, but not today. Too much to do.

She wondered why this affected her so badly when the trauma she'd been part of aboard Garfield hadn't. Because this was personal, that was why. For all the Skreesh's destruction, none of it had been focused on Valri Gibb. The bastards who pulled off the assault in her flat had called her by name. The drones used to carry out the attack were destroyed now, and there wasn't a thing she could do about it. Except resign.

"I'm not resigning," she said. "Fuck those bastards. They want me, they can damn well look me in the eye when they pull the trigger."

"It won't get that far," Underhill said. But her tone was one of defeat. Frances clearly knew anything that could happen once could happen again. "Not if I can help it."

"Where are they now?" Valri wanted to know. "Brooks and—"

"The investigation is under way. I'm not directly involved, you know."

"But you made statements, right? Moral support and all that?"

"I told them I thought they were good soldiers and they could be returned to duty—eventually. That's literally all I can say on it."

"Good soldiers. Yeah, I guess so. Kill enemies and break shit. That's what soldiers do. So why did I become an enemy?"

"You made a call; someone didn't like it. And didn't have the juice to change it through the proper channels. So…Boom! It went further than that, though."

"How much further?"

"It's enough to fill a newspaper. The powers that be figured out that this was the new normal, and a world under ice isn't one that lends itself to thousands of different ways to manage money. On-Star went poof and other firms followed. The military doesn't have a financial management division capable of stabilizing the global economy. We might have to create one. There's a lot of people hurting on Earth, and when the hurt rises, so does the need for a scapegoat."

"So I'll make another call someday and someone won't like that either. And another and another and another. I want to start training on the rifle range again. Three, four days a week. Can you set that up?"

"I will train you myself."

"No, you won't. You'll find me a good teacher though. Right?"

"Done and done."

Two quick knocks at the door, then Basil Matsouka's head popped in. "Ma'am. The judge is here."

"Send him in. Witnesses, too."

The ceremony was brief. The oath of office, short. Everyone shook her hand afterwards and called her "Madame Secretary."

CHAPTER 36

THE GOOD NEWS as far as Brooks was concerned was that they got to endure their conditioning in more or less familiar circumstances. The OMP moved them into private quarters, the details of which would be familiar to any UEF officer. The bad news was that he and Rosenski underwent their trials separately. He had no idea where they put her or how she was doing. He didn't have the time or energy to think about her often or for long. He was in too much pain for that.

They tagged him with electrodes to measure his responses, then put him through a physical training regimen the likes of which he'd never encountered. Pushups, sit-ups, core crunches, leg lifts, and running in place for hours without a break. Every day, white-coated lab techs took readings and made notes on a slate, while two OMP police looked on with varying levels of amusement. Sometimes they moved him to a proper gym and watched him climb obstacles, shoot targets, lift weights, and cycle through all the exercise machines. His implants took up the slack. The alien gear released endorphins, improved his oxy circulation, gave him the strength of three men, and nearly unlimited endurance. He broke the leg press twice. He ran on a treadmill until the belt snapped at high speed, then retained enough control to back flip off the device onto the floor and not stumble or fall.

He maintained enough sense to see it as a grand experiment instead of a punishment. He felt sure they were experimenting with him, pushing him to limits he'd never approached, just to see what the implants could do. He approved. He'd never tested himself like this. None of them had. And there were ten UEF soldiers with these gizmos lodged in their bodies. What kind of mission could ten super-soldiers carry out?

They followed the physical tests with mental ones. They put him in escape rooms to see if he could defuse a bomb or rescue a hostage or kill an enemy. The tested whether his responses differed if he saved himself or a random bystander. They took his clothes and dropped him on an electrified floor, then jolted him until he used a safe word...a word which didn't work half the time.

There were punishments for when he didn't cooperate. Electric shocks. Intense pain. Smells he couldn't describe that made him want to barf. One thing he discovered was that they couldn't actually move his body for him. They could take away his muscle control and leave him there while they wracked him with cramps or muscle spasms in a pool of his own waste, but whatever Sleer tech did, it didn't turn a human being into a robot. They had drones for that. Good to know, he supposed.

Twenty-two days after the workouts began, they brought him home. His apartment in Primate Alley. He checked on the neighbors, Reagan and Binil. All gone. The whole building seemed to be empty except for him.

He was making coffee in the kitchen when the front door chimed and opened after a moment. A bedraggled Sara Rosenski entered and slouched to the sofa, followed by an exuberant Frances Underhill. "Simon! We're home! Where you at, boy?"

"In here." Simon set his cup aside and prepared two more. He flopped into a comfy chair as he sipped. Sara sniffed experimentally at hers, but Underhill set her cup aside.

"My dudes. My fam! Up and at 'em, slugabeds, we have a shit ton of work to do."

"Blow it out your ass, sir!" Brooks yelled.

Underhill said a word that he couldn't have pronounced and Brooks jumped up, jolted by an electric shock. In a flash, the coffee was on the floor. "You bitch!" She shocked him again and again and a third time for good measure. Brooks climbed out of the chair and stood at attention. Rosenski sighed and did the same. Brooks frowned as he saw the difference in how they were being treated. Underhill was making an example of him. Creep.

"Don't make me do that again, Simon. It wastes my time and hurts you, and I don't want to hurt you. I like you. Here, take my cup."

"Oh, are we friends now?"

Underhill grinned like a fool. "We are absolutely on a first name basis. Hell, we are family! Feels good, huh?"

"Feels like I got my joints scrubbed with wire brushes," Rosenski said. "Like my brain got scrambled with razor tape."

"How does anyone with such great hair get away with lying, blackmail, and torture the way you do, Captain?" Brooks asked.

"It's not the hair, it's the headset," Underhill said. She even tapped her headgear to make her point. The silver comm band snugged against her head perfectly, her blue-black mane hanging straight down her back. "Anyway, Colonel Yousaf believes that you have demonstrated sufficient levels of adaptability and that we can start moving you both into places of responsibility again. Unfortunately—," she said, even as Rosenski opened her mouth to ask a question, "—there's no way we can let you back in with the *Ascension* crew. Katsev and Rojetnick were beyond unhappy, but they recognize the need for accountability in the ranks. But there are plenty of opportunities for competent, experienced combat crews. We'll find one for you."

"What about getting permission from your pal, ZERO? I take it he's still not talking to anyone."

"Not that I've heard. Frankly, I don't think Hendricks will waste too many resources trying to restore him. Now that he has access to two battle stations worthy of the name, the last thing he wants is an AI second-guessing him."

"There's still the issue of implanted humans. The three of us, Valri, six former Hornets. Ten in all. Are you going to make everyone just disappear?" Rosenski asked wearily.

"Not at all. I'm glad you brought it up. I wasn't sure how to breach the subject."

"Which subject?"

"Advanced fighting techniques and services," Underhill said. "You're all on record as serving under intense pressure with high stakes. Even if your loyalty can be questioned, your abilities are beyond reproach. That leads us to imagine that you would do nicely in a purely combat setting. Even Brooks here—as long as he doesn't lose the plot."

Rosenski sipped her coffee. "Special ops?"

"Nope. Darker."

"Black ops?"

"Darker than that. *Negative* ops."

"What's that even mean?"

Underhill pulled off her head band and dropped it in her lap, then fiddled with her hair. When she finished, her eyes were dead serious. "It's been three years since we lost the Earth. We've built ourselves a base of operation here, but it's not the same by any measure. We know plenty about the Sleer. Three years of close observation, both of their government and their military, and careful mapping efforts of this battle ring gives us a working knowledge of their capabilities. What you two picked up from the ring around Earth helped considerably with that. Enough to start thinking about how to approach any attempt to re-take the Earth Ring. We have no such information about our new trading partners, the Movi. I'm asking you two, and a few very carefully selected individuals, to help rectify that."

"Head into Movi space? Kick a few asses?"

Underhill nodded. "Or get your asses kicked. We're working on instruments for the most part. It'll take time. But…yes. I promise we'll take care of Simon's real estate holdings while you're gone. You will have the opportunity to recruit people whose value you can demonstrate."

"People with Sleer implants," he said. "But not Valri, I'd guess."

Frances winked at him. "Naturally. I'd stay away from Val for a few months. Fairchild is keeping her grounded, but she doesn't know about your involvement and I don't see a reason to tell her."

Rosenski fidgeted and stared at her feet. "That sounds fair."

"Simon, you'll be around to handle Binil. She'll automatically be included in any effort to probe Movi space. Which means Reagan will be part of this. You three have a weird knack for figuring things out when you get together. Just keep your nocturnal activities private. The rooms have eyes and ears."

"Gah. It's not like that, man."

"What do we get in return for signing on?" Rosenski asked.

"We seal your records, you go back into general pop, we find you both a new unit to join, and life goes on. I made the case that any recon effort that doesn't include you both would have a greater chance of failure. Your choice."

Simon drained his cup. "What if we say no?"

"You're in no position to do that. Like it not, you two have made very bad choices recently. Death sentence choices, at least for Sara. And we can find a box for you to stew in for...ten years? So. I do have one question, though. How deep into the Laynies are you, Sara?"

Brooks watched silently as Rosenski crumpled into herself like a deflating tire. He'd never seen her like this. Never imagined she had weaknesses. Frau Butcher was a bona fide legend.

"No one was supposed to get hurt," she murmured.

"I know. You were just working outside the law to bring down an illegitimate government. I've heard that before. Here's what you're going to do. The mission you carried out might have knocked you out of their orbit, but when your controllers realize you're part of an elite recon group, they'll be back on you."

"How would they find out?"

Underhill snorted. "Come on, Simon. I think this proves they have their hooks into the UEF, and probably the OMP, at every level. That's above my pay grade. Layne's Brigade will give Sara another mission and she will tell me about it when it happens. If Simon Brooks receives an invitation to join the Brigade, he will accept and tell me everything he learns from his handler. Am I clear, fam?"

"Crystal."

"Excellent." Underhill got back to business. She replaced her headgear, began tapping on her slate, and missed the look Brooks and Rosenski shared. Sara flexed her knee and he tested his arm. For the first time in months, their implant-repaired bones didn't hurt.

THANK YOU FOR READING DISJUNCTION!

WE HOPE you enjoyed it as much as we enjoyed bringing it to you. We just wanted to take a moment to encourage you to review the book. Follow this link: Disjunction to be directed to the book's Amazon product page to leave your review.

Every review helps further the author's reach and, ultimately, helps them continue writing fantastic books for us all to enjoy.

You can also join our non-spam mailing list by visiting www.subscribepage.com/AethonReadersGroup and never miss out on future releases. You'll also receive three full books completely Free as our thanks to you.

Facebook | Instagram | Twitter | Website

Want to discuss our books with other readers and even the authors? Join our Discord server today and be a part of the Aethon community.

ALSO IN SERIES:

Disjunction
Dissonance
Dominion

Looking for more from Jon Frater?

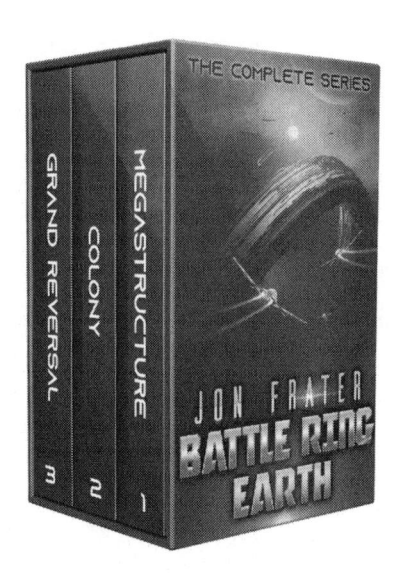

The Complete Battle Ring Earth Series Bundle is here. 1000+ pages of military sci-fi action about the defense of Earth against aliens, fighter pilots, and the last hope for mankind. Technical Specialist Simon Brooks was no soldier. More suited for the academy than combat, his assignment to a rear echelon support squadron seemed a good fit. Everything changed when the Sleer attacked Earth's newly salvaged spacecraft, UEF Ascension. In a flash, Brooks goes from fleeing a burning transport plane to piloting a broken mech and learning the habits of a fighter pilot from Lt Sara Rosenski, the terror of Nightmare Squadron. But his rising star takes a hit when he learns to talk to the Sleer AI, Genukh…and suddenly the UEF doesn't know whose side he's on. Now Brooks and Rosenski are stuck aboard Earth's Sleer weapon—the Battle Ring--and they may be all that stands between Earth and its induction into the Sleer Empire… **Experience this complete Military Science Fiction Series perfect for fans of Rick Partlow, Jamie McFarlane, and Joshua Dalzelle. Books in the Set:** Book 1: Megastructure Book 2: Colony Book 3: Grand Reversal

GET BATTLE RING EARTH NOW!

Looking for more great Science Fiction?

When the rules of war keep changing, fight for each other... Humanity has been banished to a distant star. Left to fight over resources rationed to them by mysterious machine-overlords known as Wardens. Commander Rylan Holt labors against inter-colony arms trafficking when an informant gives him horrific news. The ruthless cartel boss, Lilith, has stockpiled outlawed weapons of mass destruction. Worse, she claims to have permission from the Wardens to unleash them upon the system. When the battleship *Audacity* speeds to investigate Rylan's discovery, operations officer Scott Carrick finds himself in a trap more deadly than he could have ever imagined. His only hope of escape may lie with their most junior crewmember, a nurse named Aila Okuma, who's never seen battle. As Rylan, Scott, and Aila struggle to survive a war where the rules keep changing, they must answer a terrible question: how do they win when it seems the Wardens intend for everyone to lose?

Get Hellfire Now!

A smuggler, a spy, a brewing revolution…and a rogue agent who could destroy it all. Perrin Hightower can fly a run-down freighter through the galaxy's most dangerous wormholes blindfolded, a handy skill in her shipping business…and her smuggling enterprises. Special agent Tai Lawson dreams of leading the Ruby Confederation's spy agency. But when his partner steals a top-secret list of revolutionaries and vanishes, Tai's accused of helping his friend escape. When Tai seeks her navigation expertise, Perrin would rather jump out an airlock than help. But the missing person is her ex-boyfriend—a double agent she thought was helping the revolution. Her name's on that list, and she'll do anything to keep it secret.

Get A Rogue Pursuit Now!

"**Aliens, agents, and espionage abound in this Cold War-era alternate history adventure... A wild ride!**"—Dennis E. Taylor, bestselling author of We Are Legion (We Are Bob)

GET THE LUNA MISSILE CRISIS NOW!

For all our Sci-Fi books, visit our website.

CAST OF CHARACTERS

UNIFIED EARTH FLEET

LT CMDR JOANNE ARKADY: Lt. Cmdr. UES Gauntlet's XO. VRF pilot, veteran of the U-War with 17 kills to her name during the conflict. Her squadron call sign is "Saint." She becomes Fairchild's XO when they transfer to Gauntlet.

LT. BARROWS: A friend of Brooks. Works with the HR division on AMS-1.

LT. BRONSON. A friend of Brooks. Works in the AMS-1 armory.

LT. SIMON BROOKS: Simon began his term as the comm specialist for Hornet Squadron. He graduated to piloting a Raven soon after. He is a specialist in understanding Sleer technology.

LT. DIALLOU: Senegalese Raven pilot, runs an EWAR Raven. Was attached to Hornet Squadron before the Battle of Great Nest and remains part of the Gauntlets.

CMDR RAY FAIRCHILD: Cmdr. "Uncle" Ray Fairchild is Hornet Squadron's commanding officer and Simon Brooks's mentor. He's an Ace from the U-War with 105 kills to his name.

CPO RICHARD FROST: Heads the Hornets' engineering section. But he's a fully qualified VRF pilot. Manages the Engineering section on Gauntlet.

VALRI GIBB: Valri Gibb worked for a military contractor, supplying the outer planet bases before AMS-1's launch day and for months afterward. She parted with the world of civilian business to buy a military waste dump on South Pico Island in order to salve a Pegasus -class assault shuttle she calls The Beast. She met Ray Fairchild in a local bar and she joined forces with Hornet Squadron to repair and crew the shuttle. She's currently serving as the Secretary of Commerce and Interstellar Trade with EarthGov.

LT. MARC JANUS: An original member of Hornet Squadron, transferred to the Gauntlet. An excellent pilot.

CMDR. THOMAS KATSEV: Leader of Specter Squadron, and also the CAG of AMS-1. Veteran of the Unification War with 80 kills to his name. Call sign is

The Butcher. Mentored Sara Rosenski through her flight training and recommended her for the leadership position of the Nightmare Squadron when she was ready to be promoted. Currently serves as the CAG for AMS-1.

LT. KATSUTA: Pilot in Gauntlet Squadron.

LT. BASIL MATSOUKA: Valri Gibb's Chief of Staff.

LT. MORROW: Pilot in Gauntlet Squadron.

LT. LOUIS PURCELL: Member of Gauntlet Squadron, VRF pilot.

LT. JUDY "DANCES WITH GEARS" REAGAN: Hornet Squadron's chief mechanic. Reagan becomes involved in the struggle between Binil and her Movi friends to escape imprisonment by stealing the Cyclops. She graduates to piloting a Raven. She has a romantic relationship with Simon Brooks.

LT. BRIAN ROBERTS: Raven pilot in Hornet squadron. Described as young and afraid.

ENSIGN RODRIGUEZ: A friend of Brooks. Works with the food service crew on AMS-1.

CAPT. ABRAHAM ROJETNICK: the Commanding officer of Alien Megastructure-1 aka Ascension.

LT. CMDR. SARA ROSENSKI: Leader of Nightmare Squadron. Was mentored by Cmdr Katsev through her flight training and still remains close to him. Call sign is Frau Butcher (The Butcher's Wife).

LT. SIMMONS: A friend of Brooks. Works on the Flight Ops deck of AMS-1.

LT. CMDR. SKELLINGTON: Leonard "Skull" Skellington is Hornet Squadron's intelligence officer. He's a UEF military specialist with the rank of Lieutenant Commander. He has full clearance for just about anything aboard the AMS-1 except for the most classified stuff. Currently serving as Gauntlet's sensor chief.

LT. SMITHERS: A friend of Brooks. Works with the AMS-1 Quartermaster.

LT. ANYA SOLOVOYA: Attached to Gauntlet after the Battle of Great Nest. She's an excellent VRF pilot. Her call sign is "Ghost." She is Ukranian.

GEN. EISENBERG: CIC of UEF Ground Forces.

FLT ADM. HART: CIC of UEF Space Forces.

MCPO AMIR: Runs the communication department on AMS-1.
LT. CMDR MARISSA HART: Runs the Flight Ops deck on AMS-1. Daughter of Adm. Hart.

OFFICE OF MILITARY PROTOCOLS

GENERAL HENDRICKS: Hendricks is the OMP commandant of South Pico Island. He works closely with the Sleer in the vain hope that he can influence their leaders to accommodate Earth's interests.

CAPT. FRANCES UNDERHILL: A close friend of Valri Gibb, and the OMP officer assigned to *Gauntlet*.

LT. COL. YOUSAF: Department head of the Great Nest OMP espionage group known as the "Chick Pit," and Underhill's former CO.

CYCOMM UNITY

BINILSANETANJAMALALA Considered royalty on her home worls, BInil is a young girl who learns she is a psychic "scrambler" and wants to join her world's military. Then she finds herself exiled and makes common cause with fellow Movi prisoners to escape. She falls in with Lt. Reagan and is adopted into the UEF.

SLEER EMPIRE

EDZEDON : Fleet Master Nazerian, science officer. Nazerian maintains a curiosity about human culture and history but relies on Edzedon to explain what he can't discover for himself.

GROSSUSK: Supreme Commander of the Sleer forces.

KHITEN: A Sleer trade functionary assigned to EarthGov.

METZEK: A Great Servant of Science and Ship Master in the Sleer forces. He was assigned to investigate Vega, located a derelict Sleer base, and decided to preserve it.

MORUK: Executive Commander of the Sleer forces.

NAZERIAN: Tall Lord and Fleet Master of the Sleer effort to recover the AMS-1 years ago. Now part of the Sleer high command and a confidant of Great Lord Moruk.

ZOLIK: Metzek's Executive Officer.

MOVI KINGDOM

CLEO: One of Sora's henches from prison. She spent a decade as a dancer in the Movi royal court.

HORVANTZ: An officer of the Royal Movi Naval Intelligence Corps. His current assignment is to present as the head of the Dal-Cortsuni trade delegation to Great Nest.

FLIGHT ADMIRAL SORA LAAKSHIDEN: A former flag officer in the Royal Movi Navy, she lost her title and rank when she was captured and sent to a Cycomm penal colony.

MIRALED MAKJIT: An officer of the Dal-Cortsuni trade delegation to Great Nest.

SELLIK: One of Sora's henches from prison. Quick to anger with a short temper she tends to use violence to solve every problem.